The Memory of You

Center Point
Large Print

The Memory of You

A Sanctuary Sound Novel

Jamie Beck

CENTER POINT LARGE PRINT
THORNDIKE, MAINE

This Center Point Large Print edition
is published in the year 2019 by arrangement with
Amazon Publishing, www.apub.com.

The text of this Large Print edition is unabridged.
In other aspects, this book may vary
from the original edition.
Printed in the United States of America
on permanent paper.
Set in 16-point Times New Roman type.

ISBN: 978-1-64358-298-6

Library of Congress Cataloging-in-Publication Data

The Library of Congress has cataloged this record
under Library of Congress Control Number: 2019942054

To my oldest friend, Joanna, who has helped celebrate my happiest moments and supported me through my worst. Thanks for being bold enough to talk to a stranger while walking home from school all those years ago.

Preface

Dear Reader,

Thank you for picking up this book! I've been looking forward to introducing you to Sanctuary Sound and the circle of friends known as the Lilac Lane League for some time. The idea for this series came about after watching the news following the devastating explosion at the concert of a singer in England. I remember thinking about how easily my own teenagers could fall victim to a similar incident. That led to me wondering about how victims and their families survive such events and how different people might respond to trauma. Thus began the seeds of the stories for Steffi, Claire, and Peyton, each of whom has her own trauma to overcome.

Steffi is one of the toughest, most resilient heroines I've ever written. And while her story is a powerful one, it certainly comes out of a place of darkness. In my research for this tale, I was not only taken aback by the staggering number of women who are sexually assaulted in the United States every year, but I was also struck by some minds' powerful reactions to such trauma.

While I consulted a number of sources and two psychologists to construct this plot, I am not a psychologist, and it is possible that I have misinterpreted some of what I learned, so I own those mistakes. As this is ultimately intended to be a hopeful story about learning to ask for help and facing one's fears, I've taken some liberties for the purpose of storytelling. If you are interested in learning more about these topics, I've included a list of some research materials I reviewed at the end of this book.

In Stefanie Lockwood, I hope I've done credit to all the women who have suffered trauma and bravely battle every day to reclaim their lives and decide what will define them.

Regards,
Jamie Beck

Chapter One

Never regret anything that once made you happy.
The deathbed advice imparted years ago by her
mother had comforted Steffi in the wake of many
mistakes. Today those words drifted back as she
turned down Echo Hill Lane, the narrow, tree-
lined cul-de-sac where her next appointment,
and many happy memories, lived. Then again,
that old lesson didn't quite apply to her current
predicament, because her regret had nothing
to do with the time she'd spent here with Ryan
Quinn and his family, and everything to do with
leaving them all behind.

She parked her Chevy van across the street
from the white Dutch colonial that had been like
a second home in her teens. Once she killed the
engine, she sat in the driver's seat, shaking out
her hands, anticipating her first real conversation
with Mrs. Q. in a decade. She'd forfeited this
family's comfort after she'd ghosted Ryan in
college. If her brothers could see her now, they'd
never stop teasing.

But today wasn't about her discomfort. Today
was about a job—one she and her childhood
friend turned business partner, Claire, needed to
keep their home-remodeling business growing.

"Here goes nothing," she muttered, then blew

out a breath and opened the door. She buckled her tool belt before trotting across the lawn to the shade of the home's small portico. The familiar apple-red front door prompted a shallow smile as she gave it three sharp knocks. She inhaled the pungent aroma of the nearby Long Island Sound to settle her nerves.

Mrs. Q. opened the door, her lively smile curling the edges of her wise blue eyes. The tall woman still exuded confidence, although she now had a decade's worth of new wrinkles. Gray strands frosted her blonde hair. Warm memories rushed into the space between them, but Steffi fought the urge to press her hand against her heart.

The scent of freshly baked snickerdoodles wafted outside while they faced each other for the first time in forever. Steffi couldn't hide now, like she had at that near run-in with Mrs. Q. the summer after she'd broken up with Ryan, when he'd stayed in Boston for an internship.

She'd stopped by the pharmacy to pick up last-minute items for her summer-abroad trip—the one Ryan had talked her out of taking the prior summer—and spied Mrs. Q. at the checkout line. She'd camped out behind the chips until Mrs. Q. had left, grieving anew the loss of their special friendship.

Until recently, Steffi had lived in Hartford and had not bumped into the Quinns during visits with her family, which was why her pulse now throbbed with uncertainty.

"Stefanie, you've hardly changed. Come on in before my last batch of cookies burns." She waved Steffi inside—minus the hugs of yester-year—and then strolled ahead, straight back toward the kitchen.

Distracted by familiar sights and sounds—the creaky, original wide-plank floors, the sisal carpet running up the stairs that led to Ryan's room—Steffi bumped into the cardboard boxes stacked near the base of the stairwell. "Oof."

"Watch yourself!" Mrs. Q. called.

An oversize, handsome photograph of Ryan with his daughter, Emmy, sat on the mantel. His smiling brown eyes and cocoa-colored hair kept him as handsome as ever. Val—his lucky wife—got to wake up to that grin every day. Steffi rubbed her chest as she made her way to the kitchen.

Mrs. Q. gestured toward the platter on the counter with her spatula. "Have one."

"Thanks." Steffi nabbed a thick, warm cookie, then stood in the kitchen—with its same old cherrywood cabinets and green granite—feeling sixteen years old again.

As she swallowed the last bit of cookie, she wondered if those boxes meant the Quinns were moving. Did they want renovations to make the home more attractive to a young buyer? It shouldn't matter, yet the idea of anyone other than the Quinns living here was like setting fire to her favorite scrapbook.

She couldn't say that, of course. "You look great, Mrs. Q."

"Thanks. You too." She transferred the last batch of cookies to a cooling rack. "We're both adults now. Call me Molly."

"Okay." Steffi mentally tested it, but it was hard to think of Mrs. Q. as Molly. Especially with so much unsaid between them.

"Molly" turned off the oven. "So tell me, how are you?"

"Same as always." Not exactly true, but she wasn't about to confess that life now was nothing like she'd once imagined. Standing in this kitchen, she couldn't escape the irony of her running off to pursue a "big" life, yet ending up back at home, while Ryan and his legal career thrived in a major city with his family.

Molly crossed her arms. "Sanctuary Sound must seem sleepy after life up in Hartford."

"Not really." She hoped that would be the last half truth she'd need to utter. "It's nice to be home."

Her hometown—five thousand residents nestled on the central Connecticut coastline—certainly differed from city life. She'd hurried home two or so months ago, eager to surround herself with the familiar, after . . .

12

"No boyfriend left behind?" Molly's voice pulled her out of that rabbit hole. Her even gaze betrayed no bitterness—probably because Ryan had given her a beautiful grandchild—but Steffi didn't like the conversation heading in this direction.

"Nope." She dug her fingernails into her palms while she recalled the cruel way she'd dumped Ryan. To this day, thinking about that made her stomach burn as much as it had back then when she'd ignored his calls and texts. Now seemed like a good time to change the subject. "No time for that, anyway. Claire and I are super busy getting things off the ground."

"It's brave of you girls to start your own business."

"The town's little renaissance made it the perfect time to take the risk."

"We've certainly seen an influx of newcomers." Molly's brittle smile and tone carried the same hint of disenchantment as Steffi's dad and other longtime residents bemoaning the armada of wealthy young families who'd sniffed out the undervalued, aging homes near the beach. But those whom old-timers saw as outsiders, Steffi deemed target customers.

Molly set the empty mixing bowl and spoon in the sink, along with the cookie sheet.

"Most of the old gang has up and gone." Molly's gaze turned distant, perhaps wishing both of her kids hadn't moved away. "It's the curse of a small-town childhood. You think the rest of the world is more exciting, taking for granted the deep relationships that make life rich."

Steffi had come to understand *that* better with age. She almost asked about Ryan, because not talking about him seemed awkward and cowardly. Something stopped her, though. "I should look at the back porch and familiarize myself with it again so I can determine the project's scope."

Converting a screened porch to a family room would be a straightforward job, and a nice addition to the gallery of work she could show prospective clients.

"I'll come with you so we can talk through my ideas." Molly untied her apron and hung it neatly on its hook. She cast a hesitant glance at the dirty bakeware abandoned in the sink but walked on.

Steffi covered a smile, recalling how nasty-neat Molly had always been. Ryan had driven his mother crazy with his piles of shoes, clothes, sports gear, and the trail of crumbs he and Steffi had left behind whenever they'd raided the cookie jar and the junk food cabinet after soccer practice.

When she followed Molly through the kitchen door onto the screened porch, the distant wail of an ambulance siren split the air.

A sudden burst of sunlight—or something—blinded Steffi. Time shifted to a slow pulse while short, sharp breaths chafed her lungs.

That's wrong. There shouldn't be sunlight.

Should be black. No sun. Not even moonlight.

Something—a shadow—lurking at the edges . . .
cold metal, grunting, cigarette smoke and pain . . .

"Stefanie?" Molly's touch broke through Steffi's haze. "Are you okay?"

A trickle of the perspiration gathering along Steffi's hairline rolled down her temple. "Yes."

She forced herself to focus on the clusters of terra-cotta pots, which overflowed with sunny-yellow begonias, on the flagstone floor. Then she noticed the faux rattan outdoor sofa and two gliders that had replaced the old teak furniture Steffi remembered.

"You looked stricken." Concern colored Molly's eyes. She reached out as if to pat Steffi's shoulder, then withdrew her hand uncertainly.

Steffi shrugged off Molly's unspoken questions. She couldn't answer them even if she wanted to, which she didn't. "Lost in thought, I guess."

"About what?"

Steffi reached for her notebook, avoiding Molly's questioning gaze. As always, remembering any detail of her zone-outs was like trying to catch fog. "Ideas for the project."

Molly hesitated, a disbelieving look crossing her face, then clasped her hands together. "Let me get you some water."

Steffi waited on the porch and caught her breath. She'd been losing track of time now and then for the past few months. Her hazy moments

15

didn't follow a discernible pattern, so she chalked them up to the aftereffects of her most recent concussion.

She'd suffered multiple concussions throughout her high school and college soccer career. Then, three months ago, she'd taken another harsh blow to the head when some assholes jumped her in an alley at gunpoint, beat her unconscious, and made off with her purse.

A sudden burst of acid surged up her esophagus, but she breathed through the burning sensation. Molly returned and handed her a glass of water, which she chugged.

Determined to wipe that worried look off Molly's face and be professional, she flipped to a clean page of her notebook and said, "Tell me what kinds of finishes you envision."

Molly blinked but didn't press her concerns. "Nothing modern. I'd like the windows and floors to blend in with the 1940s construction, if possible. Same with the exterior."

Steffi opened the screen door to go out to the yard and look at the structure. Molly shadowed her. Together they squinted in the August sunlight. "Shouldn't be hard to match these double-hung windows and standard-shingle siding. I'm thinking we pull out all the floor-to-ceiling screens and build half walls and windows, unless you prefer a series of French doors?"

"I'd like it to be bright and have views of my

garden." Molly pointed to her massive pink polyantha rose bushes. "One set of doors is fine. Add as many windows as you can include without making it impossible to heat in the winter."

"No problem." Steffi went back into the screened porch, which was formed on two sides by exterior walls of the house, and two sides of screening. She crossed to the longest section of shingled wall and pointed over at the kitchen door on the shorter wall. "We'll remove that door to create an opening there, and another one here, for better flow." She pounded on the section of wall that would lead into the hallway beside the stairwell.

"Good idea." Molly checked her watch and bit her lip. She flitted her hands after clearing her throat. "Ballpark me . . . How much, and how long will it take?"

"Depends on whether you want to connect to the home's HVAC or go with the new portable units, among other things." She put away her notebook and withdrew a tape measure to verify her estimates.

"I'm not picky. Functional and basic is fine." Molly's gaze darted to the kitchen door and back again. "What's the timing on all of this?"

"Maybe six to eight weeks. We're working right on the slab and can keep much of the porch framing and roof, which saves time and expense."

"Great." Molly crossed to the kitchen door, pre-paring to go inside while Steffi continued measuring. "Let's get it started ASAP."

Steffi remained on the porch, tape measure retracting. "Molly, I haven't even given you a bid."

Molly waved that comment away. "Honey, I know you'll be fair."

Surprise tugged at her brows. "Do you mind if I ask what's the rush?"

Molly stood in the open doorway and cast Steffi a peculiar look before affecting a half-hearted shrug. "Ryan and Emmy are moving in. We'll need the extra space sooner rather than later."

"Ryan's moving home?" A steady rush of heat rose from Steffi's toes to her head. Her body tensed into the defensive posture she'd assumed as her team's goalie, ready to jump or run or do whatever it took to protect the net—or, in this case, her pride and heart. Ryan was coming home? And why hadn't Molly mentioned Val?

Before Molly could expound, the front door slammed open, and a young girl's voice called out, "Memaw, I smell cookies!"

Five seconds later, little Emmy Quinn raced into the kitchen and skidded to a halt.

Ryan tossed his keys on the walnut entry table that had long ago given him the small scar toward the back of his head and kicked off his flip-flops,

18

keeping the damp, sandy beach towels slung over his shoulders.

"We're home," he called out, as if Emmy's dash to the kitchen hadn't already warned his mom of an oncoming storm. And Emmy was a storm these days—a raging sea of emotion that could turn from frothy giggles to waves of hysterics without notice. Val's decision to run off with her new lover had done a real job on their daughter, leaving him and his family groping to fill the void.

He didn't relish moving in with his parents but couldn't deny the comfort of coming home to fresh-baked cookies and his mom's support. More important, her help with Emmy would be invaluable; and more than anything, Emmy needed a positive, stable woman in her life.

He glanced at the unpacked boxes, sighed, and kept walking. Those could wait another thirty minutes. Sharing warm cookies with his daughter would be a better use of his time.

The transition from their eclectic suburb outside Boston to the tiny beach community of his childhood wouldn't be a cakewalk. Next week he'd start his new job, and Emmy fourth grade at a new school, which was sure to bring another round of highs and lows while she struggled to make new friends. Between now and then, he hoped he and his parents could swaddle Emmy in some old-fashioned love and discipline. Two things Val had never consistently provided their child.

He rounded the corner and spotted Emmy standing in her flamingo-pink swimsuit, brunette curls springy as ever as she tipped her head from side to side while staring out to the porch.

"What's up, buttercup?" Ryan swiped a cookie for himself and took a giant bite.

"Who's that?" Emmy pointed outside, past his mother, to a woman—*to Steffi Lockwood?*

He nearly dropped the cookie as his hand fell to his side. Why the hell was Steffi hanging out with his mother? Before he realized what was happening, he found himself standing in the middle of the patio. "What's going on here?"

Those brusque words scraped along the scarred part of his soul.

"Ryan Andrew Quinn! What kind of greeting is that?" His mom cast him "that look" she gave when she expected him to behave. She then leaned toward Emmy, who'd followed him onto the porch. "Emmy, this is Miss Lockwood. She's going to turn this porch into a room for you to hang out in with your new friends."

Steffi fiddled with her tool belt, looking like she'd rather be anyplace other than in Ryan's sight line. *Good.* "Hi, Emmy. You can call me Steffi."

"Miss Lockwood is fine," Ryan said without thinking. A quick glance at her ring finger suggested she'd never married. No surprise. Com-

20

mitment hadn't been her strong suit, and he didn't need his daughter getting overly familiar with another woman who didn't keep her promises.

"Hi." Emmy gave Steffi a serious once-over, her gaze snagging on the tool belt before lingering on the black-and-turquoise work shoes. Quite a different look from Val and her friends, none of whom would be caught dead sporting overall shorts, a freshly scrubbed face, and a ponytail. Emmy then turned toward his mother. "Can we paint the room pink, Memaw?"

"I don't think so, Pooh. But maybe your dad will paint your bedroom pink." She smiled at Emmy, whose head bobbed with excitement.

"Yes! Please, Dad. Please, please! The same pink as my room at home." Her big hazel eyes fixed on him. If he dared say no, the waterworks would start.

Not that he had time to paint a picture, much less a bedroom. But Emmy probably needed something familiar in a time of tumult. If pink walls would hit "Pause" on the behavioral regression he'd noted since Val had split, he'd have to make time. "We'll see, princess."

"Maybe Mom will help." Her hopeful smile shoved his heart through a meat grinder.

He wouldn't discuss Val in front of Steffi, so he deflected. "Let's leave these two out here to finish their discussion."

"Actually, hand me those dirty towels before

21

you get sand everywhere." His mother bundled the towels in preparation for her sprint to the laundry room. "I've already given Stefanie my thoughts. Why don't you weigh in? I'm sure you have an opinion about space for a big-screen TV or some such." She glided past him, patting his cheek on her way. "Emmy, come sit at the table and I'll pour you some milk for those cookies."

Ryan thought to turn his back on Steffi, because even unpacking his moving boxes would be preferable to dealing with her. Then he decided he'd better not hand her the satisfaction of seeing him agitated. That'd only give her the misimpression that she held sway over him, which she didn't. She hadn't in many years.

If memories of how she'd blown him off still nicked his heart like a razor blade, it was only because he might mourn the fact that the girl he'd cherished had turned into a bitch.

He widened his stance and crossed his arms, reminding himself to play it cool. "I'm shocked to see you here."

"Yeah, well." She adjusted her overalls. "I was surprised to get the call."

"I'm sure you were." He stretched his stiffening neck, the litigator in him coming to the fore. With a cold smile, he asked, "What made you come? Morbid curiosity?"

"No." She stood still, unflinching now, with a slight tip of the chin. "I need the work. Claire and I

22

just got our company off the ground. I can't afford to say no to anyone."

"That must be uncomfortable for you, given how much you like your freedom." *Damn.* Guess he couldn't keep his cool. His sarcasm constituted the first blow of an argument they should've had years ago. Now it'd be pointless. He should change the subject. "How *is* Claire?"

Claire McKenna, the childhood friend who, along with Steffi and Peyton Prescott, had formed the middle school triumvirate known as the Lilac Lane League. They'd all remained close friends until Peyton stole Claire's boyfriend . . . or so he'd heard.

"She's doing well." Steffi's expression remained alert and somewhat wary.

"Really? Even after her boyfriend dumped her to run off with Peyton?" He shook his head with a derisive chuckle. "So much for the Triple L's infamous loyalty."

He empathized with Claire's pain, having suffered through duplicity more than once.

"Peyton didn't set out to seduce Todd, and I know she feels horrible about hurting Claire."

"Are you *defending* Peyton?" Actually, that shouldn't surprise him. He clenched his jaw and released it, momentarily picturing himself striding toward Steffi and backing her up against the wall until she trembled or groveled.

Her sigh was less than satisfying. "I'm not

happy about all of that, but Peyton didn't get together with Todd until after he left Claire."

"Left Claire for Peyton," Ryan reminded her.

"I know, but Peyton's like a sister. I hate what she did, but I don't hate *her,* so I'll forgive her even though it's hard. As for Todd, Claire is better off without him. He obviously didn't love her. When she realizes that and meets someone new, maybe she'll forgive Peyton so we can all be friends again."

"Don't count on it," he grumbled.

They stared at each other, their entire history now ringing in their ears at a pitch not audible to any other human. Was she so naive as to think that moving on could erase the pain of wasted love? Perhaps that was what she told herself to ease her own guilt for how she'd treated him.

The pause in conversation gave him an opportunity to study her. The ponytail—reminiscent of her soccer days—suggested she still wore her chocolate-brown hair in a simple, long, blunt style. Her hazel eyes, flecked with gold and framed by heavy, dark brows, flashed her emotions like always. The cute oval face that had imprinted itself on his heart looked nearly the same as his memory of her, except for the absence of her playful smile. Those work shorts proved years of playing soccer and doing manual labor had kept her legs toned as ever, too.

She swallowed hard before clearing her throat.

"Your mom wants the finished space to have lots of windows and a French door. That's as far as we got."

"Well, it's her house, so I have no opinions." He turned to leave before he did or said something even less kind.

"Ryan."

Hearing her say his name stopped him for a second, but he didn't turn around.

She sighed again. "I think she wants this to be someplace you and your daughter can be comfortable, so if you want a big TV or whatever, I'd like to know so I can plan for it."

He glanced over his shoulder. How many evenings had he and Steffi hung out here, candles lit, listening to rain on the roof while making out? Every spot in the whole damn house contained a shared memory, some better than others. There'd been a time when he would've bet nothing could've come between them. He'd considered himself the luckiest in love until she'd broken and humbled him.

Between that and Val's recent whopper, he'd taken a hard look at his judgment of people lately. "I won't be here long enough for that to matter."

He didn't know how true that was, but he'd hoped he'd find his own place in six or so months. For now, he needed to conserve money to pay for his divorce. In his mind, Val didn't deserve one cent of his hard-earned paycheck, especially not after leaving her daughter behind to move in with her sugar daddy. The court would probably disagree.

When Steffi had left him, he'd cried and prayed and secretly hoped for a reconciliation. When *Val* bailed, he'd shed no tears. Instead, he'd put their house on the market the next day rather than waste emotional energy on another woman who didn't want him. He'd found a new assistant public defender job in Hartford and decided to take advantage of a rent-free situation until he had a better idea of what to expect. In the meantime, his mom wasn't just the cheapest after-school day care around but also the most reliable.

"I'm sorry about your marriage—" Steffi sputtered.

She should be sorry. He wouldn't have hooked up with Val if he hadn't been on the rebound from Steffi's head games. Granted, Val's unplanned pregnancy during senior year had pushed that relationship someplace it probably shouldn't have gone, although he couldn't regret having Emmy. His daughter gave him purpose and filled his life with immeasurable love. "My marriage is off-limits. I advise you to let it lie."

"Noted, Counselor." The sharp edge in her voice goaded him, so he faced her fully for another stare-down. Being a lawyer who regularly contended with criminals and cops made these kinds of contests too easy. She dropped her gaze, then looked up again, her expression softened. "Listen, it looks like I'll be here working for a couple of months, so it'd be nice if we could get off on a better foot. Maybe we could even be friends."

He snorted. "No, thanks. Friendship requires trust, and I don't trust you. So you can go back to treating me exactly like you did in college. Pretend I don't even exist. It gutted me back then, but now it suits me fine."

Bam! For three seconds, the overdue release of pent-up anger made him feel ten feet tall. But then her slumped shoulders and red cheeks reversed his high, sinking him as low as a man could go.

She smoothed her shortalls again, her face now a mask of indifference.

"I'm sorry I hurt you, especially since it seems to have changed you into someone I might not like." She unwound her tape measure and started walking along the far edge of the patio. "I'll do my best to stay out of your way."

He'd changed, no doubt. She'd started that ball rolling. Then his wife and his job had exposed him to even more injustice, making him cynical and, sometimes, bitter.

Steffi had been just shy of twenty when she'd blown him off. A decade ago. They'd both been different people then, and maybe she'd changed, too. Maybe she even regretted how she'd handled things. But he certainly had more important things to worry about than her or any lingering hurt feelings.

He couldn't make himself apologize for snapping at her now, so he pointed to the right corner of the room. "Might be nice to have my fifty-five-inch screen mounted over there."

She paused and glanced at him. "I'll be sure to factor that in."

"Thanks." He needed a shower. The damp, sandy suit had started to make him itch. "See you around."

He walked into the kitchen to find Emmy fingers-deep in a mug of milk and soggy cookie crumbles. Little sugar puddles lay scattered on the table all around her.

"You'd better wipe all that up before Memaw comes back. She won't stand for that kind of mess." Unlike Val, who'd never cared much about the messes Emmy left. In fairness, he hadn't trained his daughter to be tidy, either.

"Okay," Emmy said, dunking another cookie.

"That's enough, princess." Ryan removed the platter, although he was probably too late to prevent a tummyache. "You're going to get sick. When you finish here, come up and help me unpack some of our boxes, okay? Then I need to do some reading for a while. But maybe we can go to town and get pizza for dinner."

She shrugged, neither excited nor unexcited by the offer.

"I'll take you to my old favorite, Campiti's. You'll love it."

Emmy kicked her feet beneath the table. "Did Miss Lockwood used to hang out here a lot?"

"Yeah." He scratched the back of his neck. "She grew up here in town, like me."

"Memaw says she was a special friend."

"Did she?" *Just great.* A nice piece of circumstantial evidence to prove his mom had an ulterior motive with this remodeling plan. She'd always loved Steffi. She'd even pooh-poohed the breakup, claiming Steffi needed a little space to grow up.

If his mom thought Ryan had any interest in women right now, she'd lost her mind. He'd have to be extra careful to make sure Emmy didn't make room in her heart for Steffi, because being disappointed by Steffi Lockwood was as certain as the sugar high those snickerdoodles were about to give his daughter.

Chapter Two

Steffi wiped sweat from her brow, laboring to breathe in the oppressive midday humidity. Finally alone, she measured out the potential second access point again, managing to write it down this time. Ryan's words kept boring into her thoughts, messing with her focus. *"It gutted me back then, but now it suits me fine."*

At nineteen, she hadn't known how to break up with the only boyfriend she'd ever had. The man she'd lost her virginity to and spun future plans about for so long that the restless feelings she'd begun experiencing as a freshman in college had made her hate herself. The catalyst had been when he'd convinced her to scrap her summer-abroad plans so they could spend time together before being separated for another nine months. For twelve weeks, she'd corralled ten-year-olds on the lumpy town field at a local summer soccer camp while daydreaming about Barcelona. Hot, aggravating, monotonous days. Her resentment had made Ryan's attention and affection suffocating.

Freedom beckoned, but she couldn't end it in person because he would've asked too many questions. He'd already proved he could talk her into or out of anything, so she'd known she'd have to take drastic steps to convince him to let go.

Her stomach tightened now as if she were back in her dorm at UConn, chewing her nails while staring at her phone as it pinged over and over after he'd returned to his school in Boston. Each deleted text and unanswered voice mail had made her hug herself and rock with doubt, despite her teammates' claims that it would be fine. More than that, they'd turned her breakup into some kind of feminist mission. After all, guys ghosted girls all the time, didn't they? She'd wanted a clean break, hadn't she? They'd convinced her that she couldn't give him any wiggle room or she'd never get the chance to explore the world.

Meanwhile, Ryan's messages had cycled from concern to dismay to anger. Deep down, she'd known he deserved much better. And instead of the relief she'd expected after cutting herself free, she'd limped through those early weeks as if half of her was missing. But as weeks had turned to months, she couldn't then reach out and apologize. When Peyton had informed her that he'd taken up with Val, that had sealed their fate.

How foolish of her now to think they could be friends. *"I don't trust you."* Given her behavior, she could hardly blame him. She got cramps whenever she imagined how he'd felt to be blindsided with that freezeout. Even now, she buried her face in her hands and drew a deep breath.

The squeak of the kitchen door opening caused

her to look up. Emmy Quinn wandered outside, leaving the door wide open.

"What's a 'special' friend?" Emmy's precocious gaze glided over Steffi for the second time that day. Her coloring and face might resemble her father, but her impudent personality had to come from Val. Ryan didn't usually provoke others for a thrill. Emmy clearly did.

"I'm not sure." Steffi had never had intimate conversations with kids, and she didn't need her first time to be with Ryan's daughter.

Emmy huffed. "Memaw says you were my dad's special friend."

"Oh." Had Molly lost her mind? "Well, we had a lot in common. We both played soccer for our high school, and we both liked to go sailing, so we hung out a lot back then."

Emmy pursed her lips as her gaze slid to Steffi's Timberland work shoes. She wrinkled her nose. "You don't dress like a girl."

Steffi smothered a smile while deciding Emmy needed a little lesson in feminism. She made a show of patting her overalls and tool belt. "Hmm. I'm a girl, and I'm wearing clothes, so I'm not sure I understand what you mean. Far as I know, there's no such thing as dressing 'like a girl.'"

Emmy's head dipped backward as her eyes rolled heavenward. The child was petite despite her age, her diminutive size at odds with a big personality. She waved her hands at her pink floral swimsuit and sparkly flip-flops. "Girls wear pretty colors and dresses." Then she scowled at Steffi's footwear again. "And fancy shoes."

"I suppose some girls do."

"My mom does." Emmy's eyes filled with challenge.

Steffi couldn't care less about Val or the woman's clothes, but she knew how it felt to lose your mom before you're ready. Steffi had been twelve; Emmy was barely nine and scared and probably in a whole lot of pain.

"I met your mom once." Steffi reflected back six years ago when she'd bumped into Ryan and his young family at the town "Caroling on the Green" on Christmas Eve. Dainty but buxom, Val turned heads with her blonde curls that framed cool blue eyes and a sensual smile. "She's very pretty."

Emmy nodded, and Steffi could see little pools forming in her eyes. *Shit.*

"Hey, while you're here, I could use some help." She tossed the tape measure at Emmy, who seemed too surprised by the gesture to catch it. It clattered to a halt at her feet. "I'll be blasting through this wall here, and I need to know how big the opening should be. Want to be my assistant?"

Emmy stooped to pick up the tape measure and then began playing with it. Tears gone. Mission accomplished.

"This whole wall?" she asked.

"That would be nice, except I'm pretty sure the stairs are right behind this part." Steffi pounded on the wall. "I think I can only open up that side."

Emmy stretched her skinny arms as wide as she could. "Like this?"

"Yes, about that wide." Steffi pulled her notepad back out, pretending to take her seriously. "How many inches is that?"

Emmy stretched the tape measure the full span of her arms. Oddly, she rose onto her tiptoes while doing so, causing Steffi to cover another smile. Emmy then set the tool on the floor and squatted to read the markings. "Forty-nine and two little marks."

Steffi pretended to write that down. "That's a good size."

Emmy smiled and pushed the tape back into the roll.

"Don't shove it. Just press that black button and it will roll right up." Steffi pointed.

Emmy squeezed it with both hands, grinning when the metal measure snapped back into place. She then pulled it out and snapped it back again.

"Don't play with it. It's a tool, not a toy." She extended her hand. "I'll take that back now."

"How will you break the wall?" Emmy asked.

"With a sledgehammer."

Emmy looked like she didn't believe Steffi. "You can't hammer down a whole wall."

"I can with a sledgehammer. It's this big." She used her hands to estimate its length and the size of the head. "You need both arms to swing it."

"Cool!" Emmy craned her neck to get a better look at Steffi's tool belt. "Can I try?"

"We'll see."

"Emmy!" Ryan's holler made its way outside before he did. He appeared, hair still damp from a shower, wearing khaki shorts and a formfitting gray T-shirt. He'd opted not to shave the little bit of stubble on his jaw. The shock of seeing him again, up close and personal, made every part of her body thrum. She held her breath, waiting to hear what else he would say. "What are you doing out here? I asked you to come help me unpack boxes after you finished cleaning the cookie mess."

Emmy cocked her hip and crossed her arms. "I helped Miss Lockwood measure." She gestured to the shingled wall. "We're going to tear down this whole wall with a sledgehammer!"

Ryan slid Steffi a side-eye glare. "That doesn't explain why you came out here in the first place."

"She says you took her sailing, Dad," Emmy replied, throwing the counselor's interrogation offtrack. "Will you take me sailing?"

For a second, Ryan's face paled. Steffi wondered if he was thinking of the picnics they'd packed, or the beer they'd sneaked, on the used 1980 Pearson 26—*Knot So Fast*—that Ryan's dad had bought him for his sixteenth birthday. Eyeing his daughter, Ryan hitched his thumb over his shoulder in the direction of the door. "March upstairs and shower. We can talk about sailing after you unpack your boxes."

Emmy stomped her foot. Had she learned that from her mom, or did all little girls play that card? "You don't have to yell."

Ryan raised his arms from his sides. "I'm not yelling."

Emmy tossed Steffi a "Can you believe this guy?" look, at which point Steffi gave up trying not to laugh at the tiny spitfire who would cause Ryan to gray prematurely.

Following a nonchalant shrug, Emmy sauntered inside, leaving Steffi alone with Ryan.

"What are you doing?" He peered at her with the same irritation he'd had when she'd accidentally bleached his soccer shirt. Funny how, despite the years and tears, his expressions were still so familiar.

"She came out here asking me questions about the past. What was I supposed to say?"

"How about 'I'm sure your dad can answer that for you,' or something like that?"

"I'm sorry, Ryan. I was being friendly. She's got to be confused and lonely and scared." She turned her palms upward in question. "I thought it'd be nice to give her some attention and make her feel helpful."

He crossed his arms and stepped closer, lip curled. "On the surface, that does sound nice—thoughtful, even—until I remember that you're great at making people feel like they matter to you, until they don't. I don't want my daughter getting attached to you when I know you'll vanish from her life once you get bored."

Although Steffi admired Ryan's desire to protect Emmy, she also refused to be his dumping ground.

She pushed at his shoulder. "Enough already. I've apologized for the past. I'm not proud of how I acted back then, but I can't change it, either. I was nineteen, for God's sake. How about you at least give me a little break for being a stupid teenage girl who was in over her head? As for now, your mom hired me to do a job. I'll be here every day for six to eight weeks, so I'm going to run into Emmy. I won't go out of my way to involve her, but I also won't ignore her if she comes to talk to me. If you don't want to try to be my friend, that's your choice, but that doesn't give you the right to treat me like gum under your shoe. Now, if you'll excuse me, I need to find your mom and say goodbye."

She brushed past him before he could smack her with another hurtful retort.

Molly wasn't in the kitchen or living room, so Steffi decided to text her a note and be on her way. Once she got outside, she found

Molly weeding her flower beds surrounding the hydrangea bushes. "Oh, there you are. I'm done for today. I'll work up a bid by tomorrow."

Molly waved a hand. "Just a formality. And I'm not too worried. My mother left me some money when she died two years ago that's itching to be put to use. The key is to get started right away."

Steffi smiled, grateful that Molly didn't hold a grudge. She welcomed the opportunity to rebuild some semblance of their old relationship, and she needed the work. On the other hand, her being here could make things very hard on Ryan. "Molly, I appreciate this chance, but I'm not sure my working here every day is something Ryan's too jazzed about. Maybe I should recommend someone else for the job."

Molly stood and removed her gardening gloves. "Nonsense. I love my son, but he's got to learn to let go of things."

"Like you managed to do?"

"Honey, you were a young girl. Young girls make lots of mistakes . . . this I know from experience." She winked. "Some of us need to go far and wide before we find our way home. With a limited supply of old friends in our lifetime, it's worth giving them a second chance, don't you think?"

"Thank you for that." Steffi nodded, although she'd pretty much blown any right to call Ryan a friend, and he surely didn't see her as one.

He didn't trust her. Maybe he never would, but maybe she owed it to him to try, even if he rejected her. At the very least, that kind of penance might help her overcome lingering guilt about the way things had ended. "I'll shoot you an estimate and some window options, and then we'll go from there. Red oak floors for that space will cost a couple grand, plus labor. Do you want those, or do you want to use a seal over the flagstone floor?"

"I suppose there's a certain charm to keeping the stone floor, and it never hurts to save a few dollars."

Overhead, a window squeaked open, and Emmy pressed her face to the screen. "Memaw, can you help me unpack my boxes?"

Molly looked up, shading her eyes with one hand. "Close that window unless you want your room to turn into a sauna."

"What's a sauna?" Emmy bounced her nose off the screen a few times, apparently enjoying the springy sensation.

"Never mind. Just close the window. You'll split that screen. I'll be up in a minute." Molly looked at Steffi once the window sash slammed shut. "I hope I'm not too old for all this. I love my son and Emmy, but there's a reason women my age can't have kids."

"Good luck!" Steffi smiled, thinking she liked little Emmy Quinn a lot.

She slid into the driver's seat of her sweltering car, its leather practically fusing with the skin on the back of her thighs. Before starting the engine, she checked her calendar. She'd promised her brother Benny she'd be his training partner for the New York City Marathon this fall. He'd scheduled a four-mile circuit for tonight, so it shouldn't be too bad, even in this heat.

Ben was the youngest of her three older brothers and the only one who still lived nearby. They thought alike: efficient, calm, can-do spirits. Their eldest brother, Matt—a typical firstborn overachiever—lived in Miami and worked as an orthopedic surgeon. He'd never married. Neither had Chris, who currently worked as an assistant strength-and-conditioning coach at the University of Mississippi. Ben—also unattached—worked with their dad at Lockwood Hardware.

Nobody gave a second thought to the fact that none of her brothers were in serious relationships, but she felt pressure—like there was something wrong with *her* for not finding love.

Sometimes she thought life would be easier if she'd been born a guy. She seemed to fit in better with their humor and sensibility than with that of most women she knew. Well, other than Claire and Peyton, which was another reason why she couldn't turn her back on Peyton. Molly's advice about old friends drifted back.

People hurt each other and made big mistakes

now and then, but if they felt remorse, the mistakes shouldn't erase every good thing they ever did. And maybe if Steffi could help Claire forgive Peyton, then there was hope that Ryan might one day forgive her.

Ryan loved Campiti's pizza. Salty cheese. Tiny pepperoni that crisped into little shells filled with puddles of spicy oil. Cherikee Red cherry soda, an old favorite and still just as delicious. The smell of tomato sauce and teen hormones mingling together in the venerable joint. All these things triggered a sort of time warp, reminding him of being young and hopeful, for a change.

The place retained its original decor. Black-and-white-block vinyl floors. Bold yellow Formica booth-style tables aligned along a wall with a poorly done mural of a scene from Naples. Pizza still served on waxed paper. He'd spent a lot of time here with his teammates and Steffi. Good memories. The kind that made the bad ones that much harder to understand.

Emmy sat across from him now, her short legs swinging from her bench seat, face smeared with the orange hue of pizza grease.

"Do you like it?" He wiggled his brows and took a huge bite, having waited long enough to know that the cheese wouldn't burn the roof of his mouth.

Emmy nodded. "Yes, but it's loud in here."

"You're right." He took another mouthful, noticing the hum of the exhaust fans, the barking laughter of a group of kids, and the cashier yelling a takeout order to the pizza maker. "Fun, right?"

Emmy shrugged. "I wish Mom was here. She might like *this* pizza."

Ryan almost choked on his drink, so he pounded the center of his chest. The only food Val liked to consume involved lettuce, sushi, or wine. She might be willing to try fancy artisanal pizza in a high-priced Italian restaurant, but he'd only gotten her past Campiti's front door one time.

"If she visits, you can bring her here."

Emmy smiled broadly. "Let's call her now and ask her."

He still hadn't figured out how to handle conversations about Val with Emmy. After explaining the divorce to their daughter, he and Val had told Emmy she'd be living with him for "a while." He hadn't liked Val's hedge, but Emmy had been so distraught that he hadn't had the heart to take away all her hope at once. Truthfully, he couldn't bear to see the pain of a mother's rejection in his daughter's eyes. For now, he'd let Emmy believe that her mother might change her mind. Maybe Val would surprise him and ask for shared custody.

Ryan pushed aside his pizza, unable to enjoy it, thanks to a healthy case of indigestion. "It's

Friday evening, honey. I doubt she's available."

"Try, Dad." Emmy frowned. "I miss Mom."

Every time he heard those three words, he disliked Val a little more.

"You're what?" Ryan sank onto the corner of the bed while his wife packed her last suitcase. He knew he should be unhappy about the end of his marriage, but they'd been treading water for the past three years for Emmy's sake. This latest pronouncement, however, stunned him.

"I'm leaving Emmy with you. John doesn't want the responsibility of raising her right now. We're young. He wants to travel and enjoy his early retirement."

The forty-two-year-old ex-banker and his golden parachute were making off with Ryan's wife. La-di-da. He couldn't give a damn, except that his daughter's heart would be shattered into pieces he might never be able to mend.

"Val, you can't abandon Emmy."

Val zipped up her bag. "I'm not abandoning her. I'm leaving her with her father. I put in nine years here, managing the day-to-day while you pursued law school and your career. Now it's my turn to have a life."

"Fine." He rose from the bed. "But you tell her. I won't be the heavy."

He should've known Val would wiggle her way out of a confrontation with vague answers that left Emmy with an inaccurate understanding

43

of how her life had been turned upside down. Unfortunately, that small crack had left enough room for Emmy's hope for some kind of reconciliation to flourish.

"Dad?"

"Sorry."

Emmy stuck her hand out, palm upward. "I want to call Mom."

Reluctantly, he withdrew his phone and dialed Val, then handed Emmy the phone and prepared for the worst.

"Mommy!" Emmy's face lit up as she instantly reverted to the sort of baby talk Val had always encouraged as cute.

He couldn't make out what Val was saying, but the mere sound of her voice on the other end of the line made his stomach burn.

"Can you come visit us soon?" While Emmy drew a breath, he winced at her use of the word "us." "We can bring you to this funny pizza shop. It has yellow tables and a bad painting on the wall."

Ryan watched Emmy's hopeful expression melt like a candle giving in to the flame.

"Can I come to London? I want to see Princess Kate!" Her little brows puckered as she struggled not to cry. Seeing his daughter tying herself into a pretzel for her mother's affection snapped something inside.

He gestured for the phone.

"Daddy wants to talk to you. Will you come visit *after* London?" Emmy's chin wobbled at whatever Val said next. "Okay."

She handed Ryan the phone and then toyed with her pizza.

"Val," he said, rising from the table to march outside and tell her off.

"Ryan, I'm running late. I can't talk now. I'll call Emmy tomorrow. In the future, Friday nights aren't the best."

He burst through the swinging door, onto the sidewalk. "Oh? Please share with me a list of *convenient* times to converse with your daughter. I'm sure that will do wonders for her self-esteem, you heartless—"

"Don't start. You can't pull these strings and make me feel bad. I've been a good mother. Man up and be her father for a while."

"You. Are. Unbelievable."

"I could say the same to you. You knew I wouldn't want to come down there for pizza."

"Of course I did, but your daughter begged to talk to you. I won't be accused of standing between you two. But keep this up and pretty soon she won't be asking for you at all. In fact, maybe that's the best thing that could happen." He punched the phone off and scrubbed a hand through his hair, his body strung tight with wanting to hit something.

Three deep breaths later, he smoothed his hair

and returned to Emmy. He threw thirty bucks on the table. "Come on, let's go get some ice cream. I know the best place."

She slid off the prefab bench and followed, but her smile hadn't returned. He crouched to hug her. "I love you, sweetheart."

She wrapped her arms and legs around him, so he stood and carried her out of the store and the next two blocks to Gopher's ice-cream shop. She didn't say a word but laid her head against his shoulder and people-watched along the way. Given her age, he knew she'd let him carry her now only because she was sad. She always got clingier when Val let her down. He had no idea how to help her through this, but he held tight every step.

Sanctuary Sound's central business district consisted of a green commons surrounded by streets, with colorful shop awnings and multiple restaurants, most of which had been around for more than a generation. The townsfolk knew almost everyone by sight, although an influx of vacation homeowners had breathed fresh life into the area.

He noticed the newly laid brick sidewalks, a chic Asian-fusion restaurant that must've opened in the past few months, and a fancy women's apparel store. Of course, the old guard remained—Mother of Purl yarn shop, J. Patrick's Pub, and Lockwood Hardware. He suspected

Ben Lockwood still worked there with his father, although Ryan hadn't run into Ben in a few years.

He stifled a groan when he saw the line outside Gopher's. Bad planning on his part. A muggy Friday night in August—prime time for ice-cream sales. He lowered Emmy to the ground. "Think you can wait a bit? It's a long line."

"Okay."

He glanced at his watch. "Actually, it's close to eight o'clock. Almost bedtime. Maybe we should try tomorrow."

"You promised!"

Technically, he hadn't promised, but he knew she was still processing her disappointment about Val. "Okay. You want to run up and look at the ice-cream-flavor board by the front door?"

"Sure!"

"Go ahead. I'll save our place in line." He never needed to scan the list. Mint chocolate chip: his lifelong go-to.

Emmy scampered ahead and disappeared somewhere in the front of the line. A minute later she came running back. "We can skip in line, Dad. Gimme some money."

"What do you mean we can skip ahead?"

"Miss Lockwood is up front with some man. She said I can go in with them."

He shouldn't care what man Steffi was with, but his pulse kicked an extra beat anyway. Steffi's boyfriend would put a crimp in his mother's not-so-subtle machinations. "So you're going to leave me back here by myself?"

"No, silly. Tell me what you want and I'll get it for us. That way you don't have to wait, either."

"I don't know, Emmy." He didn't want Steffi and her date to do him and his daughter a favor. More important, he didn't want Emmy taking shortcuts in life. "That seems a little unfair. What about all of these other people who've been waiting patiently? How would you feel if you were one of them?"

"Dad." She crossed her arms and let her head fall back with a groan.

"Go tell Miss Lockwood thank you, but we'll wait for our turn."

Emmy scowled and stomped off with all the drama of her mother. When she returned with a pout, he said, "Listen up. You can be nice to me and make the best of our wait, or we can leave right now, because spoiled kids don't get ice cream."

Emmy sighed. "Sorry, Dad."

"Thank you." He ruffled her curls. "Now, what flavor did you choose?"

"Cotton candy."

"No chocolate?"

She shook her head. "Can I get sprinkles?"

"Sure." His teeth hurt from thinking about her choice.

Five minutes later, as they neared the entrance,

Steffi came out through the door, followed by Ben. Ryan chose not to analyze why his muscles relaxed upon seeing that she was with her brother instead of a date. He watched her lick her cone, knowing without needing to verify that she'd ordered pistachio.

"Hey, Ryan." Ben extended his hand. Tall and muscular, Ben Lockwood had been a favorite among the girls in high school, with his sandy-blond hair and dimples like his sister's. It surprised Ryan that he'd never settled down. "Been a while."

"Ben." Ryan shook his hand and nodded a silent hello to Steffi.

They looked like they'd been on a run. Something he used to do with them eons ago when they'd all played soccer. He assumed their next stop would be their dad's, where they'd drink a beer and engage in something competitive like poker or horseshoes. The Lockwoods had always been doers, not talkers.

Ben looked at Emmy. "You decided?"

"Cotton candy," she repeated, smiling.

Ben put out his fist for a little bump. "Good choice."

Emmy giggled. "Are you her boyfriend?"

"Heck, no. I'm her brother." Ben winked at Emmy. Ryan had forgotten how much he'd liked Ben Lockwood. That friendship had been another casualty of Steffi's kiss-off.

Emmy looked at Ryan. "I wish *I* had a brother."

She might've if Val hadn't miscarried their second pregnancy six years ago. After that, Val hadn't wanted to try again for a long time. By the time she might've been willing, the marriage had already been showing signs of trouble.

"Do you have kids?" Emmy asked them both.

"No," they answered in unison.

"Why not?"

"Neither of us is married, for starters," Steffi said.

Not for the first time, Ryan wondered about the men who had come after him, but he brushed the pointless thought aside.

"Why not?" Emmy's relentless interrogations set the stage for a brilliant legal career someday. In that way, she took after him.

"Um." Steffi paused, casting a quick peek at Ryan. "Bad decisions and timing."

Ben ate his ice cream, but Ryan watched his brows rise in surprise. Had Steffi meant to insinuate regret about his and Steffi's demise? And if so, what kind of reaction did she expect from him? He grunted, causing Emmy to look up with a puzzled expression.

"Look, it's our turn to go inside." He nudged his daughter forward. "Let's let these two get on with their night. Say goodbye."

Emmy waved goodbye while he held the screen door open for her.

50

"Have a nice night," Steffi said, catching his eye.

Flustered, he almost smiled. "You too."

Ben waved, and then the Lockwood siblings turned to go off to wherever they planned to spend their night. He stood there, watching them leave, his body flushed from the summer heat and unexpected run-in. Steffi still had those great legs . . .

"Daddy!" Emmy called, having made her way to the counter. He let the screen door slam shut behind him. Damn if Steffi's wistful remark hadn't split a seam in his stitched-up heart. He'd better sew it back up before things began to spill out.

Chapter Three

A light breeze whistled through the leaves of the oak trees overhead, carrying the scent of the nearby seawater. Summer days like this made Steffi want to throw down her tools and jump on a bike. Or hit the beach with sunscreen, a trashy novel, and a friend.

Sighing to herself, she pried another wood strip from the exterior of the screen panels. Damaged or rotted stuff would be discarded, other things could be repurposed, and new elements would be introduced. In the end, the old house would be improved.

If only her life were that predictable. That simple.

Today she'd planned to remove all the screens, but she was running out of time. It was already nearing five o'clock. Given that Ryan preferred no contact with her, she wanted to leave before six to avoid bumping into him. She'd managed to steer clear of him these past few days, but only because she'd been meeting with Molly off-site to pick out windows and moldings and such. Now that demolition had begun, she knew they'd be forced to see each other again.

That thought caused old butterflies to emerge from their chrysalides. She rolled her eyes at herself. Since when had she become a masochist?

The wood strip she tossed onto the pile of ones she'd already removed landed with a satisfactory clatter. Dragging the back of her hand across her brow, she chugged from her water bottle as Molly's car pulled into the detached garage. Steffi heard its doors open and close while Emmy's voice chattered away. That kid could talk.

Steffi waved at them when they crossed the yard toward the back door. Molly was carrying a cake box. Predictably, Emmy followed behind her, wearing a pastel floral sundress and carrying a gift bag in her hand.

"Looks like you two are planning a party." She tried to recall if any of the Quinns' birthdays fell in August but didn't think so. "Special occasion?"

"Ryan's new job was also a sort of promotion, but with the move, we haven't had a chance to make a fuss yet."

Molly's proud smile made Steffi miss her own mother, who remained a dreamlike amalgam of watery memories, scattered photographs, and stories told by her dad and her brothers. Would her mom be proud of whom her only daughter had become—a self-sufficient if slightly lonely construction worker? Visits to her grave never settled that question.

Steffi smiled at Molly. "That's great."

"Something to celebrate in an otherwise turbulent time." Then Molly's gaze darted to Emmy and her ever-alert ears. "I must go set this down, Emmy. Don't distract Miss Lockwood while she's working."

Molly made her way inside, but Emmy lingered a bit, shaking the small pink gift bag dangling from her fingers. "I made my dad a present."

"How thoughtful," Steffi said. "What is it?"

"A cup." Emmy set the bag on the ground and retrieved an oversize coffee mug that she'd painted—in pinks, purples, and reds—at the local pottery-painting studio. "See the heart? And 'Dad' on this side. And this"—she proudly pointed at a giant white-and-yellow flower—"is a daisy because they're my favorite flower." She stuffed the mug back into the bag. "He can take it to work."

"He'll love it." Steffi grinned at the mental picture of Ryan sitting at his desk and drinking from a pink-heart mug with its enormous flower. Those butterflies fluttered again as she imagined sitting across the desk from him, his thick brown hair neatly combed, his sincere brown eyes seducing her from over the brim.

Emmy set the bag on the grass and wandered closer, craning her neck to investigate the pile of trim. "What are you doing?"

The kid treated Steffi like some kind of fascinating zoo creature. Steffi didn't mind her company, although she knew Ryan didn't welcome her involvement. "Removing the wood

54

moldings so I can take out all these screens."

She pried the final strip free and tossed it aside.

"Do you get splinters?" Emmy asked.

"Sometimes, if I forget to wear gloves."

Emmy narrowed her eyes as if trying to judge whether or not this kind of job would be worth risking splinters.

Steffi retrieved her rubber mallet to tap out the screen panels. Emmy wandered to her side and crouched, watching her tap and then nudge the first screen free.

"Can I try?" Emmy looked up, her pleading hazel eyes making it hard to say no. Steffi had warned Ryan that she wouldn't turn Emmy away. It was up to him to get her to leave Steffi alone, not the other way around.

"How about we make a deal? I'll let you help with one panel, but then you go inside and help your memaw get the house ready for your dad's special dinner?"

"Deal." Emmy nodded like a boss, apparently having inherited her dad's take-charge spirit. Then Emmy thrust out her hands for the mallet.

"Now, listen, you can't whack at it. Tap gently around the edges, and then we nudge. Okay?" She held on to the mallet while awaiting agreement.

"Okay." Emmy took the mallet in both hands and gave it a midair test swing.

"Tap it right here and here." Steffi pointed to the lower left corner of the frame. "Then I'll reach the high points, and you can help me push it out."

Emmy furrowed her little brows and tapped a little too gently at first, but then gave it some more oomph, loosening it from the post. After Steffi hit the high spots, they pushed the screen free, with Steffi keeping hold of it so it didn't crash onto the stone floor. "Good job, Emmy. Pretty soon you'll be wearing work shoes and protective eye gear."

Emmy smiled dubiously. "I don't know about *that.*"

Steffi's phone rang, interrupting their debate. *Peyton?* She hadn't called since their last awkward exchange following the mugging. "Hey. What's up?"

Instead of Peyton's voice, she heard sniffling followed by a croak. "Steffi, I'm in trouble."

"What kind of trouble?" Hopefully not the kind that would require Ryan's professional services. Peyton had always been a bit of a risk-taker— from teenage pool hopping to the occasional billiards hustle.

"I . . . I have . . ." A choked sob came through the line. Steffi's heart pounded in her ears while she waited for whatever terrible news was coming. "I have cancer."

"What?" Steffi blinked as if she'd heard wrong, one hand covering her mouth. She leaned against the porch column for support, trying to block out Peyton's crying so she could think. *Cancer.*

The word never failed to send a cold shock wave through her limbs. The disease had already claimed her mom too young. Now her friend? Her throat closed as she struggled for something to say. "How? When?"

Steffi listened to Peyton ramble incoherently— HER2 positive, chemo, Herceptin, and a string of more confusing medical lingo. She dabbed her watery eyes, hearing herself repeating, "I'm sorry. Oh, I'm so sorry, Peyton."

"Who's Peyton?" Emmy interrupted, surprising Steffi, who'd forgotten about her young audience.

She put her finger to her mouth to shush Emmy while she tried to focus on what Peyton was saying. The chirping and buzzing of birds and insects grew annoyingly loud.

"Why are you crying?" Emmy persisted.

"Not now, Emmy!" she snapped. "Go inside."

Emmy froze for a second before dashing to her gift bag, snatching it off the ground, and bolting inside. *Crap.*

Steffi smacked her forehead, then pinched the bridge of her nose and refocused on Peyton. "What can I do?"

"Pray, I guess. Not that you and I have been the most religious people." Wry humor—one of Peyton's defense mechanisms. Steffi supposed at this point any humor would be better than none.

"Will you be treated at Yale New Haven Hospital?"

"I'm staying with Logan in New York and going to Sloan. At least, that's the plan now. I know I've done things to change our friendship, but I just wanted to bring you up to speed. I know Claire won't care, but maybe you and I could meet for lunch in the city or something."

"Of course." Things might be strained because of all the romance drama, but she'd never turn her back on a lifelong friend in crisis. "Why are you staying with your brother? Where's Todd?"

Not that Steffi cared about Todd or wanted to see him. In her opinion, he belonged in a special circle of hell. As her thoughts looped, she realized Peyton hadn't answered her question. Silence stretched between them while warm summer breezes plagued Steffi with the false promise of a pleasant evening.

"Gone." Peyton's deadened tone suggested she was still in shock. "He started distancing himself when they found the lump a month ago. Told me he couldn't handle this—I think he actually used words like 'didn't sign up for this.' " Peyton sniffled, but Steffi couldn't pretend to be surprised. "He's not who I thought he was, and right now I don't want to be alone."

"I'm sorry, Peyton." Todd had now devastated two of Steffi's friends, which made him the biggest ass-wipe she knew. Her mom's deathbed advice drifted back and caused her to frown, because it didn't apply to Peyton. Peyton did—and should—regret a decision that had, for a while, made her happy. "Can I come visit this Sunday?"

"I'd love that."

"Perfect." She held her breath for a second, then tiptoed onto a minefield. "So, is this news something I should share with Claire?"

"Why bother? She hates me." Peyton's quiet words landed like deadweights filled with misery.

"She's hurt and angry, but hate? I don't believe it. I can't." A memory of the three of them huddled in a tent while camping out on the Prescott lawn resurfaced. Flashlights, caramel-coated popcorn, gossip, and *Teen* magazine. If only a night of innocent giggling beneath the stars would cure what ailed them all now. "But I don't want to overstep. If you'd rather no one else know for a while, I won't say a word."

Another long pause preceded Peyton's response. "It's not a secret. There'll be no hiding my bald head and double mastectomy."

Steffi held her tongue. Now wasn't the time for lectures or pep talks. And like the rest of the Prescotts, Peyton had always taken pride in her Pantene model–worthy hair and enviable figure. Losing them would be a blow, but even that couldn't compare with confronting her own mortality. "I wish I were with you now. I'll check in tomorrow, but plan on seeing me Sunday."

"Thanks, Steffi. Love you."

"You too." Steffi hung up and shoved the phone

in her pocket. She set one hand on the side of the house while her body begged to crumple to the ground from the weight of the news.

Cancer? They were too young to be dealt those cards. A scream locked and loaded in her throat, but she clamped her mouth shut. Steffi picked up her mallet and swung, hitting the frame too hard. She couldn't be careful now. She had to beat on something.

If Peyton survived, her life would never be the same. Everything would be seen as "before" and "after" the diagnosis. If she were lucky, it'd take years before she'd stop wondering if new mutinous cells were growing. Before she'd stop waiting for that other shoe to drop . . .

Why did bad things have to happen? Out of nowhere, you lose control of your life. You're caught by surprise, hit—

Steffi's ears rang and her vision dimmed as if the sun had ducked behind a cloud despite a clear blue sky.

Gun!

Can't fight.

My hands, my hands. No!

Cold metal. Breathe.

Sweat, pulling. Fingers gripped too tight. Stop!

The mallet landed on Steffi's foot, snapping her back from wherever she'd gone. A ghostly shiver—the hair-raising kind that takes hold when you suspect someone is spying on you—rippled through her body. Her head throbbed. She could cry from frustration—over Peyton. Over her memory problems. Over how complicated life had become.

She gave in to it all and sank to the grass, knees pulled to her chest, her chin tucked, redirecting her thoughts. Peyton had asked for prayers. Maybe God would listen to Steffi's this time.

The sound of another car rolling along the gravel driveway caused her to stand and brush away the grass and dirt. Ryan was home, but he must've gone in through the front door to avoid seeing her.

Steffi roused herself so she could pound out the last panel and get out of Dodge. She picked the mallet off the ground and began to bang the lower corner, when Ryan stormed out to the patio, tie loosened, sleeves pushed halfway up his forearms, eyes blazing.

He planted his hands on his hips. "Did you yell at Emmy?"

"No." Steffi stopped to twist her neck twice before she nudged the first corner loose. "She interrupted my call. I motioned for her to be quiet. When she didn't listen, I was firm."

While she'd been talking, his rigid spine softened. He narrowed his gaze and studied her face. "What's wrong?"

"Nothing," she said, covering, tapping on the final corner of the frame.

"Your eyes are red." He waved two fingers up and down between his brows. "You're doing that scrunchy thing you do when you're upset."

She supposed they'd always know these little details about each other. Old habits, tics, and preferences—like the mint chocolate chip ice cream he'd probably ordered the other night. She'd never been able to hide much from Ryan, and maybe telling him would be good practice for telling Claire.

The words formed a lump in her throat, so she coughed them up before they choked her. "I was on with Peyton. She's been diagnosed with breast cancer."

Her voice cracked open as those words, once spoken, cemented the reality she'd rather deny.

Ryan's shoulders fell, and the tension tugging at his jaw released. Years ago, he would've wrapped her in one of his generous hugs. Instead, he rubbed his chin before scrubbing the back of his neck and then crossing his arms. "I'm sorry to hear that."

"Are you?" She felt her nostrils flare and fought the stinging in her eyes. The antagonism brewing inside had less to do with Ryan than it did with the news itself, but she couldn't argue with a diagnosis. She *could* argue with a man. "A few days ago you'd written her off as irredeemable, just like me. I would've guessed you think people like Peyton and me deserve this kind of punishment."

His head tipped back as if she'd punched him in the nose. "My whole career is about *fair* prosecution and sentencing. I'm the last person to advocate capital punishment."

Death. He'd said it in a roundabout way, but it still hit Steffi in the chest as hard as any swing from her mallet. His pinched expression suggested he wished he'd thought harder before blurting that out.

"She's not going to die!" Steffi shouted, more at the sky than at Ryan, and then took a hard swing at the screen frame, sending it clattering onto the patio.

Ryan had rarely seen Steffi lose her shit. Between her mom's death and her dad and brothers toughening her up, he used to tease her about the liquid steel in her veins. Seeing her in a fragile state threw him, although he should've realized Peyton's diagnosis would bring back agonizing memories of her mother's cancer. "Peyton's a fighter. Her family has the resources to get the best doctors and treatment. She'll survive. I'm sure of it."

"Then why'd you say what you said?" she demanded, her voice bleak.

He shrugged, suddenly thirsty as hell. "Seems the only way I know how to talk to you now is to argue. Sorry."

They stood a few feet apart, speechless. His

breath burned inside his chest as he fought his old inclination to comfort her.

Steffi tossed the mallet on the grass and bent over to drag the screen off the patio.

Unable to think of anything else to say, but unsure of whether to leave her alone in this state, Ryan made himself useful and lifted the other side to help her carry it off the porch. "Will you be okay?"

"Yes." She swiped some of the hairs off her face that had pulled free from her ponytail. "Thanks."

Her one-word replies didn't surprise him. "Okay. Guess I'll see you later."

He turned to go inside, but before he reached the door, she asked, "How *do* you do it?"

"Do what?"

"Defend criminals. Set them free so they can commit more crimes, hurt more people." Her voice sounded hoarse.

"To make sure everyone—not just wealthy people—gets a fair shot at justice."

"If someone doesn't want to be arrested, they shouldn't commit a crime." She affected a self-righteous expression, then frowned and muttered, "It'd be my luck that you'd end up defending those jerks who jumped me."

"What?" She'd been attacked? And why did that thought sucker punch him in the gut? "Who jumped you?"

She bent over and dry heaved, her gaze turning

unfocused. Her body quivered like it might crumple at any second—like she was there but not there.

"Steffi, you okay?" When she didn't answer, he crossed to her just in time to catch her before she collapsed. "Hey. Hey now."

He held on to her, waiting for her to regain her balance. Meanwhile, holding her in his arms opened the door to a thousand memories. The fresh summer scent of her skin, the warmth, the silky texture of her hair on his neck—all assaulted his senses. For years, holding her had been as natural as breathing, so maybe that explained why they stood there, frozen in a sort of silent semihug, neither one quite sure what to do next.

Steffi cleared her throat and eased away first. Of course she did. "I'm sorry I snapped at Emmy. I'll apologize."

Ryan waved his hands, still warm from the heat of her, like tumbled sheets after a lover leaves the bed. "I'll talk to her about respecting when people are on the phone and tell her to quit pestering you while you work."

"Look, I don't mind her, Ryan. She's funny, and feisty."

"She can be, on a good day." He chuckled, as he often did when talking about Emmy. It was weird to laugh about her with Steffi—a woman he'd once thought would be the mother of his children.

"I'm sure all the change is hard on her. I get why you want to be careful about who she gets close to. But if 'helping' me makes her feel productive and happy, isn't that a good thing? I won't become her BFF or make her any promises."

He tilted his head. "Why do you even care? Wouldn't it be easier if she stayed out of your way?"

Steffi rolled her eyes in a way that suggested she was disappointed he hadn't put it together on his own. "She's basically lost her mom. There's no changing that fact, but if I can help fill in the gap until Val comes to her senses, I'm happy to do it."

All the hairs on his neck prickled. He didn't want to discuss Val with *her,* of all people. He didn't want her pity or sympathy or help. Not for himself. And maybe not for his daughter, although he no longer felt as certain about that opinion.

The back door opened, and his mom poked her head out. "Dinner's ready."

"Be right there," Ryan replied. For a nanosecond he wondered if his mother would dare invite Steffi to stay, but she didn't. His mom simply nodded and disappeared, leaving the door cracked open.

"You should go. They want to celebrate your promotion."

That reminded him of the claim she'd made about being jumped. He wanted to know more, but now wasn't the time to press. Everything that had happened in the past fifteen minutes had siphoned some heat from his anger, leaving him slightly light-headed. "Have a good night. Give Peyton my best. And stay positive."

Steffi nodded, color returning to her cheeks and strength in her stance. He'd known she'd tap into that sooner than later. "Good night."

He wandered inside and made his way to the dining room, where his parents and daughter were seated. One hour and eleven million calories later, he was helping his mom with the dishes while his dad read with Emmy.

His thoughts meandered to Steffi again, like they'd done a few times since he'd first seen her on the back porch after so many years apart. Years during which they'd both been changed by their different experiences. Until now, he hadn't wanted to acknowledge that because it'd been easier to hate her than to wonder who she'd become. To consider that maybe she had her own set of troubles and regrets, just like him.

"Mom, did you ever hear anything about Steffi getting jumped?" He kept his eyes on the pot he was scrubbing.

"Word is she got mugged in Hartford about three or four months ago. Bad concussion, lots of bruises."

No doubt she'd fought back. Steffi never yielded. Not when her mom died and she took over managing laundry and meals for her father and brothers. Not when facing down the most fearsome strikers of any Division I soccer team. And apparently not even in the face of the impossible task of mending Claire and Peyton's broken friendship.

He wondered why his mother had never mentioned the attack, though. Of course, that would've been around the same time that he'd first become suspicious of Val and had been otherwise preoccupied with his own life unraveling. Plus, he'd pretty much instituted a "Never mention Steffi's name again" policy not long after their breakup. "Did they arrest anyone?"

"I don't think so, but I don't know." She took the wet pot from the drying rack and rubbed it dry with a dish towel. "You know the Lockwoods are private people."

"Oh, I know." It'd been his one complaint about Steffi when they dated. Emotional intimacy didn't come easy to her. After her mom's death, she'd spent the rest of her formative years living with four men, none of whom were big talkers. Ryan had sat through family dinners where Mr. Lockwood barely said ten words. What talking did occur while passing the peas generally consisted of a friendly fire of sarcasm between brothers, the likes of which he hadn't experienced with his sister and mom.

His chances of getting Steffi to share details about that attack were less than nil. Tonight he'd run her name through the system and see if he could find an open assault case and learn who was defending the perps. If it had been a random act with no witnesses or suspects, she'd probably never get closure.

Having gone years without closure about the reasons for their breakup, he could understand that particular kind of frustration. A few days ago, he might've thought turnabout was a form of fair play. Tonight? Not so much.

Chapter Four

Steffi sat on the porch swing of the vintage yellow Craftsman bungalow she and Claire were renting, sipping a cup of tea. Across the street, the Marsh boys were tossing a football in their yard. Their French bulldog, Bubba, bolted back and forth, jumping as if he had a shot at catching that ball.

The evening sun tinted the late summer sky with swaths of peach and lilac, setting the stage for a tranquil kind of mood, were it not for the memory of Peyton's wobbly voice looping through her thoughts. Steffi had never handled sorrow well, preferring to "man up" and move on. But this news—cancer—brought back too many memories she couldn't escape.

Now her friend—someone with whom she'd played on these very streets—might not exist in a year or two. Might never have the chance to repair relationships, accomplish goals, marry, have kids, or do any of the other things people their age still took for granted. The randomness and finality of it all made her head pound.

Claire's orange convertible VW Beetle pulled up to the curb, blaring Wesley Shultz's voice singing "Angela." The diminutive car suited Claire, who stood a full seven inches shorter than Steffi's five-nine frame.

She waved at Steffi before grabbing a large fabric-sample book from the passenger seat, along with her cane, which Claire had long ago dubbed "Rosie." Steffi would offer to help, but Claire's pride made her chafe at unsolicited assistance. Right now, Steffi needed to conserve her energy for the ensuing conversation.

"Gorgeous night!" Claire smiled broadly, looking like she'd stepped out of the pages of a Vineyard Vines catalog in her colorful, boxy dress and tassel-embellished flats.

Quite a different look from the tennis whites she'd worn years ago when in training. That was before Claire had been one of the victims of the sociopath who'd unloaded his gun at an outlet mall thirty minutes from town. At fifteen, she'd undergone multiple surgeries to repair all the damage the bullet had done when it shattered her acetabulum, and months of rehab before she could walk again.

Steffi remembered helping pack boxes with Claire's tennis rackets, outfits, and other gear. Mrs. McKenna had wanted all reminders of that promising tennis career put away before Claire came home. But as difficult as that time had been, what Peyton now faced would be worse, and the future less certain.

Steffi nodded, unable to speak, thanks to the increasing thickness in her throat. She couldn't predict how Claire would react to the news, but Steffi had to tell her.

Claire hobbled up the two steps to the porch and flung the thick book on the rattan chair. She fingered the leaves of the potted soft shield fern in the hanging basket. "Are things on schedule at the Quinns'?"

"Yes, taskmaster," Steffi teased, latching on to the opportunity to procrastinate. "Demolition is on track."

"I don't mean to push, but you know we've sunk everything into this business. Can't afford to fail." Claire adjusted her headband to keep her auburn hair out of her eyes and grinned again, unburdened by the bad news that had tied Steffi into a giant knot.

"We won't fail." She had never failed at anything and didn't plan to start now.

"Don't jinx us with that kind of talk." Claire's anxiety—also a side effect of what had happened to her—colored most of her thoughts. She'd remained in the bubble of Sanctuary Sound all these years. Although she'd never quite regained all the spirit she'd had before that incident, Steffi admired Claire's ability to channel her energy into a new passion. "While I was at Donatella's Tile Emporium, I met a woman who was browsing for countertops. Apparently, she and her husband just put money in escrow on a place on Hightop Road. We talked for a while, so I gave her my card. I think we'll be hearing from her."

"That's great." Steffi worked up a smile for

her eager, earnest friend, who was better at client leads and relationships than she could ever be. Their complementary skills would no doubt help them succeed.

"I wish we had a few more projects completed so we could revamp our website gallery page. But between the Quinns and this potential project, we'll have some new work to show prospective customers by Christmas. New business stress aside, this is all much more fun than working at the Ethan Allen store in Madison." Then, as if finally taking a minute to look at Steffi, she asked, "What's got your tongue?"

Steffi drew a deep breath, rocking slightly while clutching her stomach. "I spoke with Peyton earlier."

Claire's face paled so much even her freckles turned white. Her entire being stiffened as she held up one hand. "Stop!"

"Wait, Claire. This is important."

Claire covered her ears and squeezed her eyes shut. "I mean it. I don't want to know if she's getting engaged or anything else. Drop it."

"Claire!" Steffi's voice boomed with the force of a good left hook, at which point Claire's eyes popped open and she dropped her arms to her sides. Before Steffi lost courage, she blurted, "Peyton has breast cancer."

If she hadn't been watching very carefully, she would've missed Claire's thick swallow. Otherwise, Claire stood motionless and speechless for several seconds.

The world around them moved on as if that statement meant nothing. Bubba barked when Sammy Marsh bolted into the street to retrieve the errant football. The Mannings' car crunched against the gravel next door when it pulled into the driveway. Meanwhile, Steffi waited.

"I'm hungry," Claire finally said, her voice rough, as if those words had been dragged across sandpaper. "I'll fix us a salad."

She crossed to the screen door, cane thumping on the wood porch with her uneven gait, and went inside, leaving the sample book behind.

Well, that went well.

If she'd hoped that the news would've tugged at some sympathetic cord in Claire's heart and opened a door to reconciliation, she'd been mistaken. Steffi eased off the swing and snatched the sample book.

Once inside, she set it on the entry table. The tiny rented home's bright and airy appeal didn't decrease the tension. Steffi stood in the living room, counting to ten, letting her gaze wander from the creamy-white walls to the dove-gray woodwork and brick fireplace to the sparse charcoal-colored furnishings with pops of turquoise. *Breathe.*

Steffi strode to the back of the house, shoes thudding against the hardwood, where she found

Claire standing at the kitchen sink, staring blankly out the back window. Without facing Steffi, she said, "I can't forgive her just because she's sick. I don't wish cancer on her, though."

"Of course you don't." Steffi's stomach tightened when thinking of the final bit of news she'd yet to share. If Claire freaked at hearing Peyton's name, she might lose her mind when Steffi mentioned Todd. "Not that you care, but Todd left her when they got the news."

Claire's head drooped as if it couldn't bear the weight of her disappointment over who her ex had turned out to be. "He's scum, but I sure don't feel sorry for *her* about him."

"I'm not asking you to feel sorry. I'm not asking you to feel anything, Claire. I just thought you should know so you don't think that I'm keeping things from you." She leaned against the counter and stared at her friend's profile. "I'm going to New York to meet her for lunch on Sunday."

Claire snapped her gaze to Steffi. "Surely you don't expect me to come with you."

"Maybe I'd hoped . . ."

"Don't hope. And don't you dare put guilt on me." Claire's blue eyes filled with tears. "A maniac with a gun stole tennis from me, but I rebuilt a life here. A quiet life, but a good one. I was happy. I fell in love. I thought I had a marriage and kids in my near future. Then Peyton took it all away. She did that to me . . ." Claire swiped her cheek. "I get that Todd was a bastard, but she was my friend. One of my *best* friends! I'll never forgive what she did to me."

The sharp ache in Claire's voice kept Steffi from pressing. The distinctions that Peyton didn't know Todd was Claire's boyfriend when she first met him at the coffee shop and that she didn't act on her attraction to Todd until after the breakup were meaningless to Claire. They had, however, been the facts that had kept Steffi from cutting Peyton out of her life, too.

She stroked Claire's arm. "I worry that holding on to this anger hurts you more than it helps."

"I've lost my appetite." Claire moved away from her and the sink. Usually Claire ate her way through the kitchen when she got upset. Steffi had never seen anything kill Claire's appetite until today. "I think I'll take a shower and read for a while."

Claire often retreated into a book when she didn't want to deal with reality. She had been doing that since childhood, which explained the overstuffed bookshelves throughout their small home. Everything from *Soul Surfer* to *Lean In* to *The Duke and I* was on those shelves. She loved those rogue dukes.

Funny enough, prior to meeting Peyton, Todd hadn't struck Steffi as a playboy. He'd been a rather quiet local newspaper editor and Scrabble fanatic. Affectionate with Claire. In fact, Steffi had no clue why Peyton had fallen so hard for him, unless it was due to his utter fascination with *her*.

"Okay. I'll fix you a plate in case you get hungry later." Steffi sighed.

Claire nodded and then disappeared. Steffi heard Rosie thumping its way up the stairs. Then the pipes creaked once Claire turned on the water.

Steffi collapsed against the refrigerator and rubbed her forehead. She wasn't hungry, either. In fact, she needed to run. Far and fast, if possible. She dug her phone out of her pocket as soon as she finished making Claire a sandwich. "Benny . . . meet you in ten minutes for seven quick miles?"

"Sure. Come to me this time. We'll start here."

"Good, actually. Let's work Hightop Road into the route." Might as well try to see if she could get a peek at the house that could be her next job.

Forty minutes later, her pulse hammered to the rhythm of her feet against the pavement. Normally, long runs cleared her head, but no matter how hard she pushed tonight, she couldn't outrun her concern for Peyton. Concern that mingled with misty flashbacks of her own weakened mother wearing colorful scarves while putting on a brave face for her kids. Steffi had boxed those up and stowed them under her bed, occasionally using one to tie a pretty bow around a vase of flowers she would leave on her mom's grave at Christmas.

Her legs grew heavier as her thoughts darkened. She shook her head to clear those images. When she neared the top of Hightop Road, she noticed a beautiful old shingle-style home with a "Sold" sign in its yard and stopped. The sizable home—maybe thirty-five hundred square feet or so—had a wraparound porch and widow's walk. She couldn't tell from the front, but from this location, she suspected there were water views from the back of the home. If they got to remodel a kitchen and bathrooms, this could be a profitable job.

Benny caught up to her and stopped. "Jesus, you're on a tear. What are you running from today?"

It both irked and comforted her that he understood her that well. "Just checking out this house. Might be a new client soon."

Benny glanced at the house, then back at her, his head tipped to one side. "Nice, but you weren't sprinting all this way just to get a look at this house. What's wrong?"

"Oh, life." She attempted a smirking kind of smile.

He yanked her ponytail. "Don't pull that shit with me. Spill. Is it Ryan? Has he been giving you a hard time?"

"No. It's Peyton." She blinked rapidly, standing on the side of the road, fighting the tears forming. Tucking her arms at her sides, she shuffled her feet while staring at the ground. "She's sick. Cancer."

"Aw, shit. Really?" He paled. Cancer brought up bad memories for him, too. She half suspected those same memories were why two of her brothers had left town and rarely came home. Lockwoods were natural-born runners, after all. A second later Benny reached out and pulled her into a hug. "I'm sorry, sis."

His broad chest and strong arms comforted her, despite the sweaty shirt against her cheek. She released the fear and sorrow that crashed over her in waves, like the ocean far below, and nestled into the security of her brother's love.

The wordless support reminded her of earlier, when Ryan had kept her from falling. She'd wanted to cling to him then, not just because of Peyton, but because he embodied her lost innocence, lost love, and everything she wished she had back in her life. But Ryan had made his general disdain for her clear, so she'd pushed away from him even though she'd needed to be held more than she'd needed anything in a long time.

Benny squeezed her and kissed the top of her head. "How's she handling it?"

"I'll know more on Sunday." Steffi eased away. "I'm meeting her for lunch."

"I can't believe it." Benny crossed his arms and looked off into the distance, head shaking. He'd been only a year ahead of them in school, so he'd hung out with Peyton and Claire almost as much as Steffi had. This had to hurt him a little, although Steffi knew he wouldn't show much emotion. It just wasn't in the Lockwood DNA. "Tell her I'm pulling for her."

"Of course." Steffi pressed her hands to her face, then shook off as much of the sorrow as she could.

"Disaster can strike anyone, anytime." Benny frowned. "News like this makes you check your priorities, take risks . . ."

Steffi had always thought Benny's life was exactly as he wanted it. "Sounds like you've got a question mark in there somewhere. Is something up?"

He looked away. "Nah."

"Now who's hiding?" She poked his shoulder.

He batted her hand. "I'm a guy. That's what we do." And then, before she could prod further and turn it into a real discussion, he said, "Race ya back to my house."

"Hey!" she called, now chasing him to catch up, fresh salt air pumping in and out of her lungs. With each step, she thanked God for her good health. For her family and friends. For the ability to do a job she loved. All in all, her life and priorities were pretty good, as long as she didn't think about her nonexistent love life.

Ryan's surprisingly concerned expression resurfaced.

Maybe Benny was right. Maybe she should take a risk before her time was up.

• • •

Ryan dumped the file on his desk before collapsing onto his chair and scrubbing his hands through his head. His new job meant handling more serious cases, like this newly assigned rape case, *State of Connecticut v. Owen O'Malley.*

The alleged victim claimed that Ryan's client, O'Malley, had raped her. After reading through the file, Ryan had his own theory.

The victim had prior arrests for prostitution. Meanwhile, his client had an IQ of seventy. His gut told him that the victim tried to take advantage of O'Malley, and when O'Malley didn't pay, she cried rape.

His client's IQ ought to be low enough to argue diminished mental capacity, which would undercut the requisite intent needed for a guilty verdict. The really hard part was that his client had become enraged when pressed for the money and hurt the victim when he pushed her aside to flee the scene.

This wouldn't be the first case where a prostitute filed rape charges. Prostitutes did get raped sometimes, but he didn't believe O'Malley raped this one. Maybe the guy had hurt her in his angry retreat—he was a big, bulky man—but that wasn't rape. The fact that his client had become so agitated when pressed for payment supported Ryan's theory that O'Malley didn't understand that she was a prostitute.

He thumbed through the police report again.

While he read the victim statement and took notes, the phone rang.

"Val?" He looked at the clock. Emmy shouldn't be home from school yet, so she couldn't have called Val for anything. "What's up?"

"Are you free to come to a mediation meeting next Monday at nine a.m.?"

He leaned back in his chair, tossing his pencil on the desk. "What's this one for?"

"You're the lawyer. Don't ask *me* why everything needs to be so complicated." He heard her sigh and imagined her raking her hand through her hair like she did when she got frustrated. "I just want to settle the money stuff so we can move on."

The money stuff, as opposed to the custody stuff. Why she needed money was beyond him. She'd moved in with her rich lover. According to Emmy, their home was a sleek penthouse overlooking Boston Harbor and the Financial District. Probably cost a few mil.

Ryan, on the other hand, certainly wasn't rolling in dough working for the government. He couldn't get his own place until he had a better grip on his finances, so he flipped through his docket calendar. "Looks like I can make it."

"Good. See you then. And before you complain about having to come back for these meetings, remember this can be over quickly if you're fair."

Fair? In his mind, he smashed the phone against

the desk while laughing maniacally. Looking back, his entire life with Val had been a string of impulsive, out-of-control events. Rebound sex, unexpected pregnancy, quickie wedding, baby blues . . . He'd love to rein in his life, sooner than later. The first step would be giving his daughter stability. "Speaking of fairness, I know you're off having a blast and all, but could you try to remember to call Emmy every night before she goes to bed?"

"I've been calling her."

"Not last night. And you missed a night last weekend, too."

"She goes to bed at eight o'clock. I'm not always available in the evening."

"Then call her after school, but call her every day." Reminding himself that he had to have a decent relationship with Val for Emmy's sake, he swallowed his pride and softened his tone. "Don't let her think you don't care. It's brutal having to dry her tears to get her to sleep."

"Who knew you could be so empathetic? Maybe if you showed this much emotion when we were together, I wouldn't have left."

"Thank God for small favors," he mumbled.

"What?"

"Nothing. Just, please, think about Emmy."

"I do, Ryan. She's my daughter. I love her, and she knows that. She's probably playing it up to manipulate you and your mother. And speaking of your mom, make sure she isn't poisoning Emmy against me."

For the love of God. Only someone manipulative herself could dream up that scenario. "She wouldn't do that, Valerie."

"She never thought I was good enough for you. Until you get your own place, she's got unsupervised access to Emmy. I don't need her planting ideas about me in our daughter's head. I'm still her mother."

"Then act like one." He hung up without another word. He'd been so determined to succeed at love after his failed relationship with Steffi that he'd ignored all the signs that had doomed his marriage to Val.

Steffi. Their interactions this past week had him all turned around. He hadn't discovered any open criminal cases in which she was named as the victim. The cops mustn't have had enough evidence to make any arrests. Why he cared, he couldn't say.

She hadn't been part of his life for a decade. Well, no part of his real life. She'd always been lurking just beneath the surface of his memories, though. The ones he'd tried to bury deeper than a coffin. If he'd found an open case, seen who was handling it, maybe . . . maybe what? Nothing, actually. The damn divorce uncertainty had him reeling so badly that he'd grasp at any straw to think about something else.

He was staring into space when a young investigator, Billy Friday, stopped at his desk. "Hey, Ryan. Here's the report I worked up on the Haney assault case."

"Great." Ryan took it from Billy, who looked to be about twenty-five—wiry frame, with a tattoo poking out of his left sleeve. His black hair was a few shades darker than his eyes. He might look a little threatening if not for the toothy grin. "How's it going so far?"

"Pretty good." Billy crossed his arms and leaned his hip against a chair. "The only bad part is the shit my brother gives me. He's a narco. Got my mom convinced I put scum back on the street."

Ryan whistled. "I'd like to be at one of those family dinners."

"Some of the stuff I've heard around here lately makes it harder to brush that off. There's a shit-ton of repeat offenders and outright liars."

"There are also shitty cops—not your brother, of course—and lawyers out there bending the rules or outright breaking them. And rich dicks who rob the public blind but pay lawyers and bribes to get away with it. We make sure the average Joe gets a fair trial without going bankrupt."

"Truth." Billy nodded. "So I'll keep digging on that aggravated-assault case, too. See if I can find another witness to counter the prosecution's main witness."

"Great."

"See you later."

Ryan waved Billy off and tossed the file on his desk. He didn't need more work today, but he'd have to keep on top of a bunch of open cases now. If that meant taking some files home tonight, then so be it. Not like he had better plans.

Ryan's mother had left an earlier message telling him that she was taking his dad to the doctor and leaving Emmy at the house to do homework while Steffi worked. When he arrived at home, he noticed Steffi's van still parked in front of the house, while his mother's car was nowhere to be seen.

He killed the engine and let his head fall back against the seat, closing his eyes to draw a breath. Guess that trip to urgent care this afternoon wasn't an overreaction on his dad's part.

He called his mother as he exited the car, then stood in the driveway. "What's wrong with Dad?"

"Gout!" she replied, sounding shocked. "We're at the pharmacy waiting for a prescription. Be home soon, but dinner will be late."

"I can pick up fried chicken or something."

"Good idea. Let me get it on our way home. It's just around the corner from here."

"Okay, see you soon. Tell Dad I'm sorry. I hear that's pretty painful."

"I'm the one you should feel sorry for. He's

such a baby when he's sick." She clicked off the phone.

He couldn't remember a day when his mother hadn't been a frank, no-nonsense kind of woman. She'd been the "cool" mom, thanks to her open-minded attitude about teen sex and other things that drove most parents around the bend. She'd also taught his older sister, Miranda, to be savvy and assertive, take control of her sexuality, and have a healthy no-BS meter. Miranda became a wedding planner after moving to New York City with her lover, Linda. He admired his sister, although they weren't as close as he'd like. She was five years older than he was, and they hadn't lived under the same roof since he was thirteen.

His father, on the other hand, had been a bit reclusive—drinking his nightly glass of whiskey, quietly tinkering away at his hobbies, keeping largely out of view except at meals. Still, the man got a kick out of his wife's spunky attitude and took pride in both Ryan and Miranda. His mom would be able to handle life on her own, but his dad might wither if left to his own devices. It was almost as if he needed to borrow from his wife's energy to engage with others.

Ryan wondered how that felt, though—to truly love one's wife. Like most of his Boston College teammates, he'd been attracted to Val. At twenty-one, she'd looked like a starlet. They'd had sex so often he'd worried he might hurt himself. But in those first few months, he'd never taken the time to really know her. In hindsight, all that sex had been about burying the pain of Steffi's humiliating rejection. He'd thought winning Val's attention would somehow prove something to Steffi. Make her see what she'd missed. Make her jealous. In truth, he'd probably been trying to prove something to himself. In any case, his idiotic plan for revenge had turned serious when Val got pregnant.

He'd gone into his marriage with good intentions, looking for things to love about her, and for a way to build a happy life. The kind of life he'd known as a kid and always assumed he'd create for his own children.

Val had been supportive while he was in law school. Both of them worked part-time jobs to put a roof over Emmy's head and food in their stomachs. Once he got a full-time job, Val quit to be a stay-at-home mother. For a while, he'd thought they'd found a comfortable enough kind of love so that his little family might be okay.

Apparently, he'd seen what he wanted to see, because obviously things were never really okay. Love—deep love—never existed in their home. They'd both wanted something the other couldn't quite provide, so Val went and found it elsewhere. He was still searching.

He grabbed the mail on his way inside and tossed it and his keys and phone on the table.

Dropping his briefcase on the floor, he called out, "Emmy!"

When she didn't answer, he wandered to the back of the house. Through the window in the kitchen door, he saw Emmy on the patio with Steffi. His daughter looked adorable, bent over in her ruffled dress while taking instructions on the proper use of a socket wrench.

Emmy tried to screw the washer and cap on a giant bolt that fastened the bottom plate that would form the base of the new walls. He had to chuckle at his little princess getting her hands dirty.

Normally, she preferred dolls, teacups, and Disney movies to hard labor. He'd routinely come home to find Val and Emmy doing at-home manicures. Val never gave Emmy real responsibilities, though, as if keeping her dependent would prevent her from growing up. In that wish, he couldn't quite blame his ex. Days turned into weeks and months and years so fast he could barely believe how quickly the last decade had passed.

He opened the patio door, keeping his eyes on his daughter to give himself time to set his game face before he glanced at Steffi. "Hey. What's going on out here?"

Emmy picked up her head and waved. "Look, Dad! I'm building a wall."

Her eyes sparkled with pride and even a little stunned fascination. At a time when Emmy might otherwise be moody and unhappy, Ryan should be grateful to Steffi for keeping his daughter preoccupied. Part of him was, but another part worried about Emmy's fragile heart.

"That's great, princess, but is your homework finished?" He crossed his arms, looking like the killjoy he was.

"I'll do it later." She resumed winding the wrench handle, her little tongue poking its way out of the corner of her mouth while she concentrated.

Steffi peered down at the bolt. "That's it. Tug really hard with both hands to make sure it's extra tight. We don't want the wall to fall on your head."

Emmy giggled, and tugged with both hands, as instructed. Seeing her ditch dolls and glitter to happily hunker down with Steffi and a wrench tweaked Ryan's heart. How different might life have been if things with Steffi and him hadn't fallen apart?

"Let's get your homework done before you get too tired." It'd be okay if these two spent a *little* time together, but he'd have to keep an eye on this relationship. He didn't hate Steffi anymore, but he still didn't trust her. "Maybe you can help Steffi another day, as long as it's okay with her."

"Daddy." Emmy scowled. "Pleeeease!"

He shook his head. "Don't argue. Wash your hands and hit the books."

Emmy dropped the wrench on the flagstone and stomped across the patio, her skirt flouncing as she went. "Who cares about stupid social studies anyway?" she grumbled before disappearing into the house.

"Sorry you got stuck watching her. I doubt my mom intended to be gone this long." Ryan finally met Steffi's gaze. He wiped his clammy palms on the insides of his pants pockets while standing there staring into her eyes. "I know you've got a schedule to keep."

"How's your dad?" Steffi broke the spell when she dropped to her knees to finish tightening the bolt.

"Gout. He'll be fine as long as he doesn't whine too much, in which case my mom will kill him." Ryan chuckled, then caught himself and stopped.

Too late. When Steffi smiled, her dimples popped into place. He'd always liked those damn indents too much.

She joked, "I'll keep an eye on Molly so she doesn't end up needing your services."

"Thanks." He paused, seeking to prolong their conversation even as that desire bombarded him with panic. He tugged at his shirt collar, then crouched to her level. "Have you spoken with Peyton again?"

She sat back on her haunches before she answered. "I'm visiting her this weekend."

"Give her my best wishes." He stood again,

suddenly in need of air that didn't smell like Steffi's shampoo. "Is Claire going, too?"

Steffi shook her head. "No."

He nodded, unsurprised. Claire had lost a lot in her life, and he doubted much would make her willing to forgive and forget her friend's betrayal. "Must be tough to be in the middle."

"More so now, that's for sure." Steffi grabbed the final set of base plates and fitted them over another section of bolts between two posts. Once she'd slid them into place, she looked up at him and tugged at her ear. "I have something to tell you, but I don't want you to freak out."

"Oh?" His stomach tightened. No conversation that started that way ever turned into a happy surprise.

"I think Emmy's having a hard time making new friends at school." Steffi restlessly shifted her weight while waiting for his response.

He frowned. "Why do you think that?"

"During the past two days, she's talked about how much better she liked her old school and friends. That seemed pretty normal, but then today she told me something that made it obvious she's been eating lunch alone." Steffi wrinkled her nose. "She's got a strong personality and definite opinions about things. Her life in Boston sounds like it had a lot more excitement than this little town offers. Maybe she's coming off as a little bossy or snobby to the others? I don't know.

You might want to check in with her teacher."

"Or just talk to her." Ryan glanced through the kitchen door but didn't see his daughter.

"No! If you interrogate her, she'll know I told you. Isn't it better if she feels free to talk openly with me?"

"How about we keep our little détente going by you not giving me parenting advice?" He hoped that came out with less sarcasm than he felt at the moment. Her responding frown proved it hadn't.

"I remember how much I liked talking to your mom when I was younger and didn't want my dad to know everything. An adult 'friend' was an amazing gift. I'm pretty sure your mom was savvy enough to work back channels without my ever knowing." She tipped her chin up with that challenge. Did she think him obtuse now? "But you do what you want. Emmy's your daughter."

He hadn't ever analyzed Steffi's relationship with his mom. He'd been too busy being infatuated by all the little things about her to care much about whether or not she got along with his parents. He might've even egotistically assumed she was nice to them only because of her feelings for *him*. It hadn't occurred to him that she'd had her own reasons for getting close to his mom.

As if her ears were burning, his mom poked her head outside. "Chicken's here."

"Coming." Ryan turned to go inside.

"Can you join us, Stefanie?" His mom smiled,

even as Ryan tried not to stumble. He couldn't rescind her offer, but her heavy-handed meddling stopped his breath.

"Oh, that's okay. You've got your hands full," Steffi replied, sounding equally surprised.

"No, no. It's fine. Mick's upstairs in bed. He's not hungry because of 'the pain.' " She rolled her eyes. "Join us."

Steffi looked at Ryan. He'd rather die than let her think *he* was uncomfortable, so he shrugged as if he couldn't care less.

Unfortunately, she knew him too well. He saw the spark of a dare in her eyes right before she looked at his mother. "Thanks. Sounds nice. I'll be in as soon as I finish cleaning up."

Chapter Five

Steffi subdued the déjà vu of sitting at the Quinns' dining table by watching Emmy pull the skin off her drumstick and then smother another roll in butter.

"Emmy, finish your broccoli before you eat more bread," Ryan said.

That command raised his total word count for the past twenty minutes to a grand total of fifteen. Aside from "Pass the butter" and "No fries, thanks," he'd kept his eyes on his plate for most of the meal. A stark difference in mood from the years when the two of them would lock feet beneath the table just for the thrill of touching each other. At the moment, she was tempted to run her foot up his calf just to shock him into sputtering another word or two.

"Claire called me today." Molly sipped her iced tea, which she served in the same pitcher she'd used a decade ago. The plates were set on the same rooster-shaped place mats, on the same oak table, which sat on the same needlepoint carpet. So much familiarity, yet everything was different. "She's coming over on Monday with some fabric samples for drapes and pillows and things. I admit, I can't picture the room yet."

"I'll try to have the framing done by then,

which should make it easier for you to start visualizing the space," Steffi said.

"Good." Molly then flicked her gaze to Emmy. "Is something wrong with that broccoli?"

Emmy nickered like a horse. Then she cast doleful eyes Steffi's way, silently begging for help.

"Your dad never much liked broccoli, either," Steffi said, that recollection coming from the far reaches of her mind.

"But I ate it," he muttered, giving Emmy a pointed look and then saying nothing more. He took a long pull from his Bud Light.

Another failed attempt at conversation. He still hadn't breached the twenty-word mark. If he kept this up, she might have to dub him Big Mike because he was reminding her of her father. And Chris and Matt, for that matter. Thank God for Benny or she would've grown up believing no man ever spoke unless he had to for survival.

At least the chicken tasted good. Crispy on the outside, tender inside. Flaky biscuits and fries, to boot. Not the healthiest meal, but the salty, greasy comfort food hit the spot.

Emmy pushed her broccoli around the plate while Ryan continued eating and staring into space. Steffi's plan to rebuild some kind of friendship was going nowhere, just like that broccoli. Her appetite waned as she considered the most polite way to make a break for it.

Molly cleared her throat. "I've never been good

at visualizing a room. In truth, I never much cared about decorating. We didn't entertain often, so there were always more important reasons to spend or save. Maybe it's my age, or just being tired of staring at the same old stuff around here, but I'm excited about our little project." She then leaned toward Steffi. "Once the room is done, we hope to see Ryan more. He spends too much time upstairs poring over case files."

Ryan tapped his silverware on the table and shot his mother a look that could get him arrested for assault.

"Mom also says Dad's *always* working," Emmy moaned, gazing longingly at her buttered roll.

Molly raised her brows at her son, then turned her palms up as if to say, "See the problem?"

Ignoring his mother's silent reproach, Ryan spoke to Emmy. "I'm sorry I've been busy, but I have to make a good impression on my new boss. In a couple of months, I'll have a better handle on things, and we'll plan some fun activities. For now, you should focus on your transition in school."

"School's boring," Emmy huffed. "When are we going sailing like you promised? It's almost September."

"That sounds like fun," Molly encouraged. "We can pack a picnic."

"Soon." Ryan didn't spare Steffi a glance, but his pause and stiffness hinted that he was trying hard not to make eye contact with her before he smiled at Emmy. "Do you have a new friend you'd like to invite?"

Steffi's heart sank right along with little Emmy's chin. It was as if the pressure to make new friends grabbed the kid and pushed her head down.

Emmy slid a gaze at her dad. "Let's bring Miss Lockwood."

Before Steffi could decline, Ryan said, "Honey, you should bring someone your age."

"Why?" Emmy said, now raising that chin in defiance. "I want to bring Miss Lockwood."

"Thank you, sweetie, but your dad is right," Steffi interjected. "Kids around here love to go sailing. Is there anyone in your class that you'd like to get to know better?"

"No." Emmy slunk down in her chair, slipping a quick glance at Ryan before stealing a bite of that roll she'd been eyeing.

"Emmy, don't push me." He took it from her plate and pointed at her broccoli with his fork.

"You said I could bring a friend, and she's my friend." Emmy pointed at Steffi. "And she knows how to sail, right?"

Steffi nodded, having learned from Ryan. She'd learned a *lot* from Ryan on that boat, actually. Things she'd practically forgotten, it had been so long since she'd had a date.

Ryan sat, fork and knife in hand, his gaze darting around the room, seeking some escape.

Then the house phone rang, startling everyone.

"I'll get it." Molly rose and went into the kitchen. Two seconds later she returned and handed the phone to Emmy. "It's your mother."

Emmy's face brightened as she leaped off her seat, grabbed the receiver, and started walking toward the living room. "Hi, Mommy. Guess what? I'm going sailing with Daddy and our special friend, Miss Lockwood. You should come with us."

Ryan's silverware clattered to the table. "Oh, for the love of God."

He glared at his mother.

"What? *I* didn't encourage that invitation," Molly defended.

"I'm certain I never referred to Steffi as my 'special' friend." He scowled. "Inviting her to dinner and sailing is sending weird signals to Emmy . . . and now to Val."

"Don't take that tone with me in my house. I've got enough to handle now with your father." Molly stood and took her plate to the kitchen. When she didn't return, Steffi tossed her napkin on the table.

"Ryan," Steffi sighed, "don't fight with your mom. She's only trying to be polite. I should've declined the dinner invitation. I'm sorry."

"Why'd you accept?" He leaned forward on his elbows. "This can't be any more comfortable for you than it is for me."

Her mind riffled through her options and, after thinking about Peyton, settled on the truth. "I like your mom and your daughter. I hoped staying would melt more of the ice between you and me."

He sat back, one arm dropping to his lap, the other hand twisting his glass on the table. "What am I supposed to say to that?"

She shrugged. "I'm not asking you on a date, Ryan. I'm just suggesting we try to be friends. It's a small town. It'd be nice not to carry this sick feeling in my stomach every time I see you."

Before Ryan could erase the surprised look off his face, Emmy marched back into the room and handed him the phone. "Mom wants to talk to you now."

He snatched it while still looking at Steffi, then closed his eyes as if praying for patience. "Hello?"

Steffi smiled at Emmy, who stood at her father's knee, looking happy for the first time all evening. Emmy glanced over her shoulder toward Steffi and said, "If my mom sees Dad sailing, she'll have fun and we can be a family again."

The pained, panicked look in Ryan's eyes suggested he'd heard Emmy's wish. It also mirrored Steffi's queasiness when thinking about Ryan reuniting with Val.

"Of course not, Val," he said, giving a tight reply to whatever she'd said. Ryan's brows lowered. "Yes, we have a child's life vest."

Steffi thought he'd prefer some privacy, so she

removed her dishes from the table and went into the kitchen. She saw Molly outside watering her rose bushes, which left her alone to eavesdrop on Ryan.

"Yes, *that* Lockwood." Ryan's voice remained even.

There was a pause, during which Steffi couldn't help celebrate the fact that she'd gotten under Val's skin, even if Val was totally off base with her suspicion or possible jealousy. But the victory was short-lived when Steffi remembered Emmy's hopeful face and the harsh reality of the situation.

"In case you forget, I work all day," Ryan sighed. "I can't supervise Emmy every second she's here, but she won't get hurt using a wrench."

Another pause preceded Ryan saying, "I'm sure Emmy would love to spend a weekend with you," at which point Steffi heard Emmy yelp, "Yay! When, when?"

Stef imagined Emmy had jumped and clapped, too.

More silence followed.

"Happy to." Ryan sounded drained. "Here you go."

He must've handed the phone back to Emmy, because Emmy asked, "When can I visit, Mommy?"

Steffi wondered about the way Emmy reverted to baby talk with her mom. Was that normal for them or a result of the separation? Maybe both.

Ryan barreled around the corner into the kitchen, nearly knocking into her.

"Spying?" He crossed his arms.

"Not like I had much choice." She supposed she could've gone outside to chat with Molly, but she'd wanted to listen. Rude and wrong, but honest—with herself, anyway.

He gripped the edge of the sink before looking at Steffi again. His expression resembled that of a man being served his least favorite meal. In Ryan's case, that would be meat loaf. Any meat with onions, really.

He hung his head and shook it, as if disbelieving what he was about to say. "Can you come sailing on Sunday?"

"No." And not just because of his offensive demeanor.

"Five minutes ago you said you wanted to be friends, yet already you're backpedaling on me." He thrust one hand toward her, eyes brimming with disappointment. "This is why I worry about Emmy getting close to you."

"I told you earlier I've made plans to see Peyton on Sunday."

"Oh yeah." His face paled as he grimaced. "Sorry."

Determined not to be a shrew like his wife, she graciously let his insult go.

"I could go sailing *next* Sunday, *provided* you make me a promise." She raked her fingers through her ponytail. If they were ever going to be friendly, he needed a major attitude adjustment.

He crossed his arms. "What kind of promise?"

"You'll stop assuming the worst about me."

He fell back against the counter as if she'd shoved him, which she'd wanted to but hadn't. Then his face filled with an emotion she couldn't quite name—something caught between melancholy and hopeful. "Deal."

Steffi stuck out her hand without thinking, just like she did anytime she and Benny had this kind of exchange. Ryan stared at her hand before clasping it.

They shook, but neither of them immediately released hands. For two seconds, they lingered there, hands linked, eyes locked on each other—two seconds that made staying for dinner worthwhile.

Her mouth went dry. She licked her lips, drawing his gaze.

He dropped her hand, swallowing hard. "I'll tell Emmy."

Before she replied, he turned and left her alone in the kitchen with her heart resounding in her chest.

Ryan's phone buzzed in his pocket while he was presenting a motion *in limine* with regard to witness testimony. It buzzed two more times before he was finished, but he had to keep his head in the game. Judge Kramer had a tough rep, and Ryan didn't want to draw his ire. As soon as the arguments concluded, he hastened outside the courtroom to check his phone.

He didn't recognize the first number, which accounted for two of the attempts. The third ring had been his mother, whom he dialed as he strode down the hallway of the imposing criminal court building.

"What's wrong?" Had his father's gout gotten worse?

"I'm with Emmy . . . in the principal's office."

He came to a dead stop in the middle of the busy hallway. "What happened?"

"No one's hurt, but let me put Principal Lotz on the phone."

Ryan sweated in his suit. All around him, colleagues, defendants, and other people milled around.He stuck his finger in one ear so he could hear and wandered to a secluded spot near the wall.

"Mr. Quinn, this is Principal Lotz." She sounded like a principal, formal and a little disapproving.

"Hello. Sorry I didn't pick up before. I've been in court all morning. What's going on?"

"Your daughter got into a scuffle at recess with another girl. I believe it started over a swing and escalated from there. Emmy called the other girl a name before the teacher broke it up."

Ryan palmed his forehead. "Is she sitting with you now?"

"Yes."

"Can you please put her on the phone for a minute?" He inhaled and held his breath for three seconds before blowing it out in a desperate attempt to find patience.

"Yes."

A few seconds later, he heard Emmy's remorseless voice. "Hi, Dad."

"What happened today?"

"Katie Winston wouldn't give me my turn. She never takes turns, and she's always making fun of how I talk."

"What?"

"She says I have an accent."

Ah, the Boston thing. It was there, if not overwhelmingly so. "If Katie did all these bad things, why are *you* the one in the principal's office?"

"Because I called her a name, I guess." Emmy's tone turned a little proud . . . a little too like her mother's.

"What bad name?" He grabbed his forehead, bracing himself.

After the slightest hesitation, she announced, "Bee-otch."

"Emmy!" Through the phone, Ryan heard his mother mutter something, even as he imagined the gleam in his daughter's eye for having been handed an excuse to say that word again. That word Val used in jest throughout the years, and derisively when judging other women. "We'll have a longer talk later. Please hand the phone back to Principal Lotz now."

Without a word, she passed the phone, because the next voice he heard was Mrs. Lotz's.

"What happens now?" Ryan asked, fingertips rubbing his temple. "Is she suspended?"

"For the day, yes. I'll send her home with your mother. If this happens again, there will be a longer suspension. We have zero tolerance for bullying."

"I understand and support that policy. However, it sounds like this other girl wasn't blameless. In fact, it sounds like she's the real bully. Is she also being suspended?"

"No one can corroborate that part of your daughter's story."

Story. Like Emmy made it all up. Emmy was a lot of things, but she'd never been a liar. She was too sure of herself and heedless of consequence to lie about anything.

"I know Emmy can be a handful, and she's having some trouble adjusting to the new environment, but she's assertive, but not aggressive or bullying. There's a difference. And her side of the story doesn't sound far-fetched or even vague, so there's truth to it."

"The other girls took Katie's side, so my hands are tied. The teacher only caught the end of the confrontation."

"Of course the others took Katie's side.

They've all been friends for years. My daughter is the new kid."

"Perhaps you should conference with her teacher about whether she's seen ongoing issues in the classroom."

"I will, although if there have been problems, I'm at a loss for why no one notified me sooner. I'll be in touch after I have a chance to speak with Emmy this afternoon. Thank you." He hit "Off" and stuffed his phone in his pocket, then finished the walk back to his office, forcing himself to focus on his caseload until he could get home and deal with Emmy.

Ryan stormed into the house at six o'clock, dropped his briefcase on the floor, and let his whole body rest against the door for three seconds. He'd always done the right things, yet somehow his life was imploding, which was made worse, given how it seemed to be affecting his daughter. The one who apparently still hoped for her parents' reconciliation. Meanwhile, the Vals and Steffis of the world skipped through life, leaving chaos in their wake without any personal consequence.

He pushed himself off the door and made a beeline for the back of the house.

"Whoa! Slow down there, mister." His mother materialized out of thin air and set her hand to his chest. "Settle yourself before you talk to Emmy. Attacking her won't solve the problem. Besides, she's helping Stefanie clean up right now. Let them finish."

"It's not good for her to get attached to Steffi. Steffi is *not* her mother."

"But she is a woman, and she is younger than me. Emmy seems to like her, and when it comes to kids, that's so important. That's how they decide who to talk to." When he rolled his eyes, she removed her hand. "You can charge in there and make Emmy afraid and defensive, or you can cool your heels and see what Steffi can learn." His mom shrugged, as if he bought into her nonchalance, before she started up the stairs. "I need to check on your father."

Ryan counted to five and then slowly walked toward the kitchen. The window over the sink was wide open, letting the scent of his mom's rosebushes infiltrate the house. In the yard just a few feet away, Emmy was helping Steffi fold some kind of tarp. He eavesdropped for a minute while watching them work together.

"I do understand, Emmy. Better than you think." Steffi took the partially folded tarp and snapped its final fold on her own, then crouched to Emmy's eye level. "I wasn't much older than you when my mom died. I missed her so much it felt like the whole world turned into a dark black hole. Most days I wanted to jump right through that hole and follow her to heaven. I was so angry that she left me like that, even though she couldn't help it. But I kept all those feelings tight inside, like a ball right here." Steffi pointed at Emmy's stomach. "Holding all that stuff inside hurt, but it made me *feel* strong. It seemed better than crying, for sure. Then a girl named Claire moved in across the street. She was very sweet and sporty, and I liked her right away. I was lucky because she was patient with my moods. And at the end of our street was another girl our age, Peyton. Peyton was popular, but it turns out she was kind of lonely, too, for other reasons.

"Anyway, somehow that summer we all started spending time together. We gave ourselves a name—the Lilac Lane League—and we started a journal, because Peyton liked to write. We wrote down our dreams and the things that made us mad, and the things that made us laugh. Our crushes, first kisses, all that stuff. Little by little, that knot in my stomach unwound because my friends made me less lonely. That's how I know the fastest way to feel better is to make a new friend."

"You're my new friend." Emmy's voice sounded small and shaky.

"I am your friend, but you also need a friend your age. I know you miss your old gang, but try to make one new friend here, too. I promise there are nice girls. I grew up here, after all, and I'm nice." Steffi smiled and brushed some of Emmy's curls off her face.

Ryan decided to enter the conversation now, before Emmy broke down in front of Steffi or put her in a more difficult situation. He exited through the kitchen door and crossed the partially framed porch to get to the yard. "Hey there, ladies."

Emmy snapped her gaze at him, and he saw the panic in her eyes. His daughter's fear of him speared his chest like a sword. He'd failed at his marriage, and his daughter was paying the highest price. He couldn't fail her, too. He dropped to his knees and opened his arms. She flew into them in a heartbeat.

He hugged her and swayed, like he'd done when she was so much younger. Steffi quietly retrieved her toolbox and took it to her van.

"Emmy," Ryan said, once they were alone, "I'm sorry this is such a hard time for you. I want to help you, but I don't always have all the answers. I do know one thing, though. You can't call people names and expect to make friends."

She cried against his chest, each tear falling like acid raining on his heart. "Oh, princess, it'll be okay. We all make mistakes. The important thing is to apologize and try to learn from it."

"You always say that," she muttered into his shirt.

"Because it's the truest thing I know." He kissed her head.

"So why can't you and Mom apologize and make up?"

He hadn't expected that question, although maybe he should have. "It's not that simple."

"You always say *that,* too."

If a conversation with her took this much work at this age, he could barely imagine dealing with her in her teens. "You're all dirty from helping Steffi. How 'bout you go inside and clean up before dinner? I need to talk to Steffi for a second. Then I'll come in, and we can figure out how to apologize to Katie Winston."

Emmy nodded while swiping her arm under her runny nose. "Okay."

She wandered into the house just as Steffi came back from the van to get the rest of her personal things. He stood to speak with her. "I heard part of what you said to Emmy."

"I know you don't want me to speak for you, but I just—"

"It's okay. *Thank you* for making her feel like she can confide in you. I should've listened to you the other day." He crossed his arms and blew out a longbreath. "I'm in over my head doing this on my own."

"You're not on your own. You've got your parents. But even if you were, I know you can do it. She loves you. She wants to make you happy and proud."

He nodded, although he knew he was screwing it all up.

"Well, I'd better take off. Benny's expecting me for another training run."

"You guys are disciplined. I haven't had a chance to get in a good workout in three months. Pretty soon I'm going to be too soft." He patted his gut. Granted, he was still pretty fit. He could probably keep up with Steffi for a few miles, anyhow.

"I'm sure your mom would watch Emmy if you need to hit the gym or the mean streets of Sanctuary Sound." She tipped her head, grinning. "My brother might even like some male company now and then. He gets sick of my singing."

Ryan laughed. "Well, you were good at a lot of things, but singing wasn't one of them."

"You didn't used to complain." She hit his arm.

He grew quiet for a second, remembering the many times he'd listened to her terrible rendition of Lifehouse's "You and Me" in the car or on the patio. "No, I never did mind those private concerts."

The air between them turned sweet and thick with fond memories. Holding hands, soccer footwork challenges, the first time he'd copped a feel, and the light in her eyes when he had. The images almost made him want to take hold of her hand again; his heart beat with that hot desire like it had at seventeen.

"Dad!" Emmy called from the door, breaking the spell.

"You'd better go," Steffi said with a wistful smile before she turned and walked back to her car.

He watched her go and waited . . . waited . . . Just before she got to her van, she peeked over her shoulder at him again, and everything seemed a little bit brighter.

Chapter Six

Steffi approached the gold-and-graphite condominium building where Peyton's older brother, Logan, lived. Located in the diverse, artsy Chelsea neighborhood of Manhattan, it stood within spitting distance of art galleries, eclectic shops, and cafés. Perfect for a photographer with money to burn. No doubt this pad cost a couple of million, maybe more.

The Prescotts had always had money. The rambling shingle-style mansion they grew up in at the end of Lilac Lane had originally been their great-grandfather's summer home. He'd been a famous writer who'd hosted infamous parties for his celebrity friends on those hallowed grounds. His son, Peyton's grandfather, had been a spendthrift and burned through much of the family fortune.

In 1995, Peyton's father sold off forty-five acres of the original fifty-acre estate, which was when all the modest homes on Lilac Lane were built and Steffi's family moved in. Mr. Prescott then invested the money he raised through that development into other real estate deals in the tristate area. Now he'd become wealthy in his own right, restoring the family coffers.

His kids, Logan and Peyton, worked hard, but

not in the corporate arena. They inherited their great-grandfather's passion for words and art. Peyton wrote for travel magazines, and Logan was a documentary photographer. Although successful, their high-flying lifestyles were supplemented by ample trust funds. Neither, however, flaunted that privilege. In fact, in all the ways that really mattered, both were rather down-to-earth.

Just before the elevator doors closed, a huge man ducked inside with her. He barely smiled before turning to face the button panel. The doors closed. Sweat collected at her hairline as she squeezed into the corner of the elevator and . . .

Hot, smoky breath.

A gun!

Please, no.

Help. Help.

Live. Just live.

The elevator jerked to a stop, yanking her back to reality. This last concussion had really screwed with her brain. She couldn't hold on to her thoughts—if there even were any—in those trances and didn't know when the next would strike, or why.

The man strolled out without a word, unaware that her pulse was sky-high. She inhaled and jabbed the door-close button three times. Four floors later, her pulse had slowed to normal.

Surely, one mugging hadn't made her afraid to

be alone in an elevator with a guy. She'd been friends and colleagues with men her whole dang life. But she didn't have time to worry about that now. Not with Peyton waiting just a few yards away.

When the elevator opened on the sixth floor, Steffi drew a final, cleansing breath before knocking on Logan's door.

Peyton answered wearing a forced smile and gathered Steffi into a hug. "Steffi!"

Thank God the hug gave Steffi a second to adjust to Peyton's new look. She'd butchered her waist-length blonde locks into a pixie cut. She'd always been thin, but now her legs looked more like arms. Steffi remembered how the stress from weeks of waiting for answers and preparing for treatment had killed her mother's appetite and destroyed her sleep cycles. It'd wreaked havoc on the whole family.

Peyton gave Steffi a tight squeeze before releasing her. "Thanks for making the trek."

Certainly not a trek, although driving into the city required nerves of steel. Blaring horns. Cabs weaving through traffic with less wiggle room than thread through a needle's eye. And pedestrians ignoring the crosswalks, forcing her to slam on the brakes with alarming frequency. The streets of Manhattan were an animated obstacle course with life-and-death stakes. And if, by chance, you made it safely to your destination, you'd be treated to the final insult—a ridiculously steep parking fee.

"It's good to see you." It had been a year since Steffi had met with Peyton, shortly after the whole Todd debacle. Now the awkward friendship strife settled between them like a thick morning fog on the sound. Steffi pointed at Peyton's shorn hair. "The new do is sharp."

Peyton touched it with a shrug. "I figure it'll be easier to deal with losing it this way."

Steffi's mind blanked at the stark reality of what lay ahead for Peyton, preferring to skim the surface rather than drown in heavy emotional conversation. Peyton, on the other hand, tended to overshare her emotions and the truth—or at least the truth from her perspective. Today Steffi couldn't wade at the edges of intimate conversation. She'd have to swim straight to the center and hope no sharks dragged her under.

"I'm sorry. I'm so sorry you have to go through this." Unlike *some* of her memories, the ones of her mother's last months—with ascites requiring weekly draining of the abdominal-fluid buildup—could resurface with amazing clarity. Peyton was almost twenty years younger than Steffi's mother had been in this battle. Would youth and strength give her better odds? "How do you like your doctors?"

"I'm still trying to keep everyone straight. They're okay, but numb. I'm just one of hundreds. There won't be much hand-holding, despite my fucked emotional state. That's Logan's job now—taking care of me."

Steffi seized an opening to steer the conversation away from gloom. "Is he here?"

"Not at the moment."

The swanky pad, with its modern taupe-and-cream kitchen, floor-to-ceiling black-framed windows, and gray wood floors, reflected Logan's personality. Hip, handsome verging on pretty, and a touch cool. The furnishings, however, seemed like a ragtag collection of things that didn't quite go together. Had it not been for working with Claire, she might not have noticed. Logan probably didn't care because he traveled so often; this place was more like a hotel than a home.

"Sweet digs for your recovery." Steffi crossed to the wall of windows and looked down at the busy, crowded street pulsing with traffic and pedestrians and noise. "Everything at your fingertips."

"It's more human than my neighborhood uptown, and I let that lease go because . . . who knows what will happen. I'm counting on Chelsea keeping me connected to life's energy. On good days, I'll explore and write some 'behind the scenes' pieces since I can't really travel much in the foreseeable future." Her chin dropped as she quietly added, "And best of all, no one here hates me."

"I don't hate you, Peyton," Steffi assured her.

"You hate what I did. So do I. I let us all down." She shook her head, voice thickening. "I was so stupid. I don't know what I was thinking."

"You weren't thinking." Steffi approached Peyton and reached for her hand. "People don't often think when they fall in love."

Maybe love was the exception to her mom's deathbed advice. Or maybe the advice wasn't meant to be so literal. Maybe what her mom had meant to teach her was that she had to learn to forgive herself, and others, for mistakes made.

"Love." Peyton scoffed, letting go of Steffi's hand. "We should all be more like you when it comes to that."

"What's that mean?" It didn't sound like a compliment.

"You've avoided it—other than your puppy love with Ryan, which ended as soon as you had some space." Her face grew pensive. "You've kept your heart safe. I used to feel sorry for you, but now I envy you."

"Don't envy *me*." Steffi gestured toward the sofa, needing to get more comfortable if the conversation was heading in this direction.

Peyton sat on a chair, so Steffi sat across from her on a black leather sofa.

"How are you settling in back in the old hood?" Peyton's question sounded simple enough, but her square shoulders and straight spine marked her tension.

"Pretty well. We've rented a little bungalow on Forest Street. Claire fixed it up supercute. The business is up and running, but money is tight. We're on a constant hunt for new clients."

"I saw your website. Very Claire, with its preppy colors and traditional fonts." Peyton mindlessly picked at her shirt. "How do you like being partners with someone so risk averse?"

Claire's ghost crackled in the space between them.

"We complement each other." Steffi hesitated, uncertain of how to proceed. She forced herself to make eye contact with Peyton. "Does this hurt you to talk about?"

"It makes me nostalgic for when the three of us ran around town together. But I've made my bed. Don't feel like you can't talk about your life with Claire just to spare my feelings . . ." Then she added drolly, "Even if I *am* dying."

They both laughed in that self-conscious, slightly horrified way one does when making light of something painful. Peyton's dry humor had always defused tension. Right now that made Steffi grateful as hell.

"I do wonder," Peyton mused, pulling her legs up onto the cushion to sit with them crisscrossed. "Are there any eligible men in town . . . aside from your brother, that is?"

The short haircut and childlike pose made Peyton look ten years younger, throwing Steffi so off-balance she had to replay the question to answer it. "Well, actually, Ryan's back in town. At least for a while."

Peyton's blue eyes widened as her jaw dropped open. "Seriously? That should've been the first thing you told me when you got here."

"Really?" Steffi's shirt stuck to the sweat beading from the spotlight of Peyton's intensified scrutiny. "Seems like we've got more important things to talk about."

"I didn't ask you to visit so we could sit around fretting together. I want to laugh and forget for a while. Besides, Steffi, *nothing* is more important than boy talk. Wasn't that our first rule?"

Steffi grinned, remembering the league scrapbook they'd compiled. Part collage, part journal, part wish list . . . Claire had upholstered that five-inch binder with batting and a green-and-pink plaid fabric.

Throughout the years, they'd stuffed it with cards, notes, camp brochures, and photographs, but the first page had been a list of rules. The second rule had been about boy talk (a "Vegas rules" kiss-and-tell kind of group promise). The first had been about putting friends before boys—no matter what. Peyton must've thought of that one at the exact same time, because she turned her face away and stared out the window, her forehead creased.

Steffi supposed she could distract Peyton with

some gossip, even if it would be at her own expense. "Ryan and his daughter moved in with his mom. It's temporary . . . maybe six months or so. I think he's waiting to see how things shake out with the divorce before he makes any new financial commitments. For now, his mom is helping him with Emmy."

"Divorce?" Peyton's mouth dropped open. "And he has custody? Is Val in rehab or something?"

"I don't know the full scoop, but it's not rehab. Seems more like Val's having an early midlife crisis." Steffi shook her head. "It breaks my heart to see what it's doing to Emmy."

"So you've seen him and met his daughter?" Peyton's riveted attention meant she wasn't thinking about her cancer.

Despite her damp palms and tightening stomach, Steffi kept sharing, knowing more questions would follow. "I'm converting the Quinns' screened porch into a family room, so I see them every day."

"Get out!" Peyton slapped the seat cushion and excitedly stamped her feet on the floor a few times. "Holy crap, Steffi. How's he look?"

"So good," she moaned, letting her head fall back. Eyes closed, she pictured him—tie loosened at the end of the workday, briefcase in his left hand, a warm smile for his daughter. "So, so good."

Peyton's smile broadcast genuine happiness for the first time all afternoon. For those few seconds, she didn't look like a woman facing chemo. The sight caused Steffi's eyes to mist.

"Details," Peyton demanded.

"He looks exactly how you remember, except somehow more handsome with maturity. Same shortish curls, warm eyes . . . same gentle smile." Steffi didn't share that she'd seen it only once so far. "And he's an amazing father. Steady, calm, fair. I can just see his heart melting and breaking over Emmy all at once."

"I can't believe he hired you." Peyton's voice trailed off, chasing the distance in her eyes as her mind wandered.

"*He* didn't. Mrs. Q. surprised us both." Steffi grimaced. "I almost think she did it on purpose."

"She definitely did." Peyton nodded with a light chuckle. "She loved you. She probably hates Val."

"Well, I hope she isn't counting on much. Our initial reunion was a bit ugly." Steffi winced inwardly at the memory of his bitter words. "But the worst is behind us now, I think."

"He's forgiven you, then?" Peyton went fairly still, as if the answer would translate to forgiveness from Claire.

Steffi weighed her words, aiming for that narrow space between realistic expectations and optimism. "I think he's trying to let go of his

123

grudge, although he outright told me he doesn't trust me. He probably never will."

Peyton sighed, accepting the death of her not-so-private wish. "What about you? Any old feelings coming back?"

Steffi nodded. "Regret."

"I know that one." Peyton grabbed a throw pillow and hugged it to her stomach.

"I know you do." Steffi leaned forward, determined to give Peyton the same kind of forgiveness she'd like from Ryan. "I was so, *so* mad at you at first. I mean, I didn't know why you would do that to Claire when you could have had any guy you wanted. But the more I've thought about it, the more I've realized you must've really been in love, because I know that you love Claire and would never hurt her on a whim, or for an ego trip. The only explanation is overwhelming love. How could I hate you for that? We can't choose who we love."

"I thought . . . I thought he was my soul mate." She choked on those words. "How ridiculous, right? Any guy whose affections turned so suddenly couldn't be a good guy, let alone a soul mate. But I didn't know his relationship to Claire that first time we met. We'd talked for thirty minutes and had this incredible spark, and then I got caught up in something bigger than myself—we seemed to connect on this whole other level I'd never known before. I rationalized that I hadn't done anything wrong, because I didn't make him any promises or cross any lines until after he'd left Claire." Peyton sighed. "I still wake up from nightmares about the way she screamed at me the last time I saw her."

"You need to forgive yourself. We all make mistakes. For now, you need to stay positive and focus on your treatment and recovery."

"But I *need* to make amends. I want to be forgiven before I die."

"Peyton, don't talk like you're doomed. The next six or nine months will be rough, but you're going to be okay. You have to be."

"I hope, but if not . . ." Peyton looked right at Steffi. "Can you help me?"

Steffi leaned forward, elbows on her knees, unhappy to be put in this position, but not really seeing any better option. "I don't know if I can. She doesn't wish this illness on you, but she still can't forgive you. She won't talk about you with me, or anyone else, as far as I know."

"Maybe Ryan will be an example . . . she always respected him."

"It's not really the same situation." Steffi slouched back in her seat.

"Isn't it? You shredded him when you shut him out without any explanation. I know he was devastated. Logan was his friend, don't forget."

Reminders of her behavior always made Steffi gag a little. She supposed Peyton felt the same way

125

anytime she thought about Claire. Maybe their situations weren't as different as Steffi would like to believe. "I hate how I handled that."

"I get that. Trust me."

Steffi sighed and ran her hands through her hair. "I can't make any promises, but if I see an opening, I'll try again."

"Thanks. I'm sorry to ask, but she's refused my calls, emails, and even returned a handwritten letter."

"I know."

Peyton waved her hands in the air, signaling a change of subject. "Let's get back to Ryan. What's your plan to win him back?"

"Who says I'm trying to win him back?" she deflected.

Peyton simply raised one brow. "Everything from the look on your face to the color of your cheeks says so."

The front door opened before Steffi had to respond. Logan entered carrying multiple takeout bags. "Tapas delivery."

She'd forgotten how drop-dead gorgeous he was—if a bit on the pretty side. He had perfectly smooth skin, sandy-blond hair that hung below his jaw, and beautiful green eyes. Tall, slim, and always dressed sharp, she wondered what kind of woman could handle dating him.

Peyton rose from the chair. "Originally, I'd thought we'd go out to eat, but then I decided it'd be more relaxing to stay in. Hope tapas is okay with you."

"Of course." Steffi took another minute to study her friend. Pale-purple circles shadowed her eyes. Beneath a strained smile, Steffi saw fear, too. Gossiping about Ryan and Claire had been a temporary distraction at best. Steffi needed to let Peyton know she had friends who cared. "Whatever you want is fine with me."

Logan set the bags on the counter and gave Steffi a friendly hug. He then threw his arm around Peyton's shoulder and kissed her head. "How are you?"

"Good. Maybe we can take a walk and shop after lunch."

"Don't push." He began unloading black plastic containers with clear lids from the bags. "Remember what the doctor said."

"What's that?" Steffi asked.

"Nothing," Peyton interjected. "Logan's a nervous mother hen. You know the drill. I need to stay well rested and away from germs because my immune system will be so compromised."

Steffi smiled at Logan, whose sunny personality should be helpful in this situation. "I'm glad you're here for her."

Peyton clucked. "I warned him he'll be tossed off a balcony if he tries to document this process."

When Steffi looked to him for clarification,

he said, "I think we should take photos and she should keep a journal." Then he addressed his sister, "At the very least, a project would occupy us. And, who knows? It could be a great memoir or inspirational story when you're well. Photos will keep it real."

When you're well, he'd said. Yes, please, God, let him be right about that.

"He has a point." Steffi spooned a bit of seafood paella onto a plate and then forked a beef empanada.

"Can we eat lunch without talking about my cancer? This might be the last meal I actually enjoy for a long while."

"As you wish." Logan loaded his plate with chorizo and shrimp.

Peyton finished swallowing her first spoonful of paella. With a sassy look in her eye, she said, "Logan, did you know Ryan Quinn moved back to Sanctuary Sound? Apparently, he's getting divorced."

Logan's brows rose, and he slid a glance to Steffi. "Well, isn't *that* an interesting tidbit. Sounds like I need to take a road trip soon to organize a big ol' high school reunion." He speared a shrimp and winked at his sister. "I've always liked a good challenge."

"I thought alimony was capped at sixty percent of the length of time we were married?" Ryan tamped down the growl building in his chest and smiled at the mediator, Ross Wallingford, a kindly, bald gentleman wearing a pink bow tie.

"That's correct, but that's duration of payments, not the amount."

"I'm owed some support, Ryan." Val sat ramrod straight. She'd put on quite a show so far: dressed in her least expensive clothes, ditched the fancy shoes and purses and jewelry, and even toned down her makeup. To look at her today, you'd think she was two pennies shy of needing food stamps. "We were married for almost ten years, plus the fact that I stayed home with Emmy to let you be successful in your career."

Wallingford nodded with a pleasant smile. "Yes, that's part of the point of alimony."

Ryan shifted. "You worked part-time for a few years, so you've only been out of work for about six years. You're college educated and employable, and living rent-free. Meanwhile, I'm the full-time caregiver for our daughter, which means I'll be out all the money for day care. You're getting half the equity in our home. How much more do you need? For chrissakes, you can't get blood from a stone."

"You're a lawyer, Ryan. A criminal defense lawyer, for God's sake. You could quit the PD office and hire yourself out to white-collar criminals. You could be rolling in dough."

He barked a laugh, although part of him couldn't

ignore the idea for Emmy's sake. The other part might want to make a ton of money to spite Val. But that wasn't who he was or why he went to work. It had never been about money. Now, however, his capped income presented challenges he hadn't anticipated.

He gestured to Val while looking at Wallingford. "She cheats, leaves me to go live in a multi-million-dollar penthouse with her lover, leaves our daughter in her wake, and has the nerve to sit there and demand anything from me." Ryan tossed his pencil on his pad, completely aware of, yet uncaring about, his unprofessional behavior. "You are a serious piece of work, Val."

Wallingford held up his hands to staunch another tirade. "Folks, I know this is difficult. I presume you both agreed to mediation in order to avoid the lengthy and costly court battle that can ensue in these situations. Let's remember our goal, which is to come to a fair compromise so that you can both move on and concentrate on your child."

"I *am* thinking about my child. I make eighty-two grand a year. After taxes I clear a little over four grand per month. Housing near my mother, who has offered to help me watch our daughter after school, is not inexpensive. Modest Cape Cod homes are still between three and four hundred thousand. Plus bills, food, and clothes for Emmy, gas and things I need for work and my life. I won't have any disposable income at all." He looked at Val now. "You don't need my salary, Val. John is taking care of you now. Can't you just take half of the equity in the house and half of our savings and walk away? Come on . . . think about Emmy. Do you want her living in a hovel?"

For a second, he saw a waver in Val's gaze. Maybe he'd struck a chord.

Wallingford weighed in. "I will take all of this into consideration, along with the other information you both supplied, and come up with some recommendations."

Val sat back. "Thank you. So that's all for today?"

That's all, she'd asked, sitting there calm and carefree. Meanwhile, sweat dripped down Ryan's back. He knew he shouldn't let his emotions control him or this process. But anytime he looked at Val, resentment grabbed him by the throat. Her betrayal of their vows, of their daughter . . . it didn't make sense. She'd never been the perfect woman for him, but he hadn't thought her so heartless, either. He couldn't wrap his head around it, and that drove him crazy. He didn't have the energy to waste on this now, though. Not when he had to drive back to Hartford and get in a few hours of work on the O'Malley case.

"I'll get back in touch to set up another

131

meeting." Wallingford smiled at Val as if he were her grandfather. God, she could pull any man's strings. Most of his gender could be a complete sucker for a gorgeous face and a tight ass.

"Next time I'd like to attend by videoconference or something." At least that way, he wouldn't have to breathe the same air as Val. "I can't keep skipping out on my new job like this."

"That's amenable to me." Wallingford looked at Val.

She leveled Ryan with a skeptical look, as if trying to figure out what he was hiding. That would be nothing—not that she and her scheming brain would accept it. "Fine."

"Good." Wallingford stood and collected the tax returns and other documents they'd supplied. "Have a good day."

"Wait up, Val," Ryan said as he shook Wallingford's hand. "I want to talk about Emmy."

"Okay." She said goodbye to Wallingford with a sweet-as-pie smile. Once she turned her back to the older man, her expression steeled. "What?"

Ryan asked, "First, what's the deal with Block Island?"

"John has a place there. We'd like to take Emmy for the long weekend. I thought you could bring her up to Point Judith, and we'll take the ferry Saturday morning. You can come back Monday afternoon to pick her up."

He didn't want John around his daughter, but he

knew he had no say. "I'll make it work, but do me a favor. Be careful of letting Emmy get attached to John. We don't know what the future holds, and we should try to keep her from losing more people. At least until she's gotten used to the divorce."

"I could say the same to you."

He gestured toward his chest with both hands. "I'm not seeing anyone."

"Steffi?"

He rolled his eyes. "My mother hired her to work at the house. She's converting the porch to a family room. We aren't dating."

"Then what's the sailing excursion about?"

"That was Emmy's doing, not mine. I've talked with Steffi about not letting Emmy get too attached, but Steffi's working at my mother's house every day when Emmy gets off the bus, and Emmy is curious about what she's doing. She seems to enjoy helping, and she needs something to feel good about. When the project is over, it'll end. By then, Emmy should have some friends. She's struggling with the transition at school right now."

Val seemed both relieved to learn that he and Steffi weren't romantically involved, and concerned about Emmy's school situation. "What are you doing about school?"

"Trying to encourage her to invite some friends over. That's how the sailing thing started. I want her to invest in our new community instead of sitting home alone hoping our separation is temporary."

"Are you saying something to give her the impression we might reconcile?" Val's inscrutable expression might've worried him if he cared about her opinion.

"Trust me, I'm no more interested in that than you are, Val." As soon as he said it, he regretted it, because he saw the challenge it ignited. She didn't want him, but she still wanted him to want her. Val loved sex and power games. Always had. He wished he'd realized that before they'd gotten involved, and run in the other direction.

"I'll email you the ferry departure time for Saturday."

"Fine." He glanced at his watch. "Got to run."

Old habits made him lean forward to give her a kiss goodbye, but he jerked himself back before making contact. She'd gone still and held her breath.

Near miss. Without another word, he strode out of the conference room and to the elevator. His day would improve exponentially the farther away he got from her.

Ryan arrived home that evening to hear the sound of his daughter's laughter in the yard. He saw her with Steffi, who was trying to teach her how to rainbow kick a soccer ball.

Shocking as that sight was, it didn't hold a candle to seeing Emmy in shorts and sneakers. No ruffles. No dress. No pink ribbons in her hair.

Meanwhile, he knew Steffi had gone to see Peyton yesterday. Yet here she was, putting on a brave face for his daughter despite the fact that she'd probably had a rough weekend. He wanted to ask her how she was feeling. Not that Steffi would share her feelings with him, he reminded himself, and returned his attention to his daughter.

"Where's my princess?" he called as he crossed the backyard.

Emmy waved. "Hi, Daddy. I'm learning a rainbow kick."

"Great!" he said, although she'd never once shown any interest in sports, let alone soccer.

"Actually, your dad ought to teach you. He was always better than I was." Steffi tossed him the ball, which he caught.

"You finally admit it!" He laughed, having dealt with her competitive streak for years.

"Don't push it," she murmured, suggesting she had said it only to make him look good in front of Emmy. "Goalies didn't have much need for that move."

"Let's see, Daddy. Do it!" Emmy clapped.

He looked down at his dress shoes and slacks, then shrugged. It'd been a decade since he'd done one, and now he had to impress his daughter . . .

and his ex, because, clearly, she still had the skill. "Don't I get a warm-up?"

"Chicken?" Steffi crossed her arms, goading him.

Emmy joined in the taunt, flapping her little arms, crowing, *"Bwok, bwok!"*

Resigned to potential embarrassment, he set the ball down to the inside of his right foot, with his left foot stepping back so that his toes could roll the ball up his right calf. He took a breath, stepped into it, and popped the ball with a quick snap of his right heel. It arced over his head and landed a few feet in front of him.

Emmy whooped with pride, and Steffi whistled. "Look at you, Counselor. You've still got it."

He supposed sixteen years of playing a sport meant he'd always retain some basic skills. Still, almost a decade of his life had passed without setting foot on a field or buying a new pair of cleats. Soccer had given him a fantastic outlet for his energy and a sense of belonging. It'd been neglectful not to encourage Emmy to try some sports. He'd let Val control Emmy's day-to-day, which meant that Emmy attempted ballet— because she wanted pink tutus—and piano, but neither stuck, and he hadn't pushed.

Emmy set the ball by her feet and tried again, not quite mastering the necessary roll up the calf. When the ball shot sideways, she chased it.

"Maybe she can still enroll in the community soccer league. It's early, and she's new to town.

If she's inherited your talent, she could try out for a travel league next year. If not, at least it's a way to make friends." Steffi watched Emmy from beside him.

"That's a good idea. I'll make a call and see if my mom will mind driving her to and from practice."

"She could probably walk. The town fields are only a half mile or so."

That idea shocked him. In Boston, Emmy never walked anywhere. Too much traffic and generalized "stranger danger." But maybe here in the bubble of his small hometown, Emmy could experience the kind of freedom that would help her mature. "Maybe."

Steffi raised a brow. "We did all the time, didn't we?"

"We did." Kick the can. Manhunt. Hanging out at Kovall's candy store. He was always on his own with a pack of friends. "How was Peyton?"

Steffi's face paled at the sudden change in topic. "Determined not to wallow. Logan had lunch with us. He asked about everyone."

"Haven't talked to him in a couple of years." He could picture Logan, a prankster and the king of high school partying, like it was yesterday. Life had been sweet and easy then. Study. Train. Laugh. Sex. Repeat. Now it was all work—at the office, and at home with Emmy. Not much laughter lately. No sex.

"You should reach out," Steffi said. He could hardly look at her, though, because he'd started thinking about sex—or the lack of it. "He'd probably appreciate it."

"I should." And then, because he didn't want to spend too much time wading in the tides of nostalgia with Steffi or missing sex, he changed the subject. "Looks like you're making good progress." He eyed the project, telling himself not to think about sex.

"Long day, but I'm keeping on schedule."

"Emmy's not holding you up too much with soccer lessons and all, is she?"

"No." Steffi smiled. "I promised her I'd give her a few minutes if she helped me clean up. She swept the sawdust from the porch today."

He rubbed his chin playfully. "Violating child labor laws now?"

"Well, I happen to know a great defense attorney, so I think I'm in the clear."

He repressed the urge to wrap his arm around her shoulder and kiss her head, like he used to when they'd tease each other. He didn't mind a thawing between them, but he wasn't ready to be friends, or more, even if everything in his body hummed when she stood so close. When the sun glinted off the blonde highlights and the breeze teased the stray hairs to flirt with her face. When the heat of a hot September afternoon made her skin glisten, and the joy in her eyes tugged at something deep within him while she watched Emmy trying to master the rainbow kick.

He cleared his throat. "I need to change. Have a good night."

She flinched at the abrupt shift in his demeanor but recovered quickly. "I should head out, too." She called out to Emmy, "Keep practicing and I'll see how you do tomorrow."

"Okay!" Emmy smiled, and Ryan's heart beat so hard he almost cried. His day had started off so miserably. He'd really needed this picture of hope tonight, and he had Steffi, in part, to thank.

Owing her any gratitude felt like swallowing sawdust. He'd been angry for so long he didn't know how to let that go and move on. But he had to learn, and soon. For everyone's sake.

Chapter Seven

"Steffi, I forgot to pick up my prescription yesterday and I need my Coumadin. Can you run to the pharmacy for me before you go back to work?" her dad asked as she pulled up to the curb in front of her childhood home. She noticed him squinting behind the cheap black eyewear the ophthalmologist had given him to protect his dilated pupils.

Still, he had a way of making those flimsy sunglasses look cool. Her dad had always had a Clint Eastwood vibe about him. Intense, quiet, unconventionally attractive. Even now, in old Levi's, brown suede Keens, and a white cotton collared shirt, he seemed pretty hip for a guy with cata-racts.

"Let me help you inside first." She walked with him into the house.

The gray-and-white Cape Cod home hadn't changed much. Her mom's old flower beds had been replaced with a rock garden. It didn't surprise her that her dad had opted for something low-maintenance, but part of her knew he also couldn't watch the daffodils bloom, or smell the roses, without missing his wife. Other than the river rock, it looked just as it had in the nineties. Smelled pretty much the same, too. Equal parts salt water, coffee, and Irish Spring.

The only other big difference was the quietude. Four rambunctious athletes and their friends had kept things lively, even after her mom had died. One by one, her brothers had flown the coop, and then she did, too. Did her dad miss the noise, or enjoy the silence? Maybe a bit of both, like her.

Steffi settled him on the faded leather sofa, glancing at her watch because Claire would be expecting her soon, to meet with that new client buying the house on Hightop Road. "I guess you can't watch TV yet, huh?"

"Nope." He stretched himself out along the cushions. "I'll just catch a catnap. Kind of nice to take a break midweek."

Benny had mentioned that their dad had been working fewer hours this year. She supposed he was getting up there. His seventieth birthday was just around the corner. In fact, she needed to organize something with her brothers to celebrate that milestone. Finding a date when they could all travel home would be a challenge. She couldn't recall the last time they'd all been together— probably two Christmases ago.

If her mom had lived, she'd be turning sixty-eight this winter. The last birthday they'd celebrated together had been her forty-ninth. Peyton would be thirty-one on her next birthday. Steffi shivered and refocused.

She looked around at the "senior" bachelor pad, which looked a little worse for wear since he'd lived alone. Cleaning the house had always been her mother's chore, and then hers, because none of her brothers cared if they lived in a pigsty. Her dad kept it neat enough now but probably hadn't mopped a floor or wiped down the woodwork in the past year. If she weren't racing to finish the Quinns' family room, she'd come over on Saturday and spend the day with soapy buckets and a scrub brush. *Soon,* she told herself. "Can I get you anything else? Something for dinner?"

"Nah." He shifted slightly. "I'll make a sandwich."

Eating a cold sandwich for dinner by oneself sounded a little pathetic. Then again, she'd done that more often than not over the past few years. "You need to go out more, Dad. It's not healthy to spend your time alone here every night."

He grunted. That was all he would say about that, as she well knew. It wasn't the first time she'd made the suggestion, although it had been at least a couple of months since the last time.

It seemed a shame he'd never met anyone after her mom died. Never really tried, either. He'd burned through his fifties raising teens, and then his sixties running his hardware store. At sixty-nine, it seemed as if he didn't even care about women anymore. She could still picture the lemon face he'd made when she'd suggested he take Mrs. Langley, a widow, to the Prescotts' annual literacy gala.

"Fine. I'll be back in a jiffy."

"Thanks." He must've closed his eyes. Still a man of few words, but in a crunch those words always counted for something.

By the time she got through the pharmacy line, she was late for her meeting with Claire and the new client. Steffi jogged across the parking lot, hoping she could cut through some back roads to drop the meds off with her dad and still get to the client meeting before it ended. Just as she opened her van door, a nearby motorcycle engine roared to life.

Her body stilled as if she'd been flash frozen. The biker let loose a catcall whistle before his deep voice called out, "Nice sticks, little mama."

In her mind, she flipped the guy the bird, yet somehow she knew she hadn't done it. Her ears rang, and darkness crowded her vision. Sweat beaded along her hairline as her heart pulsed faster.

Gun.

Stop. Please . . . No!

Fly away . . . you're not here.

You're not here.

Blackness.

"Miss?" A hand on Steffi's shoulder startled her.

She awoke from her daze to find herself on the ground by the side of her car, the prescription bag fallen to her side, one hand clutching the open

143

door. She blew on her scraped knee. It looked worse than it felt, although she wanted to cry. To scream. To understand why the hell her brain wouldn't heal faster. At the very least, she wanted to remember where her mind wandered during those lapses.

"Are you okay?" A teen girl wearing Converse sneakers and a silver-and-leather choker had her phone whipped out, ready to call 911. "Should I call the police?"

Steffi cringed and let her hair fall to cover her face. What must she look like to bystanders? Deranged? Drunk? Fortunately, there weren't many people nearby. Just an elderly couple she didn't recognize, thank God. She didn't need old biddy gossip making its way to Benny or her dad.

"No, no." Steffi hoisted herself up and brushed herself off, careful not to touch her angry red knee. "I just tripped."

"You were really out of it, ma'am." The girl narrowed her eyes. "Are you on medication or something? Maybe you shouldn't drive."

Ma'am? On top of looking foolish, Steffi looked *old?* She stared at the girl, whose purple bangs obscured her left eye. "I'm fine, thanks. I was distracted, then a little dazed by the fall."

"Okay." The girl pressed her lips together and narrowed her eyes, but put her phone into her backpack. "Hope you feel better."

She then turned and took off without looking back.

Steffi lumbered back inside for a box of Band-Aids, glancing at her watch. *Dammit.* She placed a large square bandage over her knee before leaving the store. When she finally got in the driver's seat and slammed the door shut, she rested her forehead on the steering wheel and closed her eyes. Adrenaline ebbed from her body, which sagged as if she'd run the freakin' marathon.

The last thing she remembered was the motorcycle dude's lame remark, then nothing. Prior concussions hadn't been this bad. The fogginess hadn't been so extreme, and it had gradually improved. These new lapses—like sleepwalking in daylight—were peculiar. Of course, a direct, intentional hit to the temple with a gun was worse than the whacks she'd taken on the field. She'd been knocked out cold for some time.

Because she'd been hit on her head one too many times in her life, this might be her new normal. She could live with that if it weren't for the nagging fear that it would get worse.

When she stopped shivering, she drove home and delivered the meds to her dad, accidentally waking him from his midday snooze.

"What happened to your knee?" he asked, having now removed those protective glasses.

"Tripped. No biggie." She tossed the bag on his coffee table. "Listen, I can't chat because I'm late for an appointment. Maybe you, Benny, and I can grab dinner soon?"

"Sure," he mumbled, still a bit groggy.

She pressed a quick kiss to his forehead and then scrambled back to the van and weaved through town to the Hightop Road house.

Claire's Beetle was parked in front, so at least Steffi hadn't missed the whole meeting. She trotted up the porch steps and knocked on the door. Voices from inside echoed off the floors and walls of the empty house. Seconds later, a cute woman with hair the shade of Elmo's answered.

"Stefanie?" she asked, opening the door wide.

"Yes." Steffi extended her hand.

"I'm Helena Briggs." The name suited the tall woman with dramatic plum eye shadow. She wore her hair short, her wine-colored dress even shorter, and sported navy-blue nail polish. "Nice to meet you."

"Same," Steffi sighed. "Sorry I'm so late. I had an incident with my father."

Claire's perturbed expression transformed to concern. "Is everything okay?"

"Yes. He required some help with a doctor's appointment that took longer than expected." Claire's gaze dropped to Steffi's bandaged knee, but Steffi waved her question away. "Tell me I didn't miss everything."

"I just walked Claire through the house and discussed the issues." Helena spoke with an accent that bore a slight resemblance to Katharine Hepburn's speech. Affected, yet interesting. "We'd like to update the kitchen, master bath, and the Jack-and-Jill bathroom, open up the first floor a bit for flow, and have a consistent theme and decor throughout. That said, I don't want cookie cutter. This house won't end up looking like every TV reno project. No white cabinets or Carrara marble, God forbid!"

"Well, decor is squarely Claire's gig, but I'm excited to work on something more original. Catch me up on the big construction wish list and proposed time frames." Steffi followed the women to the generous kitchen that offered distant water views, as Steffi had suspected. Cornflower-blue cabinetry and decorative-tile countertops harkened back to the eighties. A bay window graced the breakfast nook, though, so that would remain a key feature. Steffi whipped out her notepad and started taking notes, knowing she'd need to take a quick peek upstairs before they left.

Thirty minutes later, she and Claire departed with a promise to send Mrs. Briggs a bid within a week.

On their way to their respective cars, Claire asked, "What really happened?"

"What do you mean?" Steffi feigned indignation at the implication that she'd lied.

"You were late but didn't give details about your dad. Was that a cover, Steffi?" Claire's brow popped up in that knowing way as she pointed at Steffi's knee. She suspected the truth.

"Not entirely. I had to drive him home from the eye doctor, and then he asked me to get his blood thinner because his prescription had run out . . ." She trailed off, with a slight shudder from recalling finding herself on her knees in the parking lot.

"What?" Claire's alert gaze homed in. "You just shivered."

Steffi closed her eyes and sighed. "I don't want a lecture."

"You zoned out again?" Claire pressed her fingers to her temples as if she were holding her head together so it didn't explode from frustration. "You need to go to the doctor. Promise me, Steffi. This isn't just about our business. This is your *health*."

"I don't have two days to give up to appointments and tests when, ultimately, there isn't much they can do about postconcussion syndrome." The repeated mantra was growing tiresome, even to her. Somewhere in the recesses of her possibly damaged brain was the recognition that fear of her diagnosis being something worse kept her from picking up the phone and making an appointment.

"You need the tests in case there is some bigger problem," Claire insisted, giving voice to Steffi's subconscious. "What if it's a brain tumor or something?"

"I'm only thirty. I don't have cancer." As soon as she said it, she remembered Peyton.

Based on Claire's sharp inhale and vexed expression, she must've shared that thought. They exchanged a sober look before Claire said, "Please make an appointment."

Surely, two of the Triple Ls couldn't get cancer at the same time. "Please stop pushing me."

"Lecture over." Claire tossed her purse into her car and heaved a resigned sigh. "Let's grab Chinese for dinner, and you can tell me about Ryan and Emmy."

"Huh?"

"You've been rather cheery lately, so I think you're holding out on me."

"I'm not cheery." Steffi felt a smile tug at her mouth. "Then again, we *are* going sailing on Sunday. With Emmy, of course. She invited me, so Ryan couldn't say no, but I'll take any inroad I can get. I'm determined to renew our friendship, even if I have to choke on my pride a bit. Seems only fair after what I did."

Claire's brows pinched together when she grimaced.

"What now?" Steffi asked reluctantly.

"When I spoke with Molly today about the back order of her drapery fabric selection, she mentioned that Val was taking Emmy to Block Island this weekend."

"Oh?" The warmth of anticipation drained

away like the tide returning to sea. Had gossiping with Peyton about Ryan jinxed her progress? "I guess the plans changed. I didn't see Ryan or Emmy today because I left early to help my dad, then came straight to meet you."

"I'm sorry." Claire laid a hand on Steffi's arm.

"No worries." Steffi shrugged, eager to shirk off Claire's pity. "It's not a big deal."

"Good." Claire nodded but didn't look convinced as she slid onto her seat and started the engine. "I'll meet you at Hunan Wok. I'm up for lo mein."

Claire pulled her door shut and pulled away from the curb, leaving Steffi little choice.

She climbed behind the wheel of the van and rubbed her thighs, exhaling in order to release the selfish resentment festering in her chest. How perfectly awful of her not to be thrilled for Emmy, who missed her mother terribly. This turn of events should be good news, not bad. But she'd been fantasizing about taking a walk down memory lane with Ryan on *Knot So Fast*. Lazy days on his boat had been some of her happiest ever, and she could use another one of those. Dollars to doughnuts, he could, too.

She shook her head, feeling stupid for investing her emotions in his forced offer. Obviously, he hadn't given it much thought since—he hadn't even remembered to tell her the plans had changed.

By Friday, Ryan could barely keep his eyes open during the drive home. Long days with frantic people—or worse, criminals who didn't give a damn—took a toll. Not as big of one as his daughter's resistance to making new friends, though. Every night this week she'd yammered about the impending Block Island trip. Ryan ground his teeth when he thought about letting a man who lacked the integrity to steer clear of a married woman get close to his daughter. Then again, he did look forward to the downtime this weekend.

He set his briefcase on the entry table and stared at Emmy, who lay on the floor with her head propped up on her fists, watching television. "Where's Memaw?"

"In the garden, I think." Emmy barely looked up from whatever loud Disney show had her captivated.

He hadn't seen his mother, but maybe she was putting her gardening tools away in the garage. "Are you packed already?"

"Uh-huh."

He noticed a half-eaten bag of cheddar popcorn beside her, along with bits and pieces of other orange junk food strewn across the carpet. He bent down to kiss her head, picking up the stray bits. "Can I double-check to make sure you have everything you need?"

She scowled, sparing him a brief glance from

beneath those dark lashes. "I'm not a baby, Daddy."

"I know, but Block Island can be chilly in September. Let's make sure you have warm enough clothes for the evenings."

She pushed herself off the floor and stomped up the stairs ahead of him, making her exasperation known with the pounding of each tread. Her pink gingham weekend bag sat in the corner of her room. She unzipped it and started pointing out the items. "See? I have three of everything—three bathing suits, three dresses, three underpants, and three pajamas."

"Perfect for Florida," he teased, and tugged her earlobe. "Let's trade two pajamas for a sweater and pants, just in case."

"Okay." She tipped her head from side to side while choosing which pajamas to leave behind.

"Are you sure you want only dresses?" He thought about the potential activities—biking or hiking—that might take place on the hilly island. "No shorts or sneakers?"

"It's vacation, not *work*." Her solemnity forced him to stifle a laugh. She really took "helping" Steffi seriously, but years of Val's training would not be undone so quickly.

"I see." He leafed through her things. "These are pretty. Are you excited?"

Her face glowed. "Mommy says John's house has a *private* beach."

The gleam in her eye when she said the word *private* turned his stomach. Hopefully his getting full custody would weaken Val's materialistic influence in time. "I'm sure his house is very nice, although I prefer a public beach where you have lots of people, food, and music."

Emmy's frown suggested he'd cast a shadow on the glory of John's private beach, which felt like a small win. "I wish you were coming, Dad. It'd be more fun if it was me and you and Mom."

Emmy's wish crushed whole pieces of his soul.

Ryan imagined John's massive beach house with a large deck. He pictured Val sipping a cocktail while flipping through a magazine, and Emmy running around the yard or sand, giggling. John at the grill. A perfect family affair, were it not for the fact that John had usurped Ryan's family.

Meanwhile, Ryan would be alone. Worse than alone—he'd be with his parents. Not exactly how he'd envisioned his thirties.

"Don't think about me." He poked her tummy and forced a grin. "Have fun with your mom, and we'll have our own fun when we go sailing."

"Mommy says we're going sailing, too." Emmy zipped her reloaded suitcase.

Another punch to the gut. How like his ex to steal the chance to be the first to take Emmy sailing. Val didn't even like to sail, and Ryan had wanted Emmy to learn on his old boat. None of this was Emmy's fault, though, and he'd rather

153

chew off his arm than ruin her excitement. "Perfect! That way you'll be able to be my skipper next weekend."

"Okay!" She smiled up at him. "Is Miss Lockwood still coming?"

"I suppose, although I'd like you to bring a young friend, too." He wasn't convinced he could survive an afternoon with Steffi on *Knot So Fast*, so the more people the better. "Have you invited anyone yet?"

"No." Emmy didn't even look sad. Maybe he should get her to a counselor.

"I'll see if Steffi's free next weekend." He realized then that he'd never told her about the change in plans. Surely, she must know from Emmy.

"Can I go finish my show now?"

"Of course." He kissed her head and watched her bound out of her bedroom. *His* old bedroom, one now devoid of the medals, trophies, and photographs that his mom had boxed up. The room seemed much smaller than the one of his memories, where he'd made so many plans.

He sat on the corner of the twin bed and let his mind wander, thumbing through his past goals. He'd accomplished some, like the DI soccer invitation from Boston College and graduating from law school. Others, like creating a family of his own, had fallen apart.

Lately he'd been losing more battles with doubt

than normal. Had he been a good husband, or had he given Val reason to seek love elsewhere? Could he be a good father when he hadn't moved heaven and earth to keep his marriage together? Did he owe it to Emmy to give his marriage a Hail Mary? And if not, how would he provide an example of love and commitment for his daughter in the wake of a failed marriage?

He flopped backward onto the mattress and closed his eyes, his hands folded over his abdomen. The house smelled like dust and wood and those sickly-sweet vanilla candles his mom loved to burn. Soon the weather would turn cooler, and the old radiators would ping and pop as they came to life. Old houses made a lot of noises, and he used to know them all.

He'd found workarounds to some of them, like when he'd sneak out the window some nights rather than attempt the squeaky stairs. Before too long, his daughter would be a teen and test his limits. He wasn't ready for that, nor did he look forward to her first crush . . . or her first heartbreak.

Like always, broken hearts reminded him of Steffi.

Had fate driven them both back to Sanctuary Sound now for a reason? He'd never been a big believer in destiny. It had always sounded like an excuse to be selfish, or a way to avoid accountability for failures. But maybe he'd rejected the whole concept because he needed to believe that he had more control over his life than he actually did. Some joke. Now he had control over absolutely nothing. Not of his soon-to-be ex-wife. Not of his daughter's behavior in school. And not of his mother's choice of contractor.

That first day—seeing Steffi standing on the porch—he'd literally shaken with hostility. Since then, the cold anger consuming him had melted. He now kept his composure in her presence—for the most part, anyway. A month ago he wouldn't have believed he'd be lying here wondering if they could be friends again after everything that had gone down.

He sat up, frowning. He had a new boss to impress and a daughter who needed 1,000 percent of his attention. When it came to Steffi, neither destiny, fate, nor his own sheer will would give him spare time for any relationship with her. It was just as well that this weekend's sailing trip got canceled.

Resigned, he went downstairs to find his mother, who was putting a casserole dish in the oven. "Hey, Mom, I need Steffi's number."

She double-checked the temperature and looked up. "It's the same as it always was."

"Well, I deleted it from my phone a decade ago, and honestly, I scrubbed it from my memory." He stared at her, his hands on his hips, daring her to roll her eyes or do something else to express her opinion about his way of handling himself.

She surprised him by nodding in sympathy. "203-555-1204."

As soon as he heard it, he remembered calling her over and over, not knowing why she wouldn't answer. That texting and waiting—and waiting and waiting—for a response. That burning in his gut when he realized what she was doing. The pain. The emptiness . . .

Old bitterness swelled like a wave forming in the middle of the sea and gathering strength as it moved toward shore. Maybe if they actually had a grown-up conversation about why she'd left him that way, those waves wouldn't broadside him anymore.

"Thanks." He strode onto the porch, which was now fully framed. He ran his hand along a two-by-four and caught himself smiling while admiring her handiwork. Steffi had always been strong and active, so it didn't shock him that she'd chosen a career that required such indignation and precision. He punched the ten-digit phone number on his phone and held his breath.

For the first time in a decade, she answered his call.

"Ryan? Is something wrong?" Apparently, she'd never deleted his contact info.

"No." He paused, tongue-tied like he'd been at seventeen. "I just realized I hadn't told you that our Sunday sailing outing is off. Val's taking Emmy for the long weekend."

"She's over the moon."

He heard the smile in Steffi's voice. It worried him that he liked the fact she cared about Emmy. He might be able to forgive her for letting him down, but he couldn't bear it if she hurt Emmy. "She is, but I'm sorry I forgot to mention it to you. Hope it doesn't screw up your weekend."

"It's fine." She paused, as if waiting for him to say something more. "You must be looking forward to some freedom this weekend. Any big plans?"

"If sleeping in for a change qualifies as big plans, then yes." He smiled when he heard her chuckle in that low way he remembered. He could picture her dimples whenever she made that sound.

She cleared her throat. "Benny, Claire, and I are going to see the Basement Boys play at the Sand Bar tomorrow night. You're welcome to join us if you want."

"Oh, I don't know." His voice sounded scratchy, which was damn embarrassing. "Thanks, but . . . I just need some downtime, like you said before."

A beat or two passed between them before she said, "Well, if you change your mind, I'm sure Benny would love to catch up with you."

"I'll think about it." Would he? Probably about a hundred times.

"Have a good night. Maybe I'll see you tomorrow at your mom's."

His gaze went to the pile of plywood and table saw in the corner. "Don't you ever take a day off?"

"For the time being, only Sundays. I need to hire some help now that we're booking bigger jobs at the same time."

"Too bad Emmy isn't ten years older." He surprised himself with the bit of levity. Joking with Steffi was another thing he wouldn't have banked on when he'd first returned home.

Steffi tsk-tsked. "I don't know about that. She's gunning to be the boss, not an employee."

A proud grin erupted. "That's true."

Another quiet moment left space for conflicted emotions, turning his phone into a hot potato. "I'd better run. Have a nice night."

"Bye, Ryan."

He stuffed his phone in his pocket and walked out to the yard, seeking an escape from the prison of the new family room framing. Standing in the fresh-cut grass reminded him of the rainbow kicks from earlier that week. His thoughts flickered with visions of Steffi with Emmy, of yesteryear and soccer, of friends and enemies and love and hate and failure.

Ryan hated failure of any kind yet had suffered it with the two most important love interests in his life.

Steffi and Val were completely different women.

159

His relationships with them had nothing in common, either. Well, scratch that. They had one thing in common—him. Perhaps it was time to consider that *he* might be the reason things went wrong.

Two seagulls screeched overhead, racing toward shore a few hundred yards south. Boston was surrounded by water, but the sounds of the city drowned out the gulls and crickets and other peaceful things that soothed the soul.

"Daddy?" Emmy called from behind him.

"Yeah, sweetheart?" He turned and strolled back toward the house.

"Can you show me how to do that juggle thing with the soccer ball on your knees?" She stepped out of the framed opening of the former porch, wearing her sunflower dress and sandals, her springy curls as lively as her eyes.

His heart bathed in love every single time she smiled at him.

No regrets.

Val had come into his life when he needed someone sexy and brash to hold his attention and soothe his wounds, but his heart had left that relationship long before his wife had. One great thing came of the bad marriage, though. They'd produced this magnificent little person, so in that regard it had been time well spent.

Divorce handed him a chance for closure with Steffi, too. Closure and answers that might help him make sure he didn't fail at love a third time.

He should be happy. He *would* be happy.

"Go put on gym clothes." He grinned at his daughter. "I'll grab the ball."

Chapter Eight

The aging rock cover band took a break between sets, allowing Steffi to finally talk to her brother and Claire. Not that she had much to contribute to any conversation. A gnat's attention span would exceed hers tonight, thanks to her "Ryan antennae" being fully operational.

She leaned forward, pretending to be interested in Benny's story about an employee's perpetual problem with plumber's butt. She might've pulled it off if her brother hadn't caught her glancing toward the door again. She couldn't avert her eyes fast enough to avoid noticing "that look" of his—the one that said he was onto her. But honestly, did he think she and Claire *wanted* to visualize Brian's butt crack?

Thankfully, Benny remained clueless about her current obsession with whether or not Ryan would show. If he didn't, at least all the stomach clenching she'd done while sitting there hoping would give her abs of steel. If Ryan did show, what then?

She'd only seen him at his mother's house this morning when he'd strolled into the kitchen, fresh from his shower, and filled a tall YETI mug with black coffee. After a quick "Good morning," he'd made himself scarce while she worked, probably to escape being pressured to show up tonight. A disappointing conclusion, but not as bad as her other thought. The one that whispered that he hadn't been avoiding her at all. The same one that said he'd simply been preoccupied with the many things that were more important to him than her invitation.

Indifference—a worse status than being hated. Who would've guessed she'd miss being hated?

Ryan might no longer look at her with disdain, but that was a long way from wanting her company, as proved by the fact that he still hadn't walked through the door.

Benny continued staring at her while chugging his beer.

"What?" Steffi finally demanded while mirroring his stance and then taking a long drag of her own beer. Taking an offensive posture had been her go-to method of backing her brothers down.

"Me?" He snickered playfully—a frustrating sign that he hadn't fallen for her ruse.

"Yeah, you." Matt's age-old advice about braving it out rather than admitting defeat rattled between her ears. Show any weakness and the teasing only got more relentless, like the time her brothers had gotten her to climb so high into a tree that she cried when she realized she didn't know how she'd get down. Matt came up to help her, but then she endured years of teasing and the nickname "Koala" because of the way she clung to the branches. "You keep staring at me with a weird look on your face."

He shook his head, not falling for her shtick for a second. "You're the one who looks weird."

"Is my makeup running or something?" Steffi glanced at Claire while running her fingertips beneath her eyes, hoping for a little support.

"No." Claire and Benny exchanged a peculiar look, and then Claire added, "But you're wearing makeup and jewelry. *That's* sort of weird."

"And a skirt and *heels,*" Benny added, elbowing Claire as they chuckled. Since when did Claire choose Benny's side? Another cardinal rule of the Lilac Lane League smashed to pieces.

"Wedges," Steffi corrected, and instantly regretted it, more so when her brother guffawed.

She downed the rest of her beer, pretending her cohorts were both off base when, in fact, she did feel rather ridiculous, especially because Ryan hadn't come. She'd guessed he wouldn't, but that hadn't stopped the sweet fizz of hope from tickling her insides all day.

Hope—the sucker's credo. From now on, September 7 would be the anniversary of the day that she'd officially lost her wits. Unable to stop herself, she glanced at the door, proving to herself exactly how deranged she'd become.

"Another pitcher?" Her brother stood and strode to the bar for a refill before she and Claire replied.

"He's not wrong, you know. You're barely present," Claire said once they were alone. "Are you having another zone-out?"

"No. I'm just going deaf." Normally a joke would end the discussion.

Claire clasped Steffi's hand with a surprisingly firm grip. So strong it caused Steffi to look at their hands. Her own calloused, short, unpainted nails looked so different from Claire's delicate hands and perfect pink nails. At first blush, not many would pair them up as likely friends, but somehow they were stronger together because of their differences. "Did you make an appointment for a CT scan?"

"Not this again." She withdrew her hand.

Claire sat back in her chair and huffed. "Your attitude sucks. If I could fix my limp, I'd endure twenty more surgeries and hundreds of tests. We're talking about your brain! Putting it off won't make whatever's wrong easier to cure."

No one could argue that point, although Steffi wanted to. "I can't take time off when we're so busy and gaining traction. Too much on the line right now. In fact, I need to hire some indie contractors."

"Do we have the funds to do that?" Claire's doubt wrinkled her entire face.

"I can't take on more jobs without help. The margin we lose on any single project will be made up in quantity. There's no other way to grow."

"Fine. You handle that, since you're the one who'll be working with whomever." Claire rested her chin on her fist and studied Steffi. "If you're not spacing out, then tell me why you're so edgy . . . and dressed up."

"It's Saturday night," Steffi protested, noting Claire's gray miniskirt and pink ruffled top. "I've been in coveralls and work boots for weeks. Can't I look pretty once in a while?"

"Sure, but why here?" Claire glanced around the worn floors and chipped furniture of the shabby old bar, with its stale beer odor and random strings of white lights hung on rusty nail heads for "ambiance." Most of the men there wore camo shorts or faded denim, like her brother. "You don't usually like girlie clothes, and this isn't exactly a hotbed of fashion and culture."

"Doesn't mean we can't raise the standards." Steffi shrugged, giving a vaguely honest reply. "We might fail, but at least we look good while trying."

That had always been Peyton's motto. She'd rarely left the house looking less than perfect—which was hardly difficult for the Barbie doll look-alike. That was the past, though. Now Peyton sat alone in a stark apartment in the city, puking, sleeping, or crying—or all of the above. She probably didn't give two figs now about Theory's newest dress or the best hair glaze.

Steffi looked at the empty chairs at their table.

Misery stirred, swaddling her in a thick fog of melancholy. Even if she could reunite the old gang, it wouldn't turn back time to give both Peyton and her their much-needed do-overs. Had she never seen Ryan again, she supposed she could've lived out her life knowing he hated her. Now she craved absolution, like an addict reintroduced to her favorite drug. In this way, she understood Peyton's need to make peace with Claire.

Claire hadn't asked Steffi about her visit last Sunday. As pigheaded today as she'd been at twelve, when she refused to listen to Peyton's advice about removing a fake tattoo from her cheek with baby oil and ended up losing a couple of layers of skin trying to rub it off with a washcloth. Hopefully, she wouldn't live to regret her current obstinacy, too.

Steffi glanced at the stage, remembering better days. "Remember how Peyton used to jump onstage with the bands sometimes and play the tambourine?"

"Of course." Claire's lids lowered to half-mast. "She always loved stealing everyone's attention, didn't she?"

Steffi clenched her hands into fists. "She'll be queen of the chemo ward in no time, huh?"

Claire's gaze dropped to her lap. They sat in uncomfortable silence in the aftermath of the stark reminder.

Benny returned with a foamy pitcher of golden ale, blessedly oblivious to the downshift in mood. "Anyone up for darts or something? I'm getting a little antsy." He smiled while refilling their plastic cups just as the band took the stage again.

The opening bass line of the Beatles "Come Together" began when, from the corner of her eye, Steffi noticed a familiar silhouette come through the front door. Everything that had been on her mind flew out that door as her thoughts scattered and hope shimmered like pixie dust around one man.

She straightened in her chair, heart thumping, unsure whether or not to wave Ryan over. Doing so would set off another round of laughter from Claire and Benny. Acting surprised might temporarily spare her their relentless teasing, but playing coy wouldn't win her points with Ryan. Plus, he'd likely bust her for inviting him. The only reason she hadn't already told her brother and Claire about that was to avoid humiliation if Ryan had no-showed.

Her hand shot into the air, waving wildly. Claire's gaze followed Steffi's, then widened. "Ryan?"

"Mm-hmm." Steffi pasted a smile on her face, telling herself that Ryan's joining them wasn't *that* remarkable. "Emmy's with Val this weekend, so I invited him to join us tonight. I thought he needed to get out of his mom's house and socialize a bit. I figured Benny would appreciate another guy in the mix, too."

"Ha! Don't even try to pretend you did this for me." Her brother made that goofy face he often made when he busted her chops. He glanced at Claire. "Did you bring bulletproof vests or anything?"

She snickered. "Nope. I had *no* idea he might come."

Benny stood when Ryan reached the table and then slapped him on the shoulder. "Hey, man. Glad you came. Let me grab you a glass."

"Thanks." Ryan watched her brother leave, standing stiffly. He scratched his jaw, then directed his attention to Claire. He leaned down to kiss her cheek before taking the open seat between her and Benny rather than the empty one beside Steffi. "It's been a long time, Claire. You look exactly the same. How are you?"

"Still a flatterer, I see. I'm well, thanks." Claire smiled for the first time in the past twenty minutes and bumped shoulders with him. "You look great, Ryan. Fatherhood agrees with you."

"Keeps me young . . . though some days it makes me feel old." He flashed Steffi a polite smile, then looked away as if he'd been caught shoplifting.

Ryan didn't look great. He looked *amazing*. Dark jeans fitted his slim hips and firm thighs like a second skin. His untucked blue-and-white-striped

169

oxford shirt made him look three times as nice as the other men, including Benny, who wore earth-toned collarless pullovers. Ryan's brown eyes twinkled like the strands of lights around the bar, which made her heart ignite.

She even detected a whiff of some kind of cologne. That was new. He'd never worn cologne when they'd dated, but she liked that change.

"Steffi says Emmy is a hoot." Claire smiled. "Sounds like you've got your hands full."

"I do." He spared Steffi another glance; this time he nearly smiled. "Emmy's interest in the renovation has been the first time she's been curious about anything that didn't involve dolls and sparkles."

"Well, she seems to be rubbing off on Steffi, too," Claire said, gesturing vaguely toward Steffi's rhinestone earrings.

The traitor! Steffi's whole face heated, but she stopped shy of fiddling with the sparkly hoops.

Ryan's eyes quickly scanned Steffi's face, earrings, and halter top. With the right bra, even her mediocre cleavage could usually attract a little attention. Sadly, only the slight tightening of Ryan's jaw gave her any indication that he'd noticed. Of course, that constipated expression could just be him holding back laughter at her fruitless effort to look like a normal woman. To be sexy, like Val.

Benny returned with another cup and immediately started questioning Ryan about his new job, the Patriots, and other things men passed off as good conversation. Steffi feigned interest in the music, although she'd never been much of a Beatles fan. With one ear, she strained to listen to the conversation, aware with that odd sixth sense whenever Ryan glanced her way.

Claire leaned close, forcing Steffi's attention away from Ryan. "Why didn't you tell me you'd invited him?"

Steffi shrugged. "I only did it because I felt bad that Emmy left and he had no plans. I didn't think he'd come."

"How magnanimous of you," Claire teased, kicking Steffi under the table. "I'm not an idiot, you know. You've been twitchy since you started working at the Quinns'. Now I'm positive of why. You want him back, don't you?"

Inviting Ryan tonight had been a miscalculation. Benny and Claire would evaluate everything Ryan and Steffi did and said. That thought made Steffi's skin itch. But another glance at Ryan washed away her misgivings. He had come, after all. That had to mean something, and *that* was worth being mocked.

"Don't be silly," she whispered, an appalling lie. "The guy has hated me for a decade. I'm aiming to be friends again, that's all."

"Friends, huh?" Claire grinned while pointedly staring at Steffi's skirt and shoes.

"Please don't tease us. If he thinks I've got an agenda, it'll be a disaster. I just want to be forgiven, Claire. Even if I don't deserve it." Steffi hoped *her* pointed stare would draw a parallel for Claire regarding Peyton and steer her away from her suspicions.

Claire patted her arm. "Don't worry. I think the fact that he's here means he's pretty much forgiven you . . . or wants to, anyway."

"I hope so." Steffi shifted her position away from the band in an attempt to be part of her brother's conversation. Ryan spun his half-empty glass round and round on the table, his "relaxed" expression as forced as hers.

When the familiar drum-and-guitar riff of "Can't Get Enough" tore through the crowd, folks whooped and rushed the dance floor. Energy stirred all around Steffi, making her restless.

"Come on, Claire." Benny pushed his chair back and held out his hand.

She scrunched her nose and looked at her cane, shaking her head.

"I'm not dancing with my sister when there's another option." Benny set her cane on the table. "I promise I won't wear you out too much."

He grasped her hand and yanked her up, lifting her feet off the ground as he marched them to the dance floor. Surprisingly, Claire didn't fight too hard. Benny might not be Claire's brother, but they were as close as siblings. If anyone could make her forget about the ache in her hip long enough to enjoy the music, it'd be him.

Within a few seconds, they disappeared into the undulating crowd.

Steffi's knee bounced beneath the table while she smiled at Ryan and groped for something to say. Reminiscing wouldn't be wise. Small talk felt wrong. How long would it be until she and Ryan could have a casual conversation without layers and layers of things left unsaid distorting their words and intentions? Her tongue seemed to fill her whole mouth now, so she said nothing and bobbed her head to the beat of the song.

More couples rushed past the table on their way to the dance floor until it seemed as if she and Ryan were the only people still seated.

"Should we dance?" he ventured.

She popped off her chair as if he'd hit an "Eject" button, because anything had to be better than sitting there like two awkward middle school kids. "Sure!"

Ryan followed her to the dance floor, where they were absorbed into the mass of partiers. At first, they stood side by side with as wide a berth as possible, eyes on the band, self-consciously swaying while shuffling their feet. It took a certain level of concentration to dodge other people's elbows and avoid trouncing toes while simultaneously trying to watch Ryan's expressions using only peripheral vision. But within thirty seconds, the music and energy siphoned Steffi's tension, giving her the courage to face Ryan.

When they were younger, they'd used fake IDs to sneak into Dusty's Roadhouse two towns west of Sanctuary Sound. In those days, they'd danced so close their bodies were as one, unlike now. Their relationship had ended well before her twenty-first birthday, so being on this hometown dance floor together tonight was a first. The notion of sharing a new first with Ryan prompted a smile she didn't try to hide.

Their past might be riddled with pain, but the future could be different.

Her gaze wandered nervously, propelled by a myriad of sensations as the sensual effect of dancing pooled in her core, reminding her of the security of his embrace. The tenderness of his touch. The heat of his kiss.

Those memories clouded her mind—in a good way, for a change. Loosened her up enough to risk moving closer. Thanks to her daydreaming, she wasn't sure if she'd lost her balance, been knocked forward by another dancer, or if she'd subconsciously acted out her fantasy. In any case, she fell against Ryan's chest.

When the lead singer belted the refrain, the irony of the lyrics wasn't lost on Ryan, especially not with Steffi's body pressed against his. He couldn't count the number of times he'd held her by the waist, but *this* time the shock of it awakened every nerve ending. She blinked up at him, her cheeks as pink as one of Emmy's dresses.

He couldn't help but smile. Rarely did Steffi look bewildered or at a loss, but he welcomed the momentary vulnerability even as he knew she wouldn't let it last long.

Up close, he stared into the warm brown tones of her irises limned in gold, made even prettier for the depth, compassion, and regret that came with age and experience. He still didn't trust her, but he couldn't keep pretending he didn't wish he could. Wish they could be friends. Wish . . .

"Sorry." She eased from his grip, finding the song's beat again. To his chagrin, he missed the weight and heat of her. "Lost my balance."

He nodded, unable to speak because an unholy stew of beer, hormones, and memories pickled his brain. The song ended to rampant applause. He thought to make a break for the table, but his hesitation doomed him the instant the band transitioned to the classic Eagles ballad "Best of My Love."

All around them, the crowd paired up and began the slow sway couples manage on a tiny dance floor. Claire and Ben were still dancing and laughing, which left him no easy excuse to bow out.

"Thirsty?" His voice croaked just a touch as the

lead singer began his best Don Henley impression.

Steffi shook her head and glanced around, then looked at him. "Shall we keep dancing?"

Trapped.

Yes. No!

Why did I come?

Answers. He'd come for answers.

"Sure." He held out his arms, his skin prickling in anticipation of her touch.

She clasped one of his hands and then settled her other hand on his shoulder. For a few measures, neither made eye contact nor said a word. The melody wove them together, and it seemed equally natural and uncomfortable to hold her this close. He wondered if, like his, her throat was dry. Her back sweaty, her heart squeezing hard in her chest?

The lyrics drifted around them like a catalyst for a long-overdue conversation. Damn, it was a sad, sad song. No wonder he'd punched it off whenever he heard it on the radio.

"It's weird, right?" Steffi's face was so close that the heat of her breath brushed against his jaw. The hint of some kind of grapefruit or lime perfume wafted around them. She didn't need it—or earrings or makeup or those heels—to be attractive, but he liked it. Not because of how she looked, but because he knew that she'd done it for him. Arrogant, perhaps, but he still knew her . . .

a fact that both comforted and terrified him.

He remembered she'd asked him a question. "What's weird?"

"This. Us." She grimaced. "Dancing. Talking. A few weeks ago, I'd never have predicted it."

He grunted. "Me neither."

"I'm glad, though." She took a deep breath, and he felt her hand flex on his shoulder. "I meant it when I apologized and asked if we could be friends."

He could simply accept her apology, but he needed more. She owed him a better explanation than the simple one she'd shouted at him a couple of weeks ago on the back patio.

"Why, Steffi? Why'd you blow me off that way instead of talking to me and giving me a chance to fix things? And don't just say you were too young and couldn't handle it." When she didn't answer, he asked that nagging question that had always haunted him. The one that had caused him to spend too many nights drinking that first semester. "Was there another guy?"

He swallowed hard, his heart bruising itself against his ribs while he waited. Maybe he didn't want the answer. In some ways, it might be easier to never learn the truth.

"There wasn't anyone else." She frowned.

"Oh." Relief loosened the knot in his chest. "I assumed that was the real reason why you couldn't face me."

"No. I told you, I wanted freedom." She wrinkled her nose. "That sounds lame, but if I'd have spoken to you, you could have talked me out of it if you'd wanted to, just like you talked me out of Barcelona. I needed to be my own person for a while, and I didn't think you'd let me go unless I made you hate me. I've regretted that ploy almost since I made it. If I could go back and do things differently, I would."

"But you'd still have wanted out." Those words dropped from his lips with the unmistakable sound of dejection before he thought better of them.

"Yes." She looked away.

Even after all these years, her answer smarted more than it should. He'd always wished she'd regretted her decision, not just the *way* she'd done it. Hell, an uncharitable part of him had sometimes fantasized that she'd spent nights alone, crying over old photographs.

Her soft voice broke that train of thought. "It was never about you, Ryan. It was about me. As much as I loved fantasizing about a life together, it sometimes felt like my whole future was set before I even got a chance to know my options. I didn't want to be the small-town girl who'd only had one boyfriend . . . who'd only known a small-town life. I kept thinking of my mom. Of how she'd grown up in Sanctuary Sound, married her high school sweetheart, and died in that house by fifty, having never seen or experienced anything else.

"I know she loved my dad and us kids, but I overheard her talking to Aunt Jess once about how she was really sad that she was going to die without visiting the Louvre, seeing the Grand Canyon, or knowing the thrill of realizing other personal dreams. I don't know why, but that summer trip to Spain was a trigger. As my twentieth birthday got closer, I kept thinking, What if I'm halfway through *my* life already? Is this all there is? Is this all I'll know? It scared me. I needed to see more so I'd know that my life and choices were based on more than habit and familiarity."

Her emotion-thick voice tugged at his empathy, and he found himself holding her a little closer. Her explanation, while understandable, didn't erase the pain she'd caused, but that context certainly shone a new light on their past.

Unlike her, he'd gone farther away to college. His family had traveled more widely. He'd been content, thinking they'd explore the world together. But she'd been sheltered—maybe even smothered—by her dad and brothers . . . and, to some extent, by him.

"What are you thinking?" she asked.

She'd been honest, so he owed her the same. "I wish you would've at least written me a letter at some point just to explain all that. It sucked to have no clue . . . no closure. And if I'd understood . . ."

He thought of how he'd channeled his pain into the comfort of another woman. "I might've been patient. Things might've turned out differently." Of course, he'd never wish away Emmy.

"I was ashamed and embarrassed, and then once I knew I'd succeeded and you hated me, there wasn't anything to say or do to make it better."

"I almost got in my car and stormed your campus, but pride kept me in Boston."

"And then you met Val." Her gaze dropped over his shoulder.

His body recoiled at the mention of his ex-wife. So much so, Steffi probably felt his muscles tighten. "Actually, I'd known her for a couple of years. Val was a cheerleader, so she'd been at all of my games. She came on strong once she'd heard I was free, and my broken ego welcomed her attention. She was about as opposite of you as could be—blonde, girlie as hell, treating me like some kind of God—which made her perfect at the time. Not so perfect as time went by, though. Obviously."

"Her loss." Steffi flashed an ironic smile. "Trust me, I know."

He almost tripped over her words. If she'd truly missed him, it meant that their love hadn't been a figment of his imagination. It hadn't been one-sided. "So you never met anyone special in all these years?"

"No one that made what I did worthwhile."

Another sheepish smile emerged. "Turns out maybe my mom's choices were a lot smarter than I realized."

Ryan hesitated to read between the lines. That way lay danger, especially when it came to matters of the heart. But maybe the time Steffi had taken to discover what she wanted had taught her that she'd actually had everything she'd needed. She'd just learned it too late.

Now they were back in Sanctuary Sound. Both single. Both starting over.

Much as he wanted to resist it, he could feel the hand of fate in play. John crossed Val's path so Ryan would end up here now. Emmy had taken to Steffi so quickly. He didn't *know*, though, just like he wasn't sure whether this battle between his heart and mind was one worth fighting.

He'd come tonight for answers, although those answers only led to more questions—ones without easy answers. The most important of which was: Had he ever really gotten over Steffi Lockwood?

Her arm settled over his shoulder. His leg slid between hers as he turned her in a circle. When their bodies fitted together almost as if they'd never been apart, he suspected he knew the answer, even if he wasn't ready to admit it aloud.

Chapter Nine

It could've been the familiarity of their bodies finding the rhythm together, or his musing over her explanation, that caused Ryan's softening, but for those precious beats of time dancing in close comfort, Steffi held her breath. When the final notes of the ballad faded and his self-awareness returned, he eased away from her, and the invisible fence between them reassembled.

"Think I'll sit the next one out," he said, gesturing toward the table.

"Sure." She remained still on the floor even after he'd started toward the table, as if standing there could extend the dance that ended too soon.

When she reached the table, Ryan refilled her glass and then retreated to small talk. "So, do you and Claire have your eye on any interesting projects?"

"We're submitting a bid for a substantial renovation on Hightop Road. I need to hire another set or two of hands before we can really grow."

He nodded, staring into his cup again. Then he glanced at her with a funny look in his eyes. "Gretta Weber told my mom she's putting her mom's house on the market soon."

"Really?" She sat forward, alert, her heart thumping back to life after its postdance slump.

He knew that Wedgewood-blue cottage at the end of his street had long been her favorite house in town. "When?"

"Soon, I guess. Gretta wants to move her mom into a nursing home because she can't take care of her there. Dementia . . ."

"That's sad." Steffi's sympathy for the Webers, while genuine, quickly took a back seat to her interest in getting her hands on that house. "I wonder if they've already got a broker, and how much they want."

She doubted she could afford it for herself, but maybe she could remodel and flip it.

When she and Ryan had been younger, they'd agreed that, if they ever had the chance, they'd make it their home. She'd walked past it a zillion times, always noting things she would change. Move the garden here. Put in flagstone pavers there. Add a flower box beneath the second-story dormer. Build an in-ground fire pit. The sweetness of those youthful dreams throbbed painfully in her chest, the same way indulging in sugary icing, while delicious, produced a toothache. Ryan and she had been starry-eyed about their future with the zeal reserved for teen invincibility.

Those old dreams were dead, but she might at least have a hand in making the place sparkle.

"No idea. It can't be in great shape, though. I doubt Mrs. Weber did much maintenance in the past decade. In fact, I bet they've never updated the place once in all these years."

"Just imagine it cleaned up." Her eyelids grew heavy with pleasure from the thought of restoring it. "That's one of my favorite front porches of all time."

The front door sat on the right side of the home, with the wide porch running to the left along the front. It had two thick white columns, a porch swing, and French doors that probably led directly into the living room. The whole place looked to be no more than twelve hundred square feet. A story and a half, with a shed-style dormered roofline, and ivy climbing up one side. She'd pictured so many lazy nights with Ryan on that swing.

"You should buy it," Steffi blurted out.

His brows rose. "I can't buy anything until my divorce is final. At this rate, mediation expenses, alimony, and day care will likely eat up the equity I got out of my last house."

"I'm sorry, Ryan." She sipped her beer, her mind torn between fantasies about the cottage and consolation for Ryan's dilemma. She couldn't let go of her idea. "But seriously, how perfect would it be for you to be on the same street as your mom? Emmy could hop off the bus and hang with your parents for a couple of hours, which means no day care. And you'd be waterfront and easy biking distance to the marina."

His expression turned glum, but he kept quiet.

"You don't agree?" she asked.

"In my experience, it's better not to waste time wishing for things you can't have, that's all." A shallow grin appeared before he gestured with one hand. "But you go ahead and dream away if it makes you happy."

Dreaming about that house had always made her happy. Staring at it and projecting had softened the blow when he'd left for college a year ahead of her. Ironically, back then she'd been convinced he'd meet someone new in Boston and dump her. He'd promised the distance wouldn't break them up. Promised he'd love her forever and that someday they'd get married and buy that house.

But Steffi had destroyed that love, and now the cottage would become some other young couple's dream.

Benny and Claire returned to the table then and flopped onto their chairs with sweat-soaked hair. Steffi noticed Claire rub her hip while Benny dabbed his forehead with a napkin.

Steffi turned to Claire, firing words out like a machine gun. "We need to talk. The Weber cottage is going on the market, and I want to buy it and flip it."

"Are you insane?" Claire's eyes flashed her disbelief. "Real estate speculation isn't our business plan. We do work for hire."

"I know, but it's such a great little house, there's no risk! I know it'll be snapped up, especially after we renovate. Perfect location. Unique. And small enough to be more affordable for most."

"No." Claire shook her head. "There's no such thing as a risk-free flip. And you have no idea how much work needs to be done, or what kinds of nightmares are hidden in those ancient walls."

"That's what an inspection is for." She looked to Ryan and Benny for support. "Tell her. This could be a great opportunity, especially if we can avoid paying broker fees."

Benny held up his hands. "Don't look at me."

"Chicken!" Steffi barked.

"Hey, I don't want any blame if it goes south." Benny smiled and chugged some beer.

Steffi waved him off, aware of Ryan's intent stare. She gripped Claire's forearm. "Let me ask Gretta what she's thinking in terms of price. If it's not astronomical, I'll take a look to see if the house is salvageable. Don't say no yet. Just trust me."

"I have trusted you. A 'quit my job, moved out of my parents' house to rent a place with you, and invested in a new business' level of trust. I keep trusting you even though you refuse to go back to the doctor. Now you want to take this kind of chance? Seriously, Steffi, I really wonder what's going on in your head."

"Doctor?" Benny frowned before Steffi could

defend herself. "Why do you need a doctor?"

Bother. Now she'd have to deal with her over-protective brother on top of dealing with her anxious friend.

"I don't," Steffi said at the same time Claire answered, "She zones out a lot."

Steffi ignored both men, who were both staring at her with some measure of concern.

"Like a seizure?" Ryan's brows pulled tight.

"No!" She hadn't actually seen herself in a trance, but seizures came with convulsions, saliva, and other complications that she would have to notice, didn't they? That couldn't be her problem. Head trauma couldn't cause them . . . could it? "The concussion from last spring has left me a little fuzzier than prior ones."

"How much fuzzier?" Ryan had some experience with concussions.

"Fuzzy enough to upset Claire." When neither man looked pacified by that attempted joke, she insisted, "It's not *that* bad. Momentary lapses."

"Get it checked, Steffi," her brother commanded. "Does Dad know?"

"No, and don't tell him. I don't want him worrying." She whipped her gaze to Claire and waved her index finger. "Just for this, now I'm definitely calling Gretta."

"Call whomever you want, but we only have so much cash on hand. First you want to hire help, and now you want to buy a house? You must think Monopoly money will pay for these things." Claire crossed her arms.

"Ha ha." Steffi chugged her drink.

"It's not funny," Benny said. "Promise me you won't ignore it."

"I'm not a kid. I can handle my own health care, thank you very much," Steffi grumbled.

Fortunately, the conversation ended when Melanie Westwood, a divorced brunette MILF, appeared out of nowhere and laid her hand on Benny's shoulder. "Hey, you."

His flirtatious smile appeared, which meant he'd be leaving them for his regular booty call. Steffi didn't love their ongoing no-strings fling, but she didn't judge them, either. Maybe casual affairs were the only kind a Lockwood could sustain. She'd made do with them for years without feeling like she'd missed out on much . . . until she'd been handed front-row seats to watching Ryan and Emmy.

Benny nodded to the group as he rose from his chair. "I'll catch you all later."

As he wandered away with Mel, Claire shifted in her chair, reaching for her cane. "I'm kind of beat, too. Do you mind leaving early, or maybe Ryan can give you a ride home?"

Going home at nine thirty on a Saturday night made Steffi remember why she'd initially wanted to leave her small-town life. She didn't look at Ryan but guessed he bristled at the thought of being left alone with her. "It's early, Claire. Stay another half hour."

She shook her head. "The dancing wore me out, and my hip and leg are throbbing. I want to lie down."

"Oh." Sometimes she suspected Claire used her injury to get out of doing things she didn't want to do. The uncharitable thought might be disloyal, but still . . .

"I'll take you home," Ryan offered.

She felt a smile pop into place before she could rein it in. "Are you sure?"

He nodded and sipped his beer, casting his gaze downward.

"Thanks." She looked at Claire. "Guess I'll see you at home later."

Claire nodded and gave Ryan a friendly hug goodbye.

"I'll see you to your car," he told her.

Steffi watched them go out the door, unsuprised by Ryan's gallantry. Sanctuary Sound wasn't dangerous, and it wasn't late by any stretch—but better safe than sorry. Another random act of violence might break Claire. If only Steffi hadn't left that bar in Hartford alone . . . her stomach clenched.

Ryan returned, giving her something more pleasant to think about. Now that she was alone with him, an awkward silence expanded while she fidgeted and fumbled for a way to reestablish a familiar rapport. The people at the table behind them laughed raucously, and a couple to their left was three seconds shy of jumping each other's bones right there in the bar. Meanwhile, crickets populated their table.

What had made her think they could fall into old patterns? They were different people. Strangers in some ways. They'd need to tear down to the studs to rebuild whatever they might become to each other from here. "Do you want to go hang with Benny and Mel and meet some new people?"

He shook his head. "I don't have time to invest in new people right now."

"I bet a lot of women here would like to change your mind." As soon as she said that, she regretted it. Either he'd think she had no interest in him whatsoever, which wasn't true, or he'd think she was testing his interest in her, which also wasn't true. She'd filled the empty space with thoughtless conversation because she still had no idea how to talk to him.

"Not interested." He tilted his head, staring at her. "I've got to make sure my daughter is okay before I think about dating."

Fair warning.

She leaned forward, wishing she could squeeze his hands or give him a hug. She'd never shared the warm and easy bond with her own dad that she'd witnessed between Ryan and Emmy.

"You're a good dad. Even better than I imagined you would be."

"I hope Emmy thinks so." His doubtful smile surprised her. The old Ryan Quinn hadn't been insecure about anything. Nor should he have been.

"She does."

Ryan scratched his neck. "She misses her mom."

"Of course. But when she's older, she'll realize how lucky she is to have you."

"I'm not so sure. She's off with Val and John at a beach house with a private beach, where she'll be showered with gifts and babied by her mom. Emmy likes pretty things, just like Val, and she likes to be the center of attention." He slowly tore the cocktail napkin into small pieces. "From now on, Val will be the fun parent who gives her cool stuff, while I'll be the disciplinarian with expectations and 'boring' values. Maybe my daughter will grow to resent me, just like Val— and you—did."

He immediately dropped his gaze and stared into his cup, his neck flushing. His statement didn't require a response, because she knew there was no way he wanted to have that discussion here, let alone have it with her.

She pushed her empty cup away. "Let's take a walk or something. I can't hear myself think in here."

Ryan gulped his beer and stood. "Fine by me."

191

· · ·

Ryan followed Steffi out to the sidewalk. By this hour, the sleepy town had mostly rolled up for the night. Dim lighting from the few streetlights turned the plate glass windows of closed-up storefronts into mirrors. The empty streets transformed the public green into an intimate space, with leaves overhead whistling in the breeze.

His arm tingled with the memory of being slung over her shoulder hundreds of times while walking these streets. She strolled beside him, hands clasped behind her back, long legs keeping pace with his. Familiar, yet different. Those differences weren't the only reason why they couldn't pick up where they'd left off, but they also meant he shouldn't assume a reunion would be doomed to failure again.

"Want to grab a quick bite?" he finally asked.

"Actually, do you think we could sneak around the outside of the Weber home without waking Mrs. Weber?" She kept her eyes on the sidewalk ahead. "I'd love to take a closer look."

His foolish heart sank a little. Here he'd been thinking about them—a bad habit that had started up again the second he saw her on the porch. Meanwhile, she'd been fixated on her work.

"In the dark?" He stopped walking.

"Our eyes will adjust." She grabbed his forearm but then immediately let go. "I won't be able to sleep if I don't check it out."

He pointed toward his car. "I guess we'll go, then."

They drove the two miles to Echo Hill Lane in silence. Like every other interaction with her, being locked in the car was both familiar yet uncharted. Learning the whole truth about the past had unlocked a part of his heart, releasing his resentment and making him slightly dizzy. It had also led to sharing his fears about Val and John, although he regretted spouting that revelation. Now he had so many thoughts swirling through his mind he didn't know what to say.

He pulled into his parents' driveway and killed the engine. Mrs. Weber lived across the street and six houses down at the end of the cul-de-sac. The narrow lane would be littered with acorns and other small hazards that could turn Steffi's ankle in those shoes. "Should I get a flashlight?"

"No. I don't want to scare her. If she sees a big flashlight, she might think a burglar is looking for a way in."

"She probably sleeps like the dead. Isn't she close to ninety and near deaf?"

"The flashlight on my phone should be enough." Steffi climbed out of his car and trotted ahead, peering back at him over her shoulder with a wide, childish grin. "I'm so excited."

When Ryan's mom had shared Gretta's news over breakfast, his mood had dimmed as if a cloud had passed over the sun. He couldn't comprehend the sharp sense of grief, too caught up in remembering the way they used to dream—picking wedding songs, choosing baby names, and all the other stuff that flows along the raging river of young love.

They'd imagined Saturdays on the boat followed by romantic evenings on that porch. Kids in the little yard with its tire swing nestled deep in the backyard by the path to the beach. Never did they stop and think about work or money or health issues, much less about the possibility that they'd break up. Those innocent dreams were the best kind, and maybe the death of them, no matter how silly, had needed to be mourned.

"Oh, look!" She brought her hands to her chest before whispering, "Just like I remember."

He raised a skeptical brow. It looked much worse than he remembered. The full moon shone enough light to reveal that a new paint job wouldn't be enough to update the exterior. Patches of wood rot scarred the clapboard siding. The wood-shingle roof curled in all the wrong places. The roofline itself sagged around the dormer like wet cardboard. And his mother would be appalled at the tragic state of the flower beds and the boxwood and mountain laurel hedges.

He trailed behind Steffi while she poked at some fungi, spot-checked some of the windowsills, and crept onto the porch to peer through the French doors. She looked confident and engrossed, which made him smile. She loved what she did, as did he. They'd both been lucky in that way.

"It's too dark to see much, but look at that massive river rock fireplace." She sighed like a woman in love. "I *have* to get this house."

Even teardowns in this neighborhood cost a few hundred grand. "Maybe you shouldn't get your hopes up."

She snapped her head around and frowned at him. "Same advice twice in one night. When did you become a pessimist?"

He shrugged without answering.

Steffi crossed her arms. "Better question: *Why* did you become one?"

"Life." He chuckled, although it wasn't funny.

"That's a cop-out. From where I stand, your life is mostly good. A great career, a great kid, a great family, and great health." She slapped his arm. "Stop the glass-half-empty attitude, or I'll call you Eeyore."

He grimaced. "Please don't."

"Don't make me," she teased. When she leaned against one of the columns, her expression turned more sympathetic. "It must be really difficult to be in limbo, especially with Emmy."

"Don't pity me now."

"I don't. I only meant that you have to get her through big changes pretty much on your own."

"My mom's been great, although I'm dreading

Monday. Emmy was thrilled to go to Block Island. She'll have a tough time leaving Val. It'll be like starting the separation all over again." Ryan let loose a sigh as if it would blow away his concern.

"Maybe Val will realize how much she misses Emmy and ask to share custody. That would make Emmy happier."

"It would, although I don't know that *I* want that now. We live in different states, and I started a new job. Shared custody would be tough." He grimaced. "More importantly, I don't trust Val not to flake out again. And I don't want John having much influence on my daughter."

This time when Steffi clasped his arm, she didn't release him so fast. He liked her touching him way more than he should. "For what it's worth, Ryan, I think you did the right thing for Emmy by coming home. Your mom is amazing and supportive, and this town is idyllic."

"That's what I'm hoping." He remained still, mostly because, if he moved, she'd let go of his arm. "It's amazing how much has stayed the same."

"In all the important ways. Of course, some things have changed, like this house and us." And then, as if she'd said too much, she let go of him and wandered around the side of the house, so he followed.

His thoughts slid into dangerous territory as curiosity about how sex with Steffi would differ

196

now that they both had more experience. He'd been her first, she his second. *His* first had hardly been worth remembering, though. In all the ways that mattered, Steffi had been his true first because, with her, it had been lovemaking, not just sex.

He could still remember their first time clearly. They'd sailed *Knot So Fast* out for the day and anchored off the shores of the Thimble Islands. They'd done that before, but on that day, the water was particularly calm, and they'd planned to "do it." One of the most erotic memories of his life was watching her strip out of her swimsuit and sprawl across the little bed under the bow. The anticipation had made him hot and hard and barely able to stand up. Even now, the memory made his lower half stir.

Just ahead, Steffi stopped and rested her hands on her hips. "Jeez, is this the path to the beach?" She used her arms to bushwhack the overgrown flora, unconcerned with mud on her shoes or messing her hair. "Come on. I want to see the condition of the seawall."

She disappeared into the bushes, so he followed until they both popped out onto the seawall. Several feet below lay a narrow strip of rocky sand.

They stood beside each other, gazing at the gentle waves lapping against the shore beneath a cloudless, starless sky—a stark backdrop for a moon as white as snow. The slightly eerie scene befitted winter better than early autumn.

"I loved summers here," Steffi said, breaking their private musings. "Claire, Peyton, and I made so many plans staring at that moon."

Ryan turned to her, shamed that he'd forgotten to ask for an update on Peyton because he'd been too consumed with his own troubles. "How is Peyton?"

"Brave as ever." Steffi's brow furrowed, and she removed her shoes. She then lowered herself to sit on the wall, letting her legs dangle over the edge, with her bare feet suspended above the rocks. "I wish she was undergoing treatment at Yale New Haven so I could help her, but she prefers Sloan. They've got amazing doctors, but she needs more emotional support than Logan can give. I could kick myself for letting our friendship fade these past couple of years."

The temperature continued dropping, or maybe the turn in conversation only made it feel colder.

Ryan sat beside her, close but not touching. "It faded because of Claire?"

"Partly. But even before that, we'd started to lose touch. She traveled so much, and our lives went in different directions." Steffi glanced over at him, her eyes sparkling with tears.

Regrets could suffocate a person. He knew. He had his own. "You can't change the past, but you can be there for her now."

"I want to, but she doesn't want visitors now that she's starting treatment. She's blaming the exhausting regime of meds, but I don't think she wants to be seen so weak and . . . altered."

"So think of something else you can do to support her." He stared to the horizon, as if the answers to their problems were hidden somewhere in the vast expanse, waiting to be revealed. "What does she want or need that you can give her?"

"She wants to mend fences with Claire, but Claire won't even ask about Peyton. I can't believe she'd let her die without making peace."

Ryan drew in a deep breath of the brackish air. "You can't make Claire forgive Peyton. That's up to Peyton to earn."

"Kind of like how I'm forcing you to forgive me." She offered a sheepish smile and kicked her foot against his.

"Kind of like that." Time slowed while they held each other's gaze, shoulder to shoulder, flashbacks floating around them like dandelion fluff. He suppressed the sudden urge to kiss her there in the moonlight.

As if spooked, Steffi jumped off the seawall, leaned over to pick up some small rocks, and tossed one into the sea. "I had no idea coming home would put us back in each other's orbit, but I'm glad it did."

He frowned to himself because she'd had to put

distance between them to say those words. That much about her *hadn't* changed.

"Hmph." He scratched his head while watching her throw each rock, one by one. "Why *did* you come back?"

"To start my own business." She bent down and found a few more rocks. Her careful attention remained on the task—a tactic to prolong avoiding his gaze.

"You didn't like working for a big construction company?"

"It was fine." She pitched another one, this time with more force than before. "I wanted out of the city."

"Because of the mugging?"

She stared across the moonlit path on the sea, toward the spot where the iron-gray water met the slate-gray sky. "I'd been thinking about it before then."

His brief investigation hadn't turned up any open legal case, so he'd let it drop. He had enough on his plate. But after tonight, he wanted more details about that assault, even though he knew they might be hard to hear. "What exactly happened?"

Steffi cleared her throat and pitched another rock. This one went farther than the others. "I'd gone with some coworkers to a neighborhood bar. We played pool all night, and I'd won a bunch of money. By one o'clock, I was tired, but the guys I'd gone with weren't ready to go, so I decided to walk home. I only lived six or so blocks away, and I'd done it before without trouble." She rubbed her collarbone. "My guess is that the guys who robbed me must've been in the bar and overheard us talking. When they saw me settling my tab, they must've slipped outside ahead of me. There was a narrow alley one storefront down from the bar. That's where they got me. After that, I don't really remember much. I fought, but they were bigger and stronger . . . and they had a gun . . ."

Gun? *Jesus.* "You didn't get a good look at them?"

She didn't answer. She was rubbing her arms, her body appearing to cave in on itself while shivering.

"Steffi?" He waited, but she remained locked in silence, unaware of anything going on around her.

This behavior must be what had Claire concerned. *Was* it some kind of seizure? Had these episodes begun before the attack? That would explain how she—a typically aware and strong woman—fell victim to attackers.

Ryan jumped down from the seawall and approached her from behind. "Steffi."

As soon as he touched her shoulder, she whirled on him, screaming, "Stop!"

Her elbow connected with his jaw, sending

him stumbling backward against the seawall. He rubbed his cheek, stunned.

"Oh my God, Ryan. I'm sorry. I'm so sorry!" She rushed forward, then stopped. "I didn't mean to hit you. I—you startled me—I thought . . . I don't know. I don't know what I thought."

He recalled the milder daze he'd witnessed in his mom's yard the day she'd first learned about Peyton. Were they connected? "Where do you go during these episodes?"

"What?" She was staring at his jaw, her eyes filled with shame.

"I called your name twice. Were you remembering something about the attack?"

"No. Maybe. I don't know, but it's better to forget about it."

"How can you say that?" He held his arms wide. "Don't you want justice?"

"In theory, sure. But there were no witnesses, and I didn't get a look at them, so I don't waste time thinking about justice. Besides, I don't want to be defined by that event. It's over. I've moved on." With a perturbed tone, she muttered, "Why? Are you itching to defend them?"

"Don't deflect. This is serious. Maybe your brain is trying to tell you something."

"It's telling me I'm tired. Overworked. Stressed. Concussed. Whatever. It's not a big deal. People space out now and then, especially people who've had lots of concussions." Her face was tight, her movements jerky and quick. "I don't want to talk about this."

He frowned. Something about the edge in her voice tickled his intuition. There was more to it. Either she knew it and didn't want to share it with him, or she didn't really remember where she went during these lapses. "The best way to get people to stop asking about it is to follow up with your doctor."

She'd always had a tendency to procrastinate doing unpleasant things, so it didn't surprise him when she said, "I'm busy."

"Bullshit." Even in the darkness, he could see her clearly. Powerful and confident as ever— rejecting any whiff of weakness. "Are you scared they might find something wrong?" Maybe epilepsy, or something worse.

"No. Between the concussions, all the work stress, and now Peyton's condition, it's no wonder I'm having trouble. Maybe it will get better, or worse, but no medicine or surgery can fix those things. Once life settles, I bet it gets better. Why bother with doctors?"

"Because you don't know what you're talking about." He ran his hand through his hair to keep from shaking some sense into her. "Maybe you're right, or maybe it's something else. Something that *can* be fixed."

She shrugged. "Anything's possible, I guess."

"Steffi." He squeezed her shoulders. "Find out."

She stared up at him, her eyes shining like the surface of the water beside them, and her annoyed expression transformed to a smile. "Thanks."

"For what?" He let her go, even though part of him had thought to pull her closer.

"For caring." She gestured toward the path back to the Weber home and hefted herself to the top of the seawall. "A few weeks ago you wouldn't have."

He followed behind her in silence. She'd spoken the truth. And yet, even more surprising than that was discovering he could forgive her and be a friend. Forgiveness might be freeing if he weren't starting to look at her like he used to. If he weren't, once again, feeling like his heart only found its rhythm when it synchronized with hers.

Despite his resistance, the town, the memories, his daughter's fascination, and his mother's meddling had affected him. Out of the blue, he mumbled, "Maybe there's hope for Peyton and Claire, after all."

Steffi looked over her shoulder as they emerged from the path into the Weber backyard, and flashed a quick grin. "Thank God I won't have to call you Eeyore. I was going to hate that."

Chapter Ten

Steffi paid Brian, one of Benny's hardware store employees, in cash for helping her install the windows for the Quinn project. He'd been great in a pinch—and hadn't flashed any plumber's butt—but now she owed Benny a favor for giving Brian the half day off to help her. She needed her own crew going forward or she'd be doing her brother's laundry for a decade. She waved goodbye as Brian pulled the beet-red Lockwood Hardware van away from the curb. Then she returned to the back of the house to finish up for the day.

The bright, crisp late-afternoon weather invited her to tip her face toward the sun and close her eyes. Life had been rather unpleasant and lonely at times. Now that was changing—becoming more vibrant like the gold-and-orange leaves overhead. Everything looked more beautiful.

When she opened her eyes, she saw Molly and Mick through the newly installed windows.

"I love the way this room is shaping up," Molly called out as they came through the French doors, the sunlight glinting off her large silver earrings. As always, she moved with efficiency, looking smart in her black corduroys and layered cream-colored shirts. Steffi would never be that chic.

"You've got some skills, girlie." Mick nodded before stalking off to the garage.

"I'm glad you're both pleased, because there's no turning back now." Steffi smiled at Molly. The space was coming together, but she still had a lot to do. This room would always be part of the house and the Quinns' lives. No matter what became of her and Ryan and where they ended up, he'd think of her anytime he wandered into this space. She'd leave something permanent behind, and *that* made her smile.

Mick emerged from the garage with his golf clubs and opened his trunk, tossing them in the back. He offered them a quick wave before pulling out of the driveway. His gout must've improved considerably.

"Thank God he's finally getting out of the house. World's worst patient," Molly said. "Anyhow, I was worried that this room would darken the kitchen, but it's so sunny. Once you break the wall into the hallway, I think it will actually brighten the dining and living room, too."

"I agree." Steffi grabbed her sponge and rubbing alcohol and began removing the black-and-yellow stickers from the windows. "This extra space will come in handy with Ryan and Emmy living here."

Molly crossed her arms, grimacing. "It can't be easy for my son to live with his parents at his age."

"He appreciates your help, but it'll be nice when he and Val settle things so he can move forward." She put a little elbow grease into her work.

"Val." Molly rolled her eyes, shaking her head. "His biggest mistake."

Molly's obvious dislike of Val pleased Steffi. It meant Molly wouldn't encourage Ryan to fix his marriage or discourage him from starting a new relationship.

"We all make them." Steffi hoped she sounded more charitable than she felt toward Val. She peeled away another set of stickers. "It's too bad about the timing, though. Ryan mentioned that the Weber cottage might come on the market. It'd be perfect for him and Emmy."

"Wouldn't it? But I doubt he'll get his finances in order that quickly." Molly's nostrils flared. "Whatever transpired between him and Val when he picked up Emmy Monday put him in a horrid mood, too, which doesn't bode well for a quick divorce settlement."

Steffi hadn't seen Ryan since Saturday when he'd dropped her off at the end of the night. Other than that terrible incident when she'd clocked his jaw, their night together had filled her with breezy hope, like the wind lifting a sail at broad reach and propelling a ship forward.

There'd been those seconds in the car when her hand had stalled on the door handle, that the air between them ignited like the old days—sweet and sexy and fraught with anticipation. She waited one breath—maybe two—but he didn't lean in to kiss her good night, not even on the cheek. That behavior warned her that, despite her wishes, he might never let himself go there with her again. Not after the way she'd burned him.

"Did Emmy enjoy Block Island?" Steffi balled up the stickers and plastic and tossed the wads into the trash can.

"I'm not sure." Molly held on to her right elbow, drumming the fingers of her right hand against her cheek. "She didn't explode with stories, like I expected."

"Really?" Steffi stilled. "That's unusual."

"Maybe she'll open up to you when she gets home from school."

"Me?" Steffi's brows shot up. "Why would she tell me anything before she tells you?"

"You're young and hip. I'm . . . well, Methuselah." Molly laughed, having never cared much about her age.

Steffi chuckled. "Hardly!"

"To Emmy I am. We're *both* old to her." Molly waved her pointer finger. "You're just less so."

She patted Molly's arm. "Well, I hope I'm half as cool as you when I'm your age."

"I wish your mother could see you now," Molly said out of nowhere. "She'd be proud."

"Would she?" Steffi barely choked those words out. Her mother had been a gentle woman. A

208

homemaker who valued her family, God, and baking, above all else. Steffi's ambition and lame skill in the kitchen probably wouldn't earn her mom's praise. Neither would her reticence to give and receive love.

"Of course she would. What mother wouldn't be tickled to raise such an independent young woman?"

"One that wanted lots of grandkids." She braced for the itchy hives that the idea of motherhood usually produced. Strangely, none appeared.

"You've got time."

Molly turned to go inside, but Steffi called out, "Molly, do you have any idea what Gretta wants for her mom's house?"

Molly wrinkled her nose. "She mentioned four hundred grand."

"For that ramshackle little bungalow?" The Quinn house would fetch more than that, but it had four bedrooms, two and a half baths, double the square footage, and was well maintained.

"It's a waterfront lot. Maybe one of these rich outsiders would ante up to raze the building, clear the trees for a view of the sound, and start from scratch."

"A teardown!" Her heart squeezed. "A McMansion would destroy the charm of this lane. That cottage should be preserved. God, I wish Ryan could buy it. I'd fix it for free rather than see it torn down."

Molly's gaze sharpened. "Could you buy it and flip it?"

"I want to, but Claire's in charge of our finances. We don't really have that kind of cash, and a big mortgage isn't in the budget."

Molly licked her thumb and rubbed at a smudge of glue still stuck to a window. "What if you found an investor?"

An investor? Steffi hadn't considered taking on a new partner. Claire might not be interested, either. But that cottage . . . "I don't know anyone with the money or interest."

"Even after this project, I'll have a decent amount of my inheritance left. Maybe I could kick in a little."

"Why would you do that?"

"To buy Ryan time to get his situation in order . . ."

Steffi's breath fell short, thanks to her quickening heartbeat. Remodeling that house for Ryan and Emmy would be almost as rewarding as if her old dreams had come true. "Would Gretta talk to me before she lists with a broker? Maybe I can convince her not to let her childhood home be torn down. If there aren't broker fees and I hand her a list of necessary improvements, I could whittle the price down."

"I'll get you her number." Molly turned away and then back again, clicking her fingernail against her front teeth. "Let's not mention this to Ryan. He'd accuse me of coddling him."

Keeping a secret from Ryan just when they were becoming friends gave her pause, but it wasn't her secret to tell. Then again, this was more of a surprise than a secret. That kind of secret was okay to keep. "No problem."

"Where are you going?" Emmy chased Steffi down the lane, hair ribbons flying in the wind as her headful of curls bounced with each step.

"To look at a house." Steffi glanced at her watch. Gretta should be waiting to let her take a cursory walk through the cottage. Steffi's mission: to pluck Gretta's sentimental heartstrings and, hopefully, collect a laundry list of problems to reduce the price.

"Are you moving there?" Emmy's breathless glee made Steffi smile.

"No. But I hope to fix it up for some nice family." Steffi pictured Emmy playing on the porch while Ryan read on the swing.

"Why can't you live there?" She zipped her lavender windbreaker when a stiff breeze blew.

"This house deserves a family, not someone like me." Steffi stopped in front of the Weber home and ruffled Emmy's hair.

Emmy examined the dilapidated cottage and tossed her a skeptical look. "It looks spooky."

"It's just neglected, silly goose. With a little TLC, it'll be beautiful."

Emmy's forehead wrinkled the same way

Ryan's did when he didn't understand someone's reasoning. "Can I come look?"

"I don't think so, honey. Mrs. Weber isn't well and might get a little too tired with extra visitors. Go do your homework, and when I get back, I'll show you pictures. If we have extra time, I'll teach you to use the nail gun so you can help me trim out your memaw's new windows."

"Nail gun!" Emmy fist pumped. "Okay!"

In a flash, she skipped back down the lane toward Molly's house.

Thirty minutes later, Steffi had to be pried out of the bungalow. She didn't covet material things often, but she adored this house. She imagined a puppy's pitter-patter across the heartwood pine plank flooring. Arched openings that allowed flow from the living and dining rooms into the small kitchen would also allow the aroma of chicken noodle soup to waft through the home. That massive river rock fireplace would be perfect for Christmas stockings and romantic evenings. Two ample upstairs bedrooms could comfortably house a couple and two kids. The first-floor laundry area was conveniently located. Those features and the flat parcel were its pluses.

It had flaws, too. Only one full bathroom, with questionable plumbing. Some of the flooring was black from wear, while other uneven parts required more than refinishing work. The yellowed rings tattooed across the ceilings suggested water damage that hadn't been addressed, and the roof needed to be replaced. The plaster walls had more cracks than the streets after a rough winter. And the kitchen and bathroom both needed a gut job. She wouldn't even talk about the odor. The combo of sickly people and cats do *not* help sell a home.

While walking back to the Quinns, she began framing an argument to convince Claire to invest in this flip. It'd be best if she didn't need Molly's help, even though her offer seemed sincere. If Gretta would sell for close to three hundred grand, Steffi could put another fifty or seventy in and then sell it in the low to mid fours. Its location would make it desirable despite its smaller size. And really, she wanted it for Ryan.

"Show me pictures!" Emmy jumped up from her spot on the living room floor as soon as Steffi entered the house.

"Okay." She took a seat at the dining table and described each photo as Emmy swiped through them.

"It's ugly." Emmy wrinkled her nose. "That furniture is *old!*"

"Try to imagine it without the furniture. And picture a brand-new kitchen and bathroom, polished floors, a newer railing up the stairs, and wider archways."

Emmy grabbed her head and shook it. "I don't know what you're talking about."

"Sorry," Steffi laughed. "I just mean that I can

go in and make the inside look new and clean. It will be a cozy beach house, maybe even as nice as the one you visited with your mom."

Emmy scowled and opened her arms wide. "That was a big house."

"I said as nice, not as big." Steffi put her phone aside and did a little digging. "Block Island is a beautiful place. Did you love it?"

"It was okay." Emmy shrugged. She slid off her chair and went to the refrigerator to get a bunch of grapes.

Steffi remained at the table. "Just okay? Did it rain or something?"

Emmy plucked a grape and tested its plumpness between her forefinger and thumb. "I don't like John. He took Mom away from us. He doesn't like me, so now my mom doesn't want me anymore, either." Emmy's flat delivery should've been easier to take than a teary one, yet the acceptance in her voice put a lump in Steffi's throat.

"Emmy, of course your mom wants you." She stroked the girl's head. "She loves you."

"I heard them." Emmy popped that red grape in her mouth and then, after she swallowed it, cupped her mouth and brashly whispered, "John's a *loud* whisperer."

"I'm sure you misunderstood." Steffi wanted to pull Emmy onto her lap and hug her, but she couldn't. She wasn't Emmy's mother or aunt or even Ryan's girlfriend.

"I'm not dumb." Emmy scowled and snatched two more grapes. "My mom asked about taking me with them to London, and he said no. He said he doesn't want to be a dad or change the itin . . . itinimerry because of me."

That ass. If Steffi had been alone, she might have thrown something at the wall. Ryan must've gone bananas when he heard. "That doesn't mean he doesn't like you, Emmy. He's not used to kids. Or maybe he has a surprise planned for your mom, and it would be a bad time to have you with them. There's always next time."

"I don't even want to go on vacation with him. He's not fun."

"He could be intimidated by you." Steffi hoped Emmy's attitude would improve if she felt a sense of power. Steffi's usually did.

"Not hardly!" Emmy rolled her eyes and put the grapes back in the refrigerator.

"Well, was the beach nice?" Steffi had been raised not to be a Negative Nellie, and it had served her well. Emmy needed a lesson in shifting her perception. "Tell me at least one good thing about your trip."

"I could see the ocean from my bedroom, but you had to go down a million steps to get to the beach. There were tons of rocks there, so I couldn't build sandcastles. And we didn't go sailing . . ."

Steffi raised a hand to stop the fire-hydrant

gush of complaints. "Hang on. How about you think harder about some of the *good* things. Did you catch a fish? Meet a new friend? Read a good book? Shop with your mom?"

"I got this new dress." She lifted the hem of her Black Watch plaid jumper.

"It's very nice for fall." Steffi noticed Emmy's black tights and ankle boots. She looked like a shrunken *Teen Vogue* cover girl. More put together than Steffi on most days.

"It's okay." Emmy shrugged. "So can we use the nail gun now?"

"Is your homework done?"

"Uh-huh." Emmy nodded, smiling for the first time in fifteen minutes.

"Okay, then. Go change and meet me outside."

Ryan passed Steffi's van, which she'd parked in front of his mom's house, before he pulled into the driveway. He hadn't seen her since Saturday night, but the way his heart just lurched made him wary. His caseload, divorce, and daughter were more than he could handle at the moment. Renewed feelings for Steffi Lockwood—not ideal. Not now, anyway.

He slammed his door shut and heard Emmy yell, "Cool!"

"Be careful and steady," came Steffi's reply.

When he rounded the corner of the house, he saw his daughter at Steffi's side holding a nail gun in both hands. He could tell by the way she was using her body to support her elbows that the gun was too heavy for her to keep steady.

Steffi helped position it along the window trim, then lent her body as support behind Emmy to absorb any kickback. When Emmy pulled the trigger, a pop resounded.

"I got a report about more child labor law violations." Ryan approached them, smiling. Seeing Emmy happy after last night's melodrama came as a relief. "I suppose you're expecting me to represent you?"

"Can't beat the price," Steffi joked.

He narrowed his eyes but grinned. Val disdained his career and had constantly pressured him to go into private practice, where he could charge huge sums to wealthy clients looking to buy their freedom. But Steffi had never cared much about wealth. She'd liked simple things and people, and valued hard work and results. No one on the girls' varsity team had trained harder.

"Look, Dad. We're trimming out windows." Emmy repositioned the gun a few inches to the right of the last nail. "Here?"

Steffi nodded and braced her again. *Pop!*

"I'm impressed, princess." Ryan kissed her head. "You know more about remodeling than I do at this point."

"That's not hard." She shrugged.

"Hey! I can change a light bulb," he teased.

"But you're right. There's not much I can teach you about this kind of work."

Emmy patted his arm. "Don't worry. You can teach me about sailing."

"Deal." He high-fived her.

"Can we go this weekend?"

He set his briefcase down because he might be standing there for a while longer. "If the weather's good, sure."

"And Miss Lockwood can still come?" Her gaze darted from Steffi back to him.

"If she's free on Sunday." A rush of heat moved up his body as he smiled at Steffi and pretended to be perfectly comfortable. Pretended that he hadn't replayed those seconds before she'd gotten out of his car Saturday night and wondered what she might have done if he'd touched her jaw or kissed her.

"Wouldn't miss it." Steffi winked at Emmy and then turned a dazzling smile on him, making his heart leap around his chest like a drunken frog.

That dimpled smile had always turned him to putty, which made it easy for her to manipulate him into doing or being whatever she needed. Now she seemed happy enough to be his friend, though. He'd forgiven her, which was all she'd asked for.

Could he be content with that? Friendship filled the space between love and hate in lots of cases, but in theirs? When it came to Steffi, his feelings seemed too strong to idle in neutral. Right now he couldn't be sure, and maybe he never would.

"Emmy, can you take my briefcase inside for me? I need to talk to Steffi alone for a second."

His daughter heaved a sigh one might expect if she'd been asked to clean a clogged toilet. "Fine."

She traded the nail gun for his briefcase and strode off, swinging the worn leather case with both hands. Stuffed with case files, its weight also threw her a bit off-balance.

"I got inside the Weber house today," Steffi said, rocking on her heels, eyes bright and wide. She looked damn cute when excited.

"You work fast." He crossed his arms to keep from lifting her off the ground in a happy hug.

"I have to if I want to keep someone from razing it." She retrieved her phone from a side pocket in her overalls. "Look!"

They scrolled through the photos, shoulder to shoulder. His whole body tingled from that contact. He nearly held his breath as he leaned in closer to view the pictures. Touching her made it tough to concentrate on what he was seeing. A breeze blew some of her hair in his face, giving him an excuse to tuck it behind her ear.

He sensed her freeze and wondered if, like him, she felt tormented.

"How much?" he asked, hoping conversation would help him clear his head.

"Four hundred, but I think I can get Gretta way down. Selling without a broker will save twenty-four grand right off the top. I told her I'd get her a rough estimate of the cost anyone else would incur to fix all the problems in the house. That's easily another forty before I even get into upgrades. If I can get her closer to three, I might be able to swing it. If I do the majority of the work, I know I can turn a profit on this one."

He clucked his tongue. "Sorry I can't help. It would be a sweet little place for Emmy and me."

"You never know. By the time it's remodeled, you might be in a different position." A twinkle lit her eyes as she dropped the phone back into her pocket.

He shrugged half-heartedly. "Well, I hope Emmy isn't holding up your progress here."

"By the time she gets home, I'm slowing down for the day anyway." Steffi tucked her hands under her armpits, just like Ben often did. "I was surprised by her lack of enthusiasm about Block Island."

That trip, he thought grimly. Emmy's satisfaction about the nail gun had let him forget about that for a few minutes. "The weekend was a bust, to say the least."

"I got that sense. Sorry."

"I'm glad they never got around to sailing because I want to be the first one to teach her. But John made her feel unwelcome. And Emmy didn't make it easy. She cried to Val about wanting us to reconcile, and Val thought I put her up to it. Emmy's been doing the same to me. It's hard to let her down. Sometimes I wonder if Val and I don't owe it to her to try again, but then I just . . . can't." He noticed Steffi suck her lips inward, as if it would be the only way to keep herself from voicing her thoughts. "For the life of me, I don't understand what the hell Val is thinking. How can this guy mean more to her than her own kid?"

"I don't know." Steffi gazed into the distance. "What I *do* know is that lots of us make terrible choices and hurt people we love. Hopefully, Val will figure that out before it's too late for her and Emmy."

"It's already too late, in my book. I've lost count of Emmy's tears this past summer."

"That must kill you." Steffi touched his arm, then dropped her hand.

"It *should* kill Val." A fusillade of insults shot through his thoughts until he remembered that he hadn't been a doting husband and he shared *some* responsibility for the divorce.

"It will eventually."

"By then the damage will be done." He raised his arms from his sides. "Emmy doubts her own mom's love. No wonder she's lost the confidence to make new friends."

"Could you meddle a little? Round back with

her teacher for suggestions about a classmate Emmy might be working well with more recently? Then you could reach out to the parents for permission to take their kid sailing, or for pizza and a movie."

Meddling was his mother's gig, not Ryan's. "Maybe."

"I can't imagine many kids would pass up a chance to go sailing." Steffi grinned. "I sure wouldn't."

"It's been a long time since I've sailed. Val was afraid of the deep sea, so my dad has kept the boat here these past several years." Ryan crossed his arms and stared at the ground. "It'll be good to take her out."

"I always loved those days on the water." She held his gaze once he looked at her again.

The sun hung suspended above the horizon, bathing them in honey-toned light. Warm and rich like the thick emotion flooding his veins. From the soft glow in her eyes and the stillness of her body, he knew she felt it, too. His heart trembled with its reawakening.

"Me too." His gaze homed in on the throbbing pulse point in her neck. Without thinking, he grabbed hold of her hand and squeezed it. "Sunday is something to look forward to. Something to make Emmy smile, too."

"Absolutely." Steffi drew a breath. "And if it's okay with you, how about you let Emmy call me

Steffi, or Miss Steffi, if you insist on a little formality? The Miss Lockwood thing is getting awkward and makes me feel old."

"Dinner soon!" came Emmy's yelp from inside the porch.

His daughter's reappearance broke the spell, so they let go of each other. He considered Steffi's request, weighing it against letting Emmy get even closer to someone he still wasn't sure she could count on. "Miss Steffi should work."

"Thanks. See you later." Steffi smiled and wandered off.

Ryan stood in the yard, watching her saunter away until she disappeared around the corner of the house. He then went inside and found his mom in the kitchen and kissed her hello. "Smells good."

"Chicken and dumplings." She patted his cheek.

"I'll change quickly." He started for the stairs, then stopped, remembering Emmy bringing home a student directory on the first day of school. "Ma, where do we keep the school directory?"

"We?" She raised her brows satirically.

"Ha ha." He winked. "I know you put it someplace 'organized,' which means I'll never find it."

She gave a little puff of exasperation, then pointed to the cabinets behind him. "It's in the drawer with the phone books."

"Phone books? No one uses those anymore." He opened the drawer, shaking his head. The thin school booklet distributed by the PTA lay on top of the yellow pages. He flipped through it and saw the names, addresses, emails, and phone numbers of all the families at the grade school.

"I do . . . and apparently now so do you."

"Fair enough. Thanks." Ryan climbed the stairs and peeked in Emmy's room before he changed. "Hey, sweetheart, how was school today?"

She looked up from her book. "Okay."

"What'd you do at recess?" That had always been his favorite part of the school day—when he, Ben, Logan, and others would hit the fields with a soccer ball or football and run off all the pent-up energy.

Emmy held up her book. "I read this."

Reading at recess? That sure wouldn't make it easier to find new friends. "Must be a great book."

"It's okay." She shrugged.

Now wasn't the time for a discussion about her social skills—or lack thereof. He needed to do some fact-finding first. He kissed her head and said, "Why don't you go down and help Memaw set the table. I'll be there in a jiffy."

"Okay." She slid off her bed and strolled by.

Chronic apathy was not in keeping with the Emmy Quinn he'd known for the past nine years. *That* Emmy Quinn embraced just about everything with marked enthusiasm. Steffi was right. He had to meddle.

He went to his room, shed the suit, and logged into the PowerSchool portal to find Mrs. Leckie's email address and put it in his contacts this time. After he fired off a quick note, he sighed. How was it possible that Steffi Lockwood cared more about Emmy's current state of mind than her own mother did? Yet Val *was* Emmy's mother, and one way or another, he had to figure out how they could work together to give their daughter everything she needed. Even if that meant he'd have to choke on swallowed pride.

Chapter Eleven

"I got Gretta down to three twenty-five. The cottage is a deal at that price because of its lot. Materials might run about fifty grand, and I'll do as much labor on my own as possible. When I'm finished renovating it, we'll list it at four forty-nine." Steffi shoved the spreadsheet across the dining table toward Claire. She then gripped her thighs beneath the table to stop her knees from bouncing.

"That sounds a little high. Plus, we can't raid all our reserves for the down payment. I need money to place orders." Claire tapped her pencil eraser mindlessly, her eyes glazing over in the face of the budget. "Our original goal for the year was to rent a storefront so I could have a showroom and carry some inventory. If we dump funds into this project, it'll put off that lease for who knows how long. Not to mention, your plan is a giant risk."

Claire pushed the papers away without studying them in detail. She sat back, arms crossed, closed off to the discussion. Risk-taking hadn't been her strong suit since her injury.

Steffi wasn't about to let that gunman steal *her* future, too. She'd spent nights awake since learning that the Weber place would be sold, and hours of time investigating it and coming up with a realistic budget.

She laid both hands on the table and leaned forward, crowding Claire. "Commercial leasing options require a multiyear commitment and personal guarantees, so they're risky, too. Rental space comes along all the time, but this house is unique. A once-in-a-lifetime chance."

"We can't make money appear from the sky." Claire raised her hands heavenward. "It's not personal."

It *was* personal to Steffi. Gretta's decision to sell whispered in her ear like a message from God. Like maybe the mugging and Ryan's divorce had a higher purpose than just sending them both home to cross paths and revisit old dreams. Perhaps they could actually rebuild them . . .

Owning that house, even for a little while, would be a start. The mere thought of it spiked her adrenaline. And if Ryan ended up living there— even without her—at least she would have helped repair some of the damage she'd done. She needed that . . . probably more than he did. "What if I took twenty-five grand from our business, combined it with twenty-five of my own money . . ."

Claire widened her eyes. "You're asking for trouble. Besides, that's just the down payment. You still need money for the reno."

"I can find an investor." Steffi hadn't mentioned Molly's offer yet, hoping to convince Claire to go all in. A partnership would be too complicated, but maybe Molly could make a short-term loan— just until the house flipped.

"Say you get the money," Claire mused. "That's a full-time project. What happens to our other projects like the Hightop Road house in the meantime? And what if, when you're done, there isn't a buyer at four fifty? It's only two bedrooms. Hardly ideal."

"If you'd looked at the numbers, you'd see I factored in the extra cost of hiring a small crew that I could oversee twice a day at the Hightop house and elsewhere. I don't mind working late nights and weekends on the cottage. And maybe I can add a small third bedroom off the back. Twelve by twelve—"

"So you're already inflating the budget!" Claire rubbed her palms across the tabletop and groaned. "Why are we even having this discussion? You obviously don't want my opinion."

"I can't take money from our business if you aren't on board. I also can't commit my time if it's going to cause problems between us." Manic energy pulsed through Steffi with such force she felt pressure building behind her eyes. "I need an answer because Gretta wants to list the house ASAP. Once a broker is involved, the cost goes up substantially, and I'll lose it."

Claire perched her chin on her fists and sighed. "Why is this so important to you?"

Steffi stared at her own hands while deciding whether she could endure more teasing about Ryan like the night they'd gone to the Sand Bar. Claire's romanticism had died when Todd betrayed her, so she could view Steffi's motives as a foolhardy mission doomed to failure. Without a crystal ball to show how Claire would react, and without a good plan for hedging her bets, Steffi went with the truth. "I want to do this for Ryan and Emmy."

Claire's hands dropped to the table, and she parted her lips. "Ryan wants to buy the house?"

"He can't commit because his divorce settlement isn't final, but it could be by the time we finish the renovations. It'd be perfect for Emmy and him."

"*Could* be?" Claire slouched into her seat, an uncommon posture for her. "I feel for Ryan and will be happy to see him settled, but this risk . . ." She drummed her fingers on the table with a faraway look in her eyes.

Steffi dropped her chin and began folding the budget. It'd been a long shot, but it still hurt to lose. At least she'd tried.

Claire leaned forward. "You *really* want me to say yes?"

"Yes!" Steffi clapped too soon, then noticed Claire's scheming expression and lowered her hands.

"I'll go along with this crazy plan if *you* schedule

an appointment to get your head checked out." She primly clasped her hands together, staring at Steffi in triumph.

"Blackmail?" Steffi elongated the pronunciation, her tone tinged with a bit of respect.

Claire nodded, eyes closed, in smug satisfaction. "You've put me off for weeks. If you expect me to take this giant risk, the least you can do is assure me there's nothing seriously wrong with your head. If something were to happen to you, I'd be stuck with all this debt and no expertise to manage that kind of project."

"You're right." She nodded, having not considered that particular risk to Claire. "If it'll make you more comfortable, I'll schedule an appointment."

"Great." Claire gestured with her hand. "Go ahead."

"Now?"

"Yes, now. I want to hear you do it. No excuses or cancellations, either. I'm not signing off on a check until this is done." Claire's even gaze brooked no compromise.

Steffi couldn't help but grin. "You know, I'm not the only one whose head should be checked."

"What's that mean?"

Steffi shrugged a shoulder. "You might talk to someone about the way you've let fear limit your life . . . your options."

"That's not fair." Claire scowled. "I live in

pain, Steffi. I can't run around like I used to."

"I'm not talking about physical activity. I'm talking about how you never go beyond a handful of coastal neighborhoods. It's like you've been afraid to be in a crowd ever since . . ." She left it unsaid.

Claire narrowed her eyes. "Stop deflecting and just make that call."

Steffi scrolled through her contacts and called Dr. Wigman's office to make an appointment. After she hung up, Claire said, "Thank you. Now I'll pray that we aren't making a huge mistake with this project. I sure hope Ryan realizes how much you're willing to risk for his happiness."

Steffi grabbed Claire's hands. "He can't know."

Claire tugged free. "He's not an idiot. He'll put two and two together."

"He knows I've always loved that house. Let him think I'm scraping the money together to buy it for myself. And you'll see . . . you're going to love decorating it. It's a gem."

"We'll see." Claire rose from her seat and grabbed her cane. "I'm meeting my parents for dinner. Want to join us?"

"No, thanks. I've got to call Gretta."

Claire shook her head. "You've talked me into some ridiculous things in the past, but this one takes the cake. I hope we don't regret it."

"We won't." Steffi and Peyton *had* often talked Claire into crazy pranks, like when they'd wrapped Principal Egan's car in aluminum foil. *This* was a plan, not a prank. A good plan. Once Claire left the house, Steffi called her secret weapon—Molly.

"Stefanie? I didn't expect to hear from you this evening." From the door squeak coming through the line, Steffi guessed Molly had walked outside for privacy.

"Sorry to disturb your evening, but I'm calling to see if you were serious about your offer to help me buy the Weber house."

After a brief pause, she said, "How much do you need?"

"Realistically, probably fifty thousand. I'm thinking you make us a short-term loan. We'll pay a better interest rate than what you're earning on it now, and your downside will be limited to that amount. That's better than if you're a partner, which could put you on the hook for the entire debt."

"How long will the rehab take?"

"Barring something unforeseen, the renovations should take four or so months. Even with some delays, if I can close within the month, we'd finish in time for the spring market."

"Ryan's finances could be settled by then," Molly mused aloud, mostly to herself.

Steffi slowly rubbed her fingers back and forth across her breastbone. Each second awaiting Molly's decision its own eternity.

"Okay, let's do it. Hopefully Ryan can jump on it by the time it's completed. If not, I'll get my money back with interest, so that's something. But remember, he can't know that we're scheming."

Steffi stared at her phone. "We're not *scheming*."

"Oh yes, we are, dear," Molly chuckled. "In more ways than one."

Before Steffi could ask what she meant, Molly said, "I've got to run. We'll talk tomorrow at the house."

Steffi set the phone aside and sat back in her chair, now certain that Molly *had* been conniving since the very beginning.

Her grin stretched from ear to ear. Steffi would repay the loan, but she would never be able to repay Molly for the chance to repair her relationship with Ryan. They were friends again, like they'd been as young kids. As long as Ryan didn't run back to Val to satisfy Emmy, Steffi might even have a chance at more than friendship.

They were different people now. Older. Wiser. More appreciative of what really mattered in life. If she could convince him to believe in her and "them" again, she knew it could be even better than before.

Steffi's stomach growled while she finished shingling an exterior wall of the Quinns' new room. She stretched her arms overhead with a yawn, then twisted from side to side to loosen the knot in her back. When Emmy emerged from the house with a bag of sourdough pretzel bites, Steffi snatched a few for herself.

"We're going sailing on Sunday." Emmy gnawed the salt off her pretzel before crunching into it.

Steffi nodded while swallowing. "I can't wait!"

"My dad forced me to invite Lisa Crawford." Emmy displayed a talent for speaking clearly with food in her mouth, although dry crumbs sprinkled from it like a fountain.

Steffi tried to recall anyone in town named Crawford but couldn't. The Crawfords must be a newer family, which meant Lisa had something in common with Emmy. "Who's Lisa?"

"A girl in my class." Emmy picked through the bag, selecting another pretzel with lots of salt.

"I figured that much." Steffi grinned. "But do you like her? Is she fun?"

Emmy brushed crumbs from her dress. "I guess."

"Is she nice?"

"I dunno." Emmy shrugged.

Steffi grabbed one last pretzel for herself. "Looks like we'll find out together, then."

"I told Memaw I want to bake chocolate chip cookies to take on the boat, but she says they can't have nuts if Lisa has allergies. Do you like nuts?"

"I do. Check with Lisa, though. Hopefully she's not allergic."

She wrinkled her nose. "Yeah."

Steffi crouched to Emmy's height. "You're not shy, so help me understand why you're not interested in making a new friend."

Emmy eyed Steffi while scrunching her nose and mouth, debating what to share. "If my parents get back together, we'll move home, and I won't need new friends. Even if they don't, we won't live with Memaw forever, so I'll still be moving *again*."

The thought of Ryan back with Val slithered down Steffi's spine like a snake, but she focused on Emmy's logic. It wouldn't be half-bad *if* the kid had her facts straight. Frankly, Steffi might've reacted the same way at nine.

"I'm pretty sure your dad plans to stay in town whenever you move out of your memaw's house." Steffi gestured for Emmy to follow her inside because she had to find Molly before she left. "He and I had fun growing up here. If you give it a chance, I bet you will, too."

"I guess." Emmy hugged the bag of pretzels to her chest.

"I know." Steffi playfully tugged at Emmy's curls. "Now, the important issue is convincing your memaw to make *two* batches of cookies so we don't run out."

Emmy giggled as Steffi opened the kitchen door.

"You two sound happy." Molly stirred the contents of the Crock-Pot and returned its lid.

Steffi's stomach growled again at the first whiff

of beef, herbs, and a hint of red wine. Ryan would miss having a daily chef on hand whenever he did move out.

Steffi's mom had stopped cooking when she got sick. Then Steffi did most of the cooking . . . if you could call grilled cheese and canned tomato soup "cooking." "We were conspiring to get you to make extra cookies for Sunday."

"Were you?" Molly's gaze fell to the bag of pretzels, and then she frowned. "Pretzels before dinner, Emmy?"

"I'm hungry," Emmy whined. "And I hate stew."

"I worked hard on this meal." Molly untied her apron and hung it on its hook.

Emmy raised her shoulders and held them there for a few seconds. "Doesn't make me like it more."

"You could still be appreciative." Molly crossed her arms.

"Sorry." Emmy didn't look very sorry, though. She raised her chin, asking, "Can I make a peanut butter sandwich instead?"

She was a pistol, this one.

Molly sighed. "Put those pretzels away. It's up to your father what you eat for dinner."

"Is he home?" Emmy asked.

"I think he's upstairs changing," Molly replied, at which point Steffi's insides lit up like a Fourth of July sky.

While Emmy tromped to the pantry to return the pretzel bag to its shelf, Steffi turned away, pretending to be studying something in the new family room while she closed her eyes and willed her jitters into submission.

"Bye!" Emmy called before skipping out of the kitchen.

Once she was out of sight, Molly muttered from one corner of her mouth, "I have a check for you."

She opened her purse and pulled out a checkbook.

"We should wait until the closing." Steffi grasped Molly's hand and squeezed it. "But thank you. You have no idea how much this means to me. Or how much I hope our plans work out for Ryan."

"I have some idea." Molly smiled, then tossed her checkbook into her purse.

Steffi looked her dead in the eye. "I swear, no matter what happens, I will pay you back."

Mick surprised them both with a rare appearance, greeting Steffi with a sharp nod. "Steffi." He wandered to the counter and lifted the lid off the stew, giving Molly a quick wink. "Smells good, babe."

"Scoot." She shooed him away, but not before Steffi noticed the pleased gleam in her eye. "I'll call you all when it's time, but you're interrupting girl talk."

He raised his hands in surrender and left the kitchen without another word, reminding Steffi of her own dad. Always around, but not really present.

Her father watched football games, made jokes, and paid the bills. But the truth was, they'd never really known each other that well. He hadn't known why going to Barcelona had been so important to her. Had no clue her favorite kind of dessert was flan, or that she'd always wanted to take a family road trip to Yosemite. Would never understand that she wanted him to look at her just once like she was the apple of his eye. And he'd never know that she'd felt sorry for him almost every day since her mom died.

The same could be said of her and her brothers. Even her closeness with Benny had sprung more from hanging around and doing things together than from any heart-to-hearts.

The Lilac Lane League had been her only exposure to the kind of openness that normal people enjoyed. When thinking about why she'd held back with Ryan, she could only conclude that he was a guy, like her dad and brothers, so she'd related to him in much that same way. For the first time, it occurred to her that he might've wanted more from her. If so, could she ever give it to him?

Once Molly was sure Mick couldn't hear, she said, "I know you'll pay me back. Now, if only I had the power to settle Ryan's situation in time to buy the house."

Molly's manipulations proved she didn't share Emmy's wish for Ryan to reconcile with Val.

"I'll give him the first option to buy it before I list it." She patted Molly's shoulder. "I'd love to see him and Emmy in that house."

Ryan entered the kitchen to get a beer from the refrigerator as she finished talking. *Note to self—avoid private conversations with Molly in the kitchen around dinnertime.*

Although the sight of Ryan lifted her spirits, she noticed circles beneath his eyes.

He hesitated, then flashed a tight smile. "Were you two talking about Emmy and me?"

"How was your day?" his mother asked.

"Don't change the subject." He glanced from his mom to Steffi. "What house?"

Steffi exchanged a silent message with Molly, then fessed up part of their plan. "Gretta agreed to sell me the Weber cottage to rehab and flip. I was just musing that it'd be awesome if, by the time I'm done, you could buy it." Steffi watched his expression change, his beer suspended in midair.

"You're going for it?" His voice pitched upward.

"I am."

"Good for you." A wide grin appeared beneath those tired eyes. "It's nice when dreams come true."

Hallelujah, she'd finally turned him back toward optimism.

"Or part of a dream, anyway." Steffi felt a flush rising to her cheeks because Ryan knew what she meant, and from the look on Molly's face, she did, too.

"Excuse me, you two. I have yet another load of laundry to fold." Molly rubbed her son's back and left them alone in the kitchen. Steffi had no doubt the laundry could've waited.

She cleared her throat, fumbling for conversation. "I hear there's another little girl coming with us on Sunday."

"I took your advice and meddled." He swigged some beer. "Now if I could get Emmy to be excited about that . . ."

Steffi recalled her conversation with Emmy. "She's afraid to make friends because she doesn't want to say goodbye again."

He lowered his beer to his side, frowning. "Why do you think that?"

"Something she said."

"Well, that sucks, but at least it's something we can fix." He leaned against the counter. "I was starting to worry that she was depressed."

Had he noticed he'd said "we" instead of "I"? And did "we" mean Ryan's family, or did he mean to include Steffi, too? "Before you get too concerned about depression, let's see what Sunday brings."

"I'm counting on it changing everything." He sighed and swigged the rest of his beer.

Steffi nodded in sympathy. *Me too, Ryan. For all of us.*

As soon as Ryan pulled into the marina parking lot, he spotted Steffi's van. Like an old movie, countless memories of summer evenings spent together on his boat unspooled. For horny teens discovering sex, his boat had provided the perfect cover—a place where they could be alone for hours, their bodies rocking together in time with the water. Even now, his libido responded with Pavlovian instinct.

"Daddy?" Emmy unbuckled herself.

He swallowed his nostalgia. "All set?"

"Yes!" She flung her door open and jumped out into the sunlight.

"Have you been on a boat before, Lisa?" he asked as he hauled the cooler out of the trunk. Emmy's teacher had mentioned that the Crawfords had recently moved to town from central Pennsylvania, so he doubted she had.

"Only rowboats," she answered matter-of-factly. On the surface, she didn't appear to have much in common with his daughter. No pink clothes. A sober personality. But she'd been polite and confident, and they were both newcomers looking to fit in.

He set down the picnic basket of fried chicken, carrot sticks and hummus, and cookies that his mother had prepared, and closed the trunk.

241

"Good morning, everyone. You must be Lisa." Steffi smiled and shook Lisa's hand. Steffi's running shorts, water shoes, and ponytail made her look eighteen again. One glimpse of her rosy cheeks and smile worked like balm to his soul. She tugged at Emmy's hair. "Aren't we three lucky ladies? Sunshine. Light wind. An awesome captain. It doesn't get any better."

A gull's cry pierced the air, punctuating her pronouncement.

"What's in the backpack?" He gestured toward the small red pack slung over her shoulder.

"A few fleece jackets in case it gets a little chilly on the way back."

"Good thought." Ryan felt Emmy at his side, which meant she still wasn't comfortable with Lisa. "Honey, grab the bag of beach towels from the front seat. Then you and Lisa can also carry this picnic basket."

Emmy hefted the bag of towels over her shoulder, and she and Lisa took hold of the picnic basket's handles.

"Steffi, I'll run ahead and check the engine, oil, uncover the sails and stuff. Can you manage the cooler and make a pit stop in the marina store to grab some ice and whatever else we might need? Maybe a tube of sunscreen?"

Emmy giggled. "Dad, we won't need sunscreen. It's not that hot."

"You can still get sunburn on a fall day from the

reflection of sunlight off the water." Her dubious expression told him she didn't buy that argument.

"One time I got sunburn while skiing," Steffi added. "Sun reflects off the snow, too."

Emmy and Lisa looked at each other and rolled their eyes, the first link of a bond forming through mutual disdain for the grown-ups' concerns. Well, at least that was something.

"Come on, girls. Let's raid the store." Steffi raised the cooler's roller bar and strolled ahead, calling over her shoulder, "It used to have the best selection of candy in town."

By the time the ladies made their way to his slip, he'd just about prepared everything. It seemed right—being back on *Knot So Fast*. The captain of his ship. It'd been tough to get excited about much lately, but standing there finding his balance against the boat's gentle rocking, he couldn't stop smiling.

After helping the girls aboard and securing the cooler and other items in the lockers below deck, he came back up, eager to introduce Emmy to one of his favorite pastimes.

Steffi finished fastening the girls' life vests, then whipped a bandanna from her back pocket and used it to secure her hair from blowing around her face. In a blink, it was 2006 again, and his heart swelled like the water around them. The fact that she was there with him sharing Emmy's maiden voyage made it more remarkable.

"I assume I'll be on point with all my old jobs?" Steffi asked.

"Please." He nodded.

She jumped onto the dock to untie the lines as the engine hummed to life. The rumbling engine, the faint odor of gas and fish, the light breeze on his face . . . everything rushed back, awakening the carefree spirit he hadn't revisited in years.

Steffi leaped back onto the boat, and they began the slow journey out of the marina.

"I thought we were sailing." Emmy frowned, her gaze moving from the top of the masthead to the outboard engine.

"We can't hoist the sails until we're away from the marina and in deeper water. Be patient." He patted her knee.

The young girls fidgeted with their life jackets, neither one having much to say to the other. He should've prepared better . . . set them on a small task to force them to work together.

Emmy peered into the cabin, then looked up with a quick smile. "Can we go downstairs? It's like a fort!"

"Go ahead and look around." Ryan remained at the tiller, guiding the small craft out to the open waters of the sound as his daughter and Lisa scurried below deck. As an afterthought, he called, "We'll call you up when we're ready to hoist the sails."

"What do you want to bet those two will spend

more time playing house down there than they will learning how to maneuver this thing?" Steffi sat a few feet away, her hands on the cushions on either side of her, face now turned toward the bow.

Despite the wind, he found himself sweating. Like a ship caught in irons, he couldn't move, his heart stuck between hope and doubt. He and Steffi could never relive the happy-go-lucky days they'd spent this way. His daughter's giggles below proved exactly how different things were. And yet . . . pointed toward the horizon, anything seemed possible.

They motored farther out. Water slapped against the hull like an uneven metronome. Tracking time. Days, months, years of their lives that had stretched—pulling them in separate directions—then rebounded like a rubber band to snap them back together. He wondered how often she, too, battled bittersweet memories.

Steffi broke his dream state when she stood. "Time for me to take over here so you can hoist the mainsail?"

"Sure." He vacated his seat so she could manage the tiller, then leaned over the stairs and called out, "Emmy, Lisa, come up if you want to see us hoist the sails."

"Woo!" came their collective voices only seconds before two small heads popped through the door-way.

"You girls sit over there." He pointed to the

245

bench near Steffi. "Today just listen and learn. After another time or two, you can have real jobs. Sound good?"

"I can help now, Dad. Ask Steffi. I'm a good helper!" Emmy scowled at him as if he'd denied her ice cream or a new Barbie.

"Be a really good *listener* for now," he said. "I'll quiz you before we head home. If you pass, you can help then."

Emmy turned to her new friend, brows pinched in concentration. "We have to pay attention."

Ryan briefly taught the girls about keeping the boat facing into the wind so that it didn't blow sideways as the sails went up. He then explained the blocks and halyard, the winch, and the function of the tiller.

"You steady?" he asked Steffi.

"Aye, aye, Captain." She winked. "Hoist away!"

He might've stumbled, blinded by the memory her words summoned. Memories, actually, of when she'd teased him with that nickname and comment below deck, when their bodies had been sweat-soaked and sated.

He cleared his throat. "Here we go!"

Like everything else about the day, it all came back to him as if he hadn't skipped a summer of sailing in his life. As Steffi kept the boat nose into the wind, he cranked up the main, then winched it tight, taking the slack out of the sail.

Emmy and Lisa's bright, eager faces stared up

at the green-and-white sail. The girls then closed their eyes, letting sea spray hit their faces as the ship skimmed across the water.

Ryan took back the tiller, and Steffi got ready to let out the jib.

"Hold up another few minutes." He killed the engine to let the wind propel the craft forward. The boat rose and fell, water slapping against its hull as the gust whooshed in their ears. He glanced at Steffi. "Now."

She hadn't needed the reminder, though. She knew *Knot So Fast* almost as well as he did. Within another few minutes, she'd raised the jib, and they were off.

"Where are we going, Dad?" Emmy asked.

"There's an archipelago of tiny islands a few miles offshore. I know of a deepwater inlet where we can drop anchor, picnic, and swim." He kept his gaze from Steffi's. He hadn't picked that spot *because* it was a reminder of the past. It genuinely provided a sheltered place for the girls to swim. Then again, he *could've* selected someplace that wasn't fraught with nostalgia.

"What about sharks?" Emmy examined the murky ocean with no small degree of terror in her eyes.

"There hasn't been a shark attack in the sound since 1961," Steffi chimed in. "That's more than fifty years ago. Your memaw would've been about your age when it happened."

"Really?" Emmy looked skeptical.

"Really," Steffi promised. "And even if there are sharks nearby, they usually eat at night, not in the day. Just remove anything shiny, like a bracelet or ring. We aren't fishing and chumming the water, so we'll be fine."

Ryan noticed Emmy's fists on her thighs. She looked at Lisa, whose placid expression seemed unconcerned, and her knuckles turned white.

"When we get there, I'll jump in first and splash around," Steffi said. "If no sharks come get me, then you'll know it's safe."

"But what if they do come?" Emmy protested.

"Your dad will save me, of course." Steffi smiled at Emmy, reassuring her while transforming Ryan into a superhero.

Emmy grinned at him. The pride in her eyes would feed his soul if he was anything close to heroic in real life. But the truth was, he couldn't even save his daughter from the pain of abandonment.

"How much longer?" Emmy asked Ryan.

"A while."

She sighed. Twenty minutes and multiple "Are we there yets" later, both girls fidgeted wildly.

Lisa turned to Emmy. "Want to go back downstairs to play?"

"Okay." Emmy bounded off the bench, completely disinterested in the birds, the other boats, or the distant view of the coastline.

Ryan supposed most kids jumped from destination to destination without taking the time to participate in everything along the way. Time couldn't move fast enough at that age. They wanted to move, grow up, and taste freedom, ignorant of the fact that the responsibility that comes with that freedom changes everything. Makes you weigh your choices and consider the consequences. In other words, it slows you down.

"Told ya,'" Steffi said, sliding onto the seat the girls had vacated. She hugged her knees to her chest, removed the bandanna, and inhaled deeply as the wind blew her hair all about. "Thanks for letting me come. I haven't sailed since . . . well, in forever. I forgot how much I love it."

"My pleasure." Unbelievably, he meant it. A shrink would have a field day with him. Maybe Val hadn't been all wrong when she'd accused him of never having fully gotten Steffi out of his system.

When they finally arrived at the old secret spot—one he could almost find without plot charts and paper charts—he and Steffi worked in unison to lower the sails, pay out the line, and set the anchor.

"I think we're good." His voice cracked. Dropping anchor had always been a prelude to sex. Their routine had been sex, swim, eat, sex again, and then sail home. Now there were two little girls in the cabin—and ten years of mistrust between them.

Sex would not be part of today's routine except for the way it curled the edges of his mind like a flame to paper.

"Should we eat first?" Steffi asked.

Apparently, *she* wasn't thinking about sex at all. "Let's eat up here. I don't want Emmy indoors all day, for God's sake."

"Agreed." Steffi cupped her hands around her mouth. "Come on up, girls!"

Seconds later, they scampered up to the deck.

"We'll eat up here, and then we'll swim." Ryan noticed Emmy cast another worried look at the water.

"The islands are pretty," Lisa remarked, looking at the small, rocky landmasses dotted with trees and homes.

"Glad you noticed." Ryan then ruffled Emmy's hair, but she kept her focus on the sea.

"You girls sit on that bench and watch for pirates while your dad and I go fix some plates." Steffi grinned.

"There aren't pirates here." Emmy rolled her eyes.

"Oh?" Steffi heaved an exaggerated sigh. "No pirates. No sharks. What *will* we do for adventure?"

Then she marched below without another word.

Emmy and Lisa giggled. Ryan double-checked their life vests and said, "Don't move from this bench."

Below deck, he and Steffi worked side by side in the tight galley, each carefully avoiding looking anywhere near the forward cabin.

"It's weird, right?" she finally said as he retrieved four water bottles from the cooler.

"What?" He hoped playing dumb would avoid an awkward conversation.

"The flashbacks. Memories." She took two water bottles from him and tossed a quick glance over her shoulder toward that cabin. "I shared a lot of firsts here with you."

Those few words sent him back in time.

"Are you sure you're ready?" he asked while peeling his blue-striped bathing suit off. They'd prepared for this. Talked about it all week. He'd thought about it at least twice per hour since they'd made the pact and brought a box of condoms.

She sat on the bed, head hunched forward so as not to knock it against the ceiling, and removed her string bikini top to reveal pert, full breasts with pretty pink tips. "Yes, totally sure."

He only half believed they'd go through with it. Now, watching her shimmy out of the bathing-suit bottoms, his heart climbed into his throat. Thrill. Fear. Wonder. A cocktail of emotion that pushed its way through his body, making him quake with anticipation.

This was it. His life would be defined as before and after this step with her. Everything between them would change, too. But it would be okay, because he loved her more than any person in his life, and she loved him. He was never more certain of that love than he was right then, when she reached out for him.

"Come on, Captain. Hoist your sail." She'd always preferred jokes and physical expressions of love to intimate conversation. With a sly smile, she wound her arms around his neck and pulled him against her naked body.

What followed could only be described as a clumsy kind of passion, marked with scorching kisses, fumbling fingers, and shaky nerves. All of that wrapped in a beautiful heat that spread from his heart through his limbs, as he claimed Steffi Lockwood his . . . for always.

The boat rocked as the water lapped against the hull, and for a while, time ceased to exist.

"Ryan? Are you okay?" Steffi asked.

"Yep." His eyes stung, so he looked away. "Lots of firsts."

He tucked two bottles beneath his armpits and grabbed two of the four plates, then turned to go above deck.

"Firsts and bests." She'd said it just loud enough that he knew she meant for him to hear her.

He took one step toward sunlight, heart pounding, then looked over his shoulder with a grin. "Mine too."

A sudden need for air made him bolt outside so

the breeze would fill his lungs again. He handed both girls a plate and water bottle, then took a seat and braced to face Steffi, now that he'd admitted something he'd never planned to say.

Chapter Twelve

Mine too. Steffi smiled to herself as she replayed Ryan's words a third time. She'd earned his forgiveness in these few weeks. She should be grateful for that and not push. But those two words had offered a hairline crack of hope, and like a field mouse, she'd find a way to squeeze through it for a chance to snuggle up to the warmth of Ryan Quinn.

She went above deck and handed him his plate, which he'd piled high with chicken, then sat beside him. Close, but not touching, although it took a lot of concentration not to let her knee wander to her left. She tormented herself with the idea of an "accidentally on purpose" graze, and then by wondering if he would flinch, move over, or allow their knees extended contact.

Her gaze locked on that inch between their thighs, her heart pounding madly, desperately, egging her to move her leg. She could blame it on the rocking of the boat if he tensed. But he might let it linger . . . he might be remembering . . .

"Aren't you hungry?" he asked, gesturing to the chicken breast she'd yet to touch.

Molly's fried chicken had been Steffi's favorite for years, but sexual frustration filled her stomach now, killing her appetite. Why had she ever given up the right to hold his hand, sit on his lap, and enjoy his kisses? He'd loved her, but she'd run from him without even knowing what she hoped to find.

"Where are the cookies?" Emmy asked.

"Don't talk with your mouth full," Ryan answered, licking the salty grease from his fingers. Steffi tore her gaze from his mouth. "Cookies come *after* we swim."

Emmy glanced over the edge of the small craft and grimaced. "Are there jellyfish?"

"Not usually." Ryan tipped his head, studying his daughter.

"What about other fish?" Lisa asked.

"Of course there are other fish in the sea." He smiled at the ancient idiom, but Steffi knew it had no real meaning for young girls. She'd also come to doubt the truth of that idea, too. "But they won't bite."

"How do you know?" Emmy asked.

"Because you're bigger than most of them, and I've done this a million times without ever getting hurt." He sighed, signaling that he'd reached the limit of his patience.

"The first time your dad brought me out on this boat, I was scared to swim, too. I mean, we *are* far from the shore, and you can't see what's down there. But then I decided I wouldn't let fear make me miss out on something fun." Steffi stood and dumped her plate in the trash. Without waiting for the others, she stripped out of her shorts and T-shirt, clambered to the stern's ledge, and dived into the water, shouting, "Fish bait!"

When she broke through the surface, she gasped. The chill made it feel as if every cubic inch of water in the inlet was crushing her chest. She sucked at the air to catch her breath.

"Holy cow," she sputtered. "It's freezing!"

Three sets of eyes stared at her from over the port-side railing. Ryan crossed his arms but wore a wide grin.

"Come on, don't leave me hanging here by myself!" Steffi stammered through chattering teeth, which probably didn't encourage anyone to join her.

"No way." Emmy's emphatic headshaking showed she was more convinced than ever that deep-ocean swimming was less appealing than a math test.

"How about you, Lisa?" Steffi hoped Lisa would persuade Emmy to overcome her fear in the same way that keeping up with Steffi's brothers had forced *her* to do so. So far, that tactic hadn't helped Steffi lessen Claire's anxiety, but, surely, she could get these two girls in the water.

Sadly, a wordless shake of Lisa's head upended Steffi's ploy.

"Ryan?" She shivered, her body refusing to adjust to the cold water. Maybe it wouldn't be the worst thing if she couldn't convince them to jump in. Not to mention how unappealing she must look with blue lips and head-to-toe goose bumps.

"Can't leave the girls aboard by themselves." A taunting smile appeared. "Sorry!"

"You will be sorry," she teased, trying in vain to splash them all with water. Her benumbed arms lacked real power, so the water barely sprinkled them. Undaunted, she swam around as if enjoying it all, doing somersaults and floating on her back—anything to pique Emmy's curiosity.

A few minutes later, the girls lost interest in watching her, so Ryan lowered the swim ladder. "You can't win 'em all."

Mere seconds shy of becoming a human pop-sicle, she swam to the stern. When she boarded, he wrapped her in a towel. Face-to-face, he pulled it snugly around her, then brushed her wet hair back from her cheeks and whispered, "Thanks for trying."

He let his thumb linger at her jaw, his eyes tender and raw. Her heart pumped twice as fast, and not because her limbs needed blood to warm up. She felt words gathering—disjointed thoughts and yearnings he should hear. She'd never been good with words. If the girls hadn't been on deck, Steffi might have kissed him right then. For now, she'd settle for standing so close that their stomachs were practically touching, and holding his gaze.

"Dad, can I steer the boat next?" Emmy tugged on Ryan's swimsuit, ruining the electric moment.

He rested a hand on her shoulder. "Sure, I'll teach you and Lisa how to use the tiller."

"Yay. I'll go get the cookies now." Emmy trotted off without waiting for his permission.

Steffi supposed he, too, knew when to admit defeat.

"I think I'll get out of this wet suit and put my clothes on." She reluctantly broke free from his grip and went to the cabin. The look in his eyes suggested he wanted to follow her below deck and help her out of her suit. *Progress,* she thought. She could build on this.

Hours later, they pulled back into the marina. While everyone pitched in to tie down the boat and cover the sails—relishing their salt-crusted hair and wind-burned cheeks—Steffi wondered why Val had given up on Ryan and Emmy. There couldn't be a better way to while away time than with this little family, nor a better man to love.

Surely, Val would see her mistake, just as Steffi had, and come running back. If she did so soon, would Ryan take her back? If not for his own sake, then for Emmy's? From what Steffi had seen, he might do just about anything to make his daughter happy. He also wouldn't be the first person to keep a marriage together for the sake of a child.

Karma might enjoy Steffi getting her heart broken by *him* this time around.

That thought infringed on her good mood as they all walked along the marina's splintered wood dock, loaded down with the empty cooler, picnic basket, and bag of mostly unused towels.

When they reached the parking lot, the girls skipped ahead to the car. Ryan popped the trunk, and she helped him pack it up.

"Girls, wait in the back seat while I walk Steffi to her car." He gestured with his head toward her van.

"You don't need to walk me. We can see the van from here." She took a few steps, but he followed anyway.

"Are you okay?" He kept his gaze on the ground about four feet ahead of them as he matched her stride.

"Better than okay. Awesome day." Or it had been until doubts about Val clouded everything. "Thanks for letting me tag along."

"Your mood nose-dived at the slip." He stopped at her van.

She could lie, but having him trust her—to look at her that way again—kept her honest. "I was thinking about things, that's all."

"Things to do with me?"

She inhaled and momentarily held her breath. "Let's not spoil the fantastic day with an awkward conversation."

"Did I make you uncomfortable?"

"No." She twisted her arms together in front

of her body. "I started thinking about Val."

"Val?" He reeled backward as if she'd struck him.

Steffi dragged her hands through her hair. "I had such a great day, but I couldn't help wondering how she walked away from you two. I'm sure she'll regret it and come back."

He shook his head. "No, she won't."

"I did." Steffi should have been mortified by the confession. She just handed him a perfect opportunity to smugly take her down a peg. Instead, she found herself staring into his eyes, seeking reassurance.

He blinked, almost as if he couldn't quite believe what she'd said. His eyes glowed with something that resembled satisfaction, but then he shoved his hands under his armpits. "She won't be back. We both left that marriage, in one way or another. I don't miss her and she doesn't miss me. My only regret is that Emmy's paying the price for our mistakes."

Steffi sighed, partly relieved, but still uncertain that Ryan, if faced with the option to rebuild his family, would walk away from Val. "I'm sorry. For all of you."

"Don't waste your time feeling sorry for me, Steffi. Better days are ahead for everyone." He opened her door and waved her into the driver's seat, smiling. "Now go shower. You smell like fish bait."

• • •

"It looks like the cookies were a hit." Ryan's mom removed the near-empty Tupperware from the picnic basket while interrogating Emmy about the day. "You must've worked up an appetite swimming."

"We didn't swim." Emmy climbed onto a kitchen stool at the breakfast bar and rested her chin on her fists. "They just tasted so good!"

"No one swam?" His mom's jaw slackened in surprise as she glanced at Ryan.

"Miss Steffi swam," Emmy laughed. "She was *freezing*."

"She might've been cold, but she wasn't afraid, was she?" Ryan squeezed her shoulders and kissed the top of her head. "I think we missed out on some fun by not joining her."

Emmy shot her grandmother one of her infamous "He's not fooling me" looks. "It didn't look like fun to me."

"At least admit that she didn't get attacked by any fish, sharks, or jellyfish. Next time we sail, I want you to get in the water." The image of Steffi climbing onto the boat—her body glistening in the sunlight—flashed for the fourth or fifth time that afternoon. If the girls hadn't been there . . .

Ryan opened the refrigerator, grabbed a beer, and popped the tab even though he wasn't thirsty. He was *antsy,* thanks to everything that had simmered beneath the surface of his interactions today.

"Go shower, honey," his mom instructed Emmy. "And please take all those towels into the laundry room on your way out of the kitchen."

Emmy's head dropped back and her shoulders slumped before she slid off the stool. "Work, work, work, Memaw. It's all we do."

Ryan spat some of the beer from his mouth when he laughed at the same time his mother replied with, "You're practically Cinderella."

Good God, they were both priceless.

Emmy dragged the bag of towels to the laundry room before she went upstairs. As soon as she was out of earshot, his mom turned to him. "How'd it go with the little girl . . . Lisa?"

"Pretty good, although they played in the cabin more than they enjoyed the open water."

"That's not surprising." His mom waved her hand. "Everything down there is miniature, like them. Did they get along?"

"Yup." He probably ought to shower, too, he thought. Maybe that would wash away the itchy restlessness clinging to him like dried sea spray.

Before he made a getaway, his mom asked, "How'd Steffi handle the girls?"

"Like a champ. She remembered everything about sailing, too." He smiled without thinking, realizing his mistake when his mom seized upon it.

"So you enjoyed the day together? You two always got along so well." She dug back into the picnic basket in search of the leftover chicken. Without meeting his gaze, she mused aloud, "Now that you're both single and back home, who knows . . ."

Just as he suspected.

"You set this up from the start, didn't you?" He waved his beer bottle toward the back porch. "There are other contractors, but you picked her on purpose. Admit it."

He couldn't even pretend to be mad at this point. If anything, he should probably thank her. He would one day, just not at the moment.

"What's that thing you advise your clients to do . . . take the Fifth?" She cocked a brow above a sly smile.

He shook his head. "You know what can happen when you play with fire, don't you, Mom?"

"There's no warmth in life without a little fire, honey." She surprised him by gathering him into a hug and giving him a squeeze, something she hadn't done in quite a while. Hell, he hadn't been hugged by anyone but Emmy in months. It felt good. It felt like home.

"I'd better get my own place soon; otherwise, you'll train Emmy to meddle, too," he teased before easing away.

"You should buy the Weber cottage when Stefanie's done renovating it."

"We'll see." That would require money, which meant he had to deal with Val. That thought soured the taste of his beer. "See you in a bit."

When he reached the top of the stairwell, he overheard Emmy talking on the cell phone Val had sent her this past week. He crept closer to her room, stopping just outside her door to listen— partly to spite Val and partly because Emmy's moods were so affected by conversations with her mom that he wanted to be prepared.

"We played house in the little cabin. It was so cool, Mommy. There was a bed and sort of a kitchen and a little potty that Dad called the head." She laughed. "Isn't that funny?"

Val probably didn't find it funny. In fact, she probably remembered some of the stories about the boat that he'd told her in the earliest days, when he'd been drowning his broken heart in cheap beer. Back when Val had found the opening she'd needed and crawled inside, wrapping herself around him. He'd taken everything she wanted to give to heal his wounds, and for a while that had worked out for both of them.

Emmy's voice snapped him from that thought.

"Yes, Miss Steffi came. She knows how to sail. She worked the jib and Daddy was steering with the . . . the tiller. Anyway, we parked by a little island. Then Miss Steffi jumped in the water and yelled, 'Fish bait!' She was funny, but she was freezing in there, so Dad made her come back on the boat and wrapped her in a towel."

Ryan brought his hands to his forehead. That overshare wouldn't make negotiating a settlement any easier. Then he heard Emmy's tone turn less pleasant. "No, Mommy. They're special *friends,* that's all. We can still be a family again."

Ryan held his breath. The plea in Emmy's voice pierced his heart. He'd failed her. Failed at the most important job and relationship of his life. Even if or when he found love again, Emmy's life would never be whole. Everything would be split: birthdays, holidays, vacations. And she'd always carry this wound around from Val's choice to give Ryan full custody.

He had to make sure he never let her down again.

"Okay, I'll find him," Emmy murmured.

Ryan heard his daughter's feet hit the ground, so he pretended to be walking down the hallway. She came out of her room and nearly knocked into him.

"Mommy wants to talk to you." She was looking at him funny now. He suspected she was thinking about her mom's insinuations about Steffi. He didn't need his daughter quizzing him before he even understood all his feelings.

Ryan held out his palm. "Go see if Memaw needs help in the kitchen." Once Emmy disappeared down the stairs, he pressed the phone to his chest for a second and prayed for patience. "Hey, Val. What's up?"

"Sounds like you had quite the triumphant day with our daughter and your girlfriend."

"Steffi's not my girlfriend. But yes, we had a great day. Why does that make you angry?" He knew why. Val was a jealous woman on many levels. After Emmy's weekend with John went to shit, the last thing his wife wanted was to hear about her daughter having a wonderful time with him and Steffi. Had he not just heard Emmy's deepest wish, he might revel in the small victory. But a hollow victory was nothing to celebrate, not to mention that he couldn't afford to twist the knife if he wanted a quick settlement. "I assume you asked to speak with me for a reason. Did you want to set up another visit?"

"I don't know my schedule."

He bit back a pointed remark about her priorities. "Is this about the settlement? I'd really love to resolve things so we can both move on."

"I bet you would. Now that Steffi's around, you probably can't wait to get out of your mom's house so you have some privacy."

He sat on all his righteous indignation. "What I want is to do what's best for Emmy, and getting her settled sooner than later is best. It's not good for her to be in limbo. She's been refusing to make friends because she doesn't know where we'll land."

At least Val took a minute to think about that. "I didn't know she was struggling this much. You

266

have to keep me informed about these things, and how she's doing at school. I want to come to parent-teacher conferences, too."

"I'll do my best."

Val sighed. "I'm not trying to drag things out, but what do you expect me to live on?"

"What do you really need? It looks like John's taking care of you in spectacular fashion."

"We're not married. If things don't work out, I'll be screwed. I'm looking for a job now."

"Really?" If she had actual doubts that things would work out with John, why the hell did she blow up the family and leave her daughter? "I thought you didn't want custody because John wanted to travel. How will you keep a job if you're off seeing the world?"

"I'm applying for virtual assistant jobs with flexible hours so I can do them from anywhere as long as I have a computer. I'm good at admin." Her defensive tone evoked a little pity. She'd put a career on hold while raising Emmy, which left her fewer options now.

"Sounds like a good middle ground." He hoped she took that the right way. "If I don't demand child support, would you forgo alimony? We could split all the other assets right down the middle."

"You don't think I deserve *any* alimony?" Her pained voice clawed at him with unexpected effectiveness, especially when it dropped to a near whisper. "It's like nothing I did for you and our family had any value."

"Of course it had value. But if I'm willing to give up any help with Emmy's financial support, can't you bend, too?"

"You never loved me." The disheartened statement smacked him in the face like a wooden plank.

He didn't understand how or why the conversation had jumped there. Untangling from a ten-year-long relationship was much more complicated—and heartrending—than he'd anticipated. "That's not true, and it's kind of irrelevant now, isn't it?"

"Not to me, Ryan." Her voice dropped again. "Not to me."

He could picture her now, forehead in her hand, staring blankly in that way she did when she felt misunderstood or unloved. With some shame, he had to admit that the fact he knew that pose so well said something unflattering about him.

Ryan closed his eyes. Alimony wasn't a measure of the love that did or didn't exist in a marriage, but apparently it was to Val. "If you insist on alimony, then can you give me a bigger share of the equity from our house?"

"What's the number?" John must've called her from another room because she then rushed Ryan off the phone. "I've got to run. Shoot me an email. But don't insult me, Ryan."

She hung up without waiting for him to say goodbye.

He went into Emmy's room and set the phone on her dresser. He couldn't keep drifting through life, letting events dictate outcomes. He had to take control of things and make some choices. Smart choices.

Tonight, after his daughter went to bed, he'd focus on the math he'd been hoping to avoid for the past two months so he could hammer out a deal with Val. He'd also do a little research to see if head trauma could cause epilepsy. Steffi hadn't zoned out today, but he hadn't forgotten Claire's remarks, either.

He'd let his wife down, but he could still be there for Emmy. And maybe even for Steffi.

Chapter Thirteen

"I'm confused." Benny reached across the table for the ketchup. He flipped the lid and drew a red circle on his burger. Behind him, yet another bug met the neon zapper. "Is this good news or bad news?"

The sun was setting earlier now, so her dad excused himself to go inside to turn on the back-yard floodlights.

"It's exactly what I expected." Steffi ripped open a bag of kettle chips and poured two fistfuls onto her plate. "Nothing has really changed since my last concussion. There aren't any growths—like tumors—to worry about, although there is a tiny bit of brain shrinkage. He said that isn't shocking, given my history of concussions and the relative severity of the last one. I could be part of a 'significant minority' of folks who experience ongoing postconcussion trouble with paying attention or depression or a bunch of stuff."

"But what about the zone-outs?" Benny grabbed a handful of chips and cracked his beer open. "I've never seen one, but Claire seems concerned."

Steffi's dad opened the slider and returned to the deck wearing a fraying gray cardigan. It made him look old. She didn't like to think of him as frail, but she supposed he'd sailed through middle age sometime ago, unlike her mom.

He took a seat in front of the plate Steffi had fixed him. "Looks good."

Her dad's lack of concern about her head injuries gave her a chance to deflect the conversation. She pointed at Benny. "Thank the grill master."

Benny took a seated bow, then pressed her again. "Steffi . . . what else did the doctor say?"

Her father smothered his burger in barbecue sauce and added some bacon on top for good measure. If he cared about the doctor's opinions, he didn't show it. He'd grown skeptical of doctors ever since her mom's cancer treatments failed.

"He didn't think my description fit with grand mal seizures, but diagnosing that is tough unless I have one in front of him, because I can't really explain what's happening to me when they occur. I lose track of time, but I'm not convulsing or anything. He said it could be psychological, from the 'trauma.' " She speared a pickle, resenting being seen as some fragile flower who couldn't deal with being mugged. "He spouted off a bunch of stuff, dissociative amnesia, PTSD, yada yada."

Benny set down his burger and affected a playful snicker. "You need a shrink?"

The Lockwood family did not believe in shrinks. They also didn't believe in UFOs, the NRA, or public displays of affection.

"No!" She glanced at her dad to gauge his

reaction. "He was just throwing out every possible explanation, that's all. That's what doctors do when they don't have a real answer."

"Yep," her dad added.

Benny shrugged. "Well, you did experience something traumatic. Maybe you haven't processed it."

"Who are you, and what did you do with my brother? And since when did you buy into psychobabble . . . or think that I'm such a wuss that I haven't gotten over what happened?"

"Don't get all worked up." Benny licked some ketchup off his finger. "It was just a thought."

"A stupid thought." She shooed a bee away. "I'm sure it's just the shrinkage. Maybe it will get better with time, or maybe it will just be the way I am from now on. I don't get headaches, and these lapses are annoying but not harmful."

"What if you're driving when one happens?" her dad asked.

She hadn't considered that possibility. "It hasn't."

Her dad nodded, brows low in thought. She could only assume that her answer satisfied whatever concern he might have for her problem.

It occurred to her, not for the first time, that her own outlook on life might be different if her mom were still living. That woman had made a big deal about everything. Maybe a little too big, too often. She'd ironed every stitch of clothing in the house, including Steffi's jeans. Those creases in the legs of her Mudds had been embarrassing at the time, but now Steffi smiled at the memory.

It had also taken her mom two days to decorate their Christmas tree because every strand of tinsel had to be perfectly placed. Her dad, on the other hand, hadn't bought a live tree since his wife died.

And whenever her mom had entertained, she'd prepared multiple dishes and side dishes to ensure that everyone had their favorite food. Most important, her mom had never shied away from a deep dive into a hard conversation or hugs . . . and probably wouldn't have run from shrinks, either.

"One last question. Is there a pattern?" Benny asked, pulling Steffi out of her reverie. It took her a second to remember where the conversation had left off.

"Not that I can tell. They're sudden and brief. No headaches or puking—sorry, Dad—or drooling or anything else." She shrugged and took another bite of her burger. Missing her mom didn't help her situation, and neither did her brother's interrogation.

"Sudden?" Benny wiped his mouth, having quickly inhaled his meal. "Like they get triggered by something?"

"Nah." She frowned, shaking her head. "It's completely random. Weird places, times of day, sometimes when I'm alone and sometimes while with others."

Benny narrowed his eyes. "There's nothing in common—no sound or scent or anything—that sets it off?"

"Not that I can tell."

"And you don't remember *anything* when you snap out of it?" Benny's scowl deepened.

She shook her head. "It evaporates. Like when you come out of a dream, and it fades before you can make any sense of it."

"A good dream or a bad one?" Benny leaned forward, eyes focused on hers.

"I don't know," Steffi snapped, appetite gone. She did know that those episodes made her uneasy. Often they'd made her sweaty and slightly queasy, to boot. "I told you, I don't remember."

"Maybe you *should* see a shrink." Benny looked at their dad. "What do you think?"

"Steffi's got a good head on her shoulders." Her dad covered her hand, even though his metaphor suggested he hadn't been paying much attention to the conversation. "If she thinks she's fine, she's fine. If it gets worse, then she'll go back to the doctor."

Benny rolled his eyes. Their dad had never forced his opinions on people. That trait—like most—had its pros and cons, but Steffi knew his ambivalence drove Benny crazy at work. She appreciated her dad's faith in her decision-making, but every once in a while, she wouldn't mind him dispensing *some* advice. Her mom and then Molly had given loads of it back in the day.

"At least say something to Matt. He's a doctor. He might have some insight here," Benny said.

"No way. I don't need him to be all over me. I went to my neurologist. He isn't jumping up and down with worry, so I won't, either." She stared at her brother. "Promise me you won't go behind my back."

"Fine." Benny pushed his empty beer away.

"Now, I hate to cut our family time short, but Claire's waiting for me. We have to finish working up a proposal tonight. I'll run with you tomorrow, Benny. Can't make it tonight."

"Just as well. I think I might've pulled a groin muscle last night." He rubbed the inside of his thigh. "I should rest for a night."

"Or lay off hooking up with Melanie Westwood for a while," Steffi mumbled, while tossing a crumpled napkin at his head.

"Ha ha." He threw it back at her.

Their dad didn't react to the banter. Sometimes she wondered if he even listened during these dinner conversations. She gathered her dirty dishes. "See you guys later!"

On the way to the kitchen, she passed her favorite photograph of her mom—the one at Candlewood Lake, where they'd rented a house for the Fourth of July weekend one year. Her mom was sitting on an Adirondack chair at sunset, reading a book, with a glass of wine on the chair's arm. Whoever took the photo must've said something that tickled her, then snapped the photo precisely at the best moment to capture the beauty of her mother's laughter. Shining eyes. Pretty teeth. Dimples.

Time was funny, the way it could slip around like quicksilver, especially when it came to grief. In the immediate aftermath of a death, the ache of loss consumes the body until you doubt you'll ever find a reason to smile again. The intensity of that yawning emptiness fades with time but can still sneak up on you in the moments when you want to hear the person's voice or advice. Nowadays, Steffi no longer yearned for her mom's touch or smile on a daily basis. But today, after lying in that noisy MRI tube, facing her own mortality, she'd thought about her a lot. Her mom would push her, like Benny.

Her dad, on the other hand, never thought his kids needed counseling, not even when their mom was sick. He always said life's hard knocks help a person grow, and shrinks coddle and over-medicate people.

The Lockwoods didn't coddle each other. That sense of independence and strength had always made her proud, but now she wondered if it had been a liability.

"I've been digging, but we're not getting lucky with this one. The whore—" Billy began.

276

"The alleged victim," Ryan corrected. He had no problem digging for evidence to discredit the woman's testimony, but he wouldn't tolerate disrespect. He and Billy weren't in a position to judge her or even understand what drove that woman to prostitution. In his book, an uneducated prostitute who is buying groceries for her kid was a better person than an overeducated politician who harasses female employees.

"Yes, her." Billy cocked an eyebrow. "Despite a bunch of arrests for solicitation, she's never filed a rape claim. I hung out around her neighborhood this week to see what else I could learn. Aside from mild recreational drug use and a scuffle with another prostitute, she's unremarkable. Then there's your client. No one overheard them transacting. And some might say that, technically, it *was* rape since O'Malley didn't pay. I feel bad for the guy, 'cause O'Malley's kinda fucked."

When Ryan grimaced, Billy said, "Bad pun, sorry. But physical evidence proves O'Malley screwed her. She's bruised from when he pushed her out of the way to run from the motel room. My gut says Owen didn't understand that he was supposed to pay, though. Too bad he freaked out instead of going to an ATM."

"Too bad our belief isn't enough, you mean." Ryan rubbed his forehead. "We can use her prior arrests for prostitution to show a pattern of behavior, but I'd really like to get my client out of solicitation charges, too. O'Malley didn't have the requisite intent, nor did he try to dupe her into a freebie. I'm convinced he just thought he was getting lucky."

Owen's low IQ would make jail that much harder for him. And then to live as a registered sex offender? The guy's life was already complicated enough.

"One thing is bugging me, though. Why didn't she get the money up front? Isn't that standard?" Billy scratched the back of his neck. "Won't the prosecution use that to argue it wasn't a pay-to-play?"

"I'm sure they'll raise it, but I'll try to shut it down. Her blood tests came back positive for drugs and alcohol, and she's no rocket scientist. If they were partying together, I can argue that she thought she'd collect at the end of the night after racking up extra services. Maybe I could even use the fact she didn't collect money up front to prove it was consensual instead of transactional."

Billy shrugged as if unconvinced. "I'll keep digging tomorrow. It's getting late, and I've got to run now."

"I was wondering about that tie." Ryan smiled. "Big plans?"

When Billy stroked the blue-on-blue striped tie, a little color filled his cheeks. "Dinner with her folks tonight. Their twenty-fifth anniversary."

"I didn't know you had a serious girlfriend.

You're as good at keeping secrets as you are at uncovering them." Ryan tossed a pencil across his desk. "Does 'her' have a name?"

Billy shoved his hands in his pockets, shoulders hunched. "Just got back together with my ex, Dina, a few nights ago."

"I can't tell if that's good or bad news."

"I guess the jury is still out. Truth is, she cheated on me with *her* ex back in June."

"Sorry. That sucks. You're a braver man than I, going back to the hand that bit you." Ryan wished he had that courage, though. Maybe then he could be with Steffi instead of being tormented by his dreams.

"It's not easy. When it first happened, she acted like it didn't mean anything." Billy's gaze wandered while he grimaced.

"What made you trust her again?"

"She kept apologizing all summer . . . swore it wouldn't happen again." Billy let out a slight chuckle. "Maybe I'm a sucker, but you know, we all make mistakes. I wasn't the best boyfriend, either. I guess I figure the only way to know for sure if I can trust her again is to trust her. I'm happier today than I was two weeks ago, so I'll keep my fingers crossed and keep looking forward."

"I hope you're right. She's a lucky woman." *Very lucky,* he thought. He wouldn't have pegged Billy as one to hand out second chances.

"I'm feeling pretty lucky, too." He flicked his tie and joked, "Except when I have to dress like this."

Ryan waved him off. "Have a good night."

He organized his file and then shut off his computer.

On his way to his car, Ryan hugged himself to keep warm in the face of an autumn wind. His thoughts turned to Billy, whose youth allowed romantic optimism to flourish.

Unlike Billy, Ryan wouldn't be spending a romantic evening with a woman his own age. Nope. His inability to trust meant the only women he'd be spending the night with were his kid and his mom.

"Thank you, Steffi." Claire hugged her. "I'm *so* relieved that it's not epilepsy or a tumor. Not that the tests solved the problem. I wish they had more answers for you."

"I'm more concerned about answers to our scheduling dilemmas." Steffi took a seat at the dining table, where Claire had strewn a bunch of estimates she'd worked up for the Hightop Road house.

"Has anyone replied to your want ad?" Claire asked.

"Yes, but they're all men."

"That never bothered you before." She began setting the estimates into piles: tile and granite, fabrics, furnishings, fixtures.

280

"I'm not bothered, but I've spent my whole career working for and with men. I wouldn't mind a few more women in the mix." She reviewed the logistics plan for the project. "You'd think a women-owned business would attract at least one."

Claire wrinkled her nose. "Is there a big pool of female construction workers around here?"

"Obviously not." Steffi scribbled some notes on the plan. "I'll put a crew together in another week or two. Perfect timing for this job and the upcoming closing on the Weber property."

"The Weber property." Claire pressed her fingers to her temples, shaking her head. "You're the closest thing I've got to a sister, and that's the only reason—*real* reason—I caved on that project. If I didn't see you falling back in love with Ryan, I would've put my foot down. But despite my cynicism about love, I'd be happy to be proven wrong in this case."

Claire would see through any denial, so Steffi didn't protest. "I'm not holding my breath. He's come a long way since last month, but he still doesn't trust me. I hurt him—betrayed him—just like Peyton did to you."

Claire's expression turned icy. "When you put it *that* way, I can hardly believe that he can be in the same room as you."

"So you don't think I deserve a chance to prove I've changed?" Steffi bristled.

"It's not my place to judge you, or what Ryan should or shouldn't do." Claire sighed. "I love you, and I know you regret the way you handled that breakup, so I want to see you get your second chance."

"Thanks." Steffi considered her last call with Peyton two days earlier. Claire's name had come up only once. Then Peyton dropped it, but not before Steffi heard the desperation in her voice. "You loved Peyton like a sister, too, and believe me when I tell you she regrets what she did. Can't you make *any* room in your heart for forgiveness?"

"Please stop pushing me." Claire balled her hands into fists on the tabletop.

"Pushing? I've tiptoed around this for a year. But Claire, there's no guarantee that her treatments will work. Are you so full of hatred that you'd let her die without talking to her? Without even giving her a chance to *apologize?* And if she dies without you two ever speaking again, can *you* live with that?" She clasped one of Claire's fists with her hand and squeezed it. "I want you to forgive her—not just for her sake and mine, but for yours, too."

Except for the rising flush in her neck and cheeks, Claire's face looked like it had been carved in stone. She withdrew her fist before she spoke, her voice brittle. "Am *I* now the guilty party and Peyton the victim?"

"That's not what I'm saying," Steffi began, but Claire cut her off.

"You two don't get it, and you don't get me. This is just like after that bullet struck. 'Claire, you'll be fine,' " Claire mimicked. "And, 'There's more to life than tennis. You have other talents.' Or my favorite, 'Claire, you *have* to go away to college. Why would you want to stay *here?*' Meanwhile, you both went off in search of more exciting lives, yet neither of you ended up any better off than me. And *still* you push, trying to convince me to do things your way. Why don't you try to understand me instead of trying to change me?" Her voice cracked.

"Relax—"

"Don't tell me to relax." Her voice turned shrill. "You don't know what it's like to be shot by a madman. To rebuild a new life after your dreams are stolen." Claire gripped her cane, staring into the distance. "To live with a daily reminder and pain. To wake from dreams that I'm healthy and playing tennis, and see ugly scars, feel the ache, and grab this." Claire shook her cane.

"Claire . . ." Steffi reached out, but Claire withdrew further.

"I don't need your pity. I made peace with it— or I had." She smoothed her hands along the tabletop. "I had carved out a pleasant life here with a job I enjoyed, a family I love, and a man I loved. Someone who overlooked my disfigurement and lived in quiet contentedness like me. I was finally happy and had 'it all'—more than either of you at the time, actually. It might not have been much by your standards, but I was planning the future . . . a family. Then Peyton deigned to return to this 'pitiful little town,' with her teasing ways, and her larger-than-life stories, and perfect, healthy body that never held her back. Just like that gunshot that changed my life, so did she." Claire thumped her fist on the table.

Steffi waited, sensing Claire had more to say.

Claire's scowl deepened, and her voice fell so low it sounded hoarse. "She already had so much, why'd she have to take Todd? And I don't care if they didn't get together until after he broke up with me. If she'd been any kind of friend, Todd would've been one hundred percent off-limits. She wouldn't have given him any signals or encouraged any hope. So don't guilt-trip me because I won't talk to her. I told you, I don't wish her harm, but I don't owe her anything, either."

Claire's gush of anguish swept away every argument Steffi might've posed, leaving her speechless. And she was right; Steffi and Peyton had been too busy making Claire "better" to have seen things from her perspective.

"I'm sorry I've been the kind of friend that made your recovery harder rather than easier. I never meant to make you feel alone, downplay what you lost, or belittle the way you chose to cope. I should've listened to you instead of trying to convince you to do things *my* way." Although heartfelt words and softness never came easily to her, Steffi scooted to the edge of her seat and held Claire's gaze. "I hear you now. I love you, whether or not you ever forgive Peyton. All I want is for everyone to be happy. For all of us to find what we need in life. I wish life—happiness—wasn't so complicated, don't you?"

"It's not complicated," Claire snapped. "Just be honest—with others and yourself. If you do that, then you should be able to get what you need."

Steffi drummed her thumbs on the table, musing softly, "That would mean I'd have to tell Ryan how I feel."

"Maybe he deserves that from you—for *you* to take the risk. It could be what gets him over his mistrust." Claire patted Steffi's hand and then pushed herself up with her cane. The lines of her face curved downward, as if the gravity of the conversation had pulled at her cheeks and mouth. In a wistful tone, she said, "You don't have much to lose at this point."

Claire turned and started for the stairs, the heavy thump of every other step drilling home the story she'd unloaded this afternoon. Steffi sat at the table and filed the paperwork her friend had uncharacteristically left behind.

Ryan had warned that Peyton would have to be

the one to find a way back into Claire's life. He'd been right.

Was Claire right, too? Could life be simpler if she was honest with Ryan?

Claire had blithely said Steffi had nothing to lose, but Steffi's pride was at stake, even though pride didn't keep you warm. Vanity could wreak havoc on a life, like a toddler throwing a tantrum.

And even if she got over that hurdle, honesty wouldn't budge two others: Emmy and Val. No matter what *she* wanted, she had no control over how those two would react.

Chapter Fourteen

"Why are you wearing that mask?" Emmy asked from where she'd drawn back the clear plastic curtain Steffi had put in the new archway between the not-yet-finished family room and the home's central hallway.

Was it four o'clock already? That meant Steffi had an hour until her appointment with Gretta. The elder Mrs. Weber had already moved into the nursing home, so Gretta agreed to let Steffi and a home inspector into the bungalow this afternoon.

"Hold up, Emmy. Don't come in here." Steffi finished wedging the insulation between the studs before climbing down from the ladder. "The fiberglass can irritate your eyes, skin, and throat."

"It looks fluffy." Emmy inched closer, fingers outstretched to touch the deceptive pink batt. She glanced up at Steffi's stern glare and whipped her hands behind her back. "Can I help you stuff it into the walls?"

Steffi studied the remaining wall—half wall, really—running beneath the windows. She supposed she could supervise Emmy without losing too much time.

"Go put on pants, long sleeves, and gloves. You'll need eye protection, too." Steffi's would be too large.

"Okay," she called, already running toward the stairs. "I'll be *right* back."

Steffi chuckled to herself.

"You have a nice way with her," Molly said. Apparently, she'd been listening from the kitchen. Now that the kitchen door and other wall had been removed, Steffi could also smell all her cooking. Today, the aroma of beef broth had piqued her hunger.

"She's pretty easy," Steffi demurred.

Molly peeked through that plastic drape and chuckled. "Oh, Stefanie, I love her dearly, but few people would call Emmy Quinn easy to handle."

"Considering all of the recent changes in her life, I think she's a marvel. No self-pity. No whining. She keeps truckin' along." In that way, she supposed she and Emmy had something in common. Of course, Emmy hadn't given up hope that her family would be reunited. Once that dream died, her attitude could change.

"That's true." Molly then teased, "She must get that from me."

"Absolutely," Steffi laughed. Molly embodied resilience. Perhaps that was why they'd always gotten along. "Has she mentioned anything about Lisa since our sailing trip?"

"They've been eating lunch together. It's a good step." Molly's expression warmed. "Ryan mentioned that you pushed him to meddle."

Steffi felt her lips part in surprise before she

could stop herself. "I didn't mean to overstep."

"Nonsense. You're helping him and Emmy. Both of their moods have improved these past several weeks."

"I'm sure that has more to do with your support than mine." She deflected the compliment. Her father didn't hand them out often, and her brothers usually dealt them with a heavy dose of sarcasm, so to her, they always sounded like false praise.

"As good as I am . . . and I *am* good"—Molly winked—"I can't take full credit. Trust me, you've played a big part in easing this transition."

Their conversation came to an abrupt halt when Emmy raced back into the room. Steffi had to smother her laughter. Emmy came to a full stop, arms and legs spread wide, wearing jeans, a pink-and-red-striped shirt, purple knit mittens, and swim goggles.

"You look prepared!" Molly exclaimed. "I'll let you two get back to it."

Steffi knew those mittens wouldn't do the job. "Molly, do you have gardening gloves that might not be too big for her?"

"Let's see." Molly disappeared into the garage and then reappeared with green-and-white gloves. "Try these."

They nearly came up to Emmy's elbows but provided better protection and mobility than the mittens.

"Come on, Emmy. Let's cover your mouth and

nose with a face mask." Steffi had more in the pack, so she fitted one securely onto Emmy's head. "Now, take the tape measure and determine the exact distance from the bottom of this row to here." She touched her fingers to the underside of the window frame.

While Emmy measured, Steffi unspooled more batt.

"Thirty-three and a half," Emmy announced.

"Is that perfect?" Steffi asked, resisting the temptation to double-check. It seemed important to trust Emmy. If she'd made a mistake, Steffi could fix the problem easily enough.

"Yes." Emmy snapped the tape measure back into place.

"Okay, come over here and I'll show you how to cut the batt with a utility knife."

Emmy watched with rapt attention, and then Steffi showed her how to properly install batt and gently push it into place. "I'll cut a bunch more to fit these sections, and you can be my stuffer."

"Okay." Emmy spun in a circle while Steffi measured and cut. When Steffi heard a muffled ringtone, Emmy stopped twirling. Her eyes went wide inside the goggles as she pulled the face mask down and removed her gloves.

"That's my mom!" She answered the phone, wearing a giant grin. "Hi, Mommy!"

After a pause, she said, "Helping Miss Steffi stuff insulation."

Steffi cut through the insulation, wishing she could see Val's face or hear her reaction. Did that woman miss her daughter yet? Was she second-guessing her decision?

"I'm not bothering her. I'm helping build Memaw's new room." She twirled a bit of her hair in her fingers, swinging her hips restlessly, the way fidgety kids do. "Am too. I helped push down screens, and I used a nail gun on trim."

She wrinkled her nose. "It *is* safe. I'm in goggles and a mask."

Another pause. "He's not home yet."

More silence. "You should come visit and help. There's still lots to do. It's a mess!"

Steffi frowned to herself. It was hardly a mess. She kept her work space neat as a pin, and the project had progressed nicely. Not that she cared about Val's opinion or approval.

"Okay, Mommy. I love you, too." Emmy hit "Off" and pushed the phone back into her pants pocket. Without skipping a beat, she put the mask and gloves back on, and then picked up a section of freshly cut batt and started working.

Steffi kept her questions to herself, but Val's motives gnawed at her. If she planned to be honest with Ryan, she ought to do so before Val changed her mind. Ryan deserved someone better than his wife, but if he wasn't dating anyone when Val came calling, he might take her back for Emmy's sake.

"Why are you breathing funny?" Emmy asked, hovering over Steffi's shoulder, wearing a frown.

"Am I?" Steffi worked to regulate her breath. "Some of the fiberglass dust must be tickling my lungs," she fibbed.

Emmy inhaled deeply, then blew it out and shrugged. "Not mine."

"Good. You don't want it in there." Steffi handed her the final section of batt. Funny thing. It could keep you toasty warm, but it could also irritate and hurt you if you weren't careful with it. "Go on, finish it up."

Suddenly, she felt claustrophobic in the Quinn house. Her appointment at the Weber home couldn't come soon enough.

Ryan pulled onto Echo Hill Lane, barely able to keep his eyes open. Some days he felt like a hero—helping the underprivileged community get justice or rescuing the wrongly accused from convictions. Other days, like today, he had a slate of clients—repeat offenders and all-around bad seeds—that he'd just as well see thrown in jail for as long as possible.

On those days, it took every ounce of integrity in his bones to provide the best defense possible. It wore him down and raised questions he didn't want to ask himself. Questions like whether the guys who hurt Steffi had been career criminals who played the system.

He was parking in his mother's driveway when, in his peripheral vision, he noticed Steffi's van down the street in front of the Weber home. The photos he'd seen hadn't quite satisfied the itch to explore that place.

Ryan left his briefcase on the front seat and locked the door before strolling down the lane and up the porch steps of the antique bungalow. He knocked on the door, then finger brushed his hair and smoothed his tie.

He heard the sound of heavy footsteps approach the door from inside the house.

"Oh, hi!" Steffi's bright-eyed smile eased his self-consciousness.

"Saw your van and thought I'd take a peek . . . if that's okay." Once again, his mouth went dry around her. It never had in the past. This limbo—a friendship complicated by uncertain yearning—had him by the throat.

"Of course. The home inspector just left . . . no big surprises, so I'm moving ahead with the sale. Now I'm sketching out some plans." She waved him inside. "In fact, I'm glad you're here. Maybe my vision will convince you to buy it when I'm done."

"You're persistent, I'll give you that." He chuckled, wishing he had the money to give Emmy a sweet little place to call home.

This place, however, smelled worse than a locker room after an August practice. He supposed that would be resolved once they removed the furniture, opened some windows, and tore out old carpets. "Give me the grand tour."

"Yay." She clapped her hands with no small amount of glee, like a grown-up version of Emmy. "Okay, so as we saw through the window, this is the main living area. It's cluttered as hell right now, but it's a decent size and anchored by that amazing hearth. Imagine it stripped of her chintz and tchotchkes, with gleaming refinished floors, a simple L-shaped sofa here, maybe a swivel bucket chair here. A nice ottoman there, and over here you could hang a decent flat-screen television."

She flashed a quick smile and motioned for him to follow her. "Then I'd widen this archway between the living and dining room by eighteen inches or more to open the flow a little. In here, I'd replace the window on the back wall with French doors for a view of the backyard. When we clear some of the overgrowth, we might even get some view of the sound. Now, picture a simple round dining table with six chairs and an updated dining chandelier. Claire has great taste, so I know she'll find something perfect to suit the home. Maybe I'd add some texture to one wall, like reclaimed wood or something, just to give it a hip look. Again, Claire is great with those details."

"That'd be cool. Trendy, though."

She shrugged, winking. "If we knew the buyer in advance, we could customize to his taste."

"Keep movin'," he urged, partly because he didn't want to fall in love with the idea of this house—or of Steffi being the one to remodel it for him.

"Fine." She gestured toward the door leading to the kitchen. "The kitchen is small and dark because it's closed in. I'd open up this wall and either do an island or a peninsula here. It would create better flow for entertaining. I think a greenhouse window over the sink would be cute, and I'd swap a single glass door for that wooden one to the backyard. Those fixes will make the kitchen feel bigger and brighter even though the floor plan won't be enlarged. I think pale-gray cabinets with white quartz counters, a farmhouse sink, maybe some funky drawer pulls or open shelves here for a bit of contemporary flair. Oil-rubbed bronze fixtures might be cool, too."

"Sounds amazing." He turned about, imagining Emmy seated at an island, waiting for pancakes. "What's through that door?"

She held open a swinging door. "A laundry area. I'd put in a pocket door here and clean it up."

"No dedicated office or den?" Not that it mattered. He wasn't really looking. Not seriously, anyway. Daydreaming. Fantasizing at most.

"No, and it's only got two bedrooms and one bath, all upstairs. That's a major drawback." She held her finger to her lips. "Don't tell Claire I said that."

He pretended to lock his lips.

"If there aren't any major structural or piping and wiring problems, and if I can salvage most of the existing flooring, I might have room in the budget to create a small powder room from a section of the laundry room." She sighed. "If I had a buyer and we could agree on a price, I might also afford to build a small office off the living room. It's always an option for someone to do down the road. Just pop a French door on the right side of the fireplace, and then just do a single-story ten-by-ten room. Small but adequate. It could even double as a guest room in a pinch."

"Let's see the bedrooms." He'd gotten caught up in this fantasy now. If Val would agree to his last request, maybe he could stretch and swing it.

"The bedrooms." Steffi cleared her throat, then led him up the narrow stairs. He followed close behind, enjoying the view of her cute ass and the intimacy of the close space. He could picture this being a nightly routine, even.

The bedroom doors flanked the landing. Each generously proportioned room had eaves that kept them cozy. The shared bathroom—which could be a drawback when Emmy hit her teens—was a decent size.

"I wish I could get rid of the tub and do a

fabulous walk-in shower, but with only one bathroom, I can't ditch the tub. I'm thinking of putting a deep soaker tub here with a waterfall showerhead over the center. I can squeeze a double vanity along this wall."

"I'm sure it'll be stunning."

"I hope so. I love the stained glass window in here. On a sunny day, it probably casts a pretty pink color in the room. Emmy would *love* that!" She smiled.

His daughter *would* love it.

He and Steffi both turned to leave at the same time, bumping into each other as they tried to squeeze through the door. "Sorry."

"My fault."

Neither moved from the tight space.

Having just toured this house through her eyes, he could picture himself here, with Emmy, and as crazy as it seemed, with Steffi, just like they'd talked about all those years ago. After a long day in court, he could return home to find Steffi in this shower, washing off the grime from some other renovation project. Maybe he'd even climb into that big tub and let the water splash over them both.

He might've groaned.

"Ryan?" She laid her hand on his chest. "Are you okay?"

He covered her hand with his own and held it there. "Hard to say."

"Do you feel it?" She swallowed hard. He could almost hear the effort.

"Feel what?" His heart thundering beneath his rib cage?

"Us, here in this house." Her eyes gleamed as she spoke even faster. "All of our old dreams suddenly possible . . . sort of. I mean, if I hadn't, well, you know."

He didn't say anything because they'd already dissected the past. He'd let go of his anger weeks ago, so he just nodded.

"Actually," she continued, looking at her toes. He tipped her chin back up.

"Actually, what?"

She licked her lips. "Maybe I'm totally off base and, if that's true, just tell me to shut up and I'll stop. But ever since we went sailing, I've been thinking about us and how we're both home again. I was wondering if . . . well, if there was any chance that maybe you'd be interested in going out sometime. Like for real. On a date." Her cheeks grew redder by the second.

"Steffi . . ." He hesitated. In many ways, daydreaming about making things work with Steffi was a lot like fantasizing about being able to afford this house. He could get too attached to the idea and then suffer massive disappointment if it failed. "I won't pretend it hasn't crossed my mind. The world's full of coincidences, but sometimes I wonder if fate brought us both back here now. I also won't pretend that none of the old feelings have resurfaced. But it's not just me taking a chance now. I've got Emmy to protect. And maybe I shouldn't consider dating until my divorce is final."

"Okay. Makes sense." She removed her hand from his chest and backed away. "Pretend I never said a thing. Friends, then. Friends is good."

She offered a fleeting smile before trotting down the stairs. He stood at the top like a coward. Like the guy who let her ghost him all those years ago without a fight—out of pride or fear or a combination of both.

She'd broken up with him because she'd wanted adventure. If he made his decisions based on safety, then he didn't deserve to be with someone like her. A minute later, he found her in the living room.

"For the record," she said without meeting his gaze, "I know you consider me a high-risk proposition, but that works both ways. *I* could get hurt this time around, especially if Val waltzes back in to reclaim her family." She put distance between them, crossing to the far side of the living room. "Like you said, you're not divorced. Any day now, she might realize what a mistake she's made."

"I don't want Val back."

"But you love Emmy, and she loves her mom. She wants you two back together." Steffi stared at him from a spot next to the hearth of the home that could be theirs if they tried and succeeded. "If there was any chance to give her back her family, you might try. I know you. I know what you value."

"Then you know I value honesty. Val cheated on me for a while before she had the balls to ask for the divorce. She didn't have the courage to walk out until she had someone else waiting. I can't respect her now, let alone take her back." He shook his head.

"She could beg. Emmy could beg." Steffi sighed. "It's *possible,* that's all I'm saying."

As he approached her, she got fidgety. "So then, why ask me out at all?"

"Because it's been torture to sit on these feelings. To wonder. At least now I know where I stand." She flashed a wan smile, then attempted a joke. "So now that you've dashed my romantic hopes, can you *at least* reconsider buying this house?"

"I can't make any promises about this house, although I'd love to say yes." Then he tossed all logic aside and came so close they were almost nose to nose. "But if the offer for dinner stands, maybe we can give that a try."

Chapter Fifteen

Steffi sat in the passenger seat of Ryan's Jeep, resisting the urge to tug at her shirt or fix her hair. She'd paired black jeans with an off-the-shoulder pale-green shirt with bell sleeves. Claire had convinced her to borrow a gold necklace and earrings, too. Honestly, Ryan had seen her turning purple in the ice-cold ocean not long ago, so it probably didn't matter what she wore tonight.

"Are you serious?" Ryan asked, a half grin spreading across his face.

He'd dressed well tonight, too. Dark denim jeans, a collared shirt, and an unstructured beige jacket. Once again, he'd worn cologne. She'd find him sexy in sweats and a T-shirt, but appreciated the effort.

"Dead serious. Wait here." She opened the passenger door and walked into Campiti's to pick up the pizza and Cherikee Red sodas she'd called in.

Another woman might try to avoid anything that would bring up the past when it wasn't exactly a point in her favor. Steffi had considered and then rejected the avoidance route. Their past—the good and the bad—was inescapably the foundation upon which anything new must be built.

Foundational cracks couldn't be ignored or whitewashed in *any* kind of renovation. They required reconstruction to ensure stability. Taking that cue, Steffi planned for their official reunion date to honor what they once were, discover how well they still understood each other, and acknowledge they were also two people who'd become strangers in many ways.

As soon as she stepped inside the pizza joint, the salty, greasy aroma of the restaurant stoked her hunger and erased her nerves. Two pizzas might've been overkill, but Ryan could eat an entire large pepperoni-and-mushroom pie by himself. Or he used to be able to, anyway.

When she returned to the car, she said, "Now let's go to the high school."

"The high school?" He turned on the ignition and checked the rearview mirror before pulling away from the curb. "Bold move, taking this trip down memory lane."

She knew he'd catch on quickly. "We might as well embrace what was. It's part of us and who we were but doesn't define who we are now or what we could become."

His crooked smile always stopped her heart. "Sounds like a plan."

Wherever the night might lead, this moment filled her with giddy happiness. Few experiences in life matched romantic beginnings—that buzz that wound its way through the body and pooled in the stomach and just below. If she could figure out how to slow the clock, she would marinate in the beginning of everything so it would sink in and season all the days to come.

A few minutes later, they pulled into the parking lot of their alma mater. The two-story redbrick building hadn't changed much this past decade, at least not on the outside. It brought back memories of the white-and-blue-tile floors and rows of bright-yellow lockers where she'd met Ryan before lunch each day. The simple pleasures, like cheering him on at his games, and he at hers.

But they were grown-ups now with real problems and responsibilities. They lacked the freedom and novelty of adolescence to sustain and thrill them.

Her hands were full with the pizzas and sodas. "Can you grab the bag from the back seat?"

"Of course." Ryan reached behind her to get the tote that had a blanket and some paper products.

Together they wandered to the stadium, which was situated not far from a winding inlet river that led to the town harbor. The picturesque setting suited them—their history, their love of sports, and the energy of youthful hope it evoked.

"Bleachers or sidelines?" she asked.

Ryan's gaze strayed to the small group of boys kicking the ball around at one end of the field. The lights had flickered to life as the sun hit the horizon and the final hints of sunshine faded from the sky. "Bleachers."

They climbed a few rows; the tinny clomp of their footsteps on metal pierced the brisk fall air.

She created a table of sorts by setting the pizza one row above the one where they sat.

"It's been a long while since I've come here." Ryan's eyes went back to the boys on the field. "How many hours did we spend that way?"

"Too many to count, and too long ago to want to consider." She opened the pizza boxes and popped the tab on her soda. "I'm still trying to process the fact that I'm thirty."

His eyes crinkled at the corners when he smiled. "It's not so bad. Besides, you look young."

"Thanks." She held her soda can as if making a toast. "To old times and new beginnings."

He tapped his can against hers. "Do you ever attend any football or soccer games?"

"No. I don't know any of the kids who play now. I'd look like some old, creepy woman coming here alone, wouldn't I?"

"Not creepy. Maybe pathetic," he said. "Kidding. I should check out the schedule and bring Emmy to a football game. She'd like the drums and tubas."

Steffi pictured Emmy decked out in blue and white—the school colors—shaking a pom-pom or cowbell, demanding popcorn, and cheering for the Blue Devils. "That does sound like fun."

"You could come, too. That way you won't look pathetic." He chomped on a slice of pizza.

Even as she batted his knee, heat spread through her chest. The Snoopy dance wouldn't be out of place after being asked on another date before this one even got started.

They ate a slice in comfortable silence, watching the boys practice footwork and tricks while some girls gathered at the edge of the field to flirt. Those girls all looked the same—long straight hair, ripped jeans, hoodies. Their laughter fanned into the night sky, raining joyful energy over the stadium, bringing back memories of the Lilac Lane League and Benny, Logan, and Ryan.

Ryan kept his gaze on the kids. "It's funny to think about how life changes—perspective, too. I had some big dreams back then. I'm not where I thought I'd be at this age."

She turned away from the kids and stared at him, head tipped. He'd accomplished a lot since high school, so she didn't know why he sounded disappointed. "Where did you think you'd be?"

"Well, I'm not giving David Beckham any competition, am I?" He chuckled. "But seriously, I'd dreamed of a pro career, or at least a coaching gig."

"I didn't know that." A nonsensical part of her felt slighted that he'd had a dream she hadn't known. "So why'd you go to law school?"

Ryan raised his brows, as if the answer was obvious. "Val got pregnant."

She shrugged. "Beckham has kids, Ryan. Why couldn't you do both?"

His incredulous expression suggested he

couldn't believe he had to explain himself to her, of all people. "We were blindsided. Who knew antibiotics could affect the pill's effectiveness? When she came to me in tears, the sudden responsibility hit me. One minute I'm a carefree college kid and player, the next I'm stepping up to be a husband and father. Pipe dreams don't buy formula and diapers. I needed to provide a good home for Val and our child. I needed a secure career, and the law appealed to my sense of right and wrong."

In Steffi's mind, she'd always envisioned Val gleefully telling Ryan the news. Somehow, she'd needed Val to be a seductress and conniver, trapping Ryan into a life he never wanted. It never crossed her mind that Val had been frightened by her situation. Truthfully, she'd been too busy feeling sorry for herself to stop to consider what Val and Ryan had sacrificed in order to give their child a chance at the white picket fence–style American dream.

"You must have really loved her . . ." Steffi grimaced at the envy in her tone.

Ryan set his crust aside. Another thing she remembered—he never ate the crusts. "I don't know."

"I do. You wouldn't have married her, and she wouldn't have wanted to keep the baby, if you weren't in love."

He shook his head, yet a melancholy smile

played on his lips. "It's not that simple. We were young and clueless. We wanted to do the 'right' thing. We had a lot of heat in our relationship, but love? Real *love?*" He wrinkled his nose in doubt. "I can't say I loved her the way a man should love his wife. Not with my whole heart and soul."

"Maybe you're just jaded now because it didn't turn out well."

"No. It was doomed from the start." He plucked a pepperoni from his slice and popped it in his mouth. "When you suffer a serious heartbreak, it's tough to really love anyone else with abandon again. A mended heart is fragile, so I think I held back a bit because I was a little afraid of what might happen if it broke again. I never gave my wife my entire heart, and that's at least part of why we failed."

He frowned now, seeming lost in his confession.

"I'm sorry." Steffi stared at her pizza, having lost her appetite. She'd cost Ryan so much. No simple dinner date would get them over the trust hurdle. "I'm truly sorry that what I did closed off a part of your heart, and that the ripple effect caused so much pain to so many. I never meant for that to happen."

Ryan shrugged. "I got Emmy, and I wouldn't trade her for any of it. Not even for you, Steffi. So don't feel sorry for me."

"I wouldn't trade her for me, either," Steffi teased, grateful for a way out of the bottomless pit of that topic. "She's a great kid. I'm glad to hear that she's been getting friendlier with Lisa."

"Me too." He chewed another bite of pizza in silence, then asked, "What about you? Did anyone in college or afterward change how you think about love?"

"No. I dated around in college, but nothing serious. I focused on sports and school."

He widened his legs and rested his elbows on his knees. "I can't believe you didn't have a single significant boyfriend in the past ten years."

"I told you, I broke up with you because I didn't want to be tied down." She blotted some grease from her lips. "I wanted to make my own way in college."

He stared at the space between his feet. "What about after that?"

One never knows how far they're willing to humiliate themselves until a test comes along. Given what he'd admitted here tonight, she decided to expose herself and hope for the best. "Honestly, when I heard about you and Val getting married, it threw me into a funk. Before that, I had this crazy idea that we could still end up together—assuming I was willing to beg. Then Peyton called me after she heard about the pregnancy from Logan. On your wedding day, I drank myself into oblivion with my teammates and had an ugly cry. I knew I deserved every bit of that bitter pill, but it sucked." Steffi stretched her legs out, hoping it might help her relax a bit. "After college, I worked with some real alpha-holes in construction. It wasn't easy to meet the kind of guy I could see myself with. I kept searching for someone who had it all—someone like you. I dated, but I never fell in love again. Seems like love was another first and best with you." She fanned herself despite the early-October chill.

Ryan reached for her hand and tugged her closer, then raised one hand to her cheek. His gaze dipped to her lips, and he leaned forward, brushing her lips with a gentle kiss. Brief and sweet, leaving her wanting so much more.

He rested his forehead against hers, their noses touching. "Thanks for telling me all that. I know you don't like to talk about your feelings."

"No, I don't," she laughed. "But I'm older now. I'm getting better . . . or at least I'm willing to try."

Ryan eased away but kept hold of her hand, allowing his chest to fill with the hope that this would blossom into something beautiful. Something more real than the fairy-tale love story he'd imagined it to be way back when. "You've changed. I mean, you're the same in a lot of ways, but you're more open."

It was one step, but could she commit? That, in essence, had been her fatal flaw. The thing that had ruined them. He couldn't give in to his feelings until he felt more certain of hers. That kiss had been a reflex and had whetted his appetite for more. But whatever happened between them wasn't just about them. Any relationship he had, whether with Steffi or someone else, would affect Emmy. He should be sure before he took a major step, or stole more kisses.

"Tell me one thing that's changed about you." She turned and straddled her legs on either side of the bleacher now, her curious expression staring him in the face.

"For the better or for the worse?"

She made a soft clucking sound. "You were sort of perfect before, so it must be for the worse."

"Fooled you, apparently." He crossed his arms, thinking he'd changed in so many ways he didn't know where to begin. "I'm more cynical now."

"Aren't we all?"

"My job keeps me mired in the shit parts of humanity. Between the criminals and the dirty cops, it's hard to be optimistic about people's intentions."

"Sounds depressing. Why not switch to corporate law?"

"It might sound weird, but this job feels like a calling. Once in a while, a case comes along where I'm the only thing standing between some poor sucker and a really bum deal. Most of my clients have never had a lucky break. At least half are decent folks who made a single bad mistake, like a bar fight. In court, I see private defense attorneys getting rich people off for the same and worse crimes. Seems to me the average Joe deserves a lawyer who cares."

Her eyes twinkled beneath the stadium lights. The chilly air painted her cheeks, and the tip of her nose, a rosy shade of red. Like her lips. The ones he wanted to kiss again.

"They're lucky to have you on their side, but I still don't know how you can defend someone you know is guilty."

"Guilt's not always so easy to define. For example, right now I've got a guy who's accused of rape." In his head, he saw Owen O'Malley's face. The perpetual confusion and frustrated anger that shone through his eyes. Ryan could hear the man's slow speech responding to questions. "I know he had sex with his accuser—DNA evidence is clear, and he doesn't deny it. The problem is, his IQ is seventy, and she's a known prostitute he didn't pay. I'm convinced he didn't understand the transaction, and she's accusing him of rape as some kind of payback." When he looked up at Steffi, her rosy cheeks now matched the color of the moon above. Beads of perspiration dotted her forehead, adding sheen to her haunted expression. Her pupils had dilated and were fixed on some distant spot.

Ryan glanced over his shoulder to see what was

happening on the field or in the parking lot, but nothing caught his attention. He turned back and gently touched her knee. "Steffi."

Her body trembled as she let out a sort of stifled whimper. He watched as she blinked, her focus sharpening on him, yet her eyes remained filled with confusion.

"Are you okay?" he asked.

"Yes." She rubbed her temple. "Sorry. Zone-out."

"I saw." Wherever she went during those lapses, she came out of them agitated. "Can you remember anything?"

"No." She shook her head briskly while playing with the generous cuffs of her sleeves. Everything about her body language signaled a desire to end the inquiry, like she was keeping something from him.

Maybe he didn't have the right to all her secrets yet, but given their past, he wanted them. He wanted to know she would confide in him. Beyond that, her insentient behavior could hurt her and others, like Emmy. "Do you remember what we were talking about?"

"Your job." She rubbed her head again. Maybe she had a headache and now wasn't the time to press her.

"I wish you'd go to the doctor."

"I went early this week. My scans show mild concussion damage, but no other physical symptoms."

"I did a little reading about brain trauma causing epilepsy. There are things called absence seizures, although those are usually prevalent in children and go away with maturity. Did he mention epilepsy?"

"He sort of dismissed it because there wasn't real evidence." She patted her head and flashed a forced grin. "The good news is I'm tumor-free!"

A healthy level of paranoia earned from years with the PD office meant he could be misreading her overly bright attitude as some kind of cover. Yet something in her manner seemed off. "Maybe you should do a follow-up to rule out other things."

"Overextended business owner here." She raised her index finger, along with the level of sarcasm. "No free time or spare change for second opinions or shrinks."

Psychologists? Had the doctor suggested that? A mental disorder? A reaction to trauma? Something else?

"Minutes ago you were bragging about how much you've changed, but if you don't get answers, that's your passive-aggressive way of avoiding things."

Every trace of humor vanished from her expression. "Watch yourself there, Ryan, or you might sound self-righteous and condescending."

"Sorry." Was she right? Did he impose his judgment on everyone around him? Or did he just want people to take good care of themselves and others? "Tell me this, did these episodes happen before the mugging incident?"

She shrugged. "No."

"So it *is* related to what happened in Hartford."

"Yes. I told you that concussion was serious."

"I'd love to look at the police file. Maybe I'd notice something they missed, or someone in my office might pick up on a clue."

"Don't bother. Besides, I tossed that file along with lots of other pointless stuff when I moved. I got attacked and robbed. It sucked. Life goes on. Don't make me a *victim*." Her voice had sharpened with each word, and her spine grew increasingly erect. "I'm not powerless or broken. It's only been a few months. This brain fog could clear up on its own."

"Okay. Okay." Ryan held his hands up. "No one would ever call you powerless, by the way."

"Good." She grinned and blew out a short breath. "Now, if you're finished interrogating me, let's clean this up and go someplace a little warmer."

Before he could respond, she leaned forward, took his face in her capable hands, and kissed him. Not an all-out passionate kiss, but the nip at his lip drove all thoughts from his head except one—desire. "Whatever you want."

Chapter Sixteen

Steffi's heart beat as if she were sprinting the stadium stairs when she and Ryan climbed her porch steps. "Claire's at her aunt's birthday dinner tonight, so she's not home. But I doubt she'll be out past ten."

"Are you trying to send me home early?" Ryan asked playfully.

"No. I just . . . I don't know. I'm being weird." The last thing she wanted was to cut their night short. She'd prefer to drag him inside and lock the door so he could never escape, frankly. Not that she could say that, or admit that her insides were shaking like an earthquake. That would make him laugh. She unlocked the door and stepped inside, telling herself to relax. Did that work for anyone? It never worked for her. "Let me find a bottle of wine. Maybe you can find something decent on TV or pick a music channel."

Ryan removed his jacket and laid it over a chair, then picked up the remote from the coffee table. "I'll do my best."

Steffi went to the kitchen and, once alone, slapped her cheeks a few times. Discomfort from the recent zone-out clung to her longer than others, but she couldn't say why. That kiss keyed her up, too. Made her almost uneasy, which didn't make much sense. She really liked Ryan. She'd loved him for years, and then loved her memory of him. She couldn't afford to let anything blow this second chance.

"Get yourself under control," she muttered to herself.

"What?" Ryan called from the other room before she heard lounge music emanate from the speakers. Mm . . . kinda sexy.

"Nothing!" Her heart would not cooperate and settle into a normal rhythm. She glanced heavenward and took two wineglasses from a cabinet. "Just talking to myself about the wine."

Steffi pinched her own arm and took another deep breath before shaking out her hands and searching for wine.

They were out of red, but she found a rosé in the refrigerator. A girl's drink. Good God, she had not planned this part well. Who knew they'd get this far on the first date? A trickle of sweat rolled between her breasts.

She nestled the bottle under her armpit and carried the glasses to the living room, where she found Ryan looking at some of the candid photos Claire had framed and scattered across the mantel.

He looked up when she came into the room. If he didn't like rosé, he hid it. "Let me. Do you have a corkscrew?"

"Screw top," she confessed. Fortunately, he'd

never been a wine snob—or any kind of snob—before. He was just good old Ryan. A guy she could trust.

He poured them each a glass and took a sip. "Shall we sit?"

"Yes."

He waited until she plopped onto the sofa, then sat beside her. Close but not touching. He rubbed his hands on his thighs more than once. His palms had to be clammy, too.

His gaze meandered around the small room—one that seemed to be closing in on her—taking in the turquoise abstract watercolor on the wall behind them. It complemented the cream-and-gray throw rug and the glass-top table with the tree-trunk base. "Did Claire decorate?"

He took up so much space on the sofa. The temperature seemed impossibly warm.

"You know *I* couldn't pull all this together. Remember my old room?" Steffi chuckled when Ryan involuntarily grimaced.

The decor of her high school bedroom could only be described as "sporty spirit." She'd strung soccer tournament medals, old cleats, and uniform jerseys to showcase her achievements. Photographs of Claire, Peyton, and Ryan were pinned to her bulletin board. A royal-blue comforter, the identical color of her soccer uniform, covered her bed. She'd installed a double set of metal school lockers for storage.

The only feminine touch in the entire room had been a crystal framed photograph of her mother and her, taken shortly before her mom's diagnosis, when she still looked healthy and happy and full of hope for the future. That photograph was Steffi's sole material treasure and currently sat on her nightstand upstairs alongside another photograph of her entire family.

"We snuck up there enough times for it to be etched in my memory." Ryan seemed even closer and larger as he sipped more wine. He deadpanned, "Fortunately, I usually had other things on my mind, so I was able to ignore the way it looked."

Her breath felt uneven. "I liked the no-frills appeal."

"Clearly, your brothers have had way too much influence on your taste." Then he fell silent, his brows furrowed as if he realized too late that maybe he'd tread upon a sad memory or truth or both.

"Well, we all did the best we could." She suspected part of her had shunned feminine things once she lost her mom, perhaps to prove to herself that she'd be okay on her own. Doing so taught her she'd survive just fine as long as she always kept moving forward. You couldn't gain momentum if you kept looking back or wallowing in "woe is me" thinking.

"At least you had three brothers to help you

when you missed your mom. Emmy's got no one."
He frowned while staring into his glass. Steffi
sensed more to his sorrow than the momentary
empathy he felt for his daughter. "That's a big
regret. I should've pushed for another kid sooner
. . . after . . ." His gaze never strayed from that
glass, and then he tossed back the rest of it in one
long swallow.

"After what?" Steffi prodded.

Ryan glanced at her, his shoulders drooping.
"We lost our son . . . a late-term miscarriage.
It was hard on us, especially Val. She wasn't
ready to try again, so I gave her space. Then
our relationship steadily faltered. Maybe it's a
blessing that we didn't have more kids, seeing
that we're divorcing. But for Emmy's sake, I
wish we did."

She'd had no idea he'd lost a child. Having never
been pregnant, she couldn't begin to imagine that
kind of grief. In the face of it, she didn't know
what to say, which was why she said something
lame. "You're young. You still have time for more
kids . . . or you could adopt someone closer in age
to Emmy."

"I need to sort out my life before I add more
kids to the mix." He set his empty glass down and
edged closer. "What about you? Is your biological
clock ticking, or did you toss it out the window
with that ugly old comforter?"

"It wasn't ugly." She shoved his knee, grinning

while trying to ignore two undeniable truths. A, that comforter *was* butt ugly, and B, motherhood wasn't something she'd given much thought to in her life. "Spending time with Emmy has been a fun peek into motherhood. But I wonder if I'd be any good at it."

"From what I can tell, you'll be a natural." He clasped her hand. The warmth and invitation of his touch simultaneously grounded her and launched her heart into the air like a glitter bomb.

"Thanks." She glanced at their hands, resisting the urge to squeeze or stroke or make any kind of movement that could cause him to let go, even as her skin grew damp. "Maybe *I* should consider adoption."

He tipped his head sideways, and his mouth curved into a seductive smile.

"Or maybe you could become a mom the old-fashioned way." He stared into her eyes as if he were searching her soul for all her secrets and fears and dreams and regrets. She felt her breathing hitch before she heard it. Then he said, "Under all the circumstances, we ought to take things slow. But I have to be honest, all I can think about right now is how much I want to kiss you again."

She nodded in agreement because she couldn't speak. Her gaze dropped to his mouth once more. He moved slowly, as if not to spook her, and cupped her neck before pulling her into a slow, deep kiss.

Tender but firm, his mouth slowly caressed hers . . . the familiar slide of tongues, yet somehow new and amazing and dizzying. He tasted like wine and pepperoni—the scent of his cologne lingered on his skin. Her body thrummed with anticipation, warming everything as she reached for this new chance to hold a piece of his heart. This time she'd be more careful with it . . . and him.

She laid her hands on his chest, her fingers grabbing his collar before sliding up and threading their way through his thick head of hair. Breathless with happiness, she held him close as he moved his mouth along her jaw to the tender spot behind her ear, yet deep inside, uneasiness threatened.

She tried to ignore it—nerves, doubts, whatever *it* was—determined to recapture some romance with the man she'd thought she'd lost forever.

"Ryan," she murmured.

As soon as she uttered his name, he moaned, and his tenderness transformed into something hot and urgent. He tumbled her onto her back, the full weight of him pressing against her, and dragged his mouth up her neck. He moved his hands quickly, assuredly, tugging at her shirt— and she froze.

She couldn't catch a breath. Spots danced before her eyes.

Gun.

Darkness. Filth.
Smoke, sweat, grunting.
Pain.
Live.
Breathe.
Live!

She became conscious that she was batting at and kicking Ryan while yelling, "No!"

He jerked back, hands in the air like a criminal, eyes filled with confusion and pain. "Sorry! I'm sorry."

Her chest heaved as she fought for air, and fought to piece together what had happened. Her memory failed her, as usual. No distinct thought to cling to. Only nausea and a vague sense of menace lingered, pushing in against her chest.

They'd been kissing. His hair had felt like tufts of silky thread in her fingers. She'd been happy . . . and then she'd disappeared.

Ryan sat on the far edge of the sofa, rubbing his hands on his thighs again, this time with some agitation. He kept his gaze on the ground, brows pinched.

"Did I hurt you?" The tears she wouldn't shed clogged her throat, making it sore.

"No."

He glanced at her, his features contorted as he seemed to be trying to understand her inexplicable behavior. "I thought, I thought you were with me . . . thought you wanted—"

"I did. I do . . ." She reached for his hand, but he stiffened.

"Then explain what happened, because I'm lost. You're giving me some pretty mixed signals, Steffi." His voice sounded distant and doubting, like he'd awakened from his own lusty haze and remembered the past. Remembered that he could not trust her.

"I can't explain it. I was with you . . . and then the next thing I know, I wasn't." Tears stung her eyes. This was the second time she'd hit him in mere weeks. Her confusion matched his, because she couldn't think of a single reason why she'd sabotaged this perfect moment between them.

"You know I'd never hurt you. I'd never take advantage of you." He stood and paced in a tight circle.

"I know." She sniffled and pushed her hair behind her ears.

"Then why did you push me away again?" He raised his hands from his sides with a frustrated shrug. "Seems you're not certain of me, or us."

"I *am* certain." She hugged a throw pillow to her stomach, hoping to quell the nausea. "Ever since you returned to town, I've been hoping for this chance with you."

"I want to believe that." He stood still, arms crossed. "But I can't help my doubts, given our past, and your behavior . . ."

She reached for him. "Please sit."

He took her hand and squeezed it, but remained standing. "It's pretty obvious I crossed a line . . . or something else is off. Either way, the best thing I can do for both our sakes is to give you some space tonight. We'll talk tomorrow."

"Ryan, wait . . . don't go. Not like this." She followed him to where he'd laid his jacket. "I want you to stay. I'm sorry. I'm so sorry. Please believe me. We can just watch TV and keep talking, but don't go."

He kissed her forehead. *Her forehead.* "I loved tonight, and really appreciate everything we got out in the open. If it was just about the two of us, maybe I'd be less cautious, but there's Emmy. Everything that affects me also affects her one way or another. If this is anything less than 'right,' then I need to be more cautious. It's been ten years. We don't need to rush anything now, do we?" He swiped the tear that rolled down her cheek with his thumb. "Don't cry. Let's just hit pause on this date and talk tomorrow, okay?"

Ten minutes later, Ryan sat in his car and stared at his parents' house. He squeezed the steering wheel to keep his hands from trembling at the horrible theory that had begun to take root on his drive home. Had her attack last spring been more than a mugging? Had it involved sexual assault? It would explain her jumpy behavior by the lake that night when he'd come at her from behind, and tonight, when she freaked out as soon as he became sexually assertive.

Was she afraid to tell him? Had she told anyone, or was she ashamed, like some rape victims who somehow blamed themselves? Victims who'd felt broken by the brutal violation—scarred inside and out. But Steffi wasn't broken. She was vibrant. She'd started a business. She was physically fit and vital, with ongoing social relationships with friends and family. He hoped he was wrong . . . but his instincts were sharp, thanks to his experience with criminals and their victims.

Could her brain have blocked the memory? Was that why she couldn't remember anything during the brief dissociative states?

He'd heard about this kind of thing from his colleagues—about rape victims whose minds protected them from traumatic memories. Defense lawyers loved it because spotty memories made victim testimony less credible. But the thought that Steffi might've been raped by two strangers in an alley made him gag. Somewhere out there, those two fuckers had gotten away with it and had gone on—possibly harming others— while she'd been suffering, most likely on her own.

In a roundabout way, he might be responsible for what happened—if not to Steffi, precisely, then to other women who'd been victimized by repeat offenders he'd helped put back on the street. It was always a risk, one he knew well. But until tonight, he'd been able to detach and justify his choices by wrapping himself in the protection of the constitutional rights of every citizen.

He released the steering wheel and dabbed at his eyes, praying he was wrong about all of it. That he was grasping at straws to avoid something else he'd rather not consider—the idea that he'd fallen for her again when she wasn't sure she wanted him.

After a quick glance at himself in the rearview mirror, he scrubbed his face with his hands to rub away his discomfort. He opened the car door and jogged beneath the canopy of leaves to go inside. When he entered the house, the aroma of buttered popcorn told him his parents had watched a movie with Emmy.

"You're home early." His mom looked up from her knitting as Ryan tossed his keys on the entry table.

Ryan nodded at her and his dad, whose gaze barely strayed from the *Blue Bloods* episode playing at least ten decibels too loud. He needed to move out of this house before *he* went deaf.

"She's got to be up early for work," Ryan fibbed. He composed his expression, hoping to evade his mother's hawkish instincts. "Emmy asleep?"

"She went up about half an hour ago." His mom pretended to return her attention to her project even as she asked, "Did you have a nice time?"

"Sure." He started toward the stairs. "See you in the morning."

"Ryan . . . is that all you have to say?" His mom gaped at him.

"Molly, he's a grown man, for chrissakes. Leave him be." His dad patted her leg and waved Ryan away.

Ryan took advantage of the moment his mother glared at her husband to finish his climb up the stairs. No light emanated from beneath Emmy's door. He slowly turned the handle, careful not to let it click, and then eased the door open to peek in on her.

"Hi, Daddy," came a loud whisper from her bed. He should've known her elephant ears would hear him creaking up the stairwell.

He crossed the room and leaned down to kiss her head. She wrapped his neck in a tight squeeze. He didn't let go for a long time, taking more comfort than he was giving tonight. "Did you have fun with Memaw and Pops?"

"We watched *Frozen*."

"Nice." He wasn't sorry to miss a seventh viewing of that one. "It's late. Get some sleep."

She propped herself up on her elbows. "What did you do, Dad?"

"I ate pizza." He hadn't told Emmy about his date because he didn't want her to get too invested before he even had the chance to see what might develop. As far as she knew, he'd simply gone out with a friend tonight. Not exactly a lie.

"That's all you did?"

He was grateful the dark room hid him wincing at the memory of Steffi's panicked response to his touch. "Pretty much."

"That sounds boring." She slumped back against her pillow. "You should've stayed home and watched the movie. We made popcorn."

"Next time." He kissed her again, grateful she was years away from the age when he'd have to really worry about her becoming the victim of some kind of sexual assault. "See you in the morning."

He closed the door and went to the bathroom. His innocent gums got a harsh scrubbing as more unpleasant thoughts wormed through his mind.

If Steffi had been sexually assaulted, she didn't owe him the truth about something so deeply personal. But a little part of him—the part that she'd hurt when she'd shut him out before—smarted. Another part knew that the failure of both of his love relationships grew from a lack of true intimacy. He couldn't accept less than that this time around, which made it a tricky situation.

Steffi stonewalled him anytime he brought up the incident. How could they rebuild anything worthwhile on half truths and a lack of trust? How did she expect to work through her painful memories—the ones that commandeered her mind and body from time to time—if she never told anyone what had happened? Never talked about it? And if she didn't remember, then she needed therapy . . . no excuses.

His work had shown him that those who attended counseling had the best shot at recovery. But Lockwoods didn't talk about their feelings, especially not with shrinks. Convincing her to seek help would be harder than getting Val to drop her alimony demand.

At this point, he knew only one thing with certainty: he couldn't help Steffi if he didn't have the facts. He didn't know what lines he might cross to get at the truth, but he suspected he would be willing to do things he'd never before approved.

He'd disdained the justifications people used to do whatever they wanted. Until now. His thoughts veered toward Billy's hacking skills— the ones Ryan warned him not to use for official investigations. Pulling that string would be a gross invasion of Steffi's privacy and also put both Billy and him at professional risk.

He sat at the edge of the bed, staring at his phone. One call to Billy and he'd have an answer by Monday. He stared some more before reaching for it. How could he invade her privacy when trust was such an important issue to him? Then again, if he was right and therapy could help her, didn't he owe it to her to find out before she hurt herself or anyone else?

He hesitated, then made a different call.

"Ryan?" Steffi's muffled voice sounded wary or tired, or possibly both.

"Did I wake you?"

"No. I just didn't expect to hear from you tonight."

Ryan scooted up against the headboard and stretched his legs out on his mattress. He closed his eyes and pictured her face. "I wanted to check on you, and to say good night." He paused, hoping the thousand questions swirling through his thoughts would quiet. "Despite how things ended, I had a good time tonight. Getting stuff in the open was a welcome step forward for me and, I hope, for you . . ."

"It wasn't as hard as I expected."

He frowned. "Was I always hard to talk to?"

"Well, you've got some black-and-white opinions about the 'right' way to view things."

"Do I?" If she believed that, she'd never be comfortable sharing anything important or controversial with him. "I'll work on that. But you trust me, right? You know if you told me something in confidence, I wouldn't judge you."

"Thanks, Ryan."

His feeble attempt to coax her confidence did nothing, so he resorted to small talk. "What time will you be banging on the walls here tomorrow?"

"No more banging. I'll be applying drywall mud and tape. I'm sure Emmy will want to help me mix the mud."

"I'll keep her out of your hair."

"I don't mind her company. She's respectful when I ask her to let me focus."

"I'm not sure how I feel about my daughter becoming more handy than I am," he joked, faking some humor while he tried to shake off his negativity.

"Welcome to the twenty-first century," she teased. They both fell silent, then she sighed. "Ryan, I have a question."

"Yeah?" Maybe this would be the opening he needed.

"Did I totally blow everything tonight?"

The ache in her voice matched the one in his chest. "No. You didn't blow anything."

Did she think he'd blame her for something she couldn't control? Never. Especially not now that he thought he could be onto the cause of her blackouts.

"Good." Relief brightened her voice. "Actually, I'd hoped if tonight had gone well that we might take Emmy to Oktoberfest on Sunday. We could do it as a friend thing. I mean, I understand why you need to protect her until we see where things lead . . ."

"It's not personal. She can't take more loss, that's all." He wanted to accept the invitation, but Steffi's unpredictable behavior gave him pause. Until she got that sorted out, perhaps he should limit the time she spent with his daughter outside this house. "Let me think about it. I have no idea if she'd be up for that; plus, I need to do a little work. But if we can't make it, let's you and I grab dinner one night this week."

"Okay." Her dejected tone caused him to close his eyes with regret. "See you tomorrow."

"Sweet dreams, Steffi." He hit "Off" and set the phone on the nightstand, and then folded his hands over his stomach. Drawing a deep breath, he stared at the ceiling as if the answers to all his questions were hidden beneath the paint.

Chapter Seventeen

"Steffi? You up?" Claire tapped on the bedroom door.

Steffi struggled to open her eyes, blinking against the bright sunlight coming through her window. "Come in."

Claire cracked open the door and poked her face inside. "Are you sick?"

"No, why?" Steffi yawned and rolled onto her back while she stretched. She'd spent most of the night awake because the hurt look on Ryan's face when she'd struck him had replayed every time she'd shut her eyes. The last time she'd looked at the clock, it'd been 5:20 a.m.

"I thought you were going to Molly's this morning." Claire stepped inside with her coffee. She'd already showered and dressed for the day. The bold pink-and-gold pattern on her skirt threatened to give Steffi a migraine.

"I am." She yawned and arched her back into a stretch.

Claire lowered her cup. "It's already ten thirty."

"What?" Steffi bolted upright and grabbed for her alarm clock. "Crap! I must've hit the alarm and rolled right back to sleep."

She slammed the clock back on the nightstand and threw off the blankets. She rummaged her drawers to find clean underwear and a long-sleeve shirt.

Claire didn't budge from the doorway. "Hang on, I want details! You were in bed when I got home. I half wondered if Ryan was in here with you. How'd it go?"

Steffi rolled her eyes and shook her head as she replied, "I'll fill you in later on how I sent him running, but right now I have to get to Molly's."

"I'm sorry." Claire's face pinched like she'd swallowed lemon juice. "I hope it wasn't as bad as you think."

"Maybe it can be salvaged, but I'm not sure." Steffi tugged the blanket up over the mattress in a half-assed attempt to make her bed, then wondered why the hell she bothered. "I need a cold shower to wake up. Save me some coffee?"

"Sure. I'll fix you a to-go cup. I'm on my way out to meet with Helena Briggs to look at kitchen counters for the Hightop Road house."

"Great. I have two guys starting on demolition over there today. I need to check on them this afternoon, too." She waved Claire off and dashed into the bathroom to engage in a record-breaking three-minute-long shower-and-go routine.

Fifteen minutes later, her stomach flipped as she crossed the Quinns' backyard. She mumbled to herself, "Be brave and friendly, despite the pity dinner date he offered." She couldn't blame him for that. What man would put up with being hit while kissing? Especially after the way she'd abused his trust in the past.

She entered the back of the house through the new French doors and went straight to the supply pile she'd left in the corner yesterday afternoon. Like a dog's, her ears remained alert for any sign of Ryan.

After dragging the box of drywall mud over to the five-gallon paint pail, she then laid out the tape dispenser, joint and mud knives, mud pan, and electric mud mixer. Once she'd organized herself, she took the other empty paint pail outside to fill it from the hose.

When she came back indoors, she found Emmy hunched over the row of supplies. Often Ryan would wander in to retrieve her, but Steffi didn't hear him in the kitchen.

"What's *that?*" Emmy pointed at the mixer.

"It's a mixer." Steffi lugged the heavy bucket of water to the center of the room. "I'm mixing drywall mud today."

"Mud?" Emmy wrinkled her nose in distaste. Today she sported pink sweatpants and a white T-shirt. Her so-called work clothes led Steffi to believe Emmy'd been waiting for her arrival. "Why do you need mud?"

Steffi transferred the mud to the empty paint pail, her body twitching at any sound, thinking each to be Ryan's footsteps. "See all the places where the sections of drywall connect? I have to

335

fill in all those cracks so it looks smooth when we paint. Those cracks get filled in with special mud and tape."

"Can I help?" This had become Emmy's daily refrain.

Most days Steffi didn't mind, but this part of the job could be tricky. She was having enough difficulty concentrating as it was, let alone having to deal with Emmy. But she was tough. She could handle this.

"A little, but this has to be done just right or the tape can bubble, so I have to do most of it. You're welcome to watch and learn, though."

Emmy's shoulders slumped, but she raised the mixer, which came up to her chest and probably weighed about a third of her body weight. "Can I mix?"

"I need to handle that, but you can help me with the sponge and water." Steffi grasped the mixer before Emmy let it drop, in her zeal to choose among the large yellow sponges. After a surreptitious glance through the opening to the living room—a fruitless one because Ryan didn't appear—she said, "Soak that sponge in the bucket of water, and then squeeze it out over the top of this mud bucket. I'll start mixing. We want the mud to be on the soupy side."

"Soupy?" Emmy grimaced again. She buried the sponge until the water was up to her elbows, and then brought it over to the mud bucket—

dripping water all over the flagstone floor—and squeezed.

Steffi fired up the mixer and let Emmy watch her stir the mud. "A little more water. Just a little, okay?"

Emmy complied. "Can I touch it?"

"Sure, but just with the tips of your fingers. It's messy, and you don't want to get it everywhere."

While Steffi heaped a scoop of the mud into the pan with the knife, Emmy tested the mud in the bucket. She got it all over one palm and then clapped her hands together to test its stickiness. Once both hands were dirty, she plunged them into the water bucket and wiped them on her shirt, creating a mess.

When Steffi began mudding and taping, her miniature shadow came to her side. A minute passed, maybe two, before Steffi broke down and asked, "Where's your dad?"

"Out." Emmy picked up another mud knife and studied it, slashing it through the air.

"Where?" Steffi blurted out, shamelessly pumping the child for information.

Emmy shrugged, completely oblivious to Steffi's anxiety. "Can I please try to fill a crack?"

She didn't have time for teaching, but she knew that Emmy missed her mother, had almost no friends, and felt completely displaced. There was no way Steffi could turn the kid away.

"Okay, let's try one small section." She set down

her things and took Emmy to the short wall beneath the windows, where she showed her how to apply the mud and scrape it. Then they taped.

By the time they'd finished that window section, Emmy had mud on her shoes and pants legs, and a little stuck to her hair from when she kept swiping it back with her hand. "I'm good at this!"

"Yep, you're pretty good for a beginner." Steffi heard the doorbell ring in the distance. *Ryan? No. He wouldn't ring the doorbell.* "But I need to finish on my own because you aren't tall enough and we can't have a lot of tape breaks."

"Boo." Emmy sat cross-legged on the ground with her chin on her fists.

Molly appeared in the archway with Val, causing Emmy to jump up at the same time Steffi nearly tripped over the bucket of mud.

"Mommy!" Emmy flung herself at her mom, but Val held her at a distance, presumably to spare her expensive clothing from the human drywall-mud missile. "What are you doing here?"

"I wanted to surprise you, honey bear. You invited me to come for pizza, right? I thought we'd go do that and maybe go shopping." Val's gaze slid up and down Steffi, making Steffi aware that she'd been gawking at Val. Val leaned down to kiss Emmy's head. "Where's your father?"

"Ryan's running some errands for me," Molly replied. "Did he know you were coming?"

"He told me I could see Emmy whenever I

338

wanted," Val replied. "I sent a text from the road."

Molly raised her eyebrows, but Val seemed unconcerned by her mother-in-law's disapproval. Her attention was now focused on her daughter's outfit. "Emmy, sweetie, you're a mess. Go clean up so we can go out."

Steffi noticed the way Emmy looked at Val with such longing, and the way she changed her voice to speak with a babyish tone. It broke her heart to see it. How could Val not want to take that pain away? Or Ryan, for that matter?

"Okay. Can Daddy can come with us?"

"Maybe." Val smiled, and patted Emmy's head as she bounded off to change.

Steffi's stomach dropped. As much as she wanted to see Emmy happy, the scene unfolding in front of Steffi was her worst-case scenario. Val's demeanor sent a clear message—she'd come back to see Ryan and, possibly, salvage her marriage.

"Would you like some water or tea?" Molly asked, flabbergasting Steffi with her graciousness.

Molly had to harbor ill will toward the woman who cheated on her son. Then again, Molly had forgiven Steffi for the way she'd mistreated Ryan. Given her own mistakes, perhaps she shouldn't be so quick to hurl mental insults at Val, or be so stunned by Molly's poise. After all, she loved her granddaughter, so she would force herself to be pleasant to Val.

"No, thank you. I'll just wait here . . . with Steffi." Val's cool gaze examined Steffi again. "Considering how much time she's spending with my daughter lately, I'd like to get to know her."

Oh damn.

"If you'll excuse me, then, I've got other things to do," Molly said before she disappeared. Steffi prayed she'd gone to make a 911 call to Ryan.

Val strolled around the room—waltzed, really, with a feminine lilt so natural it made Steffi a little jealous. She inspected the windows and the doors before she spun around on the heels of her black boots. Up close, the woman was more of a stunner than Steffi remembered from the long-ago run-in.

That time—Christmas Eve six years earlier—Val had been bundled up in coat, scarf, and hat. All Steffi had really noticed was her short stature and those blue eyes. She'd been so busy trying to run away from Ryan's hateful gaze that she hadn't had time to really observe Val or Emmy.

Today, Val wore black leggings and a camel-and-black cashmere sweater—an ensemble that showcased her figure. In the sunlight, Steffi couldn't ignore Val's delicately boned face, full lips, and lovely blonde hair. She carried herself with assured grace, too.

Val finally spoke. "Well, you certainly chose an interesting way to make a living."

"I enjoy it." Steffi decided amiability might disarm Val. She slapped more mud on the wall and scraped it, determined to avoid the trap Val must've planned during her drive down from Boston. Steffi might not be a delicate beauty, but she was a healthy, strong, independent woman who would not be cowed by an adulteress.

"I can't believe Molly hired you, or that you accepted." Val tsk-tsked. "It was very insensitive. This had to have been very awkward for Ryan."

Correction: adulteress and hypocrite.

"It was awkward for both of us at first, but we've worked through it." Steffi smirked to herself, knowing from the flash in Val's eyes that she'd just landed a small hit. Neither she nor Val could claim the moral high ground in this cat-fight, but Steffi wouldn't sit there and take shit.

"Have you?" Val approached her under the guise of inspecting the job. "And now what? You plan to pick up where you left off, and steal my daughter in the process?"

"I'm not stealing Emmy. I'm only being kind." Steffi stared at Val. "She's a great kid."

"I know," Val sniped. "I raised her."

Steffi bit back the snide remark that raced through her thoughts. She wouldn't be goaded into doing or saying anything that might hurt Emmy or Ryan.

"I know what you're thinking, you know. You think I've abandoned her and so I must be a terrible mother. But it's not true. I was a good mother . . . and wife. I put myself and my needs *last* for ten years. Supported Ryan, cared for Emmy, ran the house, worked odd jobs to help bring in money." Val glanced out the window toward Molly's garden. "Not that it mattered to him."

"If you're looking to justify your boyfriend, I'm the wrong audience, Val."

"Well, listen to you—so full of judgment. You have no idea about my marriage or me. Anything you think you know is filtered through Ryan's perspective, which remains tainted by what *you* did to him."

That remark struck hard enough that Steffi nearly rubbed her jaw from the blow. Fortunately, life with three brothers had taught her to recover quickly. "We're all grown-ups now. Don't blame me for your problems."

"Blame? There's plenty of that to go around. All I'm saying is that I'm not a bad person." Val sighed. "Bitter. Depressed. But not evil. Not heartless."

Steffi scraped mud along a joint, hoping Val would take the hint and go wait for Emmy in the living room.

Val, however, would not be deterred. "I met John at a party, and Ryan had noticed the attention John paid me. I thought if Ryan was jealous, maybe he really cared. I hoped if I made him more jealous, he'd realize that he didn't want to lose me. A stupid plan, in hindsight. When it didn't work, it became hard to walk away from a man who actually noticed me. Who was interested in what I had to say and put me first."

"I'm not your priest, and this isn't a confessional." Steffi shook her head, wishing she hadn't heard any of that. She preferred to view Val as the bad guy, but if this kept up, she'd have to acknowledge her as merely another flawed, sometimes lonely, human, much like herself. "This has nothing to do with me."

Val crossed her arms, scoffing. "It has everything to do with you."

"How do you figure that?" Steffi asked.

"If you'd been at BC, you'd know the answer." Val's gaze went to the windows again. "I remember the first time I met Ryan at a party. So handsome and sweet. Every girl on campus was after him but, my God, was he faithful to you. For two years, other girls tried to seduce him despite the fact that he was dating you . . . but I didn't. I waited. I always sensed he cared more for you than you did him, and that it would only be a matter of time before your relationship ended." She snapped her gaze back to Steffi. "I was right, wasn't I?"

Val mesmerized Steffi like a snake charmer.

The answers to so many of her questions about that dark time dangled before her like the apple in the Garden of Eden. All she had to do was keep quiet. Not a strength of hers, unfortunately.

"I did love Ryan," Steffi said. "I was very young, though. Not near ready for a lifelong commitment."

"And so off you went without a word, never looking back." Val's accusatory tone put Steffi in her place. "If you'd seen the damage you did, maybe you would've been too ashamed to be here now, pushing your way back into his life. That fall he lost so much weight and went on a weeks-long drinking bender. He was a wreck, struggling to focus on school and soccer, but I was there for him. I listened. I baked for him and took walks with him. Let him cry on my shoulder. I gave him everything I had—*everything*.

"When we first got together, I knew he wasn't quite over you. Still, I believed that, eventually, he'd see me for who I was, not just as your stand-in. That day never came. Not even when I was pregnant. He tried, I'll give him that. But I could never quite take your place in his heart . . ."

"It wasn't a competition. Ryan loved you. He married you and started a family." Even as she said the words, she couldn't lie to herself. Ryan had so much as confessed this very truth to her on those bleachers. "I'm sorry for hurting him, and I'm sorry, for all of you, that things didn't turn out better. But you can't blame me for everything that happened once you two got together."

"I don't blame you for *all* of it," Val huffed. "Tell me the truth, though. Are you hoping to win him back?"

"I don't owe you an answer."

Val stepped closer. "I deserve one, especially because it will affect my daughter."

"Did your boyfriend have to answer to your husband?" Steffi shot back, then closed her eyes, wishing she'd held her tongue.

Luckily, Emmy rushed back into the room, putting an end to the conversation. "I'm all clean now, Mommy."

Val's tense expression instantly transformed into a cheerful smile.

"There's my little beauty." Val gathered Emmy into her arms for a big squeeze. Then she amassed Emmy's hair in her hands and sighed. "If you find a comb, I'll pull these messy curls into a French braid."

Emmy's expression faltered. "All right."

Steffi hated the way Val treated Emmy like a baby doll. Before she could dwell on that, Ryan stormed into the room.

He looked gorgeous in his faded jeans and black sweater. Steffi's heart skittered from the collision of lust and fearful anticipation of what might happen next. He spared Steffi the briefest glance before turning on Val.

"Can we talk?" He gestured with his head, but Emmy stopped him.

"Daddy, Mommy came to surprise us and try that pizza. Now we can all go together." She hugged his legs like a gigantic monkey. "Please, Daddy. Please!"

Steffi noticed Ryan's hard expression soften. "Princess, Mommy drove all this way to see *you,* not me. I don't want to intrude on your special day together."

He patted her head.

"Actually, you're welcome to join us for lunch." Val smiled at him and Emmy. "If you want to, that is."

"See!" Emmy tipped her face up at him, bright with joy. "We can eat together, like we used to do."

How neatly she'd trapped Ryan.

Ryan's resentful gaze sliced through Val before he kissed the top of Emmy's head. "Sure, honey. If that's what you want, I'll come."

"Yay!" Emmy jumped and clapped. "I'll get my jacket."

Emmy dashed to the front closet, giving Ryan a moment alone—almost—with Val. Only the slight flare of his nostrils hinted at his mood. Steffi braced for his cutting remark, but he merely asked his wife, "Could you please take Emmy to the car? I'll be out in a second."

Val's gaze darted from him to Steffi and back.

"Fine." Then she smiled at Steffi, her voice sweeter than anything Molly could bake. "Nice talking with you. This room is a fabulous addition to the house, by the way. Love all the windows."

She gave a little wave and sashayed out of the room, leaving Steffi to stew in the new perspective on Ryan and Val's history and the domino effect of her own mistakes. Those few minutes with Val rearranged everything Steffi had thought she understood. Everything she thought was right and wrong. Worst of all, it made her feel unworthy of the second chance with Ryan she wanted so much.

Unsure of how to face him after last night's meltdown, she picked up the drywall knife and got back to work. She'd give everything to avoid all conversation with him until she had time to gather her thoughts.

"I had no idea she was coming," Ryan said.

"Obviously." Steffi scraped the freshly laid mud and the rolled tape over the seam. "But it's not my business, really."

He stared at her. "Are you okay?"

She could barely speak, with her throat tightening as if she'd swallowed a fistful of mud from the bucket. "Sure, but between getting here late and Emmy and Val's interruptions, I'm really behind now. I need to finish up and head over to our new project on Hightop Road to check in on my little crew."

Ryan came closer. "You look tired."

Unlike her, he looked composed.

"I'm fine." Steffi attempted a smile.

"I spent the night thinking about how our date ended." He hesitated. "It's something we need to talk more about. If you can't talk to me . . . maybe a professional . . ."

A professional? What the hell was he pushing that for? Fortunately, the horn honked from out front, saving Steffi from having to discuss shrinks. "You'd better go. I don't like your chances against two impatient women."

She hoped joking hid her disappointment that Val wasn't letting Ryan go without one last fight. Normally, she wouldn't be intimidated. The difference here was that Emmy wanted her family back together. Just like he had moments ago, Ryan might capitulate because that little girl was the one true love of his life. The only person he could still open his entire heart to.

"I know what you're thinking," he said, breaking her train of thought.

"I'm not thinking anything," she fibbed.

He crossed his arms, sighing. "We were pretty honest with each other last night. Let's not backtrack."

"Okay. What am I thinking, Ryan?"

"You think Val's here today to save our marriage and I'm going to let her."

Steffi shrugged. "I wouldn't blame you. I saw

Emmy's face just now—the hope and thrill of being with you both again. After last night, you can't possibly think I'm worth the death of your little girl's dream."

"That's a dramatic take on things. Val's here because she wants to see Emmy. Messing with you and me—that's just a bonus she got for her effort this morning."

"I know this might be hard for you to believe, but you could be wrong."

"About Val?" He grimaced like she'd suggested the absurd. "I know her a lot better than you do."

"She really loved you, Ryan. More than you loved her." She spread another batch of mud along a seam. "That's a painful kind of love."

"Trust me, I know exactly how that feels."

As if she needed that reminder. "That's not exactly fair."

"It's just the truth." He shrugged.

As much as she wanted to renew their relationship, she wouldn't stand for constant reminders of her mistakes. "The truth isn't some flag you can wave to excuse making me feel shitty again. It's not fair to keep throwing our past in my face. Everything that happened before August shouldn't matter. We either start with a clean slate and trust each other, or we don't start at all."

Probably the latter, given the way the past twelve hours had been going.

The car horn blasted again.

"I've got to go." He stared at her. "We'll talk later."

She watched him leave, disappointed that he hadn't tried to touch or kiss her.

Determined to finish the job before he and Emmy returned, she vigorously applied mud to the corner joints.

"Stefanie?" Molly called out from the kitchen before she appeared in the archway.

"What?"

"Your mother would be very proud of the way you stand up for yourself." She turned to go, then rested her hand on the trim and glanced back. "My son is guarded, but he's not hardened. Not yet, anyway. I hope you don't give up on him."

Emmy dashed ahead on the sidewalk and swung open the door to Campiti's. "Here we are, Mommy. Just like I told you. Look at that painting." She smothered giggles with her hands after pointing at the mediocre mural.

"I remember this place," Val replied, then muttered, "I think you gain five pounds just from walking through the door."

She could stand to gain ten pounds and would still be thinner than most. Not that he cared. In fact, this might be the only time in his entire life that he hadn't enjoyed coming to this restaurant. He had no idea what Val had said to Steffi, but judging from Steffi's attitude, their conversation hadn't been pleasant. He'd made matters worse by letting his irritation with Val spill over onto Steffi.

"Sit next to me, Mommy." Emmy scooted onto the hard prefab booth bench. "Do you like cherry soda?"

"I'll stick with seltzer, thanks, honey." Val scanned the menu, which was printed on the paper place mats.

Two salad sides—garden and Caesar—neither of which were particularly great. She turned it over, frowning in her search for better options.

"Can I order chicken or salmon over a salad?" She flattened the menu on the table again.

"Salmon?" Emmy shook her head. "Mommy, this is a pizza place, not a *real* restaurant. You have to eat pizza. But don't worry. It's really good."

Val's pretty smile appeared when she wound an arm around their daughter's shoulders and squeezed her before kissing the top of her head. "Okay. I'll try the pizza."

For just a second, Ryan's heart stuttered. Several months ago, he might've enjoyed being here with his wife and daughter. He'd wanted to keep his family together, despite his heart yearning for that elusive deeper connection. Now, staring at them from across the table, he mourned the loss anew. From now on, he'd be stuck trading off holidays and birthdays and vacations with his daughter. He and Val would each miss out on days, weeks, or more of Emmy's life.

The reality of divorce hit him this way, in little waves, whenever he saw an old photo or remembered a happy moment. He wondered if other divorced couples experienced the loss that way, too, and if it would fade in time.

Val tickled Emmy's nose. "Now tell me, what have you been up to? Any more sailing trips?"

"No. But tomorrow's not a workday, right, Daddy? We could go tomorrow! We could take Mommy, and I can work the tiller." Emmy's trusting Cindy Lou Who smile cast him as the Grinch, because he had no intention of sailing with Val. She, not he, had called it quits. He shouldn't have to entertain her and her games now.

"I'm sure your mom has to get back to Boston tonight, honey." He then held his hand up to signal for the waiter. "An extra-large pepperoni, well done, two Cherikee Reds and a seltzer, and . . ." He gestured to Val in case she wanted a salad.

"The garden salad, please." She offered the young waiter that gorgeous smile, which flustered the kid, as she probably hoped it would.

She constantly sought reassurance of her attractiveness, especially from other men, like John. Her flirtations had always angered him because of the disrespect, but maybe Steffi was right. Maybe she'd been desperate to provoke him because she hadn't known how else to secure his attention.

He'd lain awake many nights wishing to love her more. Searching his heart for whatever it was that was missing, and hating the little voice that whispered the name of the ghost he'd never quite escaped. The first love who now wanted a second chance. A woman who also might still be keeping one foot out the door, whether that was intentional or because she wouldn't—or couldn't—address her problem.

"I don't want to foist anything on you, but John's actually in Nebraska on unexpected business, so I don't need to rush back to Boston," Val said.

It took Ryan a second to remember what they'd been discussing before the waiter arrived and his mind had wandered. "What's in Nebraska?"

Val waved her hand. "Some Berkshire Hathaway board thing . . . I don't know."

Ah yes. The rich and famous movers and shakers of the world. People Ryan had never been particularly impressed by. Certainly not as much as they seemed to be impressed with themselves, anyway.

"Yay!" Emmy practically bounced out of her seat. "Mommy can have a sleepover!"

Ryan loved his daughter, but not enough to spend the rest of *this* day with Val, let alone another one. And if Val was angling for some kind of reconciliation, it'd be kinder not to do something she might misconstrue as an opening. "Actually, Emmy, I had planned to surprise you tomorrow.

There's a big fair called Oktoberfest in a nearby town. It'll have rides and games and crafts and stuff."

Emmy pouted. "Can Mommy come to the fair with us?"

"Well, actually, the fair was Steffi's idea. She invited us to go with her. I just hadn't had a chance to talk to you about it yet." He harbored some doubt about the impulsive decision, but he needed to draw a line in the sand with these two so there'd be no misunderstanding.

Val's friendly expression cooled considerably. "I'm sorry, Emmy. But you'll have fun. You're always saying how much you like Miss Steffi."

"I'd rather go with you, Mommy." Emmy played right into Val's hands.

"Thanks, sweetie. Maybe another time." Val hugged Emmy. "I don't want to ruin your father's plans."

And just like that, she'd made him the bad guy.

"But we see Miss Steffi every day. We *never* see Mommy," Emmy begged.

The waiter delivered the food and drinks, giving Ryan time to remove the knife from his heart and collect his wits.

Across the table, Emmy sat with her chin on her fists, frowning. Beside her, Val stroked her hair and snuggled her, whispering something in her ear. He rubbed his sternum, but his esophagus still burned. Val glanced at him, a question in her eyes. He could not let her manipulate him—or their child—to suit her own agenda. It wouldn't help Emmy to hold on to a fantasy about her family when he knew he couldn't give her what she wanted.

In fact, protecting Emmy from his feelings for Steffi could be a mistake. If she saw him moving on like she saw her mother with John, she'd have to start accepting her new reality.

"Don't you think it would hurt Steffi's feelings if, after she invited us to join her, we went with your mom instead?" He watched Emmy chew on the inside of her cheeks as her frown deepened. "I bet you don't want to do that after how nice she's been to you, do you?"

"No." Emmy was shifting in her seat in a way that told him she was swinging her legs back and forth like a pendulum. Her brows gathered together while she thought of another solution. "What if we all go together? That way no one has to ride alone."

Val stabbed a forkful of salad and remained silent, leaving him to do all the heavy lifting.

"That would be awkward for the grown-ups, princess. I'm sorry. If your mom had called me in advance, perhaps we could have planned something different. But I can't rearrange our schedule at the last minute."

Emmy sat back and crossed her arms, glowering. Ryan ignored the tantrum and pushed a slice of pizza in front of her. She picked at it, having lost interest in the food or in knowing whether Val liked it.

Ryan refrained from lecturing her about being melodramatic, because that would give Val another opportunity to make him the "bad cop."

"I have to go to the bathroom," Emmy announced. Val got up to let Emmy scoot off the bench and disappear around the corner.

Ryan chewed his slice in silence, unable to enjoy the salty cheese or crispy pepperoni today. He noticed that Val hadn't eaten much more than he'd managed. He couldn't take the gamesmanship for another second. "For Emmy's sake, I'm putting on a happy face today, but what's going on? Did you and John fight?"

"No. I told you. He's in Nebraska, so I decided to come down to see my daughter."

He leaned forward, elbows on the table like he usually scolded Emmy for doing. "With no warning?"

"I wanted to see you and meet the infamous Steffi. If I'd warned you, you might've made yourselves scarce," she admitted without remorse.

He tossed his napkin on the table. "You do see how manipulative that is, right?"

"Yes." She folded her hands on the table. "I see everything clearly, don't worry."

"I'm trying to have an amicable divorce and keep our daughter as happy as possible." He shook his head. "What do you want from me?"

"I don't know. Maybe some insight into why I was never enough for you. Or maybe I'm here to make sure of my feelings so I don't do to John what you did to me."

"What's that supposed to mean?" He sat back against the booth.

"I broke our vows, but you broke my heart a million times before then. I know you didn't mean to, but that doesn't mean it didn't hurt." She shrugged one shoulder. "Now I'm not sure I can trust my heart. I don't want to wake up down the road and find out that John is just a substitute, like I was for Steffi. He deserves better, and so do I."

Emmy bounded back toward the table. He could've kissed her for her good timing, because Val's last response left him reeling. He'd had the growing sense of his own role in the divorce, but he'd never thought that his doubts had been so obvious or that he'd cut Val so deeply. Had he really done such damage without realizing it? If so, he'd been almost as selfish and hurtful as Steffi had been.

"I'm sorry," he said, staring at Val and hoping she understood the full weight of his words. He then took out his wallet and threw down forty bucks. "I think I'll let you ladies enjoy the rest of the afternoon together. I can walk home. It'd be great if you could bring Emmy home by nine."

"Sounds wonderful." Val forced a smile, but he knew she wasn't happy. She spoke to Emmy, who'd resumed pouting. "We'll shop and get manicures and maybe go someplace fancy for dinner. How's that sound?"

Emmy leaned into her mother, resting her head on Val's shoulder. She looked so very young and sad that Ryan's heart actually constricted. "Good, Mommy."

"Have fun." Ryan would've kissed Emmy goodbye, but she'd molded herself to Val's body so that it would've required him to hug Val, too. Any other day he wouldn't have hugged Val for a variety of reasons, but today he avoided it because of guilt. "I'll see you later."

He exited the shop and strode down Main Street, barely noticing the cars or pedestrians. Sunshine beat down on him like a spotlight on all his mistakes. Deep down he'd known—as he'd confessed to Steffi—that he'd never given Val his all. What he hadn't known was that he'd been so transparent. That, on an ongoing basis, she'd known and suffered that bitter rejection of never being quite good enough.

That he'd never fallen completely in love with Val for his family's sake was bad enough. But even that shameful confession didn't compare with the darker truth of his heart. Despite everything—including his daughter's dearest wish—he'd rather risk another heartbreak with Steffi than force himself back into a relationship that had never truly satisfied Val or him.

He supposed the only good thing to come of lunch was the answer to the litmus test Steffi had thrown at him this morning. He pulled out his phone and called her. When she didn't answer, he left a message. "Steffi, it's Ryan. I'm sorry about earlier. You were right. Clean slate it is. I'd love to go to Oktoberfest tomorrow with you and Emmy. Call me later, please."

Chapter Eighteen

Steffi and Ryan walked one step behind Emmy, who trudged through the fairground with all the enthusiasm of a man on death row. She passed by the Magic Carpet ride with nary a pause. Her sky-high cone of cotton candy went mostly uneaten. And then there was the litany of complaints. *"I'm hot." "It's crowded." "My new shoes are giving me blisters."*

One day with her mother and Emmy had forsaken the pants and sneakers she'd been wearing lately in favor of a flouncy dress, tights, and hair ribbons. Steffi's erstwhile shadow had vanished overnight as if it never existed, leaving a fine tear in her heart.

Ryan had forewarned Steffi of Emmy's disappointment in his sending Val home. If his daughter's mood persisted today, he might rethink his priorities. After the disaster of their first date, Steffi couldn't afford another strike.

As they ambled around the gaming booths, the milk-bottle toss caught her eye.

"Hold up!" Years of goalie training gave her exceptional arm strength and aim, so she tossed five dollars on the counter and waited for her three softballs, determined to win a supersize stuffed toy. It might not win Emmy over, but it should get her to stop pouting for five minutes. "I used to be awesome at this."

"Is that your way of challenging me?" Ryan teased, his hands still on his daughter's shoulders.

"Nope. If I recall, your aim isn't any better than my singing." Steffi chuckled before she elbowed Emmy. "If I knock them all down, which prize do you want?"

Emmy shrugged, barely meeting her gaze.

She's a young kid nursing a broken heart; she's just a kid who misses her mom.

She touched Emmy's shoulder. "I know it's hard to let your heart get set on something you might not win." She didn't look at Ryan, who must've recognized the sentiment he'd mentioned more than once this fall. "You'll see, though. I'm pretty much a sure thing. My strength never fails me."

Except once.

An uncomfortable shiver awakened the hairs along her neck, but she snatched a softball and took aim. Despite Emmy's pretense of nonchalance, Steffi caught her watching from beneath her lashes, her lower lip caught in her teeth.

Steffi said a silent prayer, wound up, and then pitched the ball. Although she landed a direct hit in the sweet spot, one bottle remained standing. She suspected the game was rigged with one heavy bottle. The carnival worker reset the two capsized bottles in the exact same spots.

She turned to Emmy. "Okay, did you see which two went down?"

Emmy nodded.

Steffi stood back and let another one fly, again hitting the triangle where the three bottles connected. Once more, two went down while the same one remained upright.

"Hey," Steffi said to the booth worker while pointing at the standing milk jug, "I think that bottle is heavier than the others."

"No, ma'am," he said, but his neck broke out in red splotches.

"Then you won't mind switching it out with the top one from that other set?"

The guy looked a little stunned, but Ryan gave him a stern look, so he did it. "Sure thing, ma'am."

She knew they wouldn't put a heavy bottle on top, because it would go down with any decent hit, so she'd certainly made the best choice available. She glanced at Emmy. "Think I can do it this time?"

Emmy looked at war with herself for being intrigued, but nodded. "I guess so."

Ryan's grin grew larger. He winked at Steffi, which was all the encouragement she needed. Times like this made her lifetime of keeping up with three brothers pay off. She hauled off her final throw for another perfect shot. This time all three bottles went down.

"Wow!" Emmy hopped to the counter, planted her hands there, and hoisted herself until her feet left the ground. "Can I have that pink bunny?"

"Sure." Steffi beamed at her. Ryan mouthed "Thank you" over his daughter's head. If things were less strained, perhaps he would've squeezed Steffi's hand or given her a kiss. Maybe some-day . . .

The booth runner spoke to Emmy. "One pink bunny coming your way."

Ryan leaned forward so the young guy could hear him easily. "How about you don't rig this game for the rest of the day, and I won't report this to anyone?"

The kid nodded. "I just work here, dude."

"I know," Ryan replied, then handed Emmy the monstrous toy, which was half Emmy's size and would certainly be a pain in the butt to tote through the fair. No wonder more people didn't try to win these things.

Emmy squeezed it, wearing a giant smile before she must've remembered that she'd rather have her mother there. Smile tempered, she politely turned to Steffi. "Thank you, Miss Steffi."

"You're welcome." Steffi wanted to ruffle her hair, or something, but wouldn't force Emmy's affections. "What will you name her?"

"What do you think, Dad?" Emmy hugged the toy again.

"Pinky Lee?" he said.

"What?" Emmy grimaced. Even Steffi had to wonder where he'd pulled that old reference from.

"Pink Panther?" he offered next.

"It's a bunny, not a panther." Emmy shook her head, the hint of a playful smile reappearing.

"EB?" Steffi ventured.

Both Ryan and Emmy turned their confused faces her way. "Huh?"

"Energizer Bunny . . . he's pink." She shrugged.

"This is a girl," Emmy said.

Steffi decided not to ask how she knew that, or why it mattered.

"Obviously, this will take more thought. In the meantime, why not let me carry that for a while?" Ryan reached for the toy. "I might not throw as well as Steffi, but I can manage that big toy a little easier than you."

"No." Emmy twisted. "I've got it."

"I like your style, kiddo." Steffi smiled.

"My lot in life is to be outnumbered by opinionated women." Ryan kissed Emmy's head.

He stood just a couple of inches from Steffi now. She could feel the warmth of him and longed to hold his hand. Instead, she shoved hers in her jacket pockets. "You're a lucky guy, aren't you?"

"Very." His eyes crinkled when he smiled. "Why don't you two go to the burger hut and order lunch? I need to make a quick stop in the men's room, and then I'll meet you."

"Sounds good." Steffi turned to Emmy, somewhat anxious about being left in charge of a small child in such a chaotic environment. "Want to hold hands? It's pretty crowded here."

"I'm okay."

"See you shortly," Ryan said before trotting off to the portable toilets at the far side of the fields.

Steffi glanced at Emmy, whose stubborn streak showed no signs of surrender.

"Let's weave through there and find a picnic table." Together they snaked through the intersection of people waiting in lines for tickets and rides and food vendors.

The unseasonably warm October day had drawn a substantial crowd. Overhead, a colorful canopy of ocher and vermilion leaves rustled in the breeze. The sound of the circus calliope filtered through the crowd, making Steffi hum along to its manic tune. Emmy straggled two steps behind, trying to keep up while clinging to the bunny.

Steffi didn't offer to help a second time. It wouldn't hurt Emmy to learn to take care of herself or, conversely, to learn the consequences of not asking for help. Of course, Steffi had yet to master that second lesson.

They found an open table near the burger shack, where Steffi would have a clear shot of Emmy while standing in line. Ryan would be back momentarily, too. "Do you want to sit here while I stand in line?"

"Okay." Emmy set the bunny on the seat beside her. "Can I have a cheeseburger?"

"Of course. Maybe fries, too?" Steffi went to stand in line, where her thoughts wandered to Ryan. They'd had no privacy today, so she couldn't tell whether he regretted dragging Emmy along.

He'd promised a clean slate, and despite Emmy's poor attitude, he'd made his intentions clear. He'd sent Val packing, making room for Steffi's hopes to bloom.

While smiling to herself, in her peripheral vision she noticed two large men with dark hair walking in her direction. They laughed loudly, and one made a mock gun with two fingers and held it to his friend's temple.

The crowd closed in as a high-pitched hum resounded in her ears.

A click echoed before a cold pistol pressed against her temple. "Don't make a sound, bitch."

"Grab her purse."

"I'll grab it all . . ."

Don't be stupid. Don't die. Please don't die.

No. No, no, no.

Fly away . . . fly away.

"Hey, lady, are you okay?" the teenage boy who'd caught her from behind asked. Had she fainted?

"I'm sorry." She clutched her purse as she wrested free of his hold. She barely met his eyes while curling her arms and shoulders inward, hoping to disappear.

Like smoke, her thoughts vaporized into thin air. She prodded her memory but could only recall seeing two large men joking with each other. Maybe her brother and Ryan were right. Being mugged and beaten might've done more than physical damage.

Ryan appeared at her side, his face drawn and tight. "What's wrong? You look lost."

"I'm okay." She rubbed her temple, willing herself to smile and hoping to avoid another interrogation about her mental health. "Low blood sugar? I'll be fine once we eat."

He looked around her. "Where's Emmy?"

"Over there." She pointed to the picnic table to see, too late, that only the bunny remained.

"Where?" Ryan asked, his voice strained.

Her heart literally stopped as her thoughts splintered in slow motion. "I told her to wait there. I could see her from here."

He started toward the table, snapping, "If you could see her, then where'd she go?"

"I don't know." Tears filled her eyes, blurring her vision as she chased after him.

Ryan whirled around on her. "So you weren't watching?"

"I was, then these guys walked by . . ." Their image flashed through her mind. "One pretended to shoot . . . and I . . . I . . ."

"You zoned out?" Ryan waved her off and called out, "Emmy? Where are you?"

Steffi asked nearby picnickers, "Did you see the little girl who was sitting here? Did you see where she went?"

"No, sorry," came the blithe response of some tween girls who could barely raise their eyes from their phones.

"I'll grab a security guard while you keep searching." Ryan took off, and all the while Steffi saw his head twisting and turning, searching for his child. The one she'd lost.

She canvassed a few more tables. Finally, one skinny kid with a waterfall cowlick said, "I saw a girl with ribbons run that way." He pointed toward the edge of the field where the portable toilets stood.

"Was she alone?"

He shrugged. "I think so."

Steffi took off toward the bathrooms, making her way through the teeming crowd, which zig-zagged across the fairground. Her typical agility eluded her. Her limbs felt stiff and rusty as her pulse pounded in her ears. She told herself Emmy hadn't been taken. Ryan could have easily missed seeing her on his way back from the toilets as he waded through the dense crowds.

When she got to the long row of potties, her heart raced faster than during any training run with Benny. She whipped her head left and right.

No sign of Emmy or her ribbons. She cupped her hands around her mouth like a megaphone. "Has anyone seen a little girl in a pink ruffled dress with hair ribbons? Dark curly hair, about this tall?"

People shook their heads or ignored her. She wrung her hands, but it didn't stop them from shaking or her legs from weakening. Then her phone rang. "Ryan?"

"I got her." His voice was rough with emotion.

Steffi collapsed against a nearby tree, palm pressed to her forehead. "Where are you?"

"Heading back to the picnic tables to get the bunny." He hung up without saying more.

She jogged back to the tables on wobbly legs. With the threat removed and her adrenaline spike draining, she barked, "What happened, Emmy? Why'd you leave?"

She hadn't meant to shout. She hadn't even meant to be angry. Panic brought out the worst in her.

"You fainted, so I went to find my dad," Emmy cried. Ryan hugged her to his chest and kissed her head, murmuring in her ear to soothe her.

Seems Steffi had given everyone a good scare.

"Oh," she replied. "I'm sorry I snapped at you. I was afraid. And I'm sorry if I scared you when I fainted."

"Can we go home now?" Emmy said into Ryan's shirt, not really looking at Steffi.

"Sure." Ryan stood, also avoiding eye contact. "Get your bunny and we'll go."

"I'm sorry," Steffi repeated stupidly, as if that would help. She didn't want to leave the fair like some quitter but had lost the will to force more "fun."

The world's heaviest silence made the five-mile drive back to Sanctuary Sound feel like a ten-hour trip. When Ryan passed the turnoff to her street, Steffi pointed. "You missed my street."

"I want to drop Emmy with my mom first, then I'll take you home."

Those words might've made her hopeful if he'd smiled or reached across the console and taken her hand. Instead, his eyes had remained fixed on the road, his brows drawn together in thought.

Steffi sighed as he pulled up to his mother's house. She turned toward the back seat. "Emmy, I'm really sorry today wasn't more fun for you. I hope we can do something else together soon. Maybe you can pick the adventure next time."

Emmy shrugged without saying much and then slid out of the car.

"Wait here, I'll only be a minute." Ryan got out of the car and walked Emmy inside. True to his word, he returned quickly and pulled away from the curb. "Is Claire home?"

"I have no idea." An hour ago, she'd have paid for time alone with him. Now she wished he'd dropped her off first. "You're mad at me, huh?"

"I'm not mad." He scowled.

She shifted in her seat. "Look in the mirror."

He glanced in the rearview mirror before sighing. "I'm upset and concerned, and I'm pissed that there's no place private where we can talk."

"It's private here in the car," she pointed out as he pulled up to her house. "I don't see Claire's car on the street, so she must be out."

"Good." He got out of the car and then followed her into the house.

She tossed her purse on an obliging chair and raked her hand through her hair. "Listen, I know I messed up. I shouldn't have left Emmy at the table, but I thought it was safe. She's nine, not four. I knew I'd see her from where I was standing. I didn't feel sick or think I would faint."

"But that's the problem, Steffi. You never know where or when these episodes will take place, and yet you won't even consider a second opinion." He inhaled and scrubbed his face, smoothing away his frustration. He tipped his head. "Could that be because you know something more about them than you're willing to share with me?"

Her body recoiled. "Where is *that* coming from?"

Something new flickered in his eyes—suspicion?—but then he refocused. "From concern. From a need to know what's happening to you so I can help. Don't run away from it. Talk to me. Get answers. Stick it out. Fight through it."

She crossed her arms. "Are we still talking about

the present, or is this you drudging up the past again?"

"Does a clean slate mean I can't point out stuff that could be a problem in the future? I want to see you well, for your sake and for your business's sake. This affects our relationship, too. And after today, I can't ignore the danger these episodes pose to Emmy. What if you're driving her somewhere and it happens? You owe it to yourself, and to me, to be honest—at least with yourself. Don't settle for living this way without trying everything possible to fix it, regardless of what others or your family might think about how that happens."

"I'm not hiding anything, if that's what you're implying."

He opened his mouth, then shut it, gazing at her through narrowed eyes. "You honestly have no recollection of the moments or thoughts just before you fainted? No guesses as to why this keeps happening to you?"

She shook her head.

"If it isn't a tumor or epilepsy, is it possible that the trauma you suffered in the spring is worse than you want to admit?"

"Quit trying to make me a victim." She turned on him while massaging the hard knot forming in her stomach.

"That's not my goal. I'm exploring . . . ideas."

She glanced over her shoulder. "You clearly have a theory. Might as well share it."

His expression tightened into a concerned frown, his eyes misting until he blinked. He clasped his elbows and paced a few steps. "I'm not a professional. You should consult with someone who is."

"You're so desperate for an answer that will 'fix' me. What if you're wrong and I'm right? What if it's mild brain damage from too many concussions? Are you willing to take that—me—on if that's the case?" She bit her pinkie nail. "I wouldn't blame you if you bailed. Your hands are already full."

"*I* don't bail!"

The granite ball in her stomach moved to her throat. She took a step back, maybe two, fighting the tears that formed behind her eyes.

"I'm sorry." He closed his eyes and drew a deep breath, then walked toward her, reaching out. "I'm sorry. I'm just feeling powerless. If there's a *chance* this can get better or be healed, let me help you. If the roles were reversed, I'd take your concerns seriously."

Ryan stared into space for a moment, tugging at his earlobe. "I'm here for you, and I'll stand by you, no matter what, but I need to know that you trust me. I need to know you'll confide in me and commit to facing the truth, no matter how scary that seems. Is that unfair to ask?"

Her gaze dropped as she shook her head. "You're always fair, Ryan."

He gathered her into a hug. "I want things to work out for us this time. Please put some faith in me, Steffi."

For the first time all day, her muscles relaxed.

Ryan stopped short of voicing his suspicions. Without proof, he wouldn't risk upsetting her more, or worse, planting a seed that could aggravate her condition.

He didn't want to read too much into the fact that none of their plans had gone well this weekend, or take it as some sign that their time had come and gone a decade ago.

"Emmy hates me now," Steffi muttered against his chest.

He kissed the top of her head and squeezed her. "She doesn't hate you. She just needs to let go of her fantasy, which will be tough if Val pulls more stunts like she did this weekend."

Steffi eased away. "I'm sorry. This isn't about me. It's about you and your daughter. I still can't believe Val doesn't want physical custody."

"Val doesn't know what she wants." He swallowed hard at the recollection of his wife's heart-to-heart at Campiti's.

She flopped onto the sofa, looking absolutely spent. "She wants you back."

He sat beside her and blew out a long sigh. "Val wants something from me that she never got. I honestly tried to be happy . . . I thought I loved her *enough*. Turns out, in marriage, that type of love won't get you through the low points." He hung his head for a second, then glanced at her. "John obviously gives her something I never could, and maybe, right now, she needs that more than anything. Maybe she can't be a good mom until her heart is whole again."

"You're being very generous." Steffi rubbed his shoulder. "Is that guilt talking?"

"Maybe a little." He grimaced, hoping that opening up to her this way would encourage her to do the same. "I wish Emmy weren't caught in the middle, and that I knew she'd end up okay."

"She will."

He stared at the ground, head involuntarily nodding. "We can't predict the future, though, can we?"

"I guess not." She gestured around the room. "I never expected to be here at thirty. Or to get close to you again."

She body-bumped his side as a shy grin emerged.

"That's been a lucky surprise." He took hold of her hand, needing to end the afternoon on a peaceful note for both their sakes.

"One good thing has come out of the past several weeks. More will follow."

"I admit I've enjoyed having Emmy to myself here." Chagrin forced a wan smile. "It'd be perfect if I hadn't screwed up her life."

"Don't shoulder all the blame for your divorce. Besides, there is a silver lining. This experience will teach Emmy resilience. Few things matter more than that." Steffi's gaze softened and fell to the floor. "My mom's death was mostly awful, but I survived it even when I didn't think I would. If she'd lived and my life had been easier, maybe I wouldn't have gone on to be so competitive in sports, gotten a scholarship, or started my own business. Not that I wouldn't rather she lived, of course. But Emmy will come out stronger, like I did. I know it. She just needs a little time."

Steffi was strong. Maybe that was why she couldn't accept the idea of needing help to heal. He thought to raise the issue again but let the moment pass. She insisted she wasn't hiding anything, which meant she might've repressed the worst memories of that night.

Theories were useless and accusations unfair. He needed proof. Proof he still couldn't get without crossing some legal and ethical lines. "I hope you're right."

Steffi snuggled up against his side and laid her head on his shoulder. "Given your impromptu lunch yesterday, are you more or less likely to settle your financial stuff with Val soon?"

"Not sure." He looked down at her, surprised by the abrupt change in conversation. "Why?"

"I'm closing on the Weber house this week. I hoped maybe you'd given more thought to buying it. I'd love to personalize the design to yours and Emmy's tastes."

"I wish." He held her, enjoying the fantasy of seeing one youthful dream realized. "I'd love it, but it's not realistic."

"I know you don't like to get your hopes up, but too much reality is kind of sad and boring. Dream a little, okay?"

He had no response to that, so he laid his cheek on her head and held her. Had he forgotten how to dream? Was a life without dreams the way he wanted Emmy to see him, or to live?

After a brief silence passed, Steffi sighed in his arms. "I'm sorry today went sideways. I had high hopes of proving that things will be different for us this time, Ryan. Different better."

"Things are different. We're older and wiser, if nothing else." Ryan grinned, then brushed her hair from her face and tucked it behind her ear. He cupped her jaw and kissed her, careful not to make any sudden moves. If he was right about what had happened to her, it could take a lot of healing before she would be comfortable with sex. He allowed himself to let the kiss linger, their tongues acting out the desire, making his skin prickle with need.

Steffi wound her arm around his neck to pull him close. But he broke the kiss before spooking her again.

"What's wrong?" she asked, nuzzling his neck.

"Nothing." He felt trapped. He couldn't discuss his suspicions, yet he wouldn't push her sexually and risk triggering another episode.

"Is there some reason you're taking things so slow?" She licked his neck before nibbling at his ear.

He stifled a satisfied moan and pulled her tight to his chest. "I'm in the middle of a divorce, Steffi. I just want us to get this right. Let's not jump into bed until we're both certain. Mutual trust."

"You still don't trust me," she said, pulling away.

"Do you trust me? I've spent plenty of time blaming you and Val for things going wrong. But I smothered you when we were together. I didn't think through my quickie wedding or fully invest in my marriage. I think we both have relationship issues to sort out."

"I do trust you, though."

He kissed her lightly, wishing he knew the best way to handle his concerns. "Thanks. But I want things to be 'different better' for us now, too, and not just because you've changed. I've got to change, too."

She graced him with a smile. "Don't change too much. You're pretty perfect, as far as I can see."

He grasped her face and kissed her again, tenderly suckling her lower lip before he dipped his tongue into her mouth. He could smell her skin and the scent of her shampoo. The heat of her mouth and her warm hands around his neck had him aching to whisk her up to her room and make love, finally, after all these years apart. He pulled away.

"Ryan?" she asked.

Had he shivered? "Hm?"

She pressed her fingers to the creases between his brows. "You look so sad."

The front door slammed open, scattering his thoughts like the pile of mail that fell to the floor. They both jolted upright as Claire thumped inside, red-cheeked and wild-eyed.

She stopped short upon finding them in the living room.

"Oh! I didn't expect you two to be back so early." She closed the front door before bending to pick up the mail and return it to the table. "I'll give you some privacy."

"Wait!" Steffi said. "What happened to you?"

Claire's disheveled hair made it look as if someone had tossed her into a barrel and shoved it down a hill. Her chin quivered. "Not what. Who!"

"Who, then?" Steffi asked.

"Peyton's ambassador, that's who!"

Peyton's ambassador?

"Logan?" Ryan sat forward. He hadn't seen him or Peyton in years. "He's in town?"

"Did you know?" Claire demanded of Steffi.

Panic etched itself across her face, tugging her features downward. "Why wouldn't you warn me?"

"Warn you of what?" Steffi approached Claire the way one might approach an injured wolf.

"Logan says Peyton's coming home after this first course of treatment to have her mastectomies and recuperate." Claire closed her eyes, her body so tense it quivered. "Surely she mentioned it during one of your *talks*."

"No, she didn't." Steffi reached for Claire's arm, but Claire pulled away. "I swear, Claire. I had no idea."

"I hope not. I really hope not. It's hard enough to know that you're still friends with her." She gestured between them with a jerky motion. "*We're* partners. You should have *my* back. I don't want to be blindsided by Peyton ever again." Claire's voice trilled.

Ryan sought to break the tension. "Why is Logan in town? I thought he lived in the city."

"Visiting his mom, I guess. I don't know. I tried to avoid him when I spotted him in Connecticut Muffin, but he followed me onto the street. As if being humiliated by one Prescott in my life wasn't enough . . . he chased me down in public to deliver that news." Claire trembled, whether from anger or sorrow, he wasn't sure. She pressed her fingers to her temples. "I can't believe she'd dare show her face around here. Why can't she leave me in peace?"

"I don't think she's trying to torment you," Steffi said. "She probably needs to regroup someplace quiet and comforting. Who doesn't want to go home when she's sick?"

"Quit defending her!" Claire thrust her index finger toward Steffi. "I doubt you'd like it if Val said she was moving to town and you had to worry about running into her. And Val didn't even do anything to you. She didn't steal Ryan . . . you threw him away!"

"Hey!" Steffi cried. "Don't attack *me,* Claire."

"Everyone, cool down." Ryan stepped between the women. "Claire, I get that you're upset, but Steffi's not your enemy. Neither am I. Let's not say things we'll regret later."

"I didn't mean it." Claire started crying in earnest. "I'm upset. I don't want to have to look over my shoulder to avoid Peyton. I don't want her here."

If Claire could've moved quickly, Ryan sensed she would've bolted upstairs. Instead, she ambled up with her cane, a steady thud echoing throughout the small home until her bedroom door closed.

"I don't even know what to say," Steffi said, still looking up the stairwell. "Mentioning Peyton around Claire is like setting off a live grenade. She can't get over the whole thing with Todd."

Ryan understood Claire. Some pain reverberates over and over until you think you might lose your mind, rupturing like a volcano at the slightest provocation.

"It takes time to process betrayal. Look at how I reacted to seeing you for the first time in years." Ryan shrugged. "She got caught unaware. And if I recall, she always had a little crush on Logan. Maybe that flustered her, too."

"Middle school crushes don't count." Steffi continued to watch the stairs and listen for activity. She looked back at him and let loose a defeated sigh. "Does it feel like we can't get five minutes of peace?"

Ryan grabbed her into a hug and gave her a quick kiss. "Look at it this way . . . going through difficult stuff together will strengthen *our* resilience, right?"

Steffi wrapped her arms around his waist and rested her cheek against his shoulder. "I wish I could help Claire. She needs to talk to someone . . . maybe a counselor."

"Maybe you could do a two-for-one?" he teased, unable to resist the easy opening.

She slapped his ass. "Ha ha."

He'd made the joke, but in truth, it wasn't funny. "Why do you think Claire should talk to someone but you won't consider it?"

Steffi eased away without a reply. Upstairs, they heard movement and then the sound of running water. Steffi stared up at the ceiling, ignoring his intent gaze.

"I'm not dropping this topic, Steffi. We can't ignore what happened earlier today," he prodded. "We need a definitive diagnosis."

"We?"

"You and me." He stared into her gorgeous golden eyes. "I think you know that a part of me always cared for you, even when I was sure I hated you. If this is going to work now, we can't back away from something because it's hard or scary. Whatever's wrong, we'll face it together. We said 'different better,' so don't run away now."

She huffed. "I won't run away, but you can't push me, either. It's my health. I need to do things my way and on my schedule."

For the hundredth time, he considered disclosing his suspicion, but the downside outweighed the upside. He needed evidence, and if he got it, he needed to speak with someone about how to broach it, too.

Alternatively, if he got his hands on the police file and turned out to be wrong, then she'd never have to know what he'd done. God, he hoped that would be the case. But if it confirmed his fears, he'd handle the fallout from going behind her back after getting her the help she needed. She'd resent him at first, but once she got better, she'd thank him.

Chapter Nineteen

The old pipes clanked overhead when Claire drained the tub, causing Steffi and Ryan to look upward again. She could offer to upgrade the plumbing for the landlord, but the quirks that made each old house unique comforted her. She'd miss the clanging if it stopped.

"I'll take off so you can talk to Claire." Ryan kissed her nose. "She needs a friend right now, and I want to make sure that Emmy understands her attitude this morning is not acceptable."

"Let me work it out with Emmy on my own." A scolding from Ryan wouldn't build trust between Emmy and her. "I'll get her to help me sand the walls tomorrow. She'll open up."

"I won't make a big deal, but she needs to learn that she can't manipulate me that way." He shook his head. "She learned that behavior from watching her mother. I've got to nip it in the bud."

"Fair enough."

Ryan walked toward the door. "Let's grab dinner this week?"

"I'll be pulling double duty now, finishing your mom's job and overseeing two others, so I'll probably work most evenings." She grimaced, then smiled as an idea formed. "If you help me demo the Weber cottage, we can order beer and pizza."

"I'll take out my frustrations on an unsuspecting wall," he mumbled.

She rested her hands on her hips. "What frustrations?"

Ryan peeked up the stairs when the floorboards creaked. "The lack of privacy, for starters."

Steffi crossed to him and laid her hands on his chest. "We could always slip away to your boat."

She sensed hesitation on his part. Despite his speech about trust and going slow, she suspected more was at play. Ever since she'd batted him off her on Friday night, he'd restricted touches and kisses to the barest, briefest interactions. Like he might break her or something.

"I'm a little old to be hiding away like that, although those are good memories, for sure." He kissed her too briefly again.

"The best." She tried to grab hold of his shirt, but then they heard Claire's door open.

When her feet hit the top of the stairs, she called out, "I'm coming down."

"Thanks for the warning!" Steffi joked, "Give us a sec to throw our clothes back on."

Ryan waited to say goodbye to Claire before he left. Once he'd closed the door, Claire said, "I'm sorry. I wouldn't have interrupted, but I'm really hungry."

She started toward the kitchen. Claire had always been a stress eater. Given her current mood, she might devour everything in the kitchen.

"It's okay." Steffi followed her. "My day was sort of a bust . . . but we got back on track at the end."

"Why was it a bust?" Claire opened the refrigerator and scanned its contents, opting for leftover mushroom quiche. "I thought you went to Oktoberfest."

"Emmy was in a petulant mood after spending yesterday with her mother. She still has her heart set on her parents reuniting, so now I'm an enemy. On top of that, I had one of my episodes and lost track of her for a bit."

Claire popped a slice into the microwave and then glanced at Steffi, eyes wide. "You didn't!"

"I did." She grimaced.

Claire folded her arms across her chest. "Is she okay?"

"She's fine." Steffi leaned against the counter. "Ryan found her within a few minutes."

"How scary."

"He was pissed at first. I'm worried he might lose patience with my problem, though, especially if his daughter could get hurt."

"He seemed okay just now." The microwave dinged, so Claire withdrew the quiche and took a giant forkful.

"That's because he thinks there's an explanation with a cure. But what if second opinions confirm that this will get worse or more frequent, like with those NFL players? Honestly, if that's the prognosis, I don't want whatever good time I have left to be ruined with worry about it getting worse. I'd rather cope day to day without knowing." There. She'd admitted her deepest fear to Claire. Maybe it wasn't brave or logical, but it was real. Now if she could just say all that to Ryan without scaring him away. "And if I learn it will get worse, how selfish would it be to ask Ryan to stick by me?"

Her doctor had given her an explanation that satisfied her. That should be enough.

"Now you're just being stupid." Claire finished the quiche, then grabbed a box of Golden Grahams from the cabinet and started eating them right from the box. "You keep focusing on the worst-case scenario, but what if you're wrong? What if there could be help?"

"Let's not talk about me." Steffi reached for a handful of cereal, too. "I'm worried about *you*. Are you feeling better now?"

"Not really." She shoved another fistful of cereal into her mouth.

"Did Logan say something specific? Did he deliver a message from Peyton?"

"No. It was just him being him . . . and the way he looks." Claire closed the box and set it on the counter.

"What's wrong with the way he looks?"

"It's annoyingly perfect, like Peyton. And then sometimes he looks at me like . . ." Her cheeks got red, and she pushed hair away from her eyes. "I don't know. It makes me uncomfortable."

Ryan's commentary drifted through Steffi's mind. "You used to *like* Logan."

"Everyone did." Claire raised her hands overhead. "I was a tween, and he was the town god."

"Fair enough." Steffi preferred Ryan's more rugged features. "I'm sure he didn't set out to make you uncomfortable."

"He gets me so tongue-tied. I couldn't think of what to say when he was talking about Peyton. I sputtered . . ." Claire covered her eyes with her hands.

Steffi tempered the smile she felt forming. Ryan might've been onto something. "Sounds like maybe you do still harbor a little crush."

"Not for *Peyton's* brother!" she insisted, now reaching for an apple and a paring knife. "I was furious that he confronted me in front of people. Dang it, I shouldn't have to defend my decision not to talk to Peyton. He's got no right to corner me in public. See! I'm still mad."

"I do see." Steffi took the knife from her hand. "Let's put this down until you're calmer."

Claire kept a tight grip on the apple. "You need to talk Peyton out of coming back here. Please, Steffi. I've tried not to put you in the middle of this, but this town is all I have. She can go anywhere and do anything. Please ask her to go somewhere else."

Steffi hugged her friend. "I'm sorry you're this upset, but we can't tell Peyton she can't come home to recover. Maybe it's what she needs to get stronger. To regroup. You've cut her out of your life, but surely you don't want to interfere with her recovery. Let's find a way to prepare you so whenever she does show up, you're not this upset."

Claire glared at her and huffed. "Thanks for nothing." She then bit into the apple and limped off.

"Claire!" Steffi watched her go to the front of the house. "Where are you going?"

"To my mom's." Claire pulled her jacket back on and tugged at the zipper.

Steffi trotted to the front door. "Don't run off. I'm sorry. Let's find another way that I can help."

"You're *not* helping. You keep pushing me to defer to Peyton, just like you push with our business. You've got me fretting about money. Now I have to worry about seeing Peyton. I don't need all this stress." Claire grabbed her cane, ranting, "My mom is on *my* side. She won't make me feel like *Peyton* is the wronged party. And if we end up baking something chocolate, all the better."

"Didn't go well?" Billy asked Ryan over lunch at a McDonald's near the courthouse.

Ryan never much liked fast food, but it was cheap, and the fries weren't half-bad.

"No." Ryan swallowed some soda, wishing he could have something stronger. "The DA's taking a hard line, and Owen won't take a plea that requires some jail time. I can't believe this could go to trial."

"This case is sort of high profile now." Billy nodded thoughtfully. "When a jury sees the size of Owen compared with her, you'll have a hard time making him look innocent."

"I know. He's like the Hulk." Ryan blew out a breath. "I wish I could put him on the stand. Hearing an IQ level is one thing, but seeing his childlike thought process in action would help me persuade them that he didn't understand the transaction."

"Why not put him up there?"

"It's rarely wise to let a defendant testify, especially one who could be easily misled and manipulated." Ryan wiped his hands with a napkin and tossed it aside. "I wish we'd have found better evidence to exonerate him."

"If only there weren't so many rules about collecting it." Billy grimaced.

The justice system afforded protections to all sides; however, Billy's hacking talents and personal contacts could be useful in other ways. His brother was a cop, after all.

Ryan glanced around to make sure no one who knew them was in the vicinity, then lowered his voice. "Billy, I need a favor . . . a personal favor, but you're free to say no. There's no pressure."

"Sounds intriguing." Billy cocked a brow, waiting for the details.

This request could get Ryan sanctioned or fired. Maybe even disbarred. He hunched forward, partly covering his mouth. "I have a friend, Stefanie Lockwood. She was mugged in Hartford near the convention center sometime during late spring. I know there were police and hospital reports, but no suspects were apprehended."

Billy's brows lowered as he tried to figure out what Ryan wanted from him. "You want me to try to ID suspects?"

"No. She's been having these . . . episodes . . . ever since the attack. She's blaming it on the concussion, but I think there's more to it. I think it has to do with stuff that happened. Stuff that might be mentioned in those reports that she isn't telling anyone. Or possibly that she's repressing." Ryan maintained eye contact with Billy, whose sympathetic change in expression suggested he understood Ryan's suspicion.

"Doesn't she have the reports?" Billy sat back in his chair, gaze steady.

"She says she tossed them when she moved. I don't know if that's true. Whenever I try to bring up the incident, she shuts down and gets agitated. It's important to her that everyone believes that she's moved on and is 'fine.' I don't know if I'm right, which is why I'd love proof before taking other steps." Ryan wrung his hands together. "Between your brother and your special 'skills,' I thought maybe you could get your hands on the police report or hospital file. I wouldn't ask if I weren't desperate."

Billy drummed his fingers on the table. "Stefanie Lockwood is the victim's name?"

Ryan nodded, clutching his stomach beneath the table.

"You can say no. In fact, you *should* say no." Ryan pressed his palms to his eyes. "Forget I even asked. What the hell was I thinking? This is wrong on too many levels."

"You're a serious rule follower." Billy balled up the sandwich wrapper and tossed it into the empty bag. "This girl must mean a lot to you for you to consider bending them."

"Steffi's my first love. We're on the verge of something good now, but I'm worried about her behavior. And it could get worse the longer it goes untreated." Not to mention how complicated any physical relationship would be if she didn't start dealing with reality. "Being powerless is driving me crazy. If I had the facts, I could convince her to get help."

"She sounds like the kind who'll be pissed that you went behind her back. Maybe you should just tell her what you think."

"What if I'm wrong and just stir up unnecessary

stress? I need to know I'm right before I say anything."

"It's a dilemma. I'm sorry, Ryan." Billy stood with his garbage in hand. "You're in a tough spot."

"*She's* in a tough spot. If *I'm* tormented thinking of it, I can't imagine what it's doing to her. But I'll figure something out without involving you. Sorry I even put you in that awkward position." Ryan's phone rang. "It's my mom. Please, God, let's not have another call from the principal's office." He motioned for Billy to go on without him. "Talk to you later."

Ryan greeted his parents before climbing the stairs to change out of his work clothes, his mother's earlier call weighing on his mind. For the first time during the course of the renovation project, Emmy had ignored Steffi. In essence, she'd ignored his lecture yesterday, too.

He'd been so smug when his daughter had rejected John. He'd actually felt a measure of vindication when that had ruined Val's vacation plans. That admission made his face tingle with heat. His divorce wasn't a zero-sum game. When Val lost, Emmy lost, too. There had to be some way they could move on separately, yet be united by mutual respect and love for their daughter.

He approached Emmy's room and entered without knocking. "How was school today?"

"Boring." Emmy sat on her bed, drawing on the sketch pad his mom had bought her. She barely spared him a glance. Her tongue poked out of her mouth while she concentrated on her work.

"What are you drawing?" He tipped the pad down to look at her sketch.

"A dress." Emmy smiled. She thrust the page closer to him, revealing a triangular-shaped dress with a loud pink-and-blue zigzag pattern. The woman she'd drawn wore blue boots and a pink scarf. "I'm going to be a designer. *Mommy* says I have good taste."

"You have great taste." He kissed her head, smiling. Childhood dreams, unburdened by the weight of responsibility, made anything seem possible. If only that time lasted longer. "I think you get that from me," he teased.

Emmy scanned him from head to toe, frowning at his outfit. "I don't think so."

"Ha ha!" He decided this conversation would be as good as any other opening into another discussion about Steffi. "The way you've been helping Steffi so much, I thought maybe you might like to be a builder."

Emmy's shoulders stiffened as she added some kind of blue fringe to the hem of the outfit she was designing. Her gaze remained on her work. She didn't so much as huff or sigh, let alone respond.

"It looks like the new family room is almost

done, huh?" he prodded. "Just needs some paint. Did you and Memaw pick out a color yet?"

"No. I don't care what color it is." She picked through the box of crayons and selected a dark-blue one. "I'm bored with helping."

Ryan sat on the edge of the mattress. "Emmy, look at me."

She sighed and stared up into his eyes from beneath her lashes, clutching a crayon until her knuckles turned white. He gently uncurled her fingers and set the crayon on the mattress.

"Why are you treating Steffi like she isn't your friend? You liked her a lot up until Saturday." He laid his hand near her legs but didn't touch her.

"I didn't like her a *lot*. I was just bored here by myself."

Three "boreds" in two minutes. A new record. If she said it one more time, he might not be able to contain the frustrated growl forming in his chest.

"Don't lie, Emmy. You liked working with her, and you invited her on our sailing trip. You made her think you were friends." He rubbed her leg, suspecting Val had planted seeds of discontent. "And don't blame this attitude on the fainting, because you were treating her badly before that happened. So what changed everything?"

"Nothing."

He wound one arm around her shoulders. "I know you've been hoping that your mom and I will get back together. We're both so sorry about the way things turned out, but we can't stay married. When you're older, you'll understand better. But for now, even though you're sad, you can't punish me or Steffi . . . or your mom and John, for that matter. Life changes, and you have to be able to adapt. To roll with it."

"That's easy for you to say when you get to decide everything." She set the sketch pad on her thighs and crossed her arms, eyes glittering with tears. "I want to go live with Mommy back in Boston. Can you 'roll with it'?"

"That's different." He couldn't catch his breath. Is that really what she wanted?

"Why? Why can't *I* have a say? Why can't we be a family again?" A tear rolled out of the corner of one eye.

His daughter's pain hammered at his chest like a judge's gavel, condemning him for all the mistakes he'd made as a husband and father. He was supposed to ease her pain, not cause it. Her tears might as well be acid for how they burned his heart. He supposed there would be many types of torture a father would undergo throughout life, and he didn't particularly look forward to learning more. When he tried to hug her, she fought him.

"Emmy, I'm doing the best I can, but I won't lie and tell you what you want to hear. Your mom and I weren't happy together, but that doesn't mean we don't love you. And that doesn't mean you can't be happy again. We'd never bring anyone new into your life that would hurt you. Steffi cares about you and wants to make your life better in any way she can," he said. "I don't know exactly what the future holds, but I care about her. I think the three of us could have fun if you stay open. Can't you try, sweetheart?"

A broken voice cried. "Mommy left me for John, and now you're picking Steffi over me."

"Oh, sweetie." He tugged her against his chest. If he squeezed her hard enough, would it strangle her sense of rejection so it didn't change her on some elemental level? "That's not true. Nobody . . . *nobody* matters more to me than you. I love you with every cell in my body. But just like you might get a little lonely and want friends, I need grown-up friends, too. And Steffi is more than a friend, or a special friend. She makes me feel . . . hopeful."

Emmy broke free and flopped back onto her pillows to stare at the ceiling, arms still crossed.

Ryan sighed and watched his daughter pout until she squeezed her eyes shut. He leaned forward to kiss her forehead. "I'll go change and let you think about what I've said. I know you have a good heart. We'll *all* be happier if you use it to be kinder to Steffi and John. In the meantime, maybe you and I can plan a special father-daughter day on Saturday. Would you like to shop for a small sewing machine and fabric so you can try making some of these creations? Anything you want, princess. Just name it."

One of her eyelids popped open.

"Can we buy a puppy?" She sat up. Wily one, she was. Plucking his heartstrings with the finesse of a concert cellist.

"What?"

"I promise to take care of it. Please, Daddy. I would be happier if I had a puppy." She rose to her knees and folded her hands in prayer.

Val had never allowed pets in the house. He couldn't ask his parents to suffer through puppy-hood, but maybe once he got his own place, he'd consider it.

"I'll tell you what. Show me that you can be responsible and kind, and then when we get our own place, we can seriously consider getting a puppy." Before he rose, he added, "Cats are easier."

She wrinkled her nose. "Cats aren't fun."

"You've got a point." He ruffled her hair, then ambled out of her room, wondering whether he'd made another mistake by striking that deal without more thought. Then again, right now he'd do anything to make her feel loved.

As he strolled the hallway, his thoughts turned to Steffi, as they often did these days. He closed his bedroom door and dialed her number.

"Hey, Ryan."

He smiled upon hearing her voice. "You sound out of breath."

"Rick—from my crew—and I just finished installing a new structural beam where we've opened up part of a wall in the Hightop Road house. What's up?"

"Nothing. I heard you didn't get a chance to talk to Emmy today."

"No, but she'll come around. Don't push her. I get her . . . it needs to be on her terms."

How alike his daughter and Steffi were in that way. "Thanks for being patient."

"Once in a while, I get it right," she joked. "I hate to cut this short, but I promised Rick we'd be done by seven."

"How about dinner tomorrow?" Ryan kicked off his shoes and stretched his legs out on his mattress.

"I close on the Weber house in the morning and planned to start demo after I leave your mom's. Order pizza and come help me."

"You're determined to make me fall in love with that house," he chuckled.

"Among other things, yes."

His heart skipped. In love with Steffi Lockwood . . . again. Little did she know that she didn't have to work too hard to make that happen. "Okay. Pizza, beer, and a sledgehammer. The makings of an interesting date."

"Makes me harder to replace."

"That it does."

"Okay, see you tomorrow!"

He set the phone on the nightstand and breathed a relieved sigh. He'd figure out how to make all the women in his life happy. Even Val, whom he probably did owe more than he wanted to admit.

As for Steffi, somehow he'd find a way to help her recover the part of herself that had been destroyed last spring.

They'd come so far in such a short time, despite the past and the mistakes and pain they each carried around like a pack mule. Every corner of his soul believed that they belonged together, and together they would heal.

Chapter Twenty

"What did you tell Mick?" Steffi asked Molly as they walked into Gretta Weber's lawyer's office.

"You think he asked where I was going?" Molly chuckled. "Honey, trust me, after thirty-seven years together, he avoids me when I'm busy in the morning so he gets out of being asked to help."

"So you're saying you've got a system." Steffi smiled.

"A good system—the key to a lasting marriage." Molly winked.

"Thank you a million times over for this short-term loan. I don't feel great about keeping the secret from Ryan, but I'm hopeful when this is all done, he'll be able to buy the place."

"I have a good feeling." Molly sounded as if she might have another trick up her sleeve, but Steffi chose not to ask. Molly had her own way of doing things, and Steffi enjoyed the surprise of letting it unfold.

Gretta stood when they entered the windowless conference room. She introduced them to her lawyer, and within thirty minutes, they signed all the documents and funded the purchase.

"Thank you so much for selling this house to

me, Gretta. I'm going to turn it into a little gem, you'll see." Steffi shook her hand again.

"I'm glad to see it go to someone who loved it as much as my mom did." Gretta's dewy eyes sparkled. "Dementia is awful. She hates the nursing home, but she couldn't live alone safely, and I'm still working full-time, so I can't move her into my tiny place with my husband, two cats, and a dog, either."

"This is best, Gretta. Your mom wouldn't want to turn your whole life upside down." Molly gave her a neighborly hug. "My kids know I never want to be a burden. When I'm too old and sick to take care of myself, I understand where I belong. As long as they love me, that's all I need."

"I hope my mom understands. It's hard to tell . . . her moods shift. She can be mean."

Steffi couldn't help but relate to Gretta's mom and the sense of vulnerability and panic that accompanies mental lapses.

"Fear can make us mean. Don't take it personally," Molly suggested. "I'll stop by and visit her this week."

"She'd love that, Molly." Gretta dug her keys out of her purse. "Well, I'd better get on with the day. Good luck with the renovations."

Steffi shook off her personal concerns. "Come by anytime and check on the progress, Gretta. I'd love to see what you think when I'm all finished."

"I will, you can count on that." She smiled.

They all exited the law offices together. Then Molly and Steffi waved Gretta off.

"See you at your house." Steffi jangled her new house keys and shoved them into her pocket before opening the van door.

"I think I'll bring home some doughnuts to throw Mick off any scent he might have." Molly smiled. "Toodles!"

Steffi nearly trembled from the thrill of owning the Weber house. Her childhood dream come true, right there in black and white on the deed. She was half tempted to play lotto—her only chance of buying the house for herself.

When she got to the Quinn house, she lugged the paint cans out of the back of the van. After she painted the family room, Claire would have the drapes installed and new furnishings delivered by the end of the week.

In her career, she'd worked on more complex and challenging projects, but none had produced so many positive changes in her life. Happiness bubbled inside, thanks to her good fortune. To be reunited with Ryan and the Quinns. To become acquainted with Emmy, which had been a pure pleasure until this weekend. To see a future filled with hope. All because of good timing and Molly's scheming.

As she stood there with the sunlight pouring through the windows, warming her skin, Steffi wished she could build something to contain all her joy so it wouldn't disappear.

"Oh, this shade of gray is almost pearlescent. It's perfect! Look at how well it goes with the stone floor. I can't wait to get the area rug down. We picked a gorgeous Surya blue-and-gray Tibetan carpet." Claire glanced around the space as if mentally placing the charcoal corduroy sectional, reclaimed-wood coffee table, and nickel-coated standing lamps she'd chosen. "It'll be cozy yet elegant. Molly will love it."

"I'm glad you're satisfied with the color. I was worried it wouldn't have enough oomph for you."

"It's exactly what I wanted. Is Molly here?" Claire asked. "I have a painting and wall hanging in the car for her approval."

"I'm right here," Molly called from a corner of the kitchen not visible from the family room. "Should I come take a look now?"

"Yes, if you don't mind. I can return them before the stores close if you don't like either." Claire took her keys from her purse.

"Let's have a look." Molly followed Claire out the back door.

Steffi had finished cleaning the sprayer and sealing the paint cans when she heard Emmy go into the kitchen. She thought to invite Emmy in to see the progress but decided to wait her out. She might not have a lot of experience with kids, but they were just little people. *All* people had a lot in common when it came to trust and friendship. One thing Steffi did know was that those two things must be earned, not forced.

Emmy did eventually wander to the doorway, eating from a bag of pretzels. She wrinkled her nose and shook her head. "It would've been prettier if it had been pink or yellow."

Steffi smiled. "If I recall, your dad said you could paint your bedroom pink. I'd be happy to teach you to do that when you're ready."

Emmy's gaze narrowed, torn between wanting to say yes and resisting the demise of her nuclear family. "Maybe."

Steffi hesitated, wanting to ask Emmy questions. Instead, she wound the hose of the sprayer and continued cleaning up her work space, pretending not to care whether Emmy wanted to speak with her.

"What's that?" Emmy asked, now stepping into the room.

She covered a smile. "It's a sprayer. It's a quick way to paint walls, although I'll still paint the trim with a brush."

Emmy's gaze remained fixed on the equipment. "If we paint my room, would we use the sprayer?"

We. A positive sign. Steffi must be doing this right. "Yes, on the walls."

"Would you let me use it?" She finally made eye contact with Steffi.

"I'd show you how, and we could see how it goes. It's not as easy as it looks and takes practice. You don't want your walls to have drips or globs or an uneven tone, right?"

"No," Emmy said.

Steffi continued to act as if they hadn't had the bad experience at the fair. Avoidance was something she'd always done well, after all.

Molly and Claire came back inside carrying the artwork. "Oh, Emmy. You're home. What do you think of these?" Molly asked her granddaughter.

"I like that one." Emmy pointed at an abstract gray, blue, and pink impasto painting.

"Me too," Molly agreed. "It'll look especially nice on that wall."

Emmy nodded and then, apparently bored with the conversation, asked, "What's for dinner?"

"You pick. Your father has other plans for dinner, and Grandpap doesn't care. I've been busy today, so I haven't made anything yet. We could just have hamburgers and Tater Tots."

"Yes, that!" Emmy jumped. "And no salad."

"Carrots?" Molly suggested.

Emmy wrinkled her nose. "I'm not a rabbit."

"Let's go find a compromise vegetable and let these ladies finish their work." Molly scooted Emmy back into the kitchen.

Steffi noticed Molly hadn't mentioned that Ryan's dinner plans involved her, so she kept quiet.

"I'll see you at home tonight?" Claire asked. She and Steffi hadn't spoken about the Logan run-in since it had happened, but Claire seemed to have found her way past it. Perhaps her mom and chocolate really did work miracles. Steffi wouldn't know about that kind of comfort. It'd been too long since she'd had a mother to lean on.

"I'm leaving here to check on the Hightop crew, then heading over to the bungalow to start demo. Probably won't get home until nine or so."

"While I'm here, let me do a quick run through the Weber home so I can start thinking up ideas." Claire shrugged, accepting defeat. "Might as well get excited about it now that we've taken the leap."

"Yay!" Steffi clapped her on the shoulder. "You're going to fall in love."

Ryan returned from the Hartford Correctional Center and climbed the stairs to his office. His shoelace had come untied, his coat unbuttoned, and his tie loosened. Some days this job got the better of him, but he'd have to pull it together for a meeting with his boss in twenty minutes.

When he arrived at his desk, he dropped his briefcase on the floor and hung his jacket on the back of his chair before slouching into it and turning on his computer. A manila envelope with his first name written in black Sharpie sat on top of his keyboard.

He turned it over, finding no note, return address, or anything else to identify its contents or who delivered it. The last thing he wanted was another unexpected surprise in his shitty day.

Using the letter opener from the desk set Val had given him when he got his first job, he opened the envelope and pulled out a police report. A quick scan of the header proved it to be *the* police report. The one he'd asked Billy to filch before he rescinded his request.

He slammed it facedown on his desk and stared blankly at the wall. His entire body went cold while his heart gathered speed in his chest. He froze like a man in the middle of a high-wire act when a stiff wind blew. What had he done? Reading the file would be a gross violation of Steffi's privacy. It'd transform him into what he'd always disdained—someone who believed that the ends justified the means.

Damn it, he regretted having the option to confirm his worst fear. If Billy had planned to ignore Ryan's wishes, he should've absolved Ryan from making the choice by simply blurting out the information. Now Ryan would have to cross the line if he wanted the answer.

Staring at the back of the report, Ryan had never felt more alone. He couldn't talk it through with anyone—save Billy. Couldn't ask his mother for advice. Couldn't predict how Steffi would react to the evidence.

He tossed the file in the trash and stared at it.

His thoughts churned, starting with Claire's concerns that Steffi's behavior was affecting their business. He sifted through his own experience with the staggering range of her mental lapses: small zone-outs in the backyard and by the lake, her freak-out when things between them got physical, and the fainting spell that caused her to lose track of Emmy.

If there was an answer in that report that would lead to healing—to a healthier, safer life for her and for them—he owed it to everyone to discover the truth. In this extreme case, perhaps the ends did justify the means.

Before he could talk himself out of it again, he snatched the file from the trash and flipped the pages over.

He'd read thousands of police reports, known dozens of sexual assault claims. Seen photographs and descriptions of the injuries inflicted on those victims. Reviewed the evidence collected by sexual assault evidence kits.

In all prior cases, it had been easy to dissociate from the faceless victims. *This* report discussed Steffi's brutal attack. Her body. Her injuries.

Her blood alcohol level had been elevated. The report stated she'd been highly disturbed yet groggy, with little memory of anything, including being found in the alley and put in the ambulance. She'd consented to letting the cops speak with the

ER doctor, who said she saw physical evidence of rape, but Steffi had, in a state of bewilderment, declined the rape kit. Steffi never mentioned rape to the officer, and he didn't suggest it so as not to taint her statement. Without a rape kit, they lacked DNA evidence to track the suspects. And with Steffi's relative incoherence and inability to recall specific details about the perps or anything else, they had little to nothing to go on.

Ryan couldn't push away images of her struggling to defend herself against two strange men, or her panic and rage as they forced themselves on her. He thought of the abject fear at having a gun held to one's head, and the pain of being knocked unconscious with it so the perps could escape. The idea of her being violated, humiliated, beaten, and left unconscious proved too much for him.

He heaved, swallowing back bile, but then reached for the trash can again and threw up. He'd never be able to unsee the photographs of her swollen eye and bruising. Never stop picturing the assault. And now he wondered if he'd be able to help her be whole again. He knew nothing about helping a person recover from that kind of trauma, including whether it was even possible.

His stomach turned again, but then sorrow hardened into fury. The justice system he believed in had failed her, and nothing he could do now would change that. Maybe she'd be better off not knowing the truth if, in fact, she didn't remember.

He inhaled slowly several times to control his racing thoughts and search for solutions. Steffi might never be "the same," but she wasn't broken. She'd moved on, whether through denial or repression. Could he move on in silence? Leave the truth alone and let her manage the blackouts?

It seemed too big a secret to keep. It would be between them now if he didn't tell her what he knew. Secrets like this could destroy a relationship.

He couldn't offer closure, but he could give her love and support. He scrolled through his contacts to find the number for Melissa Mathers, a psychiatrist he'd worked with on a few cases in Boston.

"Dr. Mathers," she answered.

"Hi, Dr. Mathers. This is Ryan Quinn, from the PD's office."

"Mr. Quinn, how can I help you?"

"I'm actually calling on a personal matter. Can you spare a few minutes to give me some advice?"

"Sure."

She remained eerily quiet while he laid out the facts of Steffi's situation.

"I can't offer a diagnosis based solely on what you've told me. It's possible she doesn't recall the sexual assault—or has an extremely fragmented, foggy recollection that's more like a dream than reality. That can happen for a variety of reasons, and there's still a lot we don't understand about how the brain processes trauma. It's also rare but possible for someone to dissociate from an extremely traumatic event. They will tend to use distancing language, referring to it as the 'event' or 'incident.' They'll avoid talking about it at all costs. Her history of concussions further complicates the matter." Melissa went into more detail about the amygdala, the prefrontal cortex, and other mechanics of what happens when your brain is in survival mode. He took notes, but his eyes kept straying to the police report, and then his stomach would burn. "I wouldn't recommend you go charging at her with these records. Get her to a doctor who can help her access and process the memories."

"I've tried, but she doesn't believe in therapy, and she doesn't think she needs it because, in her mind, she was only mugged. How will I convince her to go without telling her what I know?"

"Keep pressing the safety angle with respect to the blackouts. I can give you a few referrals."

"I'm not in Boston anymore. I'm in Connect-icut."

"A classmate of mine who specializes in trauma recovery is at Yale, if that's not too far from you."

Ryan scribbled down the contact info, thanked her for her time, and made another call. Once again he felt the hand of fate intervene. A cancellation enabled him to set up an appointment for Steffi the next day. Now he just had to get her there.

He'd do his best not to mention the file, but failing that, he'd confess what he'd done, stay with her until morning, and pray that the right kind of help could save them both. After weeks of having little to no control over so much in his life, it did feel good to finally have a plan.

He'd forgiven her mistakes, so she should forgive him this one time, especially because he'd only gone behind her back to help her.

Ryan barely muddled through his meeting with his boss, knowing that what Billy had done for him could get them in hot water. He pulled up to his mother's house, still debating his options.

His mother would know how to coax Steffi into therapy. He trusted her judgment, and she knew Steffi well. But disclosing the deeply personal history would be an even worse betrayal than what he'd already done, so he was out of luck and on his own. He popped another Pepcid and wandered toward the house.

Steffi expected him and a pizza at the Weber bungalow soon. He didn't have much time to prepare.

"Dad!" Emmy called when he came inside. "I

thought you weren't having dinner with us. We're making burgers and Tots."

"I can smell them." He kissed her head and squeezed her extra hard. God help anyone who ever hurt his daughter. He wanted to bundle her up away from the violent world to a place where she wouldn't know betrayal or harm of any kind. "I'm actually meeting Steffi in a bit. She needs my help . . ."

His voice had cracked, so he swallowed.

Emmy cocked her head like a puppy dog. Her small brown brows pinched together as she touched his face. "You look sad."

He took her fingers and kissed them. "I had a hard day."

"Then stay home now." She hugged him. "We can play a game."

He held her tight and kissed her head. "Tomorrow, okay? I promised Steffi I'd help her work on that cottage at the end of the lane. She's starting to take out all the old stuff so she can fill it with pretty new things."

It helped to think of what he planned to do as being like Steffi's work. Breaking down her mental block so that, with love and therapy, they could rebuild her wounded parts into something even stronger and more beautiful.

"Can I help?"

"Not tonight. There will be lots of ways you can help in the coming months." He smiled, grateful

414

that his daughter's frosty attitude toward Steffi might begin to thaw. Hopefully, Steffi wouldn't give them both the cold shoulder after she learned what he'd done. If so, he might not forgive himself for hurting his daughter again, too. "I need to change my clothes. Finish up your homework after dinner. When I get home, maybe we'll have time for a story or something."

"Okay." Emmy heaved an exaggerated sigh before bounding back to the kitchen.

He climbed the stairs, the task ahead dragging at him, not nearly as clear-cut in reality as it had been in theory. Few things in life ever were.

When he came back downstairs, his mother was folding a throw and laying it over the back of the sofa. "Emmy says you're off to the Weber house to help Stefanie now."

"Yep." He avoided making eye contact because his hawk of a mom would know something was wrong if she studied him too closely.

"Such a quaint old house. You really ought to buy it so you'd have privacy with the convenience of being neighbors."

"You're worse than Steffi with that refrain." He finally looked at her, a faint smile lifting the corners of his mouth.

"Great minds." She winked. "When you get back, your dad wants help moving our dresser. The family room project has inspired me to do a little rearranging elsewhere."

"This could be a late night. How about tomor-row?" He tucked the rolled-up report into his barn coat. "I'm late, so I'll see you later."

"Have fun!" she called out as he closed the door.

Fun? Not likely.

He'd consider it a victory if he returned home with his body and heart intact.

Chapter Twenty-One

Ryan strode up the porch steps of the bungalow that had been his and Steffi's dream home. Like most teens, he'd been certain of everything despite knowing almost nothing.

At thirty-one, he'd learned that dreams without commitment were just fanciful wishes. There was no foolproof plan to turn a dream into reality, either, because events beyond your control could force choices that pushed it out of reach. Even now, his good intentions threatened to destroy his new reality.

He knocked on the door before opening it and poking his head inside. "Steffi?"

"In here!" Her voice rang out from the vicinity of the kitchen before she triggered an electric screwdriver. Her jubilant tone gave him a pause. *But the appointment tomorrow . . .*

Dread and doubt shackled his ankles, slowing his trek through the living and dining rooms. When he arrived at the kitchen, Steffi was pulling a narrow upper cabinet off the wall.

"Need help?" he asked, reaching out.

"Nah," she grunted while navigating the cabinet to the ground without dropping it. "I've got this one."

Here, relaxed and doing work she loved, she

looked invincible—unlike a woman whose body had been abused. Images of her bruised legs and battered head flashed through his thoughts, prompting yet another moment of intense hatred of the men who'd brutalized her.

When she turned to greet him, her cheerful face penetrated his heart like that drill on the counter. He strode to her without a word and wrapped her in a hug.

"I like this greeting," she mumbled against his chest. He could practically feel her smiling as she snuggled inside his embrace. "But where's the pizza? The rumbling in my stomach might bring the walls down. That'd require a little more reno than I can afford."

He squeezed her harder, as if his holding her tight might keep her—and them—from breaking. In truth, he might be trying to keep himself from falling apart before he finished what he'd come here to say.

"What's going on?" she asked, her playful tone slipping to concern. "Did something happen today?"

He shook his head—not that she could see it. His throat constricted, cutting off all words.

She stroked his cheek. "Something did happen. I can tell. Is Emmy okay? Did you argue with Val?"

"No." His voice wavered. He paused, reticent to upend her whole world. "They're both fine."

"Then, what?" She held his face with both hands, her thumbs stroking his cheeks.

He glanced around, searching in vain for some-place comfortable to sit and talk. The dim, empty old rooms foretold disaster, but he couldn't turn back now. Like Pandora, he had to face the consequences of his curiosity. "We need to talk."

She stepped back and hugged herself. "Uh-oh."

"No, not like that." He reached for her hands.

"You're making me nervous. I've never seen you look so . . . so sick." She kept hold of his hands and jiggled his arms. "Just spit it out."

If only it were that simple. He had rehearsed this in his head, but in person, nothing he'd planned seemed right.

"First, I need to tell you that I love you."

The unplanned declaration lit her eyes and surprised them both. He would've rather not made that declaration now, when something so explosive would quickly overshadow the beauty of the moment. Yet nothing he'd said in recent weeks or months had rung as true in his heart.

"That must sound strange after so little time . . . two dates?" He kissed her hands. "It hit the instant I saw you on my mom's porch, but at the time, it filled me with anger. The resurgence of old feelings after the way you'd hurt me made me feel pathetic, so I pushed you away for a dozen reasons, including fear."

"Fear?"

"Of being hurt again. Of being foolish . . ." He shrugged. "But then you called me out and asked to be friends. Inserted yourself into Emmy's life and eventually mine. You're so bold. And brave."

"I haven't felt very brave. Desperate, maybe, for this second chance. Grateful, recently." She tugged him close and kissed him. "I've been holding my breath since that dance at the Sand Bar. I love you, too, Ryan. I know I hurt you before, but there's nothing to fear now. The worst is behind us."

He closed his eyes, but the worst stared right back at him anyway. He opened his eyes and hugged her again, delaying the conversation that could change everything between them. "You *are* brave. Beautiful. Strong. Talented. Fun. Invincible. You can handle anything. Together we can help each other through any crisis."

He held her face and kissed her. Tender, desperate kisses. He must've been frowning, though, because worry shone in her eyes.

"Now you're scaring me again." She studied his face, pressing her fingertips against the worry lines on his forehead. "Something really bad has happened. Are you sick?"

"I'm fine." He swallowed hard and stepped back to pace, as if walking around would jostle her into opening up. "Do you trust me?"

"Of course."

"So you know that you can tell me anything.

Confide anything." He bit his lower lip, searching her expression for any hint of her thoughts. "Because after our past and Val's betrayal, I need to know you won't withhold things from me."

She hugged herself again. "It sounds like you still think I'm keeping something from you."

He stood motionless, almost wishing she were lying, because if she remembered anything, this would be much easier to handle. The manila folder in his pocket grew heavier by the second. "Not on purpose . . . but I don't think these blackouts are due to concussions. So, if there's more to say—if there are things that trouble you or have been on your mind—just know nothing you tell me will change how I feel about you."

She took a step back and let her hands come to rest on her hips. "I've no clue what you're fishing for, Ryan."

Clear eyes, direct gaze, no fidgeting. She mustn't remember. Dammit, that made this conversation nearly impossible. "Okay, then . . . I think your episodes relate to what happened last spring, and maybe you're avoiding therapy because you don't want to be forced to think about it."

Her expression turned flinty. "Why do you keep bringing that night up?"

"Because we need to get to the root of what's messing with your life, and this problem started after that night."

Her eyes glittered. "I've gone to the doctor. *He*

didn't dismiss my theory. As for that night, I've told you all the important details."

"I know you believe that, but . . ." He held a deep breath before exhaling. "I've made an appointment with a therapist in New Haven for tomorrow. Dr. Alana Saxe. She specializes in helping trauma victims process fragmented memories."

"I'm *not* a victim." She jerked her arms out from her sides. "I'm living my life just fine, thank you very much."

"I disagree." He stood still. His heart pounded with each word that brought him closer to disclosing what he knew. The ugly truth he didn't want to reveal.

"That's your problem."

"It's *our* problem. What affects you affects me. All I'm asking is that you go talk to this doctor. See if she can help. Wouldn't you be more confident and comfortable if you could control these episodes or, better yet, end them? It'd be safer for you, and better for your business."

"And better for you," she spat. "Don't leave that out, Ryan."

He sighed. "You say that like I don't have any stake in this. But how can we have a healthy relationship if you hit me when we get close? How can I trust you with Emmy if I can't count on you to be present when watching her? It's your health, but my feelings count for something, don't they? I'm only asking you to talk to an expert and deal with the pain of what happened."

"I dealt with it. It's *over,* and so is this tired argument."

Stubborn as ever. Sometimes he found the trait endearing, like he did with Emmy. In this case, it was downright dangerous. She could hurt herself or someone else if one of those trances struck at the wrong time. He had no choice now.

The air inside the tiny bungalow turned thick and sour as he reached into his pocket and removed the manila folder. He set it on the counter. It took him a few seconds to remove his hand and remember to breathe.

"What's that?" She crossed her arms.

"The police report. The one from your . . . attack."

Her gaze homed in on the envelope, then darted back to his face. "Did they catch someone? Are *you* representing the guys who robbed me?"

"No. This isn't about my job, and there still aren't any suspects." He watched her pace in a tight circle, not even knowing what he hoped to see. If he'd thought the mention of the report would help his cause, he was wrong.

"Maybe your job has warped your perspective, and that's why you can't let *me* move on." Steffi's cheeks turned red. Perspiration dampened her skin.

"That's not it. I'm trying to help you." Resorting to coercion hadn't been his plan. The brutish tactic slid through his gut, making him sick. Weakening him such that he had to grasp the counter for support.

"Help me? By sneaking around my back?" Her deflection reminded him of how Emmy responded to being cornered. His stomach burned. He didn't want to say the words, because he had no idea how to hold her together once he did.

"I'm sorry, but I'm desperate." He closed his eyes for a second time, steeling himself to voice the truth. "You need therapy."

Her gaze darted back to the envelope. Then she shook her head.

"Steffi, meet with Dr. Saxe," he pleaded. "Please, just trust me."

"Trust?" Her breath became more rapid. "That's pretty rich coming from the guy who went behind my back."

"I needed to confirm my suspicions." He took a step toward her, but she stepped back. "Now I have proof."

"Proof of what?" Her curt tone warned him to tread lightly, but there was no turning back now.

He needed to regroup. Calm her down.

"First, come here." He opened his arms for a hug. "Let me hold you."

She shook her head more and backed up until her butt hit the counter. He didn't like boxing her in, but at least he could embrace her that way. Despite her wriggling, he pressed her to his chest, clasping her head firmly with one hand and locking his free arm around her back. His strength enabled him to keep her safely wrapped in his arms.

He kissed her temple and then murmured in her ear, grateful she wouldn't have to make eye contact with him while he told her what he knew. "Steffi, I know the truth. I know what really happened, and I can't pretend I don't now. I can't sweep it under the rug. Do you understand what I'm saying?"

"No." She shivered.

This was not how he'd wanted the evening to go, but at least if she heard it from him, she'd know, absolutely, that nothing would change his love for her. "I wish you never had to think about that night again as long as you lived. To have suffered a trauma so horrific that you've buried the memory is unimaginable. But you're not alone. Dr. Saxe specializes in sexual assault survivorship and—"

"What?" She shoved him away with such force, he stumbled. She stretched out her arms to keep him back. Her haunted face turned ruddier by the second. "Was this a revenge plan all along? Lull me into feeling safe and then make me doubt my own sanity?"

"Of course not! I love you. I'm trying to help."

"I didn't ask for your help." She stood there, her body trembling.

"You never ask anyone for help, but that doesn't mean you don't need it. Let's focus on the good news—there's help available." He picked up the envelope and held it out. "We have to face this, though. I'll stay with you tonight and drive you to Dr. Saxe's office tomorrow. I'll be with you every step of the way."

She snatched the envelope and flung it across the room. "I don't need a savior. I need someone who trusts me. And someone *I* can trust."

"*I* need someone who's open to my concerns so we can build something real together instead of something built on sand. Someone who wants answers so she won't hit me when I kiss her. Someone who won't hurt herself or my daughter in a stupor because she's too stubborn to get help." Ryan reached for her again, but she dodged him. "Steffi, don't run again. Please let's handle this like two people who love each other should. Remember we said 'different better'? That's what this is. Help me help you. For yourself, and for Emmy and me."

"If you loved me, you wouldn't sneak behind my back. You wouldn't demand I do things your way or force me to remember something awful or confirm a prognosis I don't want to hear." Tears streamed down her face as she trembled. "I'm not crazy. I'd remember if I was raped, for God's sake. Get out, Ryan. Get out!"

She'd said the word—shouted it, actually—yet

it didn't seem to register. She still looked wild-eyed with rage and denial, despite the envelope on the floor.

He reached out to grab her, but she jumped sideways. He stood still and opened his arms wide. "Okay. Calm down. We won't talk about it anymore tonight, but I'm not leaving you alone like this. We can tear out these cabinets and see how you feel in the morning."

"I don't need time. Get out and take that damn file." When he didn't move, she screamed, "I mean it! Go or I'll leave."

"Steffi, please . . ." He'd bungled this as badly as possible. Instead of making it better, he'd made it all worse. Maybe even damaged her more. Warm tears stung his eyes.

She snatched her keys off the counter and dashed out the back door. He chased after her, but she slammed the van door shut and turned on the engine before he caught up to her. She backed out of the driveway while he banged on the side panel. The tires kicked up pebbles as she sped away.

"Fuck!" he shouted at the moon.

Once again, Steffi ran from him. Last time, he'd let her go. This time he would not. He jogged back to his mom's to get his car, dialing Steffi's number while he pulled out of the driveway. Voice mail.

A quick drive-by of her dad's home and Benny's

apartment turned up empty. No surprise, actually. She wouldn't turn to them—or anyone—for comfort. He reversed course and drove past her house, relief slackening his shoulders when he saw her van parked out front.

He sprang from his car, trotted up her porch steps, and banged on the door. "Steffi, let me in!"

He heard scuffling from inside.

Claire answered. "Ryan, what happened?"

"Where's Steffi?" He craned his neck, looking over her shoulder.

"She charged in like a wild animal and went straight to her room." She stood in the doorway. "Obviously, you two had a fight."

"Can you let me in? I need to talk to her."

Claire stood aside and waved him in. He took the stairs two at a time and strode to the only room with a closed door. With his forehead pressed to the door panel, he spoke in a calm voice. "Steffi. Let me in. Please."

"Go away."

He flattened his hands against the doorframe and closed his eyes. "I'm sorry. I'm so sorry about how I handled this. I can't undo that, but please don't shut me out again. Even if you deserve to, don't. Please. I love you."

Silence.

"Steffi." He tried the doorknob, but she'd locked it. After a few minutes of waiting, he gave her the space she wanted and wandered back downstairs. She was safe—at least physically safe—for now. Whether he'd caused more harm than good had yet to be determined.

"What's going on?" Claire asked.

"Try to keep her from leaving tonight. Text me if she goes out." He turned and walked out the door without another word.

His whole body ached from regret. When he got home, he walked down the street to the bungalow, which they'd left unlocked in their hasty retreat. He went inside and stowed her tools. Before he turned off the lights, he picked up the discarded envelope from the floor. After rummaging through her tool kit for a pencil, he wrote on the outside of the envelope.

Steffi,
I'm sorry I hurt you. I do love you, despite how it might feel right now. Nothing in this file changes who you are to me, and I promise I'll be with you through this process if you let me.
Love, Ryan

He scribbled Dr. Saxe's phone number and address beneath the note, set the envelope on the counter where she would see it, then shut the lights off and locked the door behind him on his way out.

He kicked some acorns around the sidewalk as

he wandered back to his mom's, wishing he had persuaded Steffi to meet Dr. Saxe without using that file. Now he'd have to live with the fact that he'd likely destroyed their last chance at a happy ending. That would be easier to accept if he knew Steffi would get better.

"Want to tell me what happened last night?" Claire asked while fixing herself a bowl of oatmeal. "I heard you throw up twice. You look like you didn't sleep a wink. I'm worried."

Steffi hadn't been able to breathe all night, which meant she couldn't form a coherent response this morning. Now it seemed as if her legs were filled with cement as she dragged herself to the coffee maker.

Claire sat at the breakfast bar while Steffi poured herself a cup of coffee. "Obviously, the demo date with Ryan didn't go well."

"Don't say his name." Steffi blew into her coffee. She couldn't close her eyes without thinking of him pleading with her, arms open, eyes full of sorrow and certainty. Images she'd rather forget, along with the dark trepidation about her "fragmented" memory.

"Oh boy, this sounds bad." Claire added more almonds to her cereal. "Will you have to see him today, or did you finish the Quinn project?"

Work. Her one salvation—a way of putting this all out of her mind.

"I'll send JT to paint the trim. Then it's done." Thank God she'd hired a small crew the other week. "I'll manage Hightop today with Rick so it doesn't fall off schedule."

"Okay, but won't Molly be disappointed not to see you at the end of her project?" Claire spooned an extra lump of brown sugar into her bowl and stirred.

Reconnecting with Molly had been one of the most wonderful things the past seven weeks had provided. Now they'd live through another rift. This one, however, was all on Ryan. "I'll call and explain that I've got to keep other projects moving."

Claire gave her the side-eye while she ate.

"What?" she barked, refusing to defend yet another decision.

Claire swallowed her oatmeal before speaking. "I can't imagine what Ryan did to make you this angry."

"He betrayed me, that's what!" Steffi clamped her mouth closed, wishing she hadn't said anything.

"He cheated?" Claire's expression melted into a scowl. "Good Lord, what's wrong with the world when even Ryan Quinn two-times?"

"He didn't cheat. He invaded my privacy. Said . . . things I wish he hadn't. Things I don't want to know. Things that can't be right." Coffee sloshed over the side of her cup, so she set it down and wrung her hands together to stop them from shaking. She couldn't wrap her head around what he'd said. Could her mind really block that trauma out even *after* hearing it laid out with such certainty?

Claire set down her spoon. "I know you don't want to talk about it, but you're literally shaking. Talk to me, Steffi. You can't work in this condition."

Steffi's breaths came up short, just like they had every time she thought about what he'd done. About what he must've read in that report. About what her own brain would not let her see.

She remembered a gun. Fuzzy snippets. Flash images of the hospital and cops. Someone handed her water when she spoke to an officer, but she recalled nothing of what was said. She'd called her work friend Jenny to take her home from the hospital. The two weeks following the incident, she'd been on bed rest, cocooned in a dark room for the concussion. Her whole body had ached from the inside out, but time had passed in a blur of sleep and confusion. In the absence of actual memories, her imagination now conjured the worst possible scenarios.

It must've been beyond gruesome for her to bury it so deeply that she couldn't recall it even now. Why would Ryan *want* her to remember something so awful? "He got his hands on the police report—my report, from last spring."

"Was he assigned the case?" Claire frowned. "Wouldn't he have to recuse himself?"

"There is no case because there aren't any arrests." That had bothered her enough when she'd thought it was a mugging. Two rapists getting off scot-free? She ground her teeth and twisted her fingers so tight they turned white. "He had a theory so he somehow got hold of the file."

He'd never been one to break the rules before. She could report him if she wanted to spite him.

Claire shifted on her stool to face Steffi. "A theory about who did it?"

"No . . . about what happened."

"I don't understand." Claire frowned.

Ryan's desolate words seeped into her mind, saturating her with sorrow. She hesitated, afraid that saying them would make them more true—not that "more true" was a thing. Truth was truth, and until she read that file, she wouldn't know all of it.

"He thought—thinks—that . . . that I . . . I was ra—" Steffi's mouth filled with a bitter tang. She clutched the table as if to stop her body from slipping away from her.

Cigarette smoke.

Keep fucking quiet, bitch.

"Steffi?" Claire's voice cut through Steffi's thoughts.

Steffi released the table and swallowed bile.

"Did you say . . . 'raped'?" Claire's face paled and her lips parted. "Is it true?"

433

I guess so!

"Does it matter?" Steffi sniveled, swiping a tear from her cheek. "The point is that he violated my privacy. He's as bad as the criminals he represents." She stood abruptly, fleeing Claire's pitying stare, and dumped the rest of her coffee down the drain.

"Wait, Stefanie. Just . . . if you don't want to talk about the . . . thing, then let's talk about why Ryan did this."

"He thinks my blackouts will stop if I go to therapy to cope with . . . it."

"So he thinks the blackouts are what? Repressed memories poking through?"

"Basically." She closed her eyes and shook her head as if shaking off snow. "I don't know and I don't care. How does his force-feeding me horrible news make anything better? Isn't an occasional zone-out better than remembering something awful!" Her voice had risen to a screech. "How is *this* news better?"

Claire hugged her, which was unusual for both of them. But Steffi melted into her arms and broke into deep sobs.

"Oh, Steffi. I'm sorry. I'm so sorry. I don't know what else to say. How can I help?"

She couldn't. No one could. If Ryan's claims were true, would she ever see herself the same? Her body? Sex? A thousand hot showers wouldn't make her feel less dirty even though she still couldn't remember. If those memories came back, she might never fully recover. "I hate him."

Claire stroked Steffi's hair. "Don't hate him. He didn't do this to hurt you."

"Don't defend him!" Steffi broke free of Claire's hold.

"Steffi, his intentions matter. He's trying to help because he cares. Isn't that what you've wanted all this time?"

"I'm telling you, Claire, this house is a Ryan-free zone."

Claire cocked a brow and crossed her arms. "So you expect me to talk *about*—and *to*—Peyton, but you won't discuss or talk to Ryan? Tell me you see the hypocrisy. At least Ryan had your best interests at heart, unlike Peyton, who only cared about herself."

"How is it loving to demand I go to therapy in order to have a relationship with him?"

"He said that?" Claire's brows shot upward.

"Not in those words, but he's worried about everyone's safety. He even made an appointment with someone for this morning, but I'm not going. I already left a message with the doc and then texted Ryan not to bother showing up here to take me."

Claire clapped her hands to her cheeks. "The thing with Emmy must've really scared him."

Steffi couldn't deny *that*. "It scared me, too. That still doesn't give him the right to do what he did."

Claire approached her like a child trying to capture a butterfly. "I know you don't want to hear this, but just because he went about it wrong doesn't mean it can't help you."

"Don't start!" How could she talk to a therapist about something she didn't even remember? Didn't *want* to remember, either. "I have to go to work. Please don't mention this to anyone."

"Of course not, but is that best? I have to be honest. Seeing you, listening to you today . . . however you got to this place, focus on the positive. This means it *can* get better, Steffi. You just need to talk to someone who knows how to handle this. Go—go to the appointment. I'll come if you want."

"It's my life, Claire. I don't need you or Ryan making decisions for me, okay?"

Claire raised her hands. "Okay. Sorry. But at least take the day off. I could hang out, we could rent movies and get ice cream or whatever."

"How many ways can I tell you and show you that I'll. Be. Fine." Steffi snatched her keys. "See you later."

She would be fine, too. No poking for pain on a shrink's sofa. No wallowing. Moving forward. Staying focused. It'd worked for her before, and it would work again. She could get right on her own. She didn't need Ryan. She didn't need anyone.

On her way toward the Hightop project, she

passed the cemetery where her mother was buried. That had been the hardest day of her life . . . until now. Despite her affirmations, she felt loss and lost, uncertain of everything. She couldn't even trust her own thoughts because, apparently, they were incomplete and unreliable.

Two blocks later, she made a U-turn and drove back to the cemetery. She'd visited her mother's grave a few times each year: the anniversary of her death, her birthday, and Christmas. On those occasions, the stoic Lockwoods would gather to talk about memories, and they'd carpet the ground in peonies—her mom's favorite flower.

They'd leave arm in arm as if they'd been at a party, none of them talking about how, each year, they wished she was there to mark a milestone or celebrate some occasion. How some nights they'd stare at the ceiling wondering if she could see them . . . or if a warm summer breeze or a butterfly on the car was a message. They never acknowledged the gaping hole in their lives that would always exist.

Today was the first time she'd ever come to her mom for advice. If she was already losing her mind, it couldn't hurt to try talking to ghosts.

She parked the car on the road and crossed to her mother's grave. The vase was empty. No flowers. No scarf tied around it. A few fallen leaves carpeted the ground and lay scattered on the headstone.

"Hi, Mom." Steffi sat cross-legged at the base of the marker, tracing the carvings that spelled out MARCH 17, 2001. She touched her forehead to the cold stone and closed her eyes. *Something bad has happened. So bad I don't even remember it. I've tried all night, but it's like a heavy, smoky veil is guarding the memory. The idea of it is terrifying enough, so it's probably better not to remember it.*

She opened her eyes and stared at her mother's name—MARGARET CATHERINE LOCKWOOD. *What if Ryan's right and I hurt myself or someone else during one of my zone-outs? And what if I can't have sex without getting violent or crazy or sad? I'm so mad at him for going behind my back and forcing this on me. And from now on, he'll look at me and imagine what happened. He'll never see me as me again. He'll think I'm broken. Violated. Soiled.*

Absently, she hugged her knees to her chest. *I was so happy before yesterday. Why did he have to ruin everything? What do I do, Mom? I can't stand this pain. I lose no matter what I choose. You were so brave when you dealt with your cancer. I wish I were more like you and less like Dad.*

She lay on the grass, touching the headstone, watching the swirl of clouds pass overhead. A few birds flew by. A hundred yards away, she noticed another mourner visiting a loved one, looking for solace.

But there wasn't solace here. No answers. Only bittersweet memories and wishes that would never come true. She didn't know what she would do with her new reality, but there were deadlines and bills and obligations that didn't care about how lousy and confused she felt.

Perhaps it wasn't fair to expect her mom or anyone else to hand her an answer. Like most things in life, she had to make her choices on her own. Other people's opinions wouldn't change the fact that she alone would live with the consequences. She smoothed her hand over the headstone one last time. *Bye, Mom.*

As she pulled away from the cemetery, she thanked God she had demolition work to do today. Few things offered as productive a way to unleash a lot of emotion as smashing through walls.

Chapter Twenty-Two

That evening, Steffi removed the final lower cabinet from the kitchen wall in the bungalow. Her phone vibrated on the counter. She'd answered none of the many messages Ryan had left for her throughout the day. Her graveside chat hadn't provided any answers, so she still had nothing to say.

Even if he spoke the truth, she wasn't ready for it. She didn't want to remember. And she sure as hell didn't want anyone else to find out. It would be bad enough knowing that every time Claire and Ryan looked at or thought of her, the first thing they'd think about would be rape. That made her want to vomit again.

She worked feverishly now, doing her best to preserve some of the cabinets for recycling while ignoring the manila envelope he'd left on the counter. The screen door clattered as autumn breezes blew through it, but none of them cooled the sweltering bungalow. She peeled her sweatshirt off, but that didn't help much, either.

A Limp Bizkit song began playing on the Bluetooth speaker she'd brought. She cranked the volume to drown out her thoughts and began headbanging to the heavy beat as she swept debris from the floor. She bagged up the unsalvageable splintered cabinets and dragged them outside to the small rented dumpster.

No moon tonight. Just pinpricks of light against a black sky. Beyond the trees were the glassy waters of the sound. A route to sail off to someplace new and start over. A place where she had no history to overcome.

While she heaved the first bag over the edge, footsteps and a snapped twig behind her made her freeze, breath burning her lungs.

I'm alone.

Please, God.

Oh God, a gun. A gun.

Be still.

Don't die. Don't die.

"Hey!"

At the sound of the male voice, Steffi spun and swung the bag of broken wood, clocking Benny in the head.

"Jesus!" he yelled from the ground, grabbing the side of his head.

"Oh God, Benny!" She collapsed beside him, crying. Adrenaline surged through her limbs until she trembled. "I didn't know it was you. I'm sorry. Are you okay?"

"What the hell, Steffi?" He pushed her away when she tried to see the lump forming on his temple. "I called your name twice."

She couldn't stop crying, even though she never cried in front of her brothers.

"You're crying? *I'm* the one who's hurt," Benny groused.

The leafless trees in the yard surrounded her like prison bars. Tears of shame choked off her words. Bone-deep fear—the thing she hated most— gripped her stomach and clenched hard. Ryan *was* right. She was a danger to herself and others.

"Sis, settle down," Benny said when she failed to pull herself together, misreading her misery as stemming solely from hurting him. "I'm okay. I just came by to razz you for blowing off my training run tonight. Dad said he hadn't seen you in days, either."

"I'm sorry." She wiped her eyes. Then another wave of tears crested and broke open. She couldn't control the wellspring of emotion.

"What's happening?" He scooted across the grass to sit beside her. "Are *you* hurt?"

She blinked at him, gulping down snot. "I'm in trouble, Benny. I don't know what to do."

Benny's puzzled expression morphed to concern as he hugged her. "What kind of trouble?"

She couldn't tell him. Couldn't face him if he knew. He'd never look at her the same. Neither would her dad. They'd be wrecked, and for what? They couldn't help her. She'd have to save herself.

"Sis, talk to me," he pleaded.

She hugged her knees to her chest. "Ryan and I had a fight."

"About what?"

"Trust." Not exactly a lie.

Benny's face pinched. "Ryan doesn't trust you?"

With good reason, she thought. Then again, he'd proved himself to be less than trustworthy, too. "It's complicated."

"You're not making any sense." Benny gently touched his goose egg, which had swelled to the size of a golf ball. "Damn, this hurts."

Taking full advantage of a way out of his interrogation, she pushed herself upright and motioned to help him up. "Maybe you should get that looked at. You could be concussed or worse."

He waved her off, like a good Lockwood would. No need for advice or help. Lockwoods could handle anything on their own. "I'm good. Now tell me what Quinn did to upset you."

"It's fine. I'm overreacting," she lied. "I can manage my own problems with Ryan, thanks."

Benny reverted to teasing, per their norm. "Must be pretty bad for you to cry like a girl."

She hiccupped. "I *am* a girl."

"Well, don't feel bad. Not like you had a choice." He yanked her ponytail.

His playful banter made her feel less the victim and more like her old self. That's all she wanted to be—just Steffi Lockwood. Not a victim. Not damaged.

"So how about tomorrow? Join me on a ten-miler? You can burn off all your tension."

"No." She glanced over her shoulder at the light shining through the screen door. "I'm too busy now with all these new projects."

"Aw, come on. You said you'd do this with me." He set his hands on his hips. "I can't believe you're quitting on me. This is like the time you said you'd help me remodel my kitchen and then left me hanging halfway through the job."

"I sent someone to help when I couldn't take enough time off work to finish."

"Not the point." Benny's accusation echoed Ryan's point about her spotty follow-through.

"I'm sorry, Benny. I can't be in two places at once."

"Always some excuse. Guess I'm on my own." He grimaced. "You seem better now, so I'll get going."

"See you later."

"Need an ice pack." He touched his head while walking away. "If I didn't know you loved me, I'd think you were trying to kill me."

"Need to work on my aim," she called, relieved that he hadn't pressed her more about her crying jag, yet saddened, too. And curious. Did everyone in her family keep secrets? What might Benny be hiding? And why hadn't she ever sought more from them?

She went back inside the house alone, still shaken. She didn't know how to lean on people. Or ask for help. Or be vulnerable. Those traits weren't conducive to intimacy. She'd never have any loving relationship without *that*.

The manila envelope mocked her. She stared at it, recalling Ryan's face last night. His tone. His contrition. His love. She picked it up and shoved it into her sweatshirt pocket. Undecided about whether she wanted to read it, she locked up the house and went home.

"You're back earlier than I expected," Claire said from the couch, where she'd curled up with her laptop. She set it aside. "How are you?"

God, she hoped that question didn't become a regular thing from Claire. Steffi sank onto a chair. "I almost killed Benny."

"What?" Claire's mouth fell open. "Is he okay? What happened?"

"He surprised me from behind. I hit him with a bag of broken wood."

"Oh, goodness." Claire slapped her forehead.

"He's okay, thankfully." Steffi tossed the envelope on the coffee table. "But I'm not."

Claire glanced at the folder. "Is that the report?"

She nodded without a word, picking at her cuticles without looking at Claire.

"Did you read it?" Claire asked.

She shook her head.

"Do you want *me* to read it?"

Steffi shook her head. "I don't want anyone to read it. I wish Ryan hadn't. I don't want you two to think of that when you look at me. Like I'm pathetic and helpless. Powerless. Victimized."

"I'm the last person who'd think of you that way." Claire sat forward. "I'm sorry it happened. I wish it hadn't. I wish I could change it or make it better." She paused. "But it isn't the defining thing about you unless *you* let it be. Trust me, Stef, I know something about this. And if you let this file—this history—be what keeps you from being healthy and happy with Ryan, then you're giving those creeps even more power over your life than what they took that one night."

Steffi slouched deeper into the chair. If only she could've remembered anything about those men, they might've been apprehended. Murky voices and the cold barrel of the gun pressed to her temple were all she could ever recall with clarity. They got away with everything because she couldn't—or wouldn't—remember more. "Maybe."

"Well, then, *maybe* you should consider talking to that doctor." Claire leaned forward.

Steffi's phone rang. She peeked at the screen.

"Who is it?" Claire asked.

"Ryan." Steffi tucked it back in her pocket.

Claire let loose a long sigh. "I know you think that ignoring this and moving on is being strong. But wouldn't it show more strength to accept—and even grieve—what's happened? Face it head-on with the therapist Ryan found. Don't let it destroy what you've rebuilt with him. Forgive him. Lean on him. That's not weak . . . that's love."

Steffi's lungs burned as if a heat lamp had been fired up inside her chest. She dabbed her eyes and reached for the file. "I'll think about it."

Her friend had survived a gunshot wound that had robbed her of her identity. She'd overcome losing her healthy, vital body and accepted a slightly disfigured, disabled one in its place. She'd learned to deal with people's pity. She'd found a way to claim some happiness. A career. Good relationships with friends and family. And even love, until Peyton interfered.

If Claire could overcome those setbacks, surely Steffi could come back from this. Somehow recognizing their similarities—sisters in survival—made her feel less alone and less pitiful.

Claire flashed an understanding smile. "Does chocolate help you think better? I always keep an emergency supply in my room, you know."

Of course she did.

Steffi managed a genuine smile for the first time in more than twenty-four hours. "Chocolate sounds good."

"I take it you looked over the proposal I sent you this morning?" Ryan lowered the speakerphone volume while seated in his car, staring down the lane toward the bungalow where Steffi's van was parked.

447

This morning the ground had been encased in frost, sort of like his chest and heart since their argument three nights ago. She'd refused all his calls this week, but at least she hadn't broken down or curled up into a ball and hidden away. He could march down the street and beg her to talk to him, but forcing her to do anything before she was ready felt like another violation.

"I'm surprised," Val said. "I thought you wanted to avoid paying alimony."

"I've been doing a lot of thinking, especially after our lunch conversation last weekend. About the sacrifices you made. The ways you tried to create a happy home. I didn't give you my best." The golden glow lighting the bungalow windows beckoned. What might Steffi do if he knocked on the door? He shifted in his seat and rested one hand on the steering wheel. "But I know and appreciate how hard you tried for so long. You deserve to know that much."

He didn't know what response he'd expected, but it hadn't been silence.

"What would this mean for you and Emmy?" Val finally asked. "Will you be able to afford your own place?"

His gaze veered back to the bungalow. He'd never afford it now. Not that Steffi would even want him to have it after the way he'd handled everything. "I'll stay with my mom awhile longer. I can probably get a better deal in December when fewer buyers are shopping for beach homes. There are some old places and town houses I might afford once I get my bearings."

"Ryan." A long sigh preceded her reply. "There was a time when I wanted to make you suffer because I hurt so much, but I'm letting go of resentment. I didn't exactly end our marriage respectfully. And I know my choices have made it harder on Emmy and you."

"We'll figure things out. She'll be okay."

"Truth is, I'm not a great mother. Even from the beginning, part of why I had Emmy was to hold on to you. I do love her, but I'm too needy right now to have enough left over to give her everything she needs. She's not my little baby doll anymore. She's growing up. You're better suited to make sure she's not insecure like me, especially when it comes to men. And John doesn't want kids." A soft sound puffed from her lips, and Ryan almost admired her brutally honest self-assessment. He didn't totally agree with her, but he believed that she thought she was doing what was best for Emmy. "When he got back from Nebraska, he told me he wants a real commitment once the divorce is final, so I'm going to take the plunge and remarry. You're off the hook for alimony, but let's split the assets fifty-fifty. When I start making money, I'll kick in something for child support."

He still wouldn't be able to afford the bungalow

if he wanted any money for other things, but he'd take the lucky break. It came on the heels of his other lucky break this week, when Billy found a prostitute willing to testify against O'Malley's accuser. Now he could get the DA to plea-bargain and bring closure to that case, much like the closure he and Val both needed with their divorce. "Never thought I'd say this—much less mean it—but I really hope you find what you've been looking for. What you deserve."

"I hope you do, too. Even if it's with Steffi."

"Thanks." The word felt thick as it tumbled from his lips. The irony that Val had found love while it still eluded him wasn't missed.

"I guess we're really done now."

Silence settled between them. He didn't want to remain married to her, yet they'd spent a decade of their lives together. Shared some good times alongside the not-so-good ones. He couldn't pretend no part of him mourned the life they'd tried to build.

"We'll never be *done*. We've got a daughter. We're still a family." He thought he might've heard a sniffle through the line. "You want to speak to Emmy before she goes to sleep?"

"Yes, please."

"Hang on." Ryan got out of his car and went inside to find Emmy. "Your mom wants to say good night."

He handed Emmy the phone and then turned to

go upstairs to change. He bumped into his mom and her mammoth basket of laundry near the top of the stairs.

"Let me." He took the heavy basket of warm, freshly folded clothes from her and walked to her room.

"Thanks, honey. Your dad always disappears whenever I start folding the laundry." She smiled, then studied him more closely and frowned. "You've looked like hell all week. Is Val giving you a hard time?"

"No." He set the basket on her bed. "Actually, we've come to a settlement agreement. She's been fair. Seems she and John will marry once our divorce is settled."

"Huh. Well, I guess the good news is that you'll be able to sort out your finances soon. Maybe you can buy that bungalow, after all. I'm sure Stefanie and Claire will work miracles." She separated the clothes into piles on her bed, consciously avoiding eye contact. "I've missed seeing her this week. She sent one of her employees to do the trim work so she could get a jump on that project."

He guessed his mom was fishing, but he wouldn't take the bait.

"She's got a lot going on." He started for his room, then turned. "I can't afford that bungalow, even with the settlement. It'd stretch me too thin, and I want to be able to afford to travel and do other things with Emmy. If it's okay with you, I'd like to stay here a few months while Emmy gets settled and adjusted. I'll try to get out of your hair after the holidays."

His mom opened a dresser drawer and loaded his dad's boxers inside. "You stay as long as you need. And who knows, maybe that bungalow won't be too expensive when all is said and done. Have faith."

Faith. He'd lost that along the way. Failed relationships. A daughter who struggled despite his best efforts. No clear answer on how to help Steffi now that she was refusing his calls.

Emmy wandered into his mother's room. "Here's your phone, Dad."

"Thanks." He stuffed it into his pocket before he noticed a worried look in her eyes. "Is something wrong?"

Emmy's gaze darted from him to his mom and back. "Is Miss Steffi mad at me?"

"What?" He sent his mom a questioning gaze, which she answered with a shrug.

"She hasn't come back in a few days. Doesn't she like me anymore?"

Shit. His daughter had lost another woman from her life because of him.

Emmy looked so small and vulnerable, but he couldn't confess the truth. "It's got *nothing* to do with you. She's very busy with lots of projects."

"Can we go look at the cottage now?" Emmy

452

made puppy-dog eyes at him. "You promised you'd take me one night."

He shook his head. "She's busy. We can't barge in without any warning—"

"She'd love to show you around," his mom interrupted. "In fact, you could take her some of the cookies we baked this afternoon. I'm sure she needs snacks to keep her energy up."

"Mom," Ryan began, then couldn't get out of it without raising a lot of questions he didn't want to answer.

"Oh, for Pete's sake. Go for five minutes." She strode out of the room. "Come on, Emmy. We'll put some cookies in a bag."

Five minutes later, Emmy raced ahead down the lane. He could see her breath fogging in a trail above her head, her curls bouncing with each step.

Meanwhile, his stomach twisted round and round until he thought it might saw through his skin. Steffi would view this intrusion as another ambush, which wouldn't help anyone.

Emmy dashed up the porch steps and banged on the door. "Miss Steffi, it's me, Emmy!"

Ryan hung back several feet, leaning against one of the porch columns. Emmy banged on the door again before Steffi opened it.

"Emmy?" She crouched, sparing Ryan the briefest glance. "What's up?"

"I brought you a snack." She dangled the bag of cookies as a sort of peace offering.

"Double chocolate chip? My favorite." Steffi reached for the bag. "That's very nice. Thanks."

"You haven't come back to Memaw's house all week." Emmy's tone sounded almost accusatory. "Dad says you're not mad at me, but are you?"

"No." Steffi's brows drew together. "I'm not mad at you. I'm just finished with your memaw's project, and now I have new projects. But you can visit me down here after school when you see my van out front—"

He couldn't stop himself from interrupting. "How've you been?"

Her head jerked toward him like an alert bird. "Fine. I'm fine."

"Can I see this house now?" Emmy craned her neck to see inside.

Steffi cast Ryan an inscrutable look, then said, "Sure. Come take a quick peek."

"I'll wait out here," Ryan said, giving her the space she clearly wanted.

Emmy shrugged off her own confusion from his behavior and followed Steffi inside. A few minutes later, they reappeared at the front door.

"It's like a dollhouse, Dad." Emmy bounded toward him like a rabbit. "Everything is small!"

"I know. It's very cozy." He looked at Steffi, who remained standing inside the open doorway. Her crossed arms gave a clear signal that he wouldn't ignore. He did meet her cautious gaze as he said, "Sorry to interrupt you tonight, but thanks. She wanted to see the house—and you."

Steffi's nostrils flared, adding another layer to her conflicted expression. "Sure. I'd better get back to work."

Emmy's gaze bounced from Steffi to him and back, her own expression growing more puzzled by their stilted behavior.

"Good luck." Ryan then tugged at Emmy's shoulder. "We'd better go before we're late for dinner."

He looked up, praying Steffi would give him a reprieve. She kept her eyes on his daughter, smiling as she closed the door.

The closed door: a trite and overused metaphor, but apt.

He followed Emmy down the lane, back to his mother's house. The old sadness he'd grown accustomed to when thinking of Steffi returned, swallowing him whole. Once again, his love and intentions hadn't been enough.

Past experience told him that once she made up her mind to freeze him out, she wouldn't break down. She'd move on, so maybe he should, too.

"Dad?" Emmy stopped and spun toward him. "Miss Steffi didn't smile at you like normal. Did you have a fight?"

He couldn't lie. "Sort of."

"Was it because I wasn't nice at the fair?"

"No!" He hugged her to his side. "It's grown-up stuff. Nothing to do with you."

"Promise?" Emmy looked up at him with wary eyes.

"I promise. Nothing that happens between Steffi and me, or your mother and me, for that matter, has anything to do with you. Got it?"

"Got it."

They walked in silence until they reached his mother's yard. Then Emmy asked, "Can we see a movie this weekend?"

"Of course." He squeezed her shoulder.

"Maybe Lisa will want to come." Emmy skipped to the front door while he covered his excited surprise. Perhaps the scheming he'd done weeks ago had turned into a real friendship. He'd take his wins where he could find them these days, like the plea bargain he and the DA had agreed upon after Billy finally dug up a prostitute willing to testify that O'Malley's accuser had lied.

"She's welcome to come. We'll get an extra-large popcorn and sprinkle M&Ms in it." He opened the door.

Emmy nodded. "You should ask Miss Steffi to come, Daddy. Then she won't stay mad at you."

Ryan glanced back at the cottage. His heart stopped for a second when he thought he saw movement in the window. He squinted, but no one was there. Must've been an illusion.

He tipped Emmy's chin up. "You can't force people to forgive you, Emmy. You can apologize and hope they do, but if they won't, you have to accept that maybe things won't be the same."

"Like you and Mommy." Emmy scowled.

"Sort of." He sighed.

He had no idea what he looked like, but it must've been quite pathetic, because Emmy wrapped her arms around his waist. "Don't be sad. I still love you."

And just like that, a little ray of warmth shot through his lifeless heart.

Chapter Twenty-Three

Steffi couldn't stop thinking about Ryan and Emmy. Not when she removed the baseboards from the kitchen. Not when she'd taken a utility knife to the pea-green linoleum flooring. Not when she'd tugged twelve-inch strips of vinyl away from the subfloor. Not even when she had to pull out a hammer and chisel to chip at hardened adhesive.

Regardless of her focus on the tedious task at hand, images kept reappearing to distract and slow her. Ryan standing on the porch. Ryan walking with Emmy along the road. Emmy asking if Steffi was mad at her—that one hurt a new part of her heart she'd never even known existed.

"For God's sake," she muttered when tears filled her eyes. Until Monday night, she could count on one hand the number of times she'd wept— maybe two hands. In the past three days, she'd need all her toes and more to keep track.

Her confrontation with Ryan had ripped open the seam that she'd glued together when her mom died, and now all kinds of sorrow and regrets kept oozing out.

After she loaded the strips of linoleum into bags and swept the floor, she hit the lights and called it a night. She stood in the kitchen, replaying the barrage of Emmy's unending questions.

"Who picked this ugly green floor? Where will all the cabinets go? Will you have a metal sink like Memaw or one of those cool white ones that looks like a bathtub? Will you put a glass door here so you can see the backyard better? Which one would be my room if my dad buys this house? Can we paint it pink, just in case?"

From the beginning, Steffi had envisioned Ryan and Emmy here. Truthfully, she fantasized about living here with them. A little family. A happy one. Having Emmy scurrying around for five minutes renewed that wish, even though she had no idea how to talk to Ryan now. How to forgive him and ask for help at the same time.

But if she didn't figure it out, then what happened last spring would truly destroy her life. She couldn't give those men that power. She wouldn't.

She locked up the home and then drove the van to the other end of the lane and parked in front of the Quinns' place, every bit as shaky as she had that first day when she'd come to bid on Molly's project.

Nine o'clock. Not too late.

Steeling herself, she trotted across the lawn and knocked on the door, bracing to see Ryan again. *"Different better,"* she'd promised. That meant she'd have to find a way to overcome her Lockwood genes and open up to him. Be vulnerable.

She trembled on the stoop.

When the door opened, she came face-to-face with Molly. "Oh, Stefanie. I didn't expect you. Is something wrong? Didn't you get the final check?"

"I got the check, thank you," Steffi assured her. "I just wanted to give the room a once-over. Make sure JT did a good job with the trim."

Molly's eyes narrowed slightly, but she didn't call Steffi a liar. "Sure. Come on back. The whole thing turned out darling. Claire says the furniture will arrive tomorrow afternoon. I'll have to invite you girls over for a little housewarming thingy."

"Hopefully, you'll bake more of those cookies," Steffi joked as she followed Molly through the house. Her stomach plummeted in anticipation of running into Ryan, but she didn't see him anywhere.

Molly turned on the lights in the new room. "I just can't believe how much space and flow this has added. I might even have to throw a Bunco party or something."

"I'm so pleased that you love it." Steffi allowed herself to bask in Molly's joy. The room had turned out beautifully. She'd seen Claire's sketches and could envision it furnished. Picture Ryan lounging on the sofa enjoying a Patriots game. See Emmy playing a board game with friends. New tears threatened, but she blinked them back.

"I'll leave you to your inspection. I've got another load of laundry to fold." Molly patted her shoulder and disappeared.

Steffi turned in circles, wondering why she'd thought it had been a good idea to talk to Ryan here. Or at all. She didn't know how to do what he wanted, or spill her guts, or ask for help, or have a truly healthy relationship.

She checked a few spots of trim, considering whether or not it'd be rude to slip out without saying goodbye to Molly. The woman had never been an idiot. Surely, she sensed something was off. She muttered, "Double damn, this is a fine mess."

"Hey," Ryan said from the kitchen, "are you okay? Sounds like you're talking to yourself."

She stopped and shoved her hands in her jacket pockets. "Yeah. I'm good. I mean, I'm not having an episode or anything, if that's what you're worried about."

Ryan stepped into the empty room, making it suddenly seem overcrowded. He wore flannel pajama pants and a soft T-shirt. His tousled hair looked enticing, and entire parts of her anatomy sprang to life. Yet, despite the sleepy sexiness of his appearance, he also looked sad. She stifled the urge to slap him and then hold him tight. An amazing feat, given her recent lack of control.

He scratched the side of his nose. "I know you don't want to listen to anything I have to say, but since you're trapped at the moment, at least let me apologize for the way I handled everything. I never meant to make things worse for you. Or to tell you how to handle something so personal." He took another step closer to her. She kept still, wanting him close yet fearing that nearness, too. "I was scared and willing to do anything to try to solve the problem. But I shouldn't have made it about me or us when it's clearly about you. I was a giant ass, and I'm truly sorry, Steffi. So I guess now it's my turn to ask if, despite everything, we can at least be friends. If not for my sake, then for my daughter's. She's got a stiff upper lip, but I'm pretty sure she's missing you."

"I miss her, too," Steffi said. "And you."

His eyes misted. "Do you?"

She nodded, horrified that there were any tears left in her body, and that they wanted to make yet another appearance. "Actually, I didn't come here to check on the job. I came to tell you something. Claire said something I can't get out of my head."

"So you told her everything?"

She glanced away, unable to face the details. "The main points."

"What did she say?"

"She said that if I let what's happened destroy everything we've rebuilt, then those men truly destroyed my life." Steffi couldn't look at Ryan.

462

She might as well be naked standing there talking about those men. Talking about her hopes for their future. She kept her eyes down. "I hate the way you went about this, but I know you only did it to help. And you weren't wrong about how my problem might end up hurting others. I clocked Benny with a bag of wood the other night by accident."

Ryan winced. "I assume he's okay?"

"It could've been much worse, but Benny's head is harder than mine." She flashed a weak smile when Ryan chuckled. "He'll recover from it sooner than I will."

"He's always been tough." Ryan narrowed his eyes. "I know that's important to you—being tough. You overcame your mom's death and held your own against endless teasing and testing from all those brothers. Even now, in the face of what you know, you're pushing forward. But I'd never think less of you if you needed a shoulder to cry on, you know."

"Good, because I can't seem to stop crying lately." Steffi covered her face and shook her head before looking at him. "You should know, I haven't read the report."

Ryan's brows rose to his hairline. "Why not?"

She took a minute to compose her thoughts. Being confronted with it had been like getting smacked in the chest with a splitting maul. In the days since he'd left it at the bungalow, she'd stared at his name, written in some other man's hand, and cursed. She could only guess that she'd gotten rid of the original report because her subconscious didn't want it around. Her inability to remember any of it made her feel even more victimized.

"I'm still trying to wrap my head around the fact that it happened to me but I can't remember it. I mean, the details must be so horrifyingly awful for me to have blocked them out."

"I've done some research." Ryan rocked back on his heels. "Turns out that, when under extreme stress and fear, the brain focuses on only those details needed for survival. The way it encodes information in those moments can misfire or fragment the memory. Add to that the trauma, which can cause PTSD and a host of other mental issues. In exceptional cases, people dissociate from the event and repress it completely. And like with you, being told of it or seeing photos won't necessarily trigger the memory. It takes finding some kind of 'access code' that re-creates the circumstances, like a smell or something."

"So I'm not a freak? Other people have had this kind of response?"

"Many rape victims' memories are faulty; a few are repressed. Defense attorneys exploit those gaps to undermine the victim's credibility." He folded his arms across his chest. "That night you'd been drinking at a bar, feared for your life, been brutally violated, and got clocked with a gun. Any one of those things could impair your memory, but combined? No wonder you can't recall everything."

Steffi twined her hair in her fist and spun around to stare out the window while she considered that massive info dump. One thing he said had stuck out. Other victims had suffered like she had, yet *they'd* taken the stand to accuse their attackers. Unlike her, who couldn't even read the file, those brave souls fought back.

Steffi turned back to face Ryan. "I want to go back to the alley."

"Why?" His expression was pinched with doubt.

"I could accept the idea that some guys got away with mugging me. But I can't let them get away with rape because I'm too afraid to even try to remember details that could lead to finding them. Maybe going back there will be my access code, and I'll recall *something* about how they looked or things they said or an accent or anything at all that could ID them." She then swallowed her pride. "Will you go with me?"

Ryan could not love this courageous woman more. "Of course. But maybe you should talk to a doctor before we put you in a situation that could make things worse."

"I'll think about that." She breathed a relieved sigh.

"You know, even if you eventually remember

some details, the cops might not ever catch those guys. Can you live with that?"

"I'll have to, won't I?"

He wanted to hold her again. To kiss her. To wrap her up in cotton and tuck her away where nothing bad would happen again. But that wasn't life. Life was messy. Risks couldn't be avoided. "Can I ask something else?"

"Sure."

"Have you forgiven me? Can we pick up where we left off before I screwed up?" His heart stopped beating while he waited for her answer.

Her hesitation sank his hopes, leaving him cold despite the cozy temperature of the new room she'd built. "I want to, but I need to make sure I'm better. I don't want to hurt you like I did Benny. And I won't risk hurting Emmy."

"Everything you've said tonight gives me confidence that won't happen."

"Then there's the whole thing about sex. What if I can't do it? I mean, I did beat up on you that night we started down that road. I doubt you want to be celibate forever."

"I'm patient. Dr. Saxe can probably help us with that, too. In the meantime, we can *cuddle* a lot." He grinned at her because, unlike him, she hadn't been much of a cuddler.

"More threats?" she chuckled, then wrinkled her nose. "Too soon to joke?"

"It's never too soon to joke. And whether or not

we ever find those guys, you'll recover, Steffi. I'd love it if you'd let me be part of the process." He opened his arms, and she walked into them. Right where she belonged. "I meant it when I said love you. I want us to keep moving forward now, but as slowly as you need. No pressure."

While he held her tight, he felt her wipe her eyes. He raised her chin and kissed her wet cheeks. "No more tears."

"Please, God, I hope you're right. I hate the waterworks," she teased.

"On the upside, they do make your eyes sparkle." He kissed her, savoring the hot sensation. "I'm glad you came here tonight. I couldn't take another sleepless night. And the fact that you trust me . . . I can't tell you how good that feels. Now I've got something to look forward to again. And thanks to Val, I'll be completely free to make plans for our future soon."

Steffi cocked her head. "Val's signed off on divorce papers?"

"Better—she's agreed to a settlement, for Emmy's sake. It didn't hurt that she and John plan to marry."

"That was fast."

He kissed her nose. "At our age, it doesn't take forever to know what you want, does it?"

"I guess not." She smiled, looking so much like the young girl he'd never quite let go of in his dreams.

Despite his long relationship with Val, Steffi Lockwood had always been his one true love. Technically, this marked their *third* chance, and he vowed not to do anything to blow it. "I'm glad you said that."

Her face suddenly brightened. "So does this mean you can buy the bungalow?"

He shook his head. "Much as I love it, I don't want to be house poor. It'll be too expensive when you're finished, and I'll need money for other things."

"What other things?" She scowled when he wouldn't consider that purchase.

He closed one eye and glanced at the ceiling as he rattled off his ideas. "Dance lessons for Emmy. Maintenance for *Knot So Fast*. Maybe some jewelry for you."

"Jewelry?" She pulled a face. "I don't wear jewelry."

He grabbed her left hand and kissed her ring finger. "Never say never."

Epilogue

Three months later

Steffi woke to the warmth of Ryan's arm and leg across her body. She smiled, curling herself deeper into his embrace. Thanks to Dr. Saxe's help, she'd finally been able to make love with him last night. He'd been patient and tender and awkwardly sweet, exactly like the very first time they'd given themselves so completely on his boat all those years ago.

Even if she never fully recovered all her memories, this alone made the weekly therapy sessions worthwhile. She might never tell Ryan or anyone else, but she didn't hate talking to Dr. Saxe. Her brothers and dad would never let her live that down if they knew. Truthfully, she wished they'd all try a little talk therapy.

Ryan kissed the back of her head. "Are you awake?"

"Mm-hmm." She twisted in his arms, grateful that Emmy was with her mother for the weekend. "I actually promised Claire I'd go with her this morning to the cottage to make some final decisions about the landscaping. Then I have to do a walk-through with the inspector at Hightop Road, so I can't laze around."

He kissed her shoulder and stroked her hip. "Not even a little while longer?"

"It's already nine thirty. I haven't slept in this late on a Saturday in eons." She kissed him, threading her fingers through his hair. He yawned with a stretch like a giant dog enjoying a scratch behind the ears. "But I'm really excited to surprise you with something. Can you meet me at the bungalow later?"

"I like surprises." He pulled her close again. "But don't you have to see Dr. Saxe today?"

"She dropped me to twice a month because I've gone three consecutive weeks without any episodes." It still surprised her to look back and realize just how often those episodes had stolen moments from each week.

"That's great." Ryan smiled. "But do you want to pare back before you remember enough details to help the cops identify the suspects?"

"It'd be great if that happens, but for now, this is enough. We're together. The episodes aren't interfering with my life and work anymore. I'm happy." She kissed him again. "Actually, I've been thinking Claire needs to talk to someone. She's getting more prickly in anticipation of Peyton's imminent return."

"When does that happen?"

"She'll be done with the treatments at Sloan in a month, so anytime after that, I guess." Steffi sighed, having found no solution to ease Claire's anxiety. "I'm just trying to keep Claire busy with our projects. And on that note, I should get moving."

He brushed his hand along her waist and cupped her breast. "Ten minutes?"

"Since when did you ever finish in ten minutes?" she teased with a quick kiss. Then she propped herself up on her elbow. "I promise I'll make it up to you later. Meet me at the cottage at four, okay?"

"I'll be there."

Steffi heard Ryan enter the bungalow and call out her name.

"Back here!" she replied from the laundry room.

Ryan appeared in the doorway between the kitchen and the laundry room. "Man, every time I come here, I'm blown away by what you've done to the place." He glanced over his shoulder toward the kitchen. "Gretta must be stunned."

Everyone was stunned. Even Steffi couldn't believe how gorgeous it had turned out. Silvery-gray Shaker-style cabinet doors, white quartzite counters, a farmhouse sink, and some open shelving lent a cozy yet modern vibe to the space. The refinished antique-wood floors provided warmth, and the new French door to the backyard allowed sunlight to flood the space and spill into the dining room through the wider archway she'd created.

"Just painted the second bedroom." She rinsed her hands. "Go take a look."

"Sure." He wandered off while she finished organizing her things.

She tiptoed up the stairs to try to catch his reaction to the palette. "What do you think?"

He turned, his eyes wide. "Is this the Pink Panther's den?"

Steffi slapped his chest. "It's perfect for a certain young girl."

His expression faltered. "Steffi, don't get me wrong . . . this whole place is picture-perfect. It'd be a dream come true to move in here with Emmy and you, but I don't make enough money to support us all here."

"I know." She hugged him, excited to share her surprise. A few days ago, Molly had secretly offered to "forgive" her loan in order to help Ryan afford the place. Steffi had then spoken to Claire about letting Ryan and her buy the house at less of a profit than they could net with a stranger. "But you're in luck, because the current owners of the house are willing to sell it to you for a bargain price."

"But—"

"Ah, ah, ah!" She pressed her finger against his lips to stop him. "I also have it on good authority that the lady in your life is a working stiff and can help pay the mortgage."

He blinked at her, processing her suggestion.

She removed her finger slowly, hoping he wouldn't let his pride ruin this dream.

"You're ready to take that step?" He smiled.

"I've never been more sure of anything in my entire life, Ryan Quinn."

He looked around the cotton candy–colored room again and smiled so wide his face nearly split in half. "Seriously?"

"I mean, I don't want to presume anything, but we have talked about the future."

He grabbed her hands and grimaced. "If I go in on this house with you, I won't be able to buy you much of an engagement ring."

"You know I don't care about jewelry. You, Emmy, this house, and the sailboat. That's my idea of heaven."

He gathered her in his arms, lifting her off the ground and kissing her hard. "Guess we've finally built ourselves that dream life, haven't we?"

Author's Note

Because of the fascinating complexity of the mind's varied and incredible reactions to trauma, I wanted to share a bit more of my research with you. As I explain in light detail in the book, it is not at all uncommon for victims of trauma, especially sexual assault, to lose many if not all details of the incident. When in survival mode, the prefrontal cortex gets shut down by chemicals in the brain, and the amygdala takes over while the person fights to survive. Researchers still have much to learn about how and why some people might dissociate and repress traumatic memories, while others suffer PTSD, and still others remember details and move on without ongoing side effects.

While I'm far from an expert, as I understand it, most cases of dissociative identity disorder involve prolonged sexual abuse starting in childhood. On a lesser scale, there is dissociative amnesia (localized dissociation), which is rare but can occur from a single, extremely traumatic event in adulthood. While the person was conscious at the time of the event, her brain's unconscious mind represses the painful memory. There are degrees of repression, but that is beyond the scope of this work. PTSD, on the other hand, is a severe anxiety disorder resulting from exposure to traumatic events that can also include an element of amnesia.

In the course of my research, I uncovered one personal account of a thirty-year-old woman who was drinking at a bar and met a man who offered her a ride home. He brutally raped her in his car and then tossed her onto the side of the road. She was found beaten and bruised, and then taken to her parents' home. She had no memory of any of it, including the STI and HIV tests. Even the police didn't tell her about the rape because they didn't want to influence her official statement. This incredible incident provided the genesis for developing Steffi's rape story.

Because my understanding of this complicated field of study is limited, I layered the elements of alcohol use and a history of concussions to further contribute to her memory issues in order to present a plausible, if not probable, story. If you're interested in learning more about these topics, please see the list of reading materials I reviewed while writing this book.

Sources

Jules Spotts, PhD

Lisa Creane Hayden, PhD

http://www.psychiatrictimes.com/ptsd/post traumatic-stress-disorder-and-memory

http://time.com/3625414/rape-trauma-brain-memory

https://www.wearyourvoicemag.com/body-politics/emily-doe-rape

https://www.theguardian.com/lifeandstyle/2009/may/16/experience-rape

https://www.clevelandclinic.org/health/disease/9789-dissociative-amnesia (inactive)

https://www.psychologytoday.com/us/conditions/dissociative-amnesia

http://blog.souldoctors.com/rape-victims-fragmented-memories

https://thoughtcatalog.com/cj-hale/2013/06/12-things-no-one-told-me-about-sex-after-rape

https://www.mentalhelp.net/advice/relationship-between-dissociation-did-and-ptsd

https://www.rainn.org/articles/rape-kit

https://www.nimh.nih.gov/health/topics/post-traumatic-stress-disorder-ptsd/index.shtml

http://www.rrsonline.org/?page_id=944

http://www.human-memory.net/disorders_psychogenic.html

http://www.psychiatrictimes.com/ptsd/posttraumatic-stress-disorder-and-memory

https://www.lucidpages.com/rmem.html

Acknowledgments

As always, I have many people to thank for helping me bring this book to all of you—not the least of which are my family and friends for their continued love, encouragement, and support.

Thanks, also, to my agent, Jill Marsal; as well as to my patient editors, Megan Mulder and Krista Stroever; and the entire Montlake family for believing in me and working so hard on my behalf.

A special thanks to Jules Spotts, PhD, and Lisa Creane, PhD, who educated me about PTSD, dissociative amnesia, head trauma, and post-concussion problems. Also, thank you to Jason W. Nascone, MD, for helping me structure and understand Claire's hip injuries for this book and the next story in this series.

I couldn't produce any of my work without the MTBs, who help me plot and keep my spirits up when doubt grabs hold.

And I can't leave out the wonderful members of my CTRWA chapter. Year after year, all the CTRWA members provide endless hours of support, feedback, and guidance. I love and thank them for that.

Finally, and most important, thank you, readers, for making my work worthwhile. Considering all your options, I'm honored by your choice to spend your time with me.

About the Author

National bestselling author Jamie Beck's realistic and heartwarming stories have sold more than one million copies. She's a 2017 Booksellers' Best Award finalist, and critics at *Kirkus Reviews*, *Publishers Weekly*, and *Booklist* have respectively called her work "smart," "uplifting," and "entertaining." In addition to writing novels, she enjoys dancing around the kitchen while cooking as well as hitting the slopes in Vermont and Utah. Above all, she is a grateful wife and mother to a very patient, supportive family. Fans can learn more about her on her website, www.jamiebeck.com, which includes a fun "Extras" page with photos, videos, and playlists. She also loves interacting with everyone on Facebook at www.facebook.com/JamieBeckBooks.

Books are produced in the United States using U.S.-based materials

Books are printed using a revolutionary new process called THINKtech™ that lowers energy usage by 70% and increases overall quality

Books are durable and flexible because of Smyth-sewing

Paper is sourced using environmentally responsible foresting methods and the paper is acid-free

Center Point Large Print
600 Brooks Road / PO Box 1
Thorndike, ME 04986-0001 USA

(207) 568-3717

US & Canada:
1 800 929-9108
www.centerpointlargeprint.com